MW01136881

THE

SINGING

STICK

A NOVEL

PHYLLIS COLE-DAI

THE
SINGING
STICK

A NOVEL

PHYLLIS COLE-DAI

ONE SKY PRESS

Visit the author's website: PHYLLISCOLEDAI.COM
Visit the author's online community: PHYLLISCOLEDAI.SUBSTACK.COM

Editing by A. M. W. Editing
Cover design by EBOOKLAUNCH.COM
Author photo by Choke Cherry Photography & Design

The Singing Stick / Phyllis Cole-Dai—1st ed.
ISBN 978-1-7371055-4-1

In loving memory of
Pat and Peter Schneider
and
Ćekpawiŋ Darlene Renville Pipeboy

In collective remembrance
of all Indigenous children
who were forced to attend
assimilationist boarding schools

We will not forget

This they tell, and whether it happened so or not, I do not know;
but if you think about it, you can see that it is true.

HEȞÁKA SÁPA (BLACK ELK)

The great force of history comes from the fact that we carry it within us,
are unconsciously controlled by it in many ways,
and history is literally present in all that we do.

JAMES BALDWIN

What is left in one
who does not remember?
Love and music.

Not a name but the fullness.
Not the sequence of events
but order of rhythm and pitch,

a piece of time in which to exist.

HANNAH FRIES

White silence sings.

PETER SCHNEIDER

FRIDAY, NOVEMBER 6, 2020

6:12 P.M.

"Nine-one-one. What's your emergency?"

"Can you hear me?"

"Yes. How can I help you?"

"Oh, thank heaven! Please . . . my husband . . . I'm so afraid . . . he's gone missing!"

"What's your name, please?"

"Fiona Richter."

"Spell that, please?"

"R-I-C-H-T-E-R."

"And your first name?"

"F-I-O-N-A."

"Okay, Fiona, can you tell me what's happening?"

"My husband—he has dementia. I can't find him anywhere!"

"Okay. What's the address of the emergency? . . . Hello? . . . Ma'am, you still there?"

"I'm sorry . . . I can't seem to think . . ."

"Can you tell me your address, please?"

"Nine Eighty-Two Division Street."

"Ninety-Two Division Street?"

"No. Nine *Eighty*-Two, I said!"

"Nine Eight Two?"

"Yes."

"That's where you live?"

"Yes."

"What kind of dwelling?"

"A house."

"One or two story?"

"Two."

"Color?"

"This is so much nonsense! Why all the questions?"

"Please, ma'am. What's the color of your house?"

"Red. With light-yellow shutters."

"Okay. One second . . . What's the phone number you're calling from?"

"Seven-eight-one, five-five-five, oh-one-four-seven."

"Landline or cell phone?"

"Landline. Do you need my cell too?"

"Not at this time. Your husband's name?"

"Simon, spelled like it sounds. Richter, same as me. He's retired from the university."

"You say he disappeared?"

"I found him gone maybe an hour ago, a bit more. Please hurry. It's dark and snowing hard—"

"Try to stay calm, ma'am. You're giving me good information. Have you searched your home thoroughly?"

"I *told* you—he's not here!"

"Do you have a garage? Any outbuildings?"

"He's not here!"

"I'm sorry, ma'am, but I have to ask. People with dementia sometimes hide close by. Have you looked under your bushes?"

"My husband would never hide in the bushes! And not in the snow!"

"How old is your husband?"

"He turned eighty today."

"Today's his birthday?"

"We're supposed to celebrate tonight. With our daughter."

"Is your daughter with you now?"

"No. She lives down in Philly. We Zoom."

"So, are you there alone?"

"Yes."

"When you last saw Simon, did he seem upset?"

"No. He was playing his clarinet."

"Okay. What does he look like?"

"*Look* like . . . ? Five-nine, maybe. Thin, around a hundred and seventy pounds. Thick white hair, swept back from his temples. Little round wire-rimmed glasses, like John Lennon. Oh, and he wears a medical ID."

"Race?"

"White—no, wait . . . Yes, okay. We'll say white."

"Eye color?"

"Hazel."

"Any facial hair? Tattoos? Birthmarks? Scars?"

"No."

"Does he have a cell phone on him?"

"No."

"Can you recall what he's wearing?"

"His field jacket's not here. It's khaki. His hat's gone too—a bush hat made of blue tin cloth, wide brimmed, with a leather band and chin strap."

"Great description! Very detailed!"

"I have an eye for such things."

"What's he wearing beneath his coat?"

"Khaki trousers, teal polo shirt—no, wait. What day is this?"

"Friday."

"Then his shirt's forest green. And a burgundy cardigan."

"Any idea where he might have gone?"

"He takes a long walk every afternoon. Always the same route. I didn't want him to go today, what with the storm coming. But he snuck out while I was upstairs."

"So, he might just be out for a walk?"

"I've driven it, start to finish."

"But you might have missed him."

"I don't believe so."

"How long's he usually gone for, on these walks?"

"Enough of this inquisition! Can't you please *do* something?"

"Mrs. Richter, answering these questions will help us locate your husband."

"You need to get out there looking!"

"Help's on the way. I promise. But I need you to stay on the line till I tell you to hang up. Will you do that for me?"

"You're sending help? Right now?"

"Yes, ma'am. I've entered the call for service into the system. Now, what kind of shoes is Simon wearing?"

"When will somebody get here?"

"I can't say specifically, but someone from our community response team will be dispatched as soon as possible. When they arrive, please be wearing a mask when you answer the door. Now, about Simon's shoes . . ."

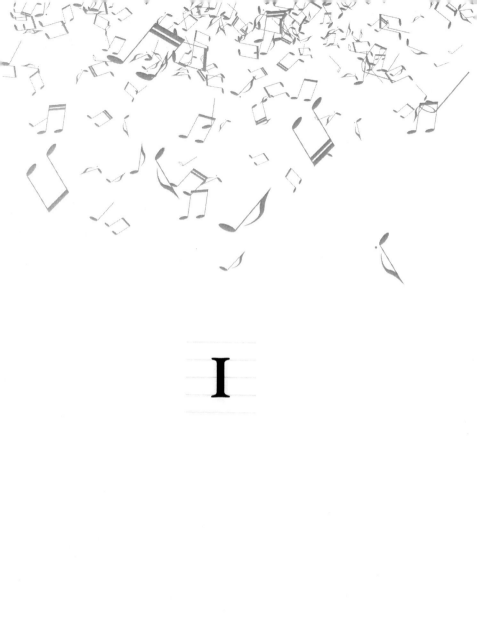

I

SPECIES OF SPIRIT

SIXTEEN HOURS EARLIER, 2:23 A.M.

SIMON JERKS AWAKE. His body is one giant knot.

Don't look, he tells himself. *You don't know what you might see.*

He senses its presence, real as flesh. If he were to reach out, he could touch it. Some species of spirit—or other unnatural spectacle—shimmering beside the bed.

Who's there? he says in his brain, half-expecting an answer. Half-expecting to hear the answer in Mama's voice.

He's a scientist. He doesn't believe in spirits. Once, when no more than a child, he'd convinced himself he'd seen one. *Her* spirit, in fact. But now he knows better. There's no credible evidence, no peer-reviewed science, to prove spirits or ghosts are real.

Entia non sunt multiplicanda praeter necessitatem. Entities must not be multiplied beyond necessity.

Still, his hair's on end. Something in this room is unearthly enough to have disturbed his sleep.

Courage, old man.

He opens his eyes to slits and peers into the dark. To his right, a streetlight glitters through tentacles of frost on a window. It's the only light to see by.

Where the hell am I?

A large quilt hangs on the near wall, above a cedar chest. Opposite the bed, along a long wall, stand a mirrored dressing table, a chest of drawers, and a rocking chair tossed with clothes.

Some other man's room. How'd I get here?

A cat's purring warmly against his ribs. Oddly reassured, Simon

7

floats a hand down beneath the blankets to scratch behind its ears. Nestled into his left side, the cat stretches a leg out of the covers and rests its paw upon his chin. He turns his head to escape the tickle.

There's a woman beside him, fast asleep, her face as close as breath.

He sits up in quiet terror. From beneath the covers, the cat meows a muffled complaint.

He's only ever lain with one woman during his marriage. And *that* woman, beside him, isn't her.

What have you gone and done, old man?

Whatever had happened here, no answer will be defensible. His Girl will never forgive him. Nor should she.

He inches away from the stranger. Reaching the edge of the mattress, he frees himself of the bedding and punches his feet into some slippers—which are right where he'd have left them, were this his room.

He pads in pajamas to the door, floorboards creaking beneath his feet.

The door is locked. No key in the keyhole.

He grabs the other man's flannel bathrobe off the hook, yanks it on, lashes it around his middle.

From the hollow beside the woman in the bed, the cat's watching him like a green-eyed sphinx.

He tries the door again. Still locked.

Trembling, he shrinks into the corner behind the rocking chair to regroup. He presses his spine into the hard angle where the two walls meet.

Across the room, beneath a wedding-ring quilt, the woman is still curled on her side like a slender comma.

Who are you? he demands of her, in his brain. *Why was I in your bed?*

The cat arches its back. It steps onto the ridge of the sleeping woman and nimbly traverses the full crescent of her before jumping onto the floor.

The woman stirs. One of her hands pats the spot where he'd been sleeping. Finding it vacant, she raises herself on an elbow.

"Sy?" comes her voice, like putty drying hard. "Where'd you go?" Her eyes sweep the dim room until she locates him in the corner. "Whatever are you doing over there?"

He marches back to the bedroom door. Rattles the knob hard.

The woman switches on the lamp on her nightstand. "Simon?"

How does she know my name?

"You need to go to the bathroom?" she asks, groggy.

"I want out!"

8

"It's the middle of the night. Come back to bed."

"You've no business telling me what to do!"

He hears her sharp intake of air. One of her hands flares high over her nightshirt—a blue T-shirt with white print on the front.

"Sy . . . it's *me* . . . Fee . . ."

With a chirrup of greeting, the cat starts rubbing against his ankles.

"How do you know my name?" he says to the woman.

"This is our house. This is where we live—"

"I don't know who you are! I don't know what I'm doing here!"

The cat walks its front paws up his leg, begging to be picked up.

"Little moocher!" the woman says with a forced laugh.

He looks down at the cat. The cat looks up at him. Big green marble eyes.

"Fritz?" he says. "That you?" He stoops to scoop up the cat. "Morning, old boy!"

He stands there, hugging Fritz to his chest.

"Forgot what I got out of bed for," he says to Fee. "What was I after?"

"I think . . . maybe . . . you were walking in your sleep."

He carries Fritz back to the bed. He bends to kiss Fee's crown, lingering in the familiar scent of her. "Morning, my Girl. We ready for another—"

"Beautiful day?" she finishes.

He cherishes this morning ritual, sprung from the soil of long marriage. But in the milky light of the lamp, a sheen of tears shows on Fee's wrinkly cheek.

"Something wrong?" he asks. There's no pain he won't spare her, if he can.

"Of course not. No. Nothing." She snatches a tissue from the box on the nightstand. "It's just that . . . well . . ." She pulls him down on the bed's edge with a sniffle. "It's *so* early, even for you."

He glances at the digital clock, beaming 2:38 in oversized green numbers. "Good God."

"Anyway . . ." She cups the side of his face in her palm. "Happy birthday, sweetheart."

"Today?"

"Today." She lifts the covers, making room. "Why don't you come on back to bed, just till we smell the coffee?"

9

ORANGE X

2:51 A.M.

DOWN IN PHILLY, Abby flips over in bed, away from the flipping numbers on the clock.

"Honey—" she murmurs to Frank, with a poke.

He grunts back in his sleep.

"You're snoring," she says.

Like a trained teddy bear, he rolls away. His snoring subsides into snuffling.

Part of her wants to wake him up. A bad dream had jolted her from a sound sleep. She needs to talk to somebody. But Frank's frazzled from his long hours at the bistro, and his alarm will soon have him up and out the door again.

Her cell phone's charging on the nightstand. She could call her mother, just to make sure the dream had been only a dream. But her mother would be scared out of her wits, the phone ringing at this hour. A middle-of-the-night phone call is never good news.

Until lately, she has always dreamed about people she's close to or spends a lot of time with. Never about her father.

Her father's like one of those unremarkable shade trees planted along the street—you don't really notice it until the city paints it with an orange X, planning to cut it down. Only when it's diseased, and you can't do anything to save it, do you begin to realize what it has provided through the years and how much its presence has mattered.

Now she dreams about him constantly.

In this night's dream, the palms of his hands had been inked red. They were pressing down, leaving handprints like blood on vital government documents—like those she'd actually mailed him a couple of days ago, in time for his birthday. She'd second-guessed herself all the way to the post office, uncertain of how he'd react and whether she was the right messenger.

The documents in the dream had caught fire. He was standing amid the spreading flames, somehow unaware of the danger. She couldn't get his attention. She couldn't make him understand. All she could do was try to escape the horror by waking herself up.

As she'd come to, a smothering terror had fallen upon her. She'd felt pinned. Her chest, crushed. Her arms and legs, paralyzed. Bizarre— she'd had no control at all, until movement returned on its own, and she could finally breathe again.

The papers should arrive in his mailbox today.

Love ya oodles & bunches ended the note she'd clipped to them. That's the way she has always signed off her letters to him.

Now that she's losing him piecemeal, she's learning how much she means it.

HELLUVA YEAR

5:57 A.M.

JOGGING against the wind up the hill to Mikey's, Victor fantasizes about which incredible dish his guy has whipped up for breakfast. Ricotta crêpes with honey, walnuts, and rose? Crème brûlée pancakes? An omelet soufflé?

It's tradition. They always eat a romantic breakfast—prepared by Mikey at dawn—on their anniversary. Just like on their wedding day.

But no.

Mikey's in the kitchen, all right. But he's guzzling a Red Bull and popping bagels into the toaster.

"Sorry," he says, ripping open Victor's love-you-forever card. Two penguins, holding hands. "I lost track of the date. But maybe I'd have remembered if we lived under the same roof!"

"Let's not get into that now," Victor says. "Okay?"

Mikey occupies the farmstead's original house. Victor lives down the lane in the studio apartment behind their shuttered farm shoppe. A five-minute run.

"Hallmark?" Mikey says, wagging the card. "You went all out."

No crème brûlée pancakes. Not even a croissant.

"What's this?" Mikey unfolds the gift certificate enclosed in the card.

"Tea subscription. Plum Deluxe. A box of artisan blends every month."

"Oh. Sweet. Thanks."

Mikey tosses the card onto the bar between them, then pivots to stick a plate of bacon into the microwave.

That infernal Old Car Horn blasts on Mikey's cell phone. *Ahooga . . . Ahooga.*

"Get that, will ya, Vic?"

Victor glances at the caller ID. He doesn't like to answer Mikey's phone, especially so early in the morning. Somebody could get the wrong idea.

But it's Jim. Jim, he can trust.

Victor answers on the fourth *ahooga.* "Hey, Jim—Victor here. What's up? . . . Wait a sec! I'll put you on speaker—"

"—running her to the ER," Frieda's old man is saying when Victor taps him on.

Mikey stiffens like a tire iron. "Oh, man! Not her too!"

Frieda's one of their last workers. Most have quit or gotten sick. She's been so careful. She's always masked up, even around the barns. When not at the farm, she's always at home with Jim, isolating.

Being careful is no guarantee against the COVID. It just means you're trying.

"Isn't Mercy out of beds?" Victor says to the tense air.

The hospital's overrun. It's been all over the news.

"Yeah," Jim says. "Well . . . they've got to make room for one more. A gurney in the hallway, maybe. I'll get back to you, soon as I know something."

"Give Frieda our love, will ya?" Mikey says. "And stay upright yourself, y'hear?"

But Jim's already gone.

"I don't think he heard you, that last part," Victor says.

Mikey drains his Red Bull. "Frieda's tough," he says. "But I'm freaking scared for her."

When Mikey's scared, Victor wears the fear around his own neck, like his dog tags on tour.

HELLUVA YEAR IT'S BEEN. First, Mikey's grandma. She died in March, one of sixteen in her nursing home, back when nobody around here knew what the hell COVID was. Then, Mikey's dad, in September. He got up one morning with a "bad head cold." He died of COVID that night, in bed, watching the Patriots.

No funerals for either of them. Only ashes and committals and wills.

COVID's done its damnedest to kill Dinky Creek too. The pandemic has disrupted their supply chains and distribution network. They've had to overhaul their business plan and revise all their marketing strategies. In May, after kidding season, they couldn't reopen to the public with their annual festival of bleating, prancing babies. They couldn't resume their weekly outdoor pizza nights either. Their tasty goat cheese specialties, baked in a wood-fired oven, used to attract a crowd in fair weather.

This time last year, the farm had been on solid financial footing. He and Mikey were even talking about expansion. Now, they're flirting with bankruptcy.

Victor spreads a jalapeño bagel with honey chèvre. "Hate to be practical at a time like this, but losing another pair of hands is tough. Especially today."

"It'd be a lot easier to manage," Mikey replies, "if we lived in the same house!"

Victor swallows his irritation with a bite of bagel. "If people find out about us, it'll hurt what business we've got left."

"You think nobody's figured us out? After thirteen freaking years?"

"*Four*teen," Victor says. "But Mikey, I've told you—they think I'm just the help. One look at me, they think they know me. They don't see a Nipmuc. They see a 'dirty Mexican.' A 'wetback.' And that wetback they see is straight."

He's been with Mikey since 2006, not long after getting home from Iraq. They'd tied the knot in 2008, in the chambers of a judge—a friend of a friend, a Republican still in the closet.

"After thirteen years—" Mikey says.

"*Fourteen*," Victor repeats.

"Thirteen, fourteen, umpteen, Springsteen—whatever! My point is, we qualify as an old married couple! But your mind's still in the closet, living Don't Ask, Don't Tell."

"Look, let's not bicker," Victor says, anxious to change the subject. "With this big storm on the way, how are we going to deal with the pad *and* make Frieda's deliveries?"

Yesterday had been fantastic for November: dry, in the mid-sixties. Unheard of around here. The perfect day, he and Mikey had decided, to pour the concrete pad for their new walk-in freezer, next to the creamery.

But now a nor'easter is blowing in out of nowhere. Could damn well warp and crack the concrete. Ruin the whole thing. The wind's already picking up, stripping trees of even their clingiest leaves. Today's predicted high had peaked just after midnight. It's only downhill from here. The low will be too damn low.

"I talked to a guy over in Martinsville," Mikey says. "He has a concrete blanket we can borrow, if we can beat the storm. How about I run over there first thing, and you pinch-hit for Frieda?"

Victor shoots Mikey a sullen look. "I'm supposed to take delivery of the freezer panels and compressor. Or did you forget that too?"

Too? he thinks, chiding himself. *Just had to twist the knife there at the end, didn't you?*

DOUBT EVERYTHING

6:37 A.M.

SIMON CONSULTS the checklist taped to the bathroom mirror. Every step of his morning routine is printed there in big bold letters, as if he were a child learning to read. Beside the mirror dangles a pencil on a string thumbtacked to the wall.

For some reason, several items are already marked off the list, including SHAVE, though he can't remember using his razor.

"Fee!" he yells. "I shave yet?"

"Check your face!" she hollers from the bedroom.

He towels the steam from a patch of mirror and leans in, rubbing the sharp angle of his chin. No stubble. He runs his hand over each cheek. Nice and smooth.

Damn dementia.

APPLY AFTERSHAVE, BRUSH TEETH, and FLOSS are also ticked off the list.

Fee hobbles in, still in her blue silk kimono, open to his threadbare Habitat for Humanity T-shirt. She's slept in that same shirt of his for years. He loves her for it.

His gaze slides down her front.

"Don't be getting frisky," she says, and she's serious. Her nose is red as a radish on her otherwise pale face. Her eyes are all teary.

"You been crying?" he asks.

"Of course not. Why would I be crying?" She grabs a brush and hair-spray from the top of the vanity and limps back into the hall.

He draws a big X beside SHOWER.

He applies deodorant.

He clips his nails.

He foregoes the trimming of his nose hairs.

He pauses at ASK FOR MEDS.

"Fee!" he yells.

"Coming!"

She shuffles back into the tiny turquoise bathroom.

"Pill time?" she asks. Not waiting for an answer, she retrieves a lime-green plastic box from the bottom of the vanity.

"My pills are in a tackle box?" he asks.

"It only *looks* like a tackle box." She inserts the small key that hangs by a cord around her neck.

"Why's it locked?"

"Hold out your hand." One by one, she deposits into his palm eight tablets and capsules of various sizes and colors.

"What are all these for?"

"Sy, we don't have time to get into that today." She fills a tumbler at the sink.

He stares into his hand. "But Fee, what *are* all these?"

"Vitamins, supplements, prescriptions—"

"I need them all?"

"Would you be taking them if you didn't? Now, be a sweetheart and swallow them down. Oh, wait . . . I keep forgetting." She refills the glass tumbler from a gallon jug.

"What's this?" he says.

"Holy water. Abby sent it up from Philly. Frank's mother had her priest bless it for you. In Latin."

"We're not Catholic."

"Frank's mother was kind to think of you. And you love Latin. So, be a dear."

"I'd rather take my pills one by one."

"Fine. Just be sure to make the sign of the cross when you're done." Winking at him.

He snorts. She plants a kiss on his cheek.

"So," he says between pills, "who's this Frank?"

"Abby's husband."

"Thought his name was Gabriel."

"That was husband number two. Last time down the aisle, you told her number three had better stick."

"Is he?"

"Is he what?"

"Sticking."

"How would I know? With Abby, everything's always fine, till it isn't. But Frank's a good boy. The *Inquirer* gave his bistro four stars."

He swishes the last of the holy water in his cup. "Blessed in Latin, eh?"

What he won't do to satisfy Gilly and his Girl. Next, they'll have him crawling on his knees to the shrine of some saint.

He washes down one final pill. "Not a word about this holy water to anybody, Fee."

"Lighten up, Professor." She relocks the medicine box and replaces it in the vanity. "The priest will bless another jug, if we want one."

"Rather liked Gabriel."

"Well, I'm happy to say you rather like Frank too."

He studies his blurry reflection in the mirror. Somehow this morning he resembles Pop, who's been dead for, what, forty years?

"*De omnibus dubitandum,*" he writes in the steam. Doubt everything.

IN THE BEDROOM, he loosens the fluffy gray towel around his waist.

How long ago had Fee taken to laying out his clothes on the bed? So humiliating, being bossed like a boy. Even more humiliating, *needing* to be bossed. These days, everything he does seems wrong.

His life as a professor is well behind him, but his habitual daily wardrobe hasn't changed: khaki pants and a plain polo shirt of a different color. Today, forest green. In cool weather, he adds this burgundy cardigan. Fee has sewn leather patches on its worn elbows. One button is hanging by a thread.

For special occasions, Fee always spruces him up in "formal wear." That thin section in the middle of the closet divides his casual wear on one end from her splashy apparel on the other. Her clothes take up three-fourths of their closet space.

When did we last go out together? Last night? Last year?

Fee has a flair for fashion, but to her credit, she has never fussed over his economy of style. She understands his desire not to trifle with things that don't matter beyond function. At the same time, he understands that, for her, clothing isn't merely practical; it's an expression of self, especially when sewn by her own hands. In that way, it's a little like him and his music, nowadays.

In the abstract, Fee's a rather plain woman. But he can't view her purely in the abstract, like one of his specimens. When she's all decked out, she can make a room just by being there, like one of his David Austin Heritage roses, a single stem sticking out of a Château Beauchêne wine bottle. No fluff. No frills. Just a fine, heady exuberance of being.

Why's a woman like her with a fool like you? The question has dogged him for more than half a century. These days, it presses on him like geological time.

They'd met by chance in 1959, in a coin-operated laundromat. She hadn't been looking for a husband. He hadn't been looking for a wife. She'd just needed quarters, and he'd had the change. In time, this impossibly delightful (and sometimes impossible) woman decided, by some quirk of fate, to hitch herself to him, a rather glum paleontologist in rumpled work clothes who preferred the company of fossils to people.

"What if I'd never proposed?" you ask her, setting her up for the schtick that both of you love but can't remember starting.

"You'd be a curmudgeon," she says, taking up her part. "And I'd be a lonesome old cat lady."

"Promise you'll never leave me?" he says, playing the straight man.

In his heart of hearts, though, it isn't a joke. Nothing about them matches. Surely one day she'll wake up and notice. Surely one day she'll have had enough.

"I'm too tired," she says, "to start over with somebody else."

"You could go it alone," he says, feeding her for the punch line.

"But who'd climb up and change the light bulbs?" Ever the funny one.

But their life together isn't so funny anymore. He's let his Girl down. Become a burden. *That* much he can recognize, even if he can no longer track the particulars of their shared days.

He remembers so distinctly events of fifteen, thirty, or sixty years ago, the footage preserved in the archives of his brain. Just don't ask him what happened fifteen *minutes* ago. That doesn't qualify him as an idiot, but it sure makes him feel like one.

If his mind has deserted him, at least the house of his body is faithfully familiar. He takes inventory as he dresses: His feet still callused. His second toes still longer than his big toes. His knees still knobby. His waist still trim enough, though paunchier than he'd like. His chest still covered with whorls of soft gray hair. His arms still bruised and scabbed, the easy bleeding a side effect of the Coumadin that Doc Willard had prescribed after his heart spell.

His face in the tilted mirror on Fee's dressing table is angular, his hazel eyes bright and sharp as thorns. His hair, once charcoal black, is almost as lily-white as the cotton handkerchief he's sliding into his pants pocket. His eyebrows are bushy and dark above his round spectacles.

Fee calls his specs his Lennons, as in John. She loves the Beatles.

He fingers the stainless-steel chain of the medical ID bracelet on his right wrist. "Simon C. Richter. Memory impaired. Easily confused. May become agitated." His current life, in a nutshell.

By design, the bracelet is impossible for him to take off. He swallows the shame of it.

Engraved on the bracelet beneath his name is his home address, along with phone numbers for both Fee and Gilly. He can't imagine how Gilly, so far away, could possibly help if he ever got lost. But neither can he imagine himself ever getting lost in a town where he has lived most of his adult life. He knows its streets and alleys like his privates.

He studies his hands—the parchment skin, the blotches of age, the gnarled knuckles, the prominent web of sinews, the rivers of veins, his wedding band. This much he'd expected of growing old.

But not dementia. Never dementia.

Dammit.

He drops his handy Swiss Army knife into the front left pocket of his khakis. Over time, the tool has worn a visible outline into that pocket of all his pants, as his wallet has done in the back.

Which day is this? What year? What idiot is playing president?

He stakes himself to the facts he's certain of: He was born on 11-06-40, like his bracelet says. On a farm outside Hardin, Nebraska. To Karl and Vera Richter. Pop's family was German. Mama was an orphan, last name of Whiteman.

"Nobody," Pop had always said, "ever told your mother who her folks were or where they came from."

Mama and Pop had gotten hitched during the Dirty Thirties. With the rest of the Richters, they survived droughts, grasshopper infestations, and black blizzards.

It was right after the dust settled that Mama's water broke in the middle of Pop's Saturday night poker game. Pop's brother—Simon Peter, who went by Pete—threw a straight flush on the table to drive them to Lincoln General. He belted out *Boop boop dittem dattem wattem chu* all the way to town. Uncle Pete's why Mama and Pop had named him Simon.

As for saddling him with the middle name Chasker, "that was for reasons," Pop had said, "nobody but your mother ever knew. You ask me, it'd better suit a horse."

THE SHRINKING CLUB

7:15 A.M.

"THE NATIONAL WEATHER SERVICE has issued a winter weather advisory for our area until noon Saturday . . ."

It's too soon for a winter storm, Fee thinks, preparing breakfast in their tiny kitchen. But pray as you might, you can't change what's coming.

At the sound of Sy's tread on the stairs, she turns down the forecast with a sigh. She'll have to tell him a hundred times today to stay inside. "No walks! Not with a nor'easter brewing!"

But if she tells him a hundred times, he'll forget a hundred times. She'll need to watch him like a hawk, or he'll go breezing out the door like the weather is plum dandy.

The diagnosis of his dementia had been confirmed for the third and final time more than a year and a half ago. That dreadful day had cleaved their fifty-three years of married life in two: Before Diagnosis and After Diagnosis. BD and AD. That's how she marks time now.

That, and Before Pandemic and Since Pandemic.

COVID-19 had locked down the city about a year AD. Since then, she and Sy have endured six months of self-isolation. Groceries delivered to the door. Takeout via Grubhub. Household necessities ordered online. Medical appointments canceled. Visits with Abby and Frank on Zoom.

She's going a little nuts, alone in the house with Sy and his condition, day in, day out. But Sy doesn't mind their seclusion. She swears he was a mountain hermit in another life. His only forays into the world now are his afternoon "peregrinations," as he calls them.

He has walked the same route through the city for decades, always

21

alone. AD, she's had to trust him not to lose his way; she's unable to tag along and chaperone him because of her hip. She *does* trust him, mostly. The same way she used to trust Abby, mostly, riding her little pink bike all by herself down to the park or over to the school. She trusts him because his memory of town remains intact. Some things, once buried, stay put, like the nest of dinosaur eggs he'd unearthed in Montana.

But that doesn't mean she never worries at the wail of a siren when her Bestie's out on his walk, or that she doesn't breathe easier once he shows up again, still in one piece.

"Wear your mask!" she always tells him as he's leaving the house.

"Mask?" he always says in bewilderment.

She then always explains, for the umpteenth time, how they're living through a pandemic.

"Oh, right."

(Like he remembers.)

"What happened to your mask?" she always says, once he returns.

"Mask?" he always says as she fishes for it in his pockets. "What for?"

Abby keeps telling her not to let him go out. "It isn't safe—for either of you. He could bring the virus home."

"Stop your fretting," Fee says. "Downtown's all but deserted. The library's closed. And the bookshop. And the coffee shop. All his usual haunts. So, why fight him? Besides, him getting out of the house does us both good."

The virus had killed Doc Willard, their family physician, back in August. He was buried without ceremony. "A community celebration of his life," the *Daily Register* announced in a front-page tribute, "will be held as soon as public gatherings are permitted."

Here it is, four months later, and the town's still waiting to say goodbye.

As soon as she'd spotted the headline about Doc's death, she'd buried the newspaper in the recycling bin. Sy didn't need to be suffering through any bad news that he'd soon forget anyway.

As for today's nor'easter, better she doesn't mention it at all. Better she just keep her eyes peeled for trouble, like a mother with her five-year-old on a playground.

The day looks far off when the world will arrive at After Pandemic. But she's dead set on arriving there as a wife, not a widow. Even if she has to drag Simon across the finish line on her knees.

As for After Dementia, there's no such place.

. . .

SHE'S SLICING STRAWBERRIES into two ramekins already brimming with blueberries and raspberries when Simon walks into the kitchen.

He glances out the window above the sink. Autumn leaves still cling to the branches of the oaks and maples, colors past their prime. "Looks like it could storm."

She points her chin toward the calendar on the fridge. "Mark off the day."

"So." He taps the name of the month beneath a vivid photo of a quilt. "It's November?"

"November *sixth*, Mr. Birthday!"

"It *is* my birthday," he says, crossing out the sixth day. He considers the calendar's year. "Guess I must be eighty. This is getting serious."

"Welcome to the club. It's shrinking fast."

"You wear eighty better than I do."

"Feed the moocher, why don't you? I'll start the eggs."

He fills the cat dish with dry chow. Fritz wends around his legs, meowing approval.

"Go easy," Fee says, dialing back the gas burner on the stove. "He's getting fat."

"Sausage?" he asks, sniffing the air.

She cracks an egg into the skillet. "Chicken links. We don't eat red meat anymore. Pour the coffee?"

"French vanilla, smells like. Why not hazelnut?"

"We're out."

"Then let's get some." He pulls out his billfold.

"Not now, Sy. Please, pour the coffee!" Another egg.

"Where's all my money?" Staring into his empty wallet.

"You don't carry cash anymore."

"How do I pay for stuff?"

"Please, Sy . . . the coffee!"

He sighs, extra loud. For her benefit, no doubt.

She pecks him on the cheek.

"Fill those, too, won't you?" She nods to two plastic pitchers beside the sink: one pink, one blue. "Remember, you're blue. For 'boy.' Make sure to drink all your water before the party tonight."

"What party?"

"Your birthday party."

"Oh, right. Eighty." He runs the faucet. "Gilly coming?"

"She can't. The pandemic."

He looks baffled.

"Never mind. We'll talk with her on the computer. She says she has a surprise."

"What kind of surprise?"

"Don't be asking questions like that on your birthday."

"Why not? I'll soon forget anyway!"

"That girl's always got something up her sleeve."

Fee scrapes a chair back from the drop-leaf table and gingerly sits down.

"Not moving well this morning?" Sy says, setting their coffee cups on their place mats.

"Just my hip." She dumps Friday's pills from her pillbox into her hand. She washes them down with orange juice.

"You work too hard," he says.

"I just need a rest."

"You and Gilly, you'll give me the surprise tonight? You won't *forget*, like *some* people?" An obvious joke at his own expense, as if to cheer her.

"Promise," she says, her voice thin and flat. "Promise and hope to die."

MORE THAN DEAD WOOD

8:45 A.M.

SIMON PARKS himself in his cane-back chair. It overlooks his bird feeders, out the side window of his den.

At the hopper feeder, a male cardinal pecks at the cracked corn. A couple of nuthatches cling to the metal mesh feeder. They're a nice little audience, to start.

Simon sets the instrument case across his thighs and runs his hand across its black leather cover.

A dog barks next door, a series of yelps that sound like pain. Across the hedge, nothing seems unusual. There's just some movement of the blinds at the near window.

He lifts the lid on his clarinet. Black wood gleams against green velvet lining. Silver keys glisten.

As a boy, he'd come so close to never playing it.

"The band director's rounding up kids," Iris tells Pop at the supper table. It's the start of fifth grade. "Why not let Simon play his mother's old clarinet? You know how fond he is of music."

Might have asked me first, *you think but don't dare say. You can't give your stepmother any guff in front of Pop.*

Iris shows Pop the mimeographed band flyer.

"Meets after school?" He crinkles the paper in his fist. "Christ. The boy's got chores."

"But Karl, it's only two days a week."

"Clarinets are for girls. And sissies."

25

That shuts her up. Relieved, you help yourself to seconds of everything.

"Iris, more meatloaf. Please." *Then,* "Iris, more potatoes. Please. And the butter . . ."

Everything but the succotash. Ugh.

Okay, so maybe you do like music. But you don't want to squeak around on Mama's old clarinet. You don't want to finger the keys Mama had played. You don't want to put your lips on the mouthpiece where she'd put hers. You don't want to learn to make sounds that would remind everyone of her and what she'd done.

No. Drums would be better. Or trumpet.

But Iris is as stubborn as a bike with a flat tire. She works on Pop throughout supper, trying to win him over.

"Damn, woman!" *Pop shoves back his chair in a huff.* "Stop twisting my arm!"

He goes to the fridge, grabs another bottle of Storz.

You expect him to head to the porch for a smoke. But he turns back to the table and snatches up the wadded flyer. Uncrumples it. Skims. The Storz sweats into the ink, making the paper bleed purple.

"Whatever the boy wants," *he says finally, dropping the flyer beside your glass of milk.*

Once Pop's out of earshot, the screened porch door slapping shut behind him, you plunk your grubby elbows on the table in defiance. "You can't make me!" *you vow to Iris.* "You're not my mother!"

That last sentence is a real zinger. You save it for moments like this.

But this time the zinger doesn't zing. No emotion flickers on your stepmother's face.

"One month, Simon. That's all I'm asking. Try band for one month, then if you want to quit, you can quit."

"Just one month?"

She raises one finger.

This is too easy. Pop, he'd be delivering a lecture right about now: "Let's get one thing straight, boy—you gotta be a fighter, not a quitter! You start with this band business, you better stick it out to the end, you hear?"

Iris stands there like she's offering you a big slice of peach pie. Straight out of the oven. With ice cream on top.

"You promise?" *you say.* "Just one?"

"Promise." *She crosses her heart, not like the Catholics do, but with a fat X over her aproned bosom.* "But you have to promise me something in return."

You fold your arms with an almighty sigh, the same exact way Pop does sometimes.

"Simon, you have to try. Honest to goodness. Like, when I cook up a new dish, and you have to take three bites before you decide you don't like it.

Sometimes you hate the first bite, but by the third, it doesn't taste half bad. Am I right?"

"Well . . ." Picturing succotash.

"Promise me?"

"If I have to."

"Pinky promise?"

You surrender your pinky. She twines hers around it and drops a kiss on your knuckle before you can rip your hand away.

Simon wrests his mind back into the present, opening the blue box of Vandoren reeds. He'd played this same brand as a boy, like Mama. First class yet affordable.

Fritz vaults from the floor onto the back of the chair. He settles there, purring, his white socks kneading the flat of Simon's right shoulder.

"Old boy," Simon says.

The first day of band class, Mr. Spitler whistles softly between his teeth at the sight of your clarinet in its case. "How'd you come by that beauty?" he asks you in front of everyone.

"My mom," you mumble.

Most members of the fifth-grade band can't afford their own instruments. They play the school's wounded loaners with broken valves and keys, minor dings and serious dents, leaky pads, lots of duct tape. One pitiful trombone is missing its slide.

Spitler arches an eyebrow. "Your mother plays?"

"Used to."

Spitler's new to town. He doesn't seem to know the stories about Mama yet, and you're not about to tell him.

"And she's letting you play this? Better treat it right, son." Spitler pulls up a chair beside you. "Has your mom taught you how to put it together yet? No? Shall I show you?"

Simon holds a golden reed to the lamplight, illuminating the "heart" between its tip and heel. Such a fragile sliver of cane. Yet when combined with breath, it can transport the soul to where it's never been.

"Mr. Spitler says my clarinet is awful nice," you tell Pop, the two of you mucking manure in the barn.

"Yeah? Good for him."

"Mr. Spitler says a clarinet's like the violin of the band. It can play low notes, high notes, everything in between!"

"That so?"

Pop screeches his metal blade over the concrete floor, ash dripping from his cigarette.

"Mr. Spitler says if my clarinet was a violin, it would be a"—you pause, dredging your memory for the word he'd used—"a Stradivarius. Sort of like, the best ever!"

"Mind your work, boy!"

"Where'd Mama get it, anyway?"

"Don't know."

"Remember how she'd call it her singing stick?"

"Christ." Pop stops and stares you down. "Why don't you go up top and start tossing down some bales?"

Slipping one end of the reed into his mouth, Simon begins to assemble the clarinet from the bottom up. Fritz fusses, disturbed on his perch, and eases off Simon's shoulder. He roosts upright on the chairback, showing off his tuxedo.

"Old boy."

Careful to protect the keys, a resonant baritone says in Simon's brain as he joins one piece of the clarinet to the next, pressing and twisting. *Don't force anything.*

After all these years, Spitler's still in his head.

"I hate new reeds," you say to Spitler, licking the tip before a lesson. "They taste like dead wood."

By this time, Spitler knows about Mama.

"You're missing it," Spitler says. "Pay attention."

That whole lesson, Spitler doesn't let you play a single note. He has you sit there, sucking on the reed, waiting for some sort of revelation.

"What's supposed to happen?" you keep asking.

"You'll know it when you taste it. And you'll taste it when you believe it's there."

"Believe what's there?"

"Something more than dead wood."

Simon reverses the smooth reed in his mouth.

His senses aren't as sharp as they used to be, but just as he finishes assembling the instrument, his tongue detects a hint of sweetness—the natural sugar of the reed. Spitler's "something more than dead wood."

Still got it, old man, Simon says, congratulating himself.

Tastes a little like life, Spitler tells him in his brain.

Simon attaches the moistened reed to the mouthpiece. All is ready now.

You're seated at the upright piano in the parlor, spotlighted in sunshine from the window. Your sheet music for solo clarinet rests on the piano's rack— here at home, the closest thing you've got to a music stand.

Spitler stands alongside you, singing the notes as you play, conducting you like a one-boy orchestra. It's another private lesson in exchange for fresh milk and eggs.

"Match my pitch," Spitler says, stopping you. "Here—in the second bar after the repeat." He sings a G above the staff, in falsetto.

You blow, trying to meet him.

"Flatten your chin," Spitler says. "Firm up, but don't bite."

Lessons like this are teaching you what it means to practice. What it means to invest yourself in what matters to you.

"Relax." Spitler rests his hand on your shoulder. "That clarinet's your friend. You're not its boss. You can't just snap your fingers and make it do what you want."

"It's so hard!"

"It's easier than it used to be, isn't it? And it'll keep getting easier. Use your ears. Listen to the clarinet's voice, like you listen to mine."

Iris stops at the parlor door. On one hip she balances a wicker laundry basket mounded with clothes from the line. "How's the lesson?"

"He's coming right along." Spitler pats you on the back. "Quite the young player!"

Iris smiles. "His mother would be proud. I know I am."

"Care to join us?" Spitler says before she can step away.

"She's too busy," you murmur so low that only Spitler can hear.

"Oh, I couldn't," Iris says.

"She's got cakes to bake," you insist on the QT.

"We could use an audience," Spitler says, ignoring you. "Or even an accompanist." He motions to a spot next to you on the piano bench.

Iris backs away. "Oh no, I couldn't."

"But Simon tells me you're the pianist in the house."

You rivet your gaze on the windmill churning out by the barn.

"I don't play so much anymore," Iris says.

"*But playing isn't something you* do, *Mrs. Richter. It's part of who you* are. *Once you learn an instrument, you never forget. And the instrument never forgets you. This piano must be pining for you! Please, join us.*"

You sneak a peek at Iris.

"*I'm sorry.*" She tucks a stray curl beneath her hairnet. "*I have to fold these clothes. Then I have a big batch of batter to mix—do you like cake, Mr. Spitler? I could give you some trimmings from the freezer.*" Her words are tumbling out now. "*They're a wonderful substitute for shortcake, if you have berries. I have so many trimmings, see. If you don't take some, they'll just get fed to the cows.*"

"*You feed cake to your cows?*" Spitler asks. "*That must be why your milk's so sweet!*"

Your mouth is watering. Nobody makes white cake like Iris. She has her own top-secret recipe. Try a piece of her cake, and you'll want to lick every last crumb and smear of frosting from your plate.

She does brisk business in birthday and anniversary orders, attracting even high-class customers from Lincoln. Pop built her a baking room by enclosing the lean-to woodshed—that cursed place where Mama did what she did—and attaching it to the back of the house.

"*I'll put a bag of trimmings with your milk and eggs,*" Iris says to Spitler. She abandons the doorway.

Spitler sinks onto the bench beside you, his back to the piano keyboard. "*That went pretty well, don't you think?*" Sarcasm so thick it could stand on its own two feet.

"*She never plays the piano,*" you say. "*Just polishes it with lemon oil. Ernie bought it for her.*"

"*Who's Ernie?*"

"*The guy she married before my pop. He died, like my mom. But different.*"

"*Different how?*"

"*He was a soldier.*"

"*Ah. The war. Sometimes it's like it never ended.*" Spitler, a veteran, looks suddenly weary around the eyes. "*I suppose playing makes Iris sad.*"

"*Maybe.*" You shrug. "*Or maybe it makes her miss him, real bad.*"

Simon plays slow notes to loosen his tongue and fingers. He works up the clarinet, from the lowest pitch to the highest, assessing his embouchure, his breath support, his tone.

Fritz leans in, rubbing his head against Simon's ear.

"Old boy."

Simon graduates to scales and arpeggios, running up and down his entire range, increasing his speed, finessing the break between registers.

Every key is working. No pads are sticking.
Sufficiently warmed up, he tunes the instrument to third-space C.
Sharp.
He pulls out the barrel a bit, plays C again.
Flat.
He pushes in the barrel.
Sharp again.
Spitler laughs warmly in his brain.

"I don't care what that Spitler fellow says," Pop says, yelling over the drumming of rain on the roof of the truck. "You can't make a living with a goddamn horn!"

You're headed home in a downpour from the hardware store in Lincoln. The old black Ford is plowing through water that is ponding in the ruts on the gravel road.

You're suffocating on Pop's cigarette smoke. The cab's thick with it, but the rain's too heavy to crack a window.

"If you plan to waste my good money on college," Pop says just as you hit a water hole too fast, "you're damn well going to waste it studying Ag." He braces himself with one thick hand against the dashboard. "Not that studying Ag would be that much better! Those bookworms on campus can't tell a bull from a cow!"

Your body tightens. "Pop, you know I don't want to be a farmer!"

You've been admitted on scholarship to the University of Nebraska, where Pop had once gone, briefly. But you refuse to suffer through courses in agronomy and animal science for his sake. This matter of your future isn't like a toy train you can pretend to like at Christmastime. You're not a boy anymore.

"I just bought another eighty acres from Dalloway, for Chrissake," Pop says. "Prime bottomland!"

"That's not on me! You've known all along how it is! What I want!"

"Somebody'd think you'd grown up in a family of bonehead musicians!"

Your knuckles are white on the steering wheel. There's no getting through to him. Pop doesn't like being told what to do or think. To him, a No Trespassing sign is an invitation to hunt. And a university degree is a sign you're no longer your own man.

If he makes you give up music, you'll find something else you can be happy doing—or at least make a living at. Because once you leave the farm, you're never coming back.

"Boy," Pop says then, "it's just . . . I just don't want you ending up like your mother . . ."

Yeah. As if music had been the death of her.

IN THE BAG OF A GOAT

9:15 A.M.

VICTOR BUMPS the van into Simon and Fee's driveway, then squeaks to a stop. He's got to replace the brake pads. Keeps putting it off.

He shifts into park but leaves the engine running. He turns up the radio to catch the latest on the brewing storm.

"Winds will be strongest Friday evening into Saturday morning, blowing at forty-five miles per hour, with inland gusts up to sixty-five miles per hour. Power outages are possible . . ."

His fingers tattoo the steering wheel.

"Ice and sleet will coat roadways before the precipitation changes over to snow. Expect significant early-season snowfall in our listening area—five to seven inches. At higher elevations, as much as a foot . . ."

Victor kills the engine and pulls his mask over his nose. He climbs out of the van and flings the door shut.

Helluva fine start to the day.

First, the nor'easter, messing with their concrete.

Then, that pathetic anniversary breakfast, topped off by Frieda.

Then, during morning chores, Meema.

He'd like to go back to bed—and take Mikey with him.

ACCORDING TO THE NIPMUC, all life began on the back of a turtle.

According to Mikey, it began in the bag of a goat.

Meema was the first doe they ever bought for Dinky Creek. A timid young thing when they got her, a petite Alpine milker with a prodigious udder. "Trixie" on her registration papers. He and Mikey renamed her after a powerful leader in his tribe, a woman who'd earned the title of clan mother for life.

This morning, choring after breakfast, he'd found Meema in the goat barn, stretched out on her side near the hayrack, knees drawn up like she'd died in a happy dream, cavorting like a kid.

"Mikey," he'd summoned in a voice full of wrong.

Her death wasn't unexpected. She was over a hundred in human years. Couldn't hear squat. Couldn't see squat. Had lost most of her teeth. But she was still queen of the herd, with enough old-lady pep to keep every goat in its place in the pecking order.

You can convince yourself that some animals, and some people, might live forever.

"It's like waking up to find that your nana's died in her sleep," he'd said to Mikey, stroking Meema's lifeless neck.

She'd been a real granny goat to the end. Not a snuggle bunny. No, sir. Scratch her on the head or rub her cheek—that was all she'd wanted.

But once, he'd flipped a metal feed bucket upside down, sat down on top, and started humming her a made-up tune. He'd coaxed and coaxed with his singing till she crawled half into his lap. She'd stood there on her hind legs, kneeling on his thighs, making goo-goo eyes, like she knew every damn goat-secret there was to know and that was the only way to tell him. Ruminant ESP.

Just that once, she'd done that.

On his knees beside Meema's body, there in the barn, he'd held it together somehow.

But Mikey . . . Mikey had lost it. "Never cried like that in my life," he said after he calmed down. "Except for when I came out to my folks and Mom threw me out."

Damn woman hasn't spoken to Mikey since.

VICTOR OPENS the rear door of the van, splitting DINKY CREEK FARM & CREAMERY in half. He grabs the Richters' half-share, the same every week: a dozen eggs, a half-gallon of milk, a log of Clover Blossom Honey Chèvre. Today he's added a brick of Maple Pecan Goat Milk Fudge for Simon's birthday.

Too bad what's happened to the old man. He isn't an easy fella to know, but once you're in, you're in for good, so long as you don't try to pick his locks.

When Simon first started to lose his memory, a couple years back, he took to playing the clarinet. Hadn't played since he was a kid, he said, but he picked it up again real fast.

Music's about all the old man's got now.

The pandemic's got all kinds of people locked up tighter than drums. Who can tell what's really going on inside all these houses. Behind all these masks.

But music . . . music doesn't lie.

Since the pandemic, Fee keeps a cooler on the back stoop. For deliveries from the farm. For goodies dropped off by him and Mikey. Maybe by other friends too.

To get around back, you have to sneak right past the window where Simon always sits and plays. The old man likes to crack that window open. Thinks he's attracting birds to the feeders.

Duck your head. If the old man sees you, he'll stop on a dime. He's shyer than a virgin in a bar. Doesn't want anybody hearing him except those birds. Doesn't think his music's any good.

But it *is* good. So good, in fact, that if not for the storm headed this way and the semi bringing the freezer, you'd settle yourself down between the bushes and listen a minute.

Music can dredge down deeper than anybody's ever been—down where you're sure nothing's left but black shit. Music can shovel all that shit up into the open. And maybe then you see it wasn't shit at all, but diamonds in the rough.

COWS AND SPIDERS AND GHOSTS

11:31 A.M.

SIMON SNATCHES another breath and pours it down the clarinet. The black wood quivers in his hands.

His den is his music lab. He's both musician and scientist, experimenting with volume and tone, searching for the sweet spot, where the music takes on a life of its own.

When he plays a high G, a fossil from the collection on his bookshelf resonates in sympathy—maybe the Mesosaurus from Brazil.

He used to believe you had to dig down deep, as through geological strata, to bring the music up. But no. It's more like tapping a spring and letting the water rise to its natural release.

This piece, "Memories of You," had been one of Mama's favorite jazz ballads. She always played it for the cows. He needs no sheet music. The melody still grows among the brambles in the unkempt garden of his memory—

Simon! Fee's voice interrupts, distant and faint in his brain.

He loves how his Girl is always with him, even when she isn't. They're a perpetual motion machine, if only in a dusty corner of his dilapidated mind.

Beside you on the piano bench, Spitler leans into your shoulder. "Does playing the clarinet make you miss your mother?"

"Pop's got Iris now."

"Your stepmother seems nice enough. I'll grant you that."

35

"*Pop says what's past is past. Dead and buried . . . Maybe we should get back to my lesson? I still got Latin before chores.*"

"*One last question: Can you remember your mother on the clarinet?*"

You bite down on your lower lip. "*Yeah. She played every night. For the cows.*"

The last time she'd played, you were only five. You'd fallen asleep up in the hayloft while she was making music down below.

"*Cows are a curious choice of audience,*" *Spitler says.*

"*She could play anything, any old way, and they'd eat it up.*"

"*Like cake?*" *Spitler chuckles.*

You remember that last time like yesterday.

Up in the loft, you'd climbed the tallest stack of bales. Almost into the eaves. So high your tummy was like feathers. From there, you sprang into empty air, as if swinging out over the creek below Donus Dalloway's cider orchard and letting yourself drop—but without the rope. On the way down, you pulled yourself straight as a pencil, to land feetfirst in the soft straw.

You scaled that cliff of bales over and over till you tuckered yourself out. Your final jump, you rolled your shoulders forward, to somersault. You failed to tuck your chin. Your body didn't spin. You plunged headfirst into the straw. Sharp stalks whipped your face.

The clumsy landing stunned you. You lay on your stomach, taking stock, before righting yourself in the straw, huffing dust from your mouth and nose.

Down below, Mama was into "Somewhere Over the Rainbow." It was a melancholy rendition, like she was crying through her clarinet. Sad as an angel who had failed. She'd never played it like that.

You sank back against the straw pile. Your scratched face was smarting, and your neck was a tad jammed, but . . . well, the day was turning out pretty swell, considering.

You let your eyelids droop—for only a second, it seemed.

But when you wakened, darkness had fallen. Mama wasn't playing anymore. The radio should have been on. It wasn't.

An unearthly screeching of owl chicks up in the rafters sent you shimmying down the ladder.

"*Barns can be awful scary,*" *you say now to Spitler.* " '*Specially at night. Everything feels turned inside out.*"

Easter Sunday, it had been. Foggy. All day long.

Later, Pop would say that on his walk home from the Big House, where Grandpa and Grandma Richter lived, he'd noticed a faint ribbon of light around the barn door. Strange. So he stepped inside.

He said he switched on the radio to calm the cows. Frank Sinatra was singing. Pop always liked Sinatra.

Pop said he stopped for a smoke, to listen. And there was her clarinet, lying in the dirt. The mouthpiece missing its reed.

He said he knew straightaway there was trouble.

He couldn't find Mama anywhere. Couldn't find you, either. That's what Pop said.

Pop always said he was huddled with Uncle Pete in the house, chewing over where you and Mama might be, when your five-year-old self burst in screaming.

"*Places look scary-different at night," you say to Spitler. " 'Specially when you're all by yourself."*

Pop said you were the one who'd led them out to the lean-to woodshed.

Said Mama was there, hanging from a low beam. She'd stepped off the chopping block. The missing clarinet reed was sticking out of her mouth.

Said Uncle Pete was the one who cut her down.

Said he himself caught Mama in his arms and carried her to the house. Laid her out on the bed with the pineapple posts. Never slept in that bed again.

"*Mama's stockings . . . they were draped over the edge of the bathroom sink," you murmur. You've almost forgotten Spitler, beside you.*

Those stockings on the sink are all you remember for sure about that night, after scrambling down the barn ladder. Everything else you think you know is what you've been told or what you've heard around the edges.

Like, how Mama had used the rope from your sled.

Spitler's hand is fast on your shoulder.

"*She used to drag my sled up Bonfire Hill," you say to the air. "She'd send me sliding down with an almighty shove."*

Why on Easter? Why in the woodshed? Why with that rope?

"*The barn . . . I almost burned it down a few weeks before she did it."*

"*That sounds scary," Spitler says.*

"*Yeah."*

After the fire, Mama had beaten the tar out of you, to teach you a lesson. And for an instant, you'd wished her dead.

That part you don't tell Spitler.

"*Mr. Spitler, what's the scaredest you've ever been?"*

"*Well, now . . ." He exhales through pursed lips. "You can't throw every kind of scared into the same hopper. I mean, I was scared all the time, fighting in the war. And far back, when I was your age, I was plumb scared of girls. And one time I thought I saw a ghost—"*

"*Ghosts aren't scary!"*

"*No?"*

"*Not to me."*

"*You've seen a lot of them?"*

"*Just one."*

You don't mean to, but you tell Spitler all about Mama laid out in the parlor of the Big House, wearing her best dress and her wedding pearls. How a dark river of mourners had flowed past her casket, the bier blanketed with flowers.

In those days, Pop never could have afforded a bronze casket with a satin pillow. The satin was the same subtle pink, almost white, as the lilacs that bloomed in spring on the weather-beaten hedge at the homeplace. But Grandpa Richter—he had the money. He must have bought that casket, to put the best face he could on the family's disgrace.

The Big House was crowded with hushed callers. "Your mother's sleeping her last sleep," grown-ups were telling you. "The kind you don't waken from till Judgment Day—if you're among the saved."

" 'And is Mama saved?' I kept asking them," you tell Spitler. "I wanted so bad for Mama to wake up!"

You remember being perched high on Pop's arm. Big people wearing black were pressing in all around. Men were muttering about why she had to do it in planting season, when Pop should be out in the fields. Women were whispering about how Pop was a catch and would soon have a brand-new mother for his poor little boy.

A roomful of black spiders spinning their sticky webs, that's what they were. And you were wishing them all gone—

"Then," you say to Spitler, "Mama, across the room, she sat up in the casket. Swear to God. I could see right through her. I said 'Pop!' and tugged his lapel. And Mama, she turned her head and looked straight at me. And I said 'Pop!'—louder this time, my arm around his neck, but he was talking with Pastor Hoff—"

Your memories spiral up and out like bats from their roost at feeding time. Spitler's hand on your shoulder is your only anchor.

" 'I didn't mean for you to die!'—that's what I wanted to yell. But all I could say was 'Look, Pop, please! Do you see?' "

"And did he?" Spitler says.

"Mama put her finger to her lips, like she was keeping secrets."

"So . . . he didn't see?"

" 'See what?' he said. Then a bunch of people got in the way, and I was squirming for a better view. And Pop . . . he just told me to shush—"

"Simon! Time for lunch!"

It's Fee's voice, for real, calling him through the door of his den.

Fritz stretches a white-socked leg over Simon's shoulder with a yawn.

EVERY TIME THE FIRST TIME

11:35 A.M.

FROM HERE, in the crusty yard of #980, Olubunmi can already hear the old man in #982 running up and down a line of music like little feet on stairs. He plays the clarinet with his window cracked.

Her heel squishes a pile of old dookie. She scrapes the sole of her boot on the dead grass.

The growling of a tree branch in the wind raises the hair on her neck. Sounds too much like a big-ass dog.

Chill, girl.

She backpedals across the yard, clutching her mailbag to her chest, ready with her pepper spray.

Beware the dogs with chummy names. They apt to be mean. Max. Mama Mae. And that mutt Buddy—he was the worst. Put her in the hospital, her last route. Surgery on her ankle. Stitches in her arms. He might have mauled her to death if that brother hadn't thrown open the door of his ride and dragged her inside. Buddy hadn't let go of her leg till the door of the Lincoln hit him upside the head.

Buddy don't bother nobody no more. Animal Control put him down.

Here at #980, they have a big ol' Rott. Name of Lucy.

"DON'T WORRY—OUR Lucy doesn't bite," the Rott's people had said, back when Olubunmi first came on the route.

Like they were righteous, telling her the dog's name. Like if that Rott ever jumped her, she'd be safe as pie, screaming "Lucy" at the top of her lungs.

Wasn't a week later, on a Saturday, she was at their mailbox when the little girl eased up to the door, inside the screen. The poor child looked so sad. Like a broken baby doll.

Olubunmi leaned down for some sweet-talk. The child reached out, as if to touch Olubunmi's dreads through the mesh. But just then, that fool dog, out of nowhere, blew through the screen like it wasn't even there.

Lord have mercy!

Olubunmi maced that dog silly. It yowled and slinked under the hedge.

"Jesus! What'd you do that for?" the mister yelled at her, running out the door. Like she'd had a choice.

He made for the garden hose. The mace in the air smelled like coffee. And nutmeg.

The woman and child made for the Rott. That dog was sniveling and crying and licking and pawing at its own face. It wouldn't let nobody come close but the girl, and the child was all wet with tears.

Olubunmi felt a world of sorrow for all the suffering—but not one bit sorry for the mace.

"I told you, our Lucy doesn't bite!" the mister said, all up in Olubunmi's face, water spouting from the end of his hose.

Hell she don't.

"Listen up," she'd told him. "You *got* to restrain your dog. Till you do, you can pick up your mail downtown."

And she could see him wanting to shove his hose down her throat.

So what'd them people do then but go and fit up an invisible fence to "secure" the Rott. Like trapping that dog in the yard was any kind of help. Don't she still have to walk into that yard every day with the mail? It's like telling a scuba diver at the aquarium, "Don't you be worrying none about them sharks you're swimming with, 'cause they can't swim out of the tank."

She told them Meadows people again: she wasn't going nowhere near their house so long as their dog was loose. Gave them the bad-eye too.

So they paraded downtown and bitched to her boss. The mister went off so loud everybody heard through the office door. Fletch don't never stick up for nobody—but for some reason, on that day, he stuck up for her. Gave them folks the what-for. Told them to tie up or shut up.

She hasn't laid eyes on that ol' Rott since. Not once.

Still . . . the air's always trembling around #980. Every drop she makes there, she lives it all over—that big black Rott coming at her, her spraying the mace. Memories of Buddy all caught up in it too.

Dog like that's got no business being in the same house as a child.

That little Meadows girl . . . she's as scarce as the Rott. Never out playing in the yard. Never out riding her bike. Never out messing with other kids. Never out to school—leastways, back before the COVID, when there *was* school.

Yeah, something in #980's just not right.

The air's a-trembling bad.

OLUBUNMI ROUNDS the tall pine with relief, glad to get off the Rott's turf. She settles her mailbag on her right hip and rushes away from #980.

She don't run, though. That would be dumb as applesauce. That Rott sees her running, it might just break loose from wherever it's at and blow through that invisible fence.

Besides, nobody looking like her should ever run in a hood like this. Not even in uniform. *Nuh-uh.*

She sinks into a good pace, boots on autopilot. No more dogs to fret over, the rest of this swing.

The sky's thickening by the minute. She's sweating in her snow gear, racing the clock against the storm. If the nor'easter hits bad enough, she can pack it in. But she's no quitter. The mail's in her hands for a reason.

On to #982. Around the low hedge. Over the gravel drive. Past the rosebushes. Across the brick walk along the porch. The old man's clarinet getting louder.

As she goes, she thumbs through #982's mail. One last check of the addresses. She always puts the handwritten mail on top, 'cause it's what matters most. Then the bills. Then the junk. All wrapped in the flats, like a taco.

The old man's getting a bunch of cards. His birthday, most like. He sure ain't sick, judging by how the house is singing.

Somebody name of "A. Richter" has sent him a flat-rate Priority Mail envelope. Must be kin.

SOME HOUSES, from a distance, they look like faces. Small windows for eyes. Front door for a mouth. Garage door, a fat old grin. Dormers for eyebrows. Vines for hair.

One house, her last route, had electric wires hanging around two second-story windows, like spectacles.

The face of a house can tell secrets about the folks living inside. The

Rott's house—it's a ranch from the '50s. Summertime, the big box at the bay window is full of pink flowers. A nice, happy lipstick smile. Right? More like the house is sticking out its tongue, warning you off.

Next door, #982's got a friendly face. Sure enough. Like your white-haired great-uncle, chilling on the porch, Sunday after church. The hedge is his painter's brush mustache, still dark and cropped close on his old-man lip. "Y'all come on up here," he says as you're passing by. "Sit down. Rest your bones a spell."

Don't matter none who you are. You're still family.

Way, *way* back, #982 had been a farmhouse, most like. Today it's smack-dab in town. Fire-engine red. Pale-yellow shutters and white gingerbread trim tone it down, keep it from being loud.

The air around #982 is kind but sassy. Like jazz. Even before the clarinet calls you up.

She takes the white porch steps two at a time.

WHEN SHE FIRST COME ON this route, she kept thinking the old lady was named Freya. Or Flora. Some *F* name nobody names their girls no more. But she's got it down now: Miss *Fiona*.

The old man was easier. Simon's her granddaddy's name. But to his face she calls him Dr. Richter. Folks say he was a big dog up at the college, back in the day. Taught old rocks and bones.

She's thinking it should have been music.

BEFORE THE COVID, she used to see Simon outside a lot. He'd be reading on the porch or messing with his rosebushes or scooping snow.

"Sorry," he'd always say when she walked up. Then he'd spout all this mumbo-jumbo about not remembering stuff, like her name. Him and his little speech always seemed so sad. So lost. Like a minor key.

So, every time, she'd say back, "Nice to meet you, Dr. Richter. I'm Olubunmi Adams." Shake his hand, like it was their first dance.

He'd always repeat her name then, real slow and fine. Like it mattered, getting it right.

She tried to help him. " 'Gift of God.' That's what Olubunmi means. But everybody just calls me Boo."

"Boo?" he'd say, eyebrows shooting up like the name didn't suit. "Is that what you like to call yourself?"

"No, sir. I prefer Olubunmi."

"Well, then, Olubunmi," he'd say with a funny laugh, "if you're bringing me any bills today, I'd be happy if you kept them."

Like, half the town's told her that same joke. Everybody acting so smart. Like they'd thunk it up themselves.

The old man, though . . . that was different. 'Cause try as he might, he couldn't do any better. His mind and all.

So, she'd always played along with his joke. Made a real show of it, grooving off down the sidewalk with her bag, like she planned to save up his precious bills till the Rapture took them to heaven.

Her act got the old man rolling. Every time.

'Cause in his mind, every time was the first time.

SHE STANDS the Priority Mail on end in the white mailbox. Leaves it sticking up, so as not to bend it.

She'd like to hand Simon his birthday mail herself. But she hasn't spoken to him none—Miss Fiona neither—since lockdown. Last time she'd seen either of them was way back in March.

That day's stuck like a needle in her mind. Cold as winter, but the front door of #982 was open wide, maybe to let fresh air through the screen. Back then, folks were saying fresh air might help guard against the COVID.

That day, she was topping the steps with her mailbag when Miss Fiona suddenly appeared at the front door and banged it shut. Like, right in her face.

Miss Fiona stood there behind the wavy glass, one hand flattened pinkish white on the pane. Her old-lady eyeballs were drilling down, making Olubunmi's insides feel all wrong, like she was bad and had to be watched.

So, she acted like she hadn't noticed Miss Fiona. Just swung around and sashayed back down the brick sidewalk like Miss Fiona wasn't on God's good earth. It was like giving Miss Fiona the bad-eye using no eyes at all.

Then Olubunmi felt a sorry kick in her heart, for thinking mean. She turned back around to throw the old lady a wave. But Miss Fiona, she was gone from the door.

Next day, Olubunmi found a note from Miss Fiona taped to the mailbox.

"My dear, please forgive my rudeness yesterday," it said, handwriting full of the shakes. "I'm only trying to keep my husband safe."

Olubunmi didn't blame Miss Fiona none. The old lady was a bit color-struck, like most white folks. And back then, in the early days of the COVID, everybody with any sense at all was acting strange, trying to keep somebody safe.

They're still acting strange.

Time to time, Miss Fiona will tape another note, like the two of them are friends. "My dear," it always starts. Not "Olubunmi" or even "Boo." 'Cause Miss Fiona still don't know her name.

OLUBUNMI HASN'T SEEN EITHER of the Richters since that day in March. But almost every mail drop, she hears Simon blowing on his sweet licorice stick. Right now, standing on the porch, she can hear him right well.

His music is part of the house, like the yellow shutters. It's the house's voice. Sure enough.

The heavy curtains inside the window are *always* closed, tight as the nation's borders since the COVID. But today an angel must have blown them open, real gentle. Only an inch or two. And in that gap, Olubunmi can see Simon through the rippled glass.

He's sitting across the little room in a cane-back chair, lit by his floor lamp. He's facing the bird feeders, out the side window. Like he's playing clarinet for that mean ol' Rott across the hedge.

There's sheet music on his music stand and a notebook too. None of it's open, though. That tune, he's either playing it by heart or making it up on the spot.

A bell goes off in her head. *Can't stand here, girl, staring in no white man's window!*

But she don't pay that bell no mind. She's digging the old man's music.

Bless him up. He's sure enough bringing the noise.

NOSING AT THE WORLD

12:05 P.M.

"Sy!"

Simon breaks off mid-measure.

His Girl pokes her head through the door of his den. *"Please,* Bestie, come eat! You've been at it for hours."

Hours?

Fritz drops heavily from the chairback to the hardwood floor. He pads toward Fee, his silver-gray tail straight up in the air.

"I'll reheat the soup," Fee says. "You want a peanut butter sandwich to go along? Or grilled cheese?"

"Peanut butter."

"With tomatoes?"

She always asks. He never answers.

How else would you eat them?

"Bring in the mail, will you?" she says.

He sets his clarinet on its three-legged stand. He pushes himself up from his chair and stretches his back. A searing ache. He's been sitting too long.

In his mind, suddenly: *A big black dog leaning out the window of a Jeep as it cruises along a gravel road. The dog's ears are flapping, its tongue hanging out, its eager nose sniffing at the country air.*

Memory? Or imagination?

He can't say.

But that sniffing dog is exactly how he wants his music to nose at the world, getting at what's real.

"Be back soon," he tells the clarinet, switching off the lamp.
At the door, he flicks off the ceiling light.
"I won't forget," he says aloud. "Promise."
Pulling the door shut behind him.

STORYBOOK HOUSE

1:11 P.M.

OLIVIA TRACES a rusty patch of hair on Lucy's black cheek. She slides her finger down the dog's thick black neck.

She used to ride Lucy like a horse. Not anymore. (She's a big girl now, Charley says.)

She rolls over against Lucy's warm belly and pops her thumb into her mouth. She sucks like a baby. Even big girls have to suck, sometimes, in secret.

The glowing red numbers on the clock beside her bed say 1:11. If she's a good girl, Charley might let her out when he comes home at 5:30. He sells cars.

"Your mom'll bring pizza after her shift," he'd told her this morning, when he locked her in her room.

His Rapunzel, safe in the tower.

"You can have two slices if you're extra good," he'd said. "You going to be extra good?"

She isn't hungry yet. But if she gets hungry before the pizza, there's a brand-new box of ramen noodles beneath her bed. Twenty-four packages. A present from Charley. She doesn't know what flavor. She doesn't care.

She needs to go potty. She's trying to hold it. There's a pail in the corner, but peeing in it makes the room stink.

"Remember," Charley'd said through the door, last thing, "I lock you in to keep the bad people out. You know that, don't you, Olivia?"

"*What* bad people?"

"The ones with the cooties. You want to catch cooties?"

She doesn't want to catch cooties. But she doesn't like being Rapunzel.

She's not as old as Rapunzel. She's only eight. And her hair's not "gold like wheat"—it's stringy brown. And if Charley doesn't stop cutting it, it'll never be long enough for a prince to climb into her window.

She grabs her binoculars and crawls off her bed.

The old man on the other side of the bushes is late. Afternoons, he always starts making his music when the red numbers say 1:00. She's already cracked her window a smidge, to hear him.

Charley doesn't know she can raise her window. It's one of her big-girl secrets.

She's figured out the screen too. That was *way* harder.

Fresh cold air puffs through the faded pink curtain. She pulls the curtain back and peeks with her binoculars through two slats in the blinds.

She made the binoculars herself, out of toilet paper tubes. She painted them purple. She uses them to spy.

Where could he be?

She shoves the window up another inch.

She plops back down on the bed and draws her furry pink blanket up to her neck. It smells like dog and pee.

She'd rather have a cheeseburger than pizza. A cheeseburger with ketchup, honey mustard, and sweet pickles. Order it on the Net. Delivery by drone. For *that*, she'd leave her window open through the most humongous snowstorm *ever*. She's sick of ramen.

She'd order a burger for Lucy, too, if she could.

But that might make Lucy poop before Charley gets home.

Lucy's pink tongue, all scratchy and wet, licks Olivia's cheek. Olivia giggles.

"No one gets you like I do," Charley always tells her.

But the old man next door just might. In her secret mind, she calls him Grampa.

She used to have a real grampa. He lives in heaven now.

Heaven might be up in the sky, with the sun and the moon. She isn't sure. She can't see it through her binoculars.

Every day, when Charley's selling cars and her mom's working her shift at the store, Olivia spies on Grampa. He sits in a chair at his window, over the hedge. He opens his window, like he wants her to hear his music, only he doesn't know about her spying. He doesn't even know she's here.

His music makes the birds at his bird feeders real happy. Red ones and gray ones and blue ones and brown ones.

While Grampa plays, she always sits real still and listens real close. The sun can't be too bright or it stabs her eyes. Then her binoculars are no good.

She always keeps her head down. She's real good at being invisible.

"Quiet as a church mouse," Charley said once, bragging her up.

"What's a church mouse?"

"A mouse that lives in a big old church. She runs up Pastor's leg when he's not looking and makes him laugh—like *this*!"

She doesn't like being a church mouse. Not at all.

CHARLEY SAID it's going to snow today. A *lot*.

That's very bad.

When it snows, Grampa lowers his window almost the whole way down, and she can't hear his music much at all.

He's just like her, locked up all alone in his little room. Except he doesn't have a Lucy. He has a cat. The cat's gray with white on her chest, belly, and paws. Her name is Shadow.

Shadow's a name Olivia made up. But it could be the cat's name, for real.

Or maybe Ashes. Or Smoke.

Olivia likes Shadow.

Shadow's a real good leaper. She jumps on Grampa's back when he bends over. And sometimes, when Grampa's sitting in his chair, playing his music, Shadow jumps up and perches on his shoulder, like a big owl on a wizard. Grampa doesn't get mad and swat her off. He lets her stay.

Sometimes, when Charley's home and making her "feel good," and Lucy's outside the door, whining and scratching—*whoosh!* she's suddenly up in the air, like in a dream. She flies like a fairy over to the red storybook house with the yellow shutters, right through the window into Grampa's room. She floats like a birthday balloon, up by the ceiling. She doesn't know how it happens, but it does, like magic.

Grampa can't see her floating up there, but she can see him down below, like Charley says God sees all His children. Especially the bad ones, who don't do what they're supposed to. They get into *big* trouble, Charley says.

She doesn't want to be bad.

So she floats up there, listening to Grampa play songs on his black stick, till Charley gets done and leaves. Then *whoop!* she's back in her bed again, and Lucy's there beside her, whimpering and washing her face with her tongue.

THE RED TURTLE

1:11 P.M.

.

SIMON STANDS AT HIS DESK, leafing through a short stack of mail. Several greeting card envelopes are addressed to him.

Must be an occasion you've forgotten.

By the return addresses, one card is from Gertie McClure. Another, from Mike and Victor at Dinky Creek. A third, from a Dr. R. Betts at the University of Chicago.

Beneath the cards, the junk. Then the *Daily Register*. The *New York Times*.

And here's a piece of Priority Mail. He smiles. It's from Gilly.

He rips the tear strip on the mailer.

Fritz bats at the strip with a frisky white paw.

Inside the mailer is a large manila envelope decorated with hand-drawn red hearts.

Valentine's Day, maybe?

On one side of the envelope, Gilly has printed: "DO NOT OPEN THIS ENVELOPE UNTIL YOUR BIRTHDAY!!!"

My birthday.

What day is today?

Doesn't matter.

He unfastens the envelope's clasp and draws out a sheaf of papers. Clipped to the top is a note.

Happy 80th, Dad!!!

Here's the first installment of your birthday present from me — more to come!
   Please look at these papers right now. Don't wait. And don't show Mom till you've read them.

   I realize you'll soon forget what's in these. Don't worry. I promise to remember for you.
   I know the kind of man you are. You value the truth. And truth never really dies, does it?

   I'll tell you more at your birthday party! (Not in person. On the computer.)

Love ya oodles & bunches,
Abby

His eyes return to "Don't show Mom." This can't be good. Gilly's never been one to keep secrets from her mother.

His curiosity quells his misgivings. He riffles through the papers. They appear to be copies of official documents and correspondence from a bygone era. Typewritten on vintage machines, with strings of longhand cropping up in the margins.

And here's a sepia-toned eight-by-ten photograph.

The sight of it shoves him down into his chair.

Memories of the day Pop took this picture rush back like a movie reel stuck in high-speed rewind. It can't be switched off.

"Stand still," Pop says, pointing his new Kodak. "Smile!"

What are you and Mama supposed to do—pose here in the yard, pretending to be as light and happy as those jackrabbits nesting only a short distance away in the patchy spring grass? Pretending that you—and Mama too—haven't just done a god-awful thing? Pretending that Pop hadn't arrived home from Lincoln in the nick of time?

"C'mon, you two!" Pop coaxes. "Say cheese."

"Why cheese?" You scowl. "That's dumb!"

Mama snatches off your cap and rakes her fingers through your hair. You shy from her touch, still smarting from her slaps. But you smell her talcum powder. A smell you love. Faintly vanilla. Clean. Safe.

"Karl," she says to Pop, "must we do this now? It's not the best time . . ."

"Won't take long."

"But it's so windy!"

"Just a few more shots!"

Pop studies the Kodak's viewfinder. All the while, those darn rabbits just lie there in the grass. Any other day, he'd be running for his twelve gauge.

"I'll get these prints developed right away," he says. "Want to make sure I know what I'm doing with this gizmo. Got to be good by Easter—Christ! So damn windy! Keeps messing with your hair!"

Mama pulls you closer. You wriggle against her.

"On three!" Pop announces.

"Mama loves you so much, Chasker," she whispers. She seldom uses your middle name out loud. Never in front of anyone else. "Smile for your father."

"One . . . two . . . chee-eeze!" Pop sings.

Empty and raw, you stare at the camera.

Shick, *clicks the shutter.*

Shick, shick.

· · ·

AND HERE'S ANOTHER PHOTOGRAPH—BLACK and white. An orchestra of young people. Mama isn't hard to spot, dressed in white, clarinet across her lap.

Someday soon, you'll be a forgotten old photo. Like her.

His eye drifts to the bass drum in the back.

GENOA INDIAN SCHOOL it says on the side.

Indian School.

Indian.

His skull is pounding.

He flips the picture, hoping for some sort of caption or note. Any kind of explanation.

"Your mother," Gilly had written along the bottom edge, in fine blue felt tip, "was a Dakota woman from the Sisseton reservation—"

Dakota.

Reservation.

His mind throws him back into the kitchen of the homeplace. To the red coffee can, high up in the cupboard, where Mama had stored her matchbooks. To the turtle, beaded red, hidden inside the battered matchbox at the bottom of the can.

That turtle wasn't a toy.

He shoots up like a man in his prime, the photographs cascading to the floor with the rest of Gilly's papers. His chair topples. His music stand tips. Sheet music flies.

Fritz darts with flat whiskers under the desk.

SIMON'S OUT of breath as he tops the attic ladder. He yanks the chain of the light fixture with such force that the end swings up and clinks against the naked bulb. That lone bulb must be loose in its socket. Or dying. It yields a flickering light.

Maybe Iris had discovered that red turtle in the coffee can when she purged all evidence of Mama from the house—a job Pop had put to her after the wedding. Or maybe she'd stumbled upon it in the course of her housework.

Either way, if Iris had found the turtle, she would have kept it. She'd have known it *had* to be kept.

And if Iris had kept it, the turtle must be up here, in the far corner, amongst the stuff his stepbrother, Colin, had shipped to him after she died.

Simon has to hurry. Time is his enemy. It has him surrounded. He'll soon forget why he's up here.

In his haste to cut across the attic, he clips his ankle on Gilly's old rocking horse. He careens against the crib. He grabs at its spindles to break his fall, but misses. His knees smack the floor, square. He buckles forward with a sharp moan.

Slow down before you break something! Fee says in his brain.

In the winking light of the faulty bulb, Simon tussles with the margins of memory.

He sets his sights on the steamer trunk his grandparents had brought over on the boat from Germany.

Too obvious, Fee says. *Iris was smarter than that.*

"Where, then?" he says aloud.

Somewhere Colin could never have found it and thrown it out—you know, not realizing that it mattered.

He picks himself up, his banged-up knees on fire.

All the boxes from the homeplace are taped shut. Except for one.

It's the train set Pop had bought that first Christmas without Mama. One of the last sets Lionel had manufactured before Pearl Harbor.

Following a hunch, Simon unwraps car after car after car.

HERE, at last, is the red caboose.

Simon pushes his spectacles higher on his nose. He lifts the caboose toward the light bulb, somehow no longer flickering. By its steady light, he peers through the tiny windows.

Triumph surges. Snug inside is the big matchbox from the coffee can.

He inspects the caboose's black undercarriage, its peacock-green roof, its red body with tarnished brass railings and ladders. No easy way to get in. Extracting the matchbox will be delicate work, like excavating a fragile fossil in the field.

How had Iris ever managed to lodge it inside the caboose? Next to impossible, like fitting a ship through the neck of a bottle.

Only a woman trying to protect another woman's secrets—and pass them on—would ever go to such bother.

He digs his Swiss Army knife out of his pocket.

SEE-THROUGH

1:21 P.M.

OLIVIA GETS up to peer through the curtains again. *Where can Grampa be?*

She's not sure, but his black stick might be a "clarinet." That's a big-people word. She read about it on the Net.

She's on the Net a lot. She can almost use it like a big girl. She can almost read like a big girl too.

The Net's fast, like melt-your-face fast. Maybe it runs on electric, like a clock. It doesn't have a cord, not that she can see, but the whole world seems plugged in.

And the Net's got all kinds of stuff. It has, like, *all* of *everything.* Like Noah's Ark. The Bible says the Ark had two of every creepy, crawly thing. It was stuffed with animals: dogs and cats and horses and giraffes and unicorns and mermaids.

The Ark must have had trolls, too, and vampires and zombies—how else could they still be around? The Flood would have taken them out, like a bomb.

Charley might be a werewolf in disguise. His body's so hairy! The Ark must have had werewolves too.

Olivia's pretty sure her mom is a witch 'cause she has a fat wart and she's always burning candles and she acts like strange stuff that should never happen is fine and perfect.

If her mom is a witch, maybe that means Olivia's a witch too. She thinks about this a lot. If she *is* a witch, she wants to be a good one. And brainy, like Hermione Granger. Only not so bossy.

She'll never be a hairy werewolf. Not if she can help it.

Maybe God's in charge of the Net. Maybe it's His castle, since God is

King, and kings live in castles. Or maybe the Net is heaven—you can't see it, but it's up there, and it's *humongous*.

Or maybe the Net *is* God.

Praying to the Net doesn't help, though.

She doesn't know how the Net works, but she needs it, like Charley says he needs her, more than anybody. Sometimes he shows her secret "big-girl" stuff on the Net, because she's "special."

She doesn't like being special.

She wishes she could tell the Net all her secrets. Or maybe she could tell Grampa. But Charley says if she tells her secrets to a single soul, they won't be special anymore. And God will be very, *very* mad.

She has to keep God happy. Or else He might write her name in the Bad People Book.

That would be very, *very* bad.

SHE DROPS down on the floor with a tablet and her crayons. Lucy's still on the bed, fast asleep, lying on her back, paws in the air.

Olivia turns her tablet sideways.

She pulls a black crayon from the box. She draws a house on the left side of the paper. *Her* house.

Now, down the middle of the paper, a thick hedge, with green.

Now, with red, Grampa's house on the right, much bigger than the black house.

She picks up orange. She hates orange.

Back in the black house, she puts Charley, with blobby eyes and a big crooked mouth and teeth like an angry pumpkin. Fat, hairy arms too. Fingers like knives.

In the red house, she puts Grampa in purple, with a smile. She puts a black stick poking out of his mouth. She gives him long purple eyelashes. Bright blue eyes. Silver hair.

She picks up white. She puts Hat Lady right beside Grampa. On the white paper, you can hardly tell she's there. When you hold the paper just right, she shines.

But Olivia wants to see her better. She puts a pink hat in one of Hat Lady's see-through hands.

Olivia smiles then. Pink's her very own favoritest color.

WHEN GRAMPA SITS at the window and plays his black stick, he thinks he's all alone, but Olivia knows better. He's never alone. Not *ever*.

Hat Lady is *always* with him.

Grampa can't see Hat Lady. Not one bit. But Olivia can.

This may be her bestest secret of all.

Hat Lady looks old, like Olivia's mom. But not as old as Grampa. Her hair is long and almost black, pulled back and wrapped in a coil. It's mussed up, like she's been out in the wind. Or maybe in a big fight.

Her clothes look real funny. Nothing like the clothes pretty women wear on the Net. More like what Olivia's mom wears. "Frumpy," Charley would say.

Hat Lady is always carrying a pink straw hat. It's decorated real nice with flowers. It's never on her head, where it belongs. Maybe it doesn't fit.

Hat Lady hovers, just like Charley says Olivia's mom does. Charley gripes about her mom's hovering, but Grampa's not bothered by Hat Lady. He never even seems to notice her. Like, she'll be standing so close to him, he *has* to feel her, right *there* . . . but *nope!* Not even when her tears drip.

Hat Lady can walk right through walls, the way Olivia can fly through windows when the fairy magic happens. Hat Lady can even walk straight through Grampa. *Whoo-ee!* So cool!

Once, on the Net, Charley showed Olivia a kind of butterfly with see-through wings, like glass. It can hide in plain sight without even trying. It doesn't have to be afraid of anything. Not even werewolves. Not *ever*.

That's the kind of creature Hat Lady is. See-through. But she's not solid, like those glassy butterfly wings.

At first, Olivia thought maybe Hat Lady was a ghost. But ghosts aren't see-through. They look like white sheets, and when they pay you a visit, they make a room go scary-cold. They make you hide under the covers and screw your eyes shut.

Hat Lady's nothing like that. She's like a foggy window with a light on the other side. She glides around real quiet. You want to get closer to her, not run away.

Maybe she's a guardian angel. But angels should have wings, right? And angels don't make tears, do they?

Besides, shouldn't an angel be able to see a little girl flying into a room and drifting up by the ceiling?

Hat Lady has eyes only for Grampa and his black stick. She wants to touch him *so bad*. But when she goes to kiss him, her lips pass right through his cheek. She can't even pat his head or tap his shoulder. When she tries, her and him get all mixed up in each other, like some crazy kind of cartoon.

Hat Lady tries to talk to Grampa too. He'll be playing his black stick, and she'll be telling him stories. But her voice is as see-through as her body is. It sort of melts into the music. You can't tell one from the other.

What Hat Lady's trying to say to Grampa must be super important, or she wouldn't try so hard. Maybe that's why she starts crying sometimes, 'cause she can't get through to him.

So Olivia wants to help Hat Lady.

"Listen real close to your music," Olivia will whisper to Grampa through the curtains at her window. She'll wave her Mystical Magical Mermaid Wand at him and use that witchy voice she always uses to cast good spells (in case she actually is a good witch).

Or if she's over in his room, floating up by the ceiling, she'll point her finger down, like all those pictures of God when He's playing at working miracles.

"Listen better!" she'll tell Grampa in her bestest God voice.

Lately, she thinks Grampa's ears might be starting to catch a hint of . . . *something*. She's not sure what. Her own witchy whispers? Hat Lady's see-through talk? Whatever he's hearing, it's making him play way better.

It's like vanilla.

Sometimes Olivia's mom lets her out of her room and tells her to do stuff. Like, bake a cake. Olivia loves baking cakes—it's messy and it's fun and she gets to be in the kitchen around grown-up stuff like matches and knives and tipsy juice. She'll stand on the step stool and dump the cake mix into a bowl and add the eggs and oil and beat it all up, then dip her finger into the batter. It's always sweet enough, but oh so *boring*, so *blah*.

So, when nobody's looking, she sneaks the little brown bottle of vanilla from the cupboard and pours a bunch in—not too much, or they might notice. Just enough that the batter tastes *way* better.

Adding *anything* can change *everything*.

OLIVIA STUDIES HER DRAWING.

Lucy needs to be in the black house.

With her pink crayon, Olivia gives Lucy a smiley face with wide-open eyes and pointy ears. Four legs. An itty-bitty tail.

She grows the itty-bitty tail into an extra-long one. That's one thing about drawing: you can always change things from how they are to how they ought to be.

But some things you can't change. Not even in pictures.

Like, she can't put Lucy in the red house. Lucy doesn't belong there.

She picks up ugly orange again.

She puts herself in the black house. Right next to pink Lucy.

She puts empty circles where her eyes should be. She doesn't give herself a mouth.

She gives herself two legs. But no arms at all.

Then she switches back to pink again.

She puts a pink Olivia in the red house, floating above purple Grampa and his black stick and white Hat Lady and her pink hat. This Olivia has real eyes and a mouth and arms . . . just an ordinary, regular girl.

Nobody "special" at all.

THE BARN

1:21 P.M.

SIMON SHOVES the big matchbox into the pocket of his cardigan. The beaded turtle remains safely inside. He suspects it's an amulet from Mama's people.

Indian people.

Dakota people, according to Gilly.

How to remember all this? How not to forget?

At the top of the ladder, he tugs the chain on the light bulb. The attic goes black. He turns around, positioning himself to descend.

Suddenly he's five years old again, the night Mama died. He's back in the barn at the homeplace, ready to climb down the ladder from the loft.

Every day of his life, his innards spew up this infernal memory. He never knows what might trigger it. But every time he's forced to relive that night, the recollection is always the same, down to the last detail.

Only, not this time.

This time, he smells smoke from a cigarette.

He follows that smoke where he has never gone.

Pop's home at last. The smoke tells you so.

The screeching of owl chicks sends you pell-mell down the ladder. You'll feel safe with Pop. More like a big boy.

As you hit the bottom rung, another bank of lights flickers on.

"Vera?" you hear Pop call.

You're about to run lickety-split toward his voice—

61

"You crazy? Shut them lights off!"

It's Uncle Pete. The creepy bite in his voice reins you in.

The barn falls back toward dark. You slink toward the low light emanating from the next bay.

"Pete? That you?" Pop blurts out. "Where you at?"

"Keep it down, will ya? I'm over here."

Filled with formless dread, you tiptoe around the wall. You duck behind a thick timber post.

Mama's spread-eagled in the dirt behind the tractor, unnaturally limp, dress up to her thighs. Uncle Pete's standing over her, muttering. His words buzz and crackle in your ears like a radio broadcast without a clear signal.

Not one sound, *you tell yourself, plugging every emotion welling up inside you.* Not a single sound.

You see Pop fall hard to his knees, the way a big person does when there's no point praying anymore. His stricken face warps into the face of some other man.

"Christ, Pete! What have you done?"

"Didn't mean to, little brother," Uncle Pete says, snapping his suspenders over his shoulders. "Swear to God."

Liar! *you think.*

Horrified, you press your cheek against the shaved wood of the post. You can't bear to look. Yet you can't look away.

Pop's rocking back and forth on his knees, wringing the skin off his hands. "Goddammit, Pete . . . how could you?"

Uncle Pete leans down, maybe to haul Pop to his feet.

Instead, he cuffs Pop on the side of the head. "Pull yourself together! We've gotta take care of this!"

Pop flies up in a rage, fists flailing. Uncle Pete ducks and dodges, not punching back. The state Pop's in, he's no real threat to anybody.

You're just a little kid, but you're tempted to jump out from your hiding place and pummel Pete with your own two dukes.

Not one move, *you tell yourself.*

Uncle Pete waits for an opening and lunges at Pop's legs, tackling him to the floor. He pins Pop's arms. Crawls astride his middle.

"Dammit, Karl—give it up! You want Simon to hear?"

Too late, you bastard, *you think.* Bastard *is a cuss word Mama always scolds Pop for.*

Pop groans in surrender. "Where's the boy at?" he says, breathing in jags, his body right next to Mama.

"The house, I figure."

Uncle Pete knows he has won. Triumph is as plain on his face as oblivion is on Mama's.

You suppress an urge to retch.

Goddamn son of a bitch, *you think—more of Pop's language. That must be about the dirtiest, wickedest thing anybody could ever say. You said it aloud once, just to test it, and Mama washed your mouth out with soap. Made you bite down on the bar.*

Uncle Pete claps Pop chummily on the cheek and slides off. "Come on—we gotta find some rope."

Pop raises himself on an elbow. "Rope?"

Uncle Pete marches along the barn wall, searching. The wall's a catchall, hung with old license plates and Pioneer Seed Corn calendars, hand tools, lengths of chain, leather straps, rat traps.

"Where's your rope, man?" he says.

Pop's still glued to the floor. "What we need it for?"

"Just tell me where it is!"

Uncle Pete abandons the wall. He weaves in and out of wooden crates and sawhorses, old tires and rusty milk cans, beat-up gas cans and cans of leftover paint, a stack of fence posts, lassos of wire, bikes resting on their kickstands.

He's headed your way. You flatten yourself skinny against the back of your post.

"Got some Manila rope in the shed," Pop offers. He sounds like "Mary's little lamb," sure to follow wherever he's told to go.

"Too thick."

Pete's so close you break off breathing.

His footsteps stop on the other side of your post, where ice skates hang by their laces from a spike. Beneath them is your sled, propped up on its runners.

"This'll do."

You hear him unfold his pocketknife. You guess what he's after: the heavy twine pull-rope attached to the sled's crosspiece.

He makes the cut.

"Clean her up," he tells Pop as he moves away, toward the cow pen.

You sneak a peek.

Pete coils the twine like a Hollywood cowboy. Then he climbs over the fence. Even from here, you can smell the hay on cows' breath.

In the middle of the pen, he fashions a noose from the rope. Curses. Unties it. Tries again, adjusting the knot, enlarging the loop.

You know from the picture shows what a noose is for. But why, when Mama's already dead?

"Done with her yet?" Uncle Pete calls.

You look back at Pop. He's there beside Mama, sweeping a tangle of hair from her vacant face. His fingertips touch her cheekbones, her lips, the tender dip between her mouth and chin.

"We'll say she hanged herself," Uncle Pete says as he tosses the noose over a crossbeam.

These words seem to break through the black ice of Pop's shock. "You can't be serious!"

"Who'll ever know?"

"But her face . . . the scratches . . ."

Uncle Pete plants a milk can beneath the dangling noose. "Rope burns will cover the bruises. Trust me. No one will ever know."

"We will know!" Pop declares, and you believe he might be growing some spine.

Uncle Pete fetches a paint-stained stepladder. "You got a better idea? Maybe you gonna turn me in?"

Pop draws a hand over Mama's eyes, closing their lids. "She was . . . my girl . . ."

Uncle Pete kicks open the feet of the stepladder beside the milk can. "She was fixing to leave you."

You straighten like an ice pick.

So does Pop. "Not a chance!" he exclaims.

"Said so herself. Meant to take your boy and run."

"The hell she was!" Pop's on his feet so fast, you don't see how he got there.

Pete storms back over the fence. He grabs Pop by the collar.

"Wake up, little brother! You two were kaputt! She didn't give a goddamn about you! She meant to join up with a band and live a whore's life on the road! You'd never have seen your boy again!"

Big fat liar! Pants on fire! Every word a whopper, flat-out ugly and mean.

Pete has Pop's face locked between his hands. "Now you listen to me, and you listen good. You're gonna help me, hear?" Pete points toward the ladder with his chin. "You hold that thing steady, and when I get her up there, you put that noose around her neck."

Pop tries to knock Pete's hands away. But Pete has him.

"We'll stand her on the milk can, see—just like she'd have done. And you put the knot behind her ear, right here." Pete jabs the spot on Pop's skull, three times, rapid-fire.

"They'll smell a rat!" Pop says, whiny again, like a bleating sheep.

"Who?"

"Sheriff, coroner . . . somebody!"

Pete shifts his hands to the back of Pop's neck and clamps down. "Dammit, Karl," he snarls through clenched teeth. "Make up your mind! Me or her!"

Pop roots his fingers into his blond hair. Fat tears dribble down his cheeks, just like they're dribbling down yours.

"Look," Pete says to Pop, "I get it—you loved her. She was something of a *looker when she dolled herself up. Sweet enough face. Eyes that could make you all weak in the knees. But her life's not worth a drop of mine!"*

You love Uncle Pete. You do. But you want Pop to clobber him. You want Pop to make him bleed.

"That's the truth, isn't it?" Pete's nose is an inch from Pop's. "I want to hear you say it. Who's it going to be—her or me?"

Please, Pop, you beg.

But Pop's body slackens. He drops his forehead against Pete's shoulder.

Pete lets go of Pop's neck and clutches him close.

"Okay, then?"

Pop pulls away. Nods.

"Only . . . not here," Pop says, wiping his face on a sleeve. "Not with the cows." His voice is a scratch. "You know how she loved to play her music out here."

"Then where?" Pete says with impatience.

Pop fumbles a Lucky Strike into a corner of his mouth. He goes to light a match with his thumbnail, but it falls in the dirt. He sends it flying with his shoe.

"Where?" Pete says again.

A second match breaks.

"Christ." Pete flicks open his Zippo and lights Pop up.

Pop takes a drag, his hand shaking bad. He blows smoke at the floor.

"Let's take her to the woodshed."

CHILDREN, Simon tells himself, still clinging to the attic ladder, *will tolerate almost any behavior on the part of the grown-ups they love. They tend to believe that the big people they belong to are heroes. They can't imagine that their big people might also be monsters.*

From that Easter night forward, he'd held his tongue. He'd broken faith with himself. He'd forced himself to live in the ocean of a lie until, somewhere along the line, he'd convinced himself that what the grown-ups were saying was actually the whole truth and nothing but: that Mama had hanged herself in the woodshed and he'd discovered her there.

He hadn't overwritten his own memory to protect Pop. And certainly not to protect Uncle Pete.

No, he'd done it to protect himself. Even now, he can barely stomach the grisly replay of that unholy hour, a fiendish contest in which everybody who mattered to him had lost.

The corpse of the drowned truth has finally floated to the surface:

Mama hadn't strung herself up on the rope from your sled in some ghastly statement of maternal rejection.

No.

Uncle Pete had killed her. Probably raped her too.

And Pop had helped him get away with it.

Simon is the only person left alive who knows the real story.

It's as if, by sampling visible remnants of rock, he has suddenly gained the vision of a long-lost continent, submerged far beneath the surface of his conscious life. Just as geologists had located Greater Adria beneath southern Europe and reconstructed its violent tectonic history.

He sees it all clearly now—not the whole truth but enough: How he had come to be and how he had been formed, deep down in the underworld. What had shattered him. What had shoved him down. What had stacked upon him, layers and layers.

The boy in the barn still exists in the old man.

Yes, he'd forgotten the truth of his life—not by choice but by reflex. By instinct to survive.

Very soon he will forget for the second and last time—through incapacity.

But this time, when he forgets, he will have known that he was loved, and the truth will be out in the open air.

BIG GIRL GETS GONE

1:27 P.M.

In Olivia's purple binoculars, Grampa steps off the porch in his coat and hat. His black stick's hanging from his neck by a thingamabob.

By the red numbers, it's way, way, *way* too early for Grampa's walk. And he *never* takes his black stick with him.

Lucy noses Olivia hard in the ribs, a ragged tug toy in her mouth, bumping Grampa from Olivia's sights.

"*Stop*, Lucy! I have to see!"

At the end of the brick path in front of his house, Grampa pauses. Then he turns right on the city sidewalk. Toward *her* house.

"What you doing, silly Grampa?"

Grampa *always* turns left on the sidewalk. He's all bass-ackwards, Charley would say.

Lucy yips and grumbles, begging to play.

"*Shhhh!*"

Hat Lady's behind Grampa, practically tripping on his heels.

"Now, where are *you* going?" Olivia asks her.

Hat Lady *always* stays home when Grampa goes out.

Hat Lady's almost unseeable in daylight. What gives her away is the straw hat in her hand—a glassy pink ring rippling the air. She's like . . . a wrinkle in the cloth of the day. Well, no. More like . . . like . . . *something*.

Things can be real even if you can't put them into words.

Maybe things without words are the realest of all.

Olivia's got Grampa in one purple tube of her binoculars, Hat Lady in the other. A few more steps, Olivia won't be able to see either of them anymore. Not from here.

She has to know what's up. Some things, you just can't *not* know.

People are a little like God that way. Snoopy! Big people, especially. They want to know everything about everybody. Till they don't.

Olivia kneels and throws her arms around Lucy. The dog purrs like a thousand fat happy cats.

"I've got to go," Olivia whispers.

Lucy whimpers.

"I know. It's not fair, is it? But you've got to stay here."

Olivia hurries to the pee pail and drops her jeans.

When she's done, she slides open her closet door. She's sure her closet has a secret entrance to a fantabulous land, like Narnia. She's checked for loose floorboards and knocked on the walls for hollow spots. Too obvious. Once she finally discovers the way in, there'd better not be monsters on the other side.

For now, though, she cares less about the world beyond her closet wall than the one outside her window. She doesn't go out of the house much at all. Her pink winter coat's buried beneath layers of books and stuffed animals and board games and Charley's special magazines. So are her stripy pink gloves. Her shiny pink boots.

She slips a package of ramen noodles into one coat pocket. She sticks her purple binoculars into another. And her pink crayon, for good luck.

She climbs onto her little-girl alphabet table. Like her little-girl chair, it's too small for her now. But it's a good stepstool, if you watch out for the wobbles.

She peers out a corner of her window.

The coast is clear.

She raises the blinds. She parts the curtains. She muscles up the heavy window, far as she can.

"I promise to come back and get you," she says to Lucy. "Don't run away."

She pushes in the cold metal thingies at the bottom of the screen. She's got to make them slide. But it's as hard as poking a camel in the eye. These thingies are made for big-people fingers, like Charley's.

But she'll show him.

She's a big girl now.

GIFT OF GOD

1:50 P.M.

SIMON'S SOMEWHERE DOWNTOWN, breathing frosty clouds. From a strap around his neck hangs his clarinet, its mouthpiece protected by a metal cap.

He doesn't remember taking the clarinet from his den.

He doesn't remember putting on his jacket and hat.

He doesn't remember leaving the house.

How did you get here? Are you out on your walk?

Why are the streets so empty?

Coming toward him is a mail carrier, bundled up in blue. A woman, maybe. Most of her dark-skinned face is concealed by a black mask.

Why's she wearing a mask? Not a hero mask that covers the eyes, like Zorro's or Batman's. More like a surgeon's, over the mouth and nose. Reminds him of the paleontology conference in Tokyo, back in 2009. Everybody in the city was masked up against H1N1.

"Hey, Dr. Richter!" the mail carrier says. "What you doing round here?"

How does she know me?

"Out walking," he manages to tell her.

"You got a gig somewhere?"

"*Gig?*"

She gestures to the clarinet, hanging off his neck. "You play real good!"

Flustered, he digs in his brain for the speech Fee had taught him for moments just like this: "I'm sorry—my name is Simon Richter. I used to teach geological sciences at the university. I have a condition that causes me not to remember well. Would you please tell me your name?"

"I'm Olubunmi Adams. Nice to meet you!"

"Olubunmi?" he says.

"You got it. 'Gift of God.' That's what it means. But everybody calls me Boo."

"That what you call yourself?"

"I like Olubunmi."

"I do too."

The woman transfers her mailbag to her opposite shoulder. Her big brown eyes never leave him. "You know, Miss Fiona—she wouldn't like you being out here without no mask."

"You know my Fee?"

"You best be getting on home, right quick, before it snows. Nasty storm coming! You do that for me?"

"Yes'm."

She passes him by. He turns to watch her go.

A half block up, she sidesteps a child in a pink parka and pink boots, dawdling on the sidewalk. A bright-pink shadow in a world of gray.

ROSES IN SOFT SNOW

2:07 P.M.

"THE VIRUS SEEMS to be spreading exponentially now," the host is saying on National Public Radio. "The worst could be yet to come, especially with winter looming . . ."

Upstairs in her art studio, Fee slumps over a quilt she's embroidering, drifting off into the hum of a dream. The words "winter looming" transpose into "winter blooming" and settle her into a la-la scene fit for a snow globe.

In the dream, she's seated on one end of a wrought-iron garden bench in front of their house. The house is painted yellow, though—not fire-engine red. Dreams can alter real-life details like that and still seem true.

It's snowing in the dream, without wind. She isn't the least bit chilled, despite wearing only a housedress and a single slipper, on her right foot. Her left slipper, she knows, is still resting beside the pedal of her sewing machine. She always runs the machine barefoot.

Sy's nearby in the yard, deadheading his roses in the soft snow. It isn't the season for blooms, yet roses of every color are streaming out of planters, climbing high trellises, cascading over windows, arching over the brick pathway, overwhelming the neighbor's garden fence . . . The scene looks stitched together, a stunning quilt of gorgeous roses on a pure-white background.

"Isn't the cold going to kill the flowers?" she calls to Sy from her bench. "Shouldn't we do something to save them?"

"Can't always save what you love," he says.

DR. BONES

2:07 P.M.

"WELL, Dr. Bones! Look at you! How you been?"

Simon's body sags with relief at the greeting, coming from behind him. Nobody but Gertie McClure ever calls him Dr. Bones.

Now he knows where he is: outside McClure's Books, on Main Street. He doesn't even have to read the sign above the store's entrance.

He turns and steps forward with open arms, requesting a hug. Gertie McClure's hugs are always tight, without trapping. They pull you into a cloud of heady perfume, floral with a tinge of coconut.

"Uh-uh! No, sir—none of that!" Gertie says, shunning his embrace. "Got to keep our distance, Dr. Bones!"

"Why?" he asks, puzzled.

"We're in a pandemic, my dear. You really should be wearing a mask."

"Should I?"

Delicate corkscrews of white hair spill out of her purple headscarf. Her matching purple face mask muffles her mellifluous voice.

Shortly after Gertie had opened the bookstore, back in the '80s, he and Fee had wandered in, lured by the hand-painted sign in the window: "Books You Don't Need in a Shop You Won't Leave." Introducing himself to Gertie that day, he mentioned he studied dinosaurs, and she dubbed him Dr. Bones. The name had stuck. And her sign's still there.

Stone-walled McLure's Books occupies one of the city's oldest buildings. It's an ancient fern in the world of independent bookstores, a rare and thriving survivor from the pre-internet age. It's also a survivor of a

New England town that, forty years ago, had been happier to tout its distant abolitionist past than to let someone like Gertie own a business on a prime piece of real estate. In those days, Sy and Fee had bought books from Gertie as an act of resistance.

Over the decades, the shop had become, for him, a refuge. Its open staircase was flanked all the way up to the third floor by a display of vintage typewriters. And up there was his favorite reading nook, an alcove with an enormous window facing the brick wall of the adjacent building. *My place,* he still thinks of it. *My chair.* Black-cherry leather, cracked with age, and comfy.

His *sanctum sanctorum.*

Every room on all three floors of McClure's is crammed full of books. The place is an absolute maze, and Gertie means you to get lost in it.

But then he actually *had* gotten lost, soon after the onset of his condition. Mercifully, he can't recall the specifics of that ordeal. Still, a residue remains of his tortured panic and the blood-cold estrangement from a place he'd always considered safe. Where he'd felt almost entirely at home. So, as much as he adores Gertie and her store, he means never to venture inside again unless his Girl has hold of his hand.

"How dare you try to pass by without stopping to say hi!" Gertie teases, her voice summoning him back to the street.

"Got better places to be," he says, carrying on like he knows exactly where he's going. And why.

"Uh-*huh,*" she says, arching a penciled eyebrow. "You tell me where you got to be that's any better than here!"

"Sign says you're closed," he says.

"That's right," Gertie says. "You can't come in. But you can't stop me coming out!"

She points at the zipper of his field jacket. "What you got hiding there in your coat?"

"Well, lookee there!" he says, flummoxed by the sight of his clarinet poking out. It's secured to his neck by a strap.

"Today's a mite cold to be busking for tips, isn't it?" she asks.

"You know how I love playing to a crowd." Forcing himself to banter.

"You lying through your gold teeth." Gertie's glittery eyes flash a smile above her mask. "Now, you be getting on home, double time, so you don't worry your missus. You know the way." She slaps a bagged book against his chest. "That's for Fee. Hold onto it tight, and it'll get to her when you do. You don't have to remember a thing."

"Another book. Just what Fee needs." He slips it into one of his deep jacket pockets. "What's she into this time? *How to Cure Dementia with Angels?*"

"*How to Put Up with Crotchety Husbands,*" Gertie jokes, wagging a finger. "A perennial best seller!"

"Keep it up, and I'll take my money elsewhere."

"Your money's no good here anyhow," she says over her shoulder, heading back inside her shop. "And don't you be dissing the angels, Dr. Bones. They're all around you!"

EMPTY PEGS

2:10 P.M.

FEE TWITCHES AWAKE, the embroidery needle still between her spindly fingers. Somehow, its tip has snapped off.

What had Sy said in the dream? *Can't . . . always save . . . those you love.*

Even in her sleep, she can't escape the hard facts.

She snatches a tissue from the box and wipes a thread of drool from her chin. She never dozes off while working on a quilt. But she's utterly spent. After Sy's episode in the night, she hadn't slept much at all. She'd spooned tightly against him, mind at a gallop, fretting over what invisible threshold they'd just crossed and what it might mean.

For the first time, her Bestie hadn't recognized her. For the first time, she hadn't known what to say or do to help him. Not since the day they'd met in the laundromat have they been such strangers to each other.

What dreadful "first" might happen next?

"Record numbers," announces a velvety voice on the radio, "are being reported in dozens of states from coast to coast . . ."

You should stop listening to the news, she tells herself as she collects a new needle. *These days, even NPR is depressing.*

"COVID is already the third-leading cause of death in the US. And for each death, there are an estimated nine people grieving . . ."

Suddenly she's struck by a conspicuous absence of sound beneath the reportage. Quiet, where Sy's clarinet should be.

She lowers the volume on the radio. The house is as silent as their street at midnight.

75

Why isn't he playing?

"Sy?" she sings out.

No reply.

She grabs up Eileen. That's what Sy (Before Diagnosis) had dubbed her hand-carved cane—as in *I lean,* a groaner of a pun. She despises having to use the cane, but she can't deny it's a help.

"Sy?" she hollers, ducking through the elfin doorway of her studio, into Abby's old bedroom.

From here, she can see out into the hall, where the attic ladder is folded down from the ceiling.

She must have been sleeping hard, not to have heard him prowling around up there.

"Sy?" she calls up from the foot of the ladder, without hope. The attic above is pitch-black.

She moves to the top of the staircase.

"Sy!" she yells down.

Please, she pleads with him—or maybe with God—as she grips the handrail. Every step down the stairs, her hip is screaming. *Please . . . please . . . please . . . please . . . please . . .*

"Sy!" she shouts when she hits the bottom.

She glances across the living room to his den. Its door is swung wide. She knows he isn't there.

"Sy?" she implores the mute house.

His field jacket and bush hat are missing from their Shaker pegs.

The tidal wave she'd spotted far out at sea crashes in. Her eyes flood.

TATTOO

2:12 P.M.

GET YOURSELF ON HOME, double time, Gertie had said, parting from Simon. *You know the way.*

But he doesn't know the way. All around him, buildings seem to stretch up, tilt to the side, sink, warp from their usual shapes.

His chest tightens.

His feet tug him to the east. He doesn't trust them.

"What am I doing here?" he cries, stamping the pavement. "Where am I going?"

"Wacko nutjob," mutters a woman tripping by in spiked red heels. She's being dragged along by a toy poodle. Their coats are identical, neon red.

Who's the crazy one? he thinks, eyeing the pair.

"Don't be mean," says a little girl in a quilted pink coat.

The girl's cheeks are like Tiffany roses, her hair like straw stubble in late summer. For a crazy instant, he believes she has read his mind.

But no. She's scowling at Red Coat.

Don't panic, Fee says in his brain. *There are more ways than one to get where you're going.*

He sets off to the west, into new, needling snow.

A RED LIGHT stops him at an intersection. Putnam and Hawthorne, the street signs say. He feels like an alien in his own town.

He punches the pedestrian button to activate the walk signal. He doubts it will do much of anything, except to promote the illusion he's in control, like pressing the close-door button on an elevator.

A bike courier whizzes by on fat tires, spattering sloppy snow.

A short man in head-to-toe black strolls up, tapping the tip of his black umbrella on the concrete. Impatient. A priest maybe. He's wearing a black mask even.

A trio of women appears, cackling over a slice of gossip.

A child in a puffy pink parka edges in beside him. She tips her head back and beams up at him, stars shooting out of her eyes.

"Hey, Pops!" cries a lusty voice from his left. "Give me a tune!"

He turns toward the voice and meets the ginger-brown muzzle of a Jersey cow—a face mask, amazingly true to life. A thick tongue curls out of the cow's mouth, licking at one nostril, giving it a good clean.

The wearer of the mask has spiked brilliant-orange hair.

Don't stare, Fee says in his brain.

How can I not? he retorts, studying himself and his distorted twin in the gold mirrors of Cow's sunglasses.

Cow's oversized overcoat, fashioned from what looks like fox fur, is golden red and lustrously fluffy. Almost obscured by fur is a tattoo in psychedelic colors, ringing Cow's neck like a yoke.

"Like it?" Cow says, drawing back the coat's collar to flaunt the line of musical notes arranged on a staff.

Cow's voice could be male. Or female. The lack of definition unnerves Simon.

Yet he's fascinated by the tiny colorful notes inked onto Cow's pale white skin. They're not a random pattern. They're actual music. He begins to sight-read, humming the tune to himself. Cow pivots by degrees as Simon croons.

"Why not give it a go on your clarinet?" Cow says, pointing at Simon's front.

That's when he notices the clarinet tucked against the plaid flannel lining of his field jacket. Strange. He never carries the clarinet out of the house. Not even out of his den.

"Oh, come on, Pops! Play with me!" Cow unfurls his (her?) full-length coat, revealing a set of wooden recorders, pocketed by size in the lining. "Go ahead—pick one! I'll play along with you!"

Inside Simon's jacket, the clarinet pulses, wanting to make music.

He eyeballs Cow's tattoo. "Maybe next time."

Cow grins and throws up a peace sign.

THE LAST TIME

2:45 P.M.

BEHIND THE WHEEL of the Rogue, Fee rubs the worry line between her brows, like Sy does in bed sometimes to help her relax. She scans the sidewalks, left and right. Left and right and left. Right.

She's living the overlap of reality and nightmare, barely holding it together.

A few blocks back, she'd almost run down a mail carrier in a crosswalk. When she slammed on the brakes, the Rogue skidded in slush. Stopped mere inches from killing.

The carrier's eyes were frozen wide in fright.

I'm so sorry, Fee had mouthed through the window.

The carrier was a black girl. Perhaps even *theirs.*

THIS IS the third time Sy's gone missing this fall, always while out for his walk.

Like a fool, Fee has always believed *this* time would be the last.

The last "last time" was only three weeks ago.

A Wednesday.

"Where've you been?" she snaps from the porch.

"What'd I do now?" he says, scuffing through the leaves up the brick path in the dark.

"I've been worried sick! You left hours ago!"

79

She limps back into the house on her bad hip. "I've got to tell Abby. She's beside herself. And Mikey and Victor are out driving around, looking for you!"

"Gilly's here?" He trails her inside, doffing his bush hat. "You didn't tell me she was coming. How long'll she be here?"

"I didn't say Abby was here!" she says, punching numbers on the phone in the front hall. "She hasn't been here in months. Not since the pandemic."

"Pandemic?" He hangs his jacket and hat on their usual pegs, then drops a kiss on her cheek with his cold mouth.

She recoils.

"Did you find him?" Abby's voice bursts into the handset, not bothering with "hello."

"Everything's fine, hon," Fee says. "He's home, just now. Would you call Mikey and Victor, tell them the news? Be sure to thank them for me!"

She wraps up the conversation quick, in no mood to talk. Abby will no doubt be pushing for more "changes."

Fee slams the phone onto the hook. She squares herself, ready to wage war.

"Simon, you can't keep doing this! I mean it!"

"Doing what?"

"Getting lost."

"Nobody's lost."

"Just the other day," Fee says, "I had all the neighbors out hunting. Even that Mr. Meadows!"

Fritz is meowing to be picked up. Sy toes the cat away.

"Meadows?"

"That prickly man next door. The one with that beastly dog."

"I wasn't lost!" He struts past her, into the living room with its three walls of built-in bookshelves.

"How was I supposed to know that?" she says, gimping after him. "You don't come home, and you don't come home, and somehow, like God Almighty, I'm supposed to know you aren't lying in a ditch somewhere?"

He wheels around. "Why would I be lying in a ditch? It's my brain that's broken, not my legs!"

"You're always back in an hour, hour and a half, at most!" She taps the ruby-studded watch he'd bought her for their fortieth. "Today you were gone for four hours! And a quarter!"

"Not possible."

"Don't believe me?"

"What the hell does it matter how long I'm gone?"

"I get so worried!"

"If you'd called, I'd have told you where I was!"

"Call you how, exactly?"

He pats his pockets for his cell phone. His face falls.

"Right," she says. "We gave it up last year. You kept losing it."

He slouches onto an arm of the couch. She can see him bridling himself, the muscles clamping in his jaw. The prominent blue vein in his temple is pulsing.

She tucks some stray wisps of hair behind her ear. She lets out a slow sigh, suppressing the sound of it, trying to tamp down her frustration. She doesn't want to fume at him. He's her Bestie. She's his Girl.

She touches his shoulder. He flinches.

"I'm sorry I yelled," she says. "We're both worked up."

"Wasn't lost," he manages to say again.

She smooths back an errant strand of his silver-white hair. "Okay." Her hand drifts down to pet the fuzz along his nape. "You could use a trim."

He lifts his head to look at her. Those sweet, serious eyes.

"I scared you," he says.

"Yes." She bends to kiss the top of his head. "Out of my wits."

"Didn't mean to." He wraps one arm around her waist and presses his face into her midriff. "I just don't know how to do this, Fee."

Well, I don't know how to do this either, she thinks now, snow melting beneath her windshield wipers.

The snow's sifting down harder. The hour seems so much later than it is.

PINK

SIMON'S UNFAZED BY the thickening snow. It has chased away many of the usual walkers and joggers on the riverside walkway. Of the remainder, most belong to Gilly's tribe of diehards. Step-counters. Run-loggers. Calorie-trackers. Buds and wires grow out of their ears. Fancy athletic shoes leave fancy prints on the whitening asphalt.

Unlike Gilly and her ilk, Simon has never walked for exercise. Nor for fun. He has always walked to think, regardless of weather.

Wordsworth and Thoreau, Beethoven and Tchaikovsky, Aristotle and Kierkegaard, Einstein and Heisenberg—all great walkers. They'd walked to write, to compose, to cogitate. Maybe, most of all, to preserve their wits. To stave off insanity. To transform loneliness into solitude. To stay grounded in the clay of their humanity.

Solvitur ambulando.

A credo that he, too, has lived by. A walk can solve almost anything.

Except dementia, he says to Fee in his brain. *Dammit.*

This walk doesn't seem like one of his ordinary, relaxed peregrinations. He's out here by some black necessity, pounding the pavement with a sense of mission. He just can't remember what needs doing.

A cyclist tinkles her bell, spinning by on the walkway.

Somebody I know? he asks Fee.

Courtesy, she says. *To avoid a collision.*

The bike's tires draw clean gray lines away from him in the snow.

Can't imagine where all this is headed, he says to Fee.

Let the future take care of itself.

Easy for you to say.

No response.

Fee?

I'm still here.

I feel so lost.

I know.

I don't want to live like this.

Don't say that.

I wake up a hundred times a day. What if I wake up, only to find I've forgotten you? Forever?

On a scenic overlook, a woman is engrossed in her phone, her elbows propped on the yellow guardrail. A stroller is parked beside her. Beneath its snow-coated canopy, a baby in a blue snowsuit reaches up with both arms, clucking to be picked up.

This calls for an observational experiment: *How long before the woman notices?*

The second hand on his wristwatch ticks to 12.

Starting now.

He brushes the snow from a concrete park bench. When he sinks onto the unforgiving seat, cold metal pokes out of his field jacket and nudges his neck. It's the protective cap on the mouthpiece of his clarinet.

The unexpected presence of the instrument somehow reassures him. He repositions it for comfort.

Snow slants down from the sky like the words of a poem. The wind is low. On a nearby ice rink, two skaters twirl and glide beneath strings of white lights.

Maybe they're lovers . . . Maybe it's Christmas . . .

The second hand rounds 9.

He resumes his observation of the woman and child just as a little girl in a hooded pink coat bends over the stroller. The older sister, he supposes. When the girl straightens, her arms are full of fussing baby.

The girl's a confounding variable. Completely unforeseen. She'll distort his informal study.

The second hand passes 12 again. The woman—presumably the kids' mother, or maybe their babysitter—is still glued to her phone.

The girl crowds the woman's body, struggling with the load in her arms. The boy's almost half her size.

"He's *so* heavy!" the girl says, dramatic as Shirley Temple.

"Just a sec." The woman's thumbs peck at her phone like hen beaks.

"Hurry, lady!"

Lady? So . . . the girl is a complete stranger. She could have run off with the tot from the get-go, and the woman, nose stuck in her screen, would have been oblivious till it was too damn late.

"I'm gonna drop him—" the girl says, her hold on the boy slipping. She fights like a painted clown to hike him higher in her pink arms.

Playacting, Simon suspects. *But why?*

Pretense or not, the girl's antics are effective. The woman snags up the boy. She bounces. She coos. She pops a pacifier in his mouth. Then she resumes her texting with her one free hand.

The second hand slips by 4. But he's lost track—how many times has that hand already traveled around the face of his watch?

The girl in pink ambles over to his bench.

"Good work, little mother," he says as if part of a conspiracy, despite his being in the dark.

"Thank you," she says, bobbing an adorable curtsy.

She shinnies up onto the seat beside him, then clambers to her feet. She stands there on the bench, sticking out her tongue, a pink statue catching snow. She reminds him of Gilly, way back when.

He wonders who she is. Why she's here, alone in the park. Why she'd labored so over the boy in the stroller.

"You tired?" she says after a minute.

"Not so much." Wracked by a sudden shiver, he socks his fists deep into his pockets.

She drops onto the seat next to him. "You *look* tired."

"A tad cold, that's all."

"Here—" Pulling off her bright-pink-striped gloves.

"Oh, they're too small for me," he protests.

"No, they're magic! See?" She grabs one of his hands to glove him up. "They fit everybody!"

Sure enough.

"What about *your* hands, missy?" he says. "I don't want you getting cold."

"We'll take turns."

She swings her shiny pink boots above the snowy walk. "Can I call you Grampa?"

"If I can call you Pink."

She giggles. "I'm Olivia. But Pink can be my last name."

"Nice to meet you, Olivia Pink."

"You like hugs, Grampa?"

"Depends on who's doing the hugging."

And just like that, she wraps him up like a bright-pink ribbon.

"What's today?" he asks when she lets go.

"Friday, silly!"

"Shouldn't you be in school?"

"Charley says I'm too smart for school. Besides, nobody goes to school anymore. The guv'ment shut them all down."

"*Gov-ern-ment*, I think you mean. Who's Charley?"

She crosses her legs, draws them up to her chest. "My stepdad. He teaches me stuff at home."

"Does Charley know where you are?"

"I'm not lost."

"Oh?" he says with hope. "Then where are you?"

"With you, silly! Want to look at some birds? Through my binoculars?"

And just like that, she pinions a purple pair of toilet-paper tubes against the lenses of his Lennons. All he can see through them are her eyes, wide and gleaming, peering back from the other end.

BIG BOARD GAME

3:45 P.M.

Olivia can see Hat Lady, sort of, through the snow.

Grampa still can't.

And Hat Lady can only see Grampa.

It's like the world's a big board game. So big, you can't see the edges.

Lots of games are being played on the board, all at the same time. But from where you sit, your game looks like the only one.

The rules of your game depend on the number of players. You and Grampa and Hat Lady make three. You've each got a game piece of a different color.

Grampa's blue. He can land only on blue squares. (Grampa must be color-blind, though. He thinks every square is blue. He keeps going where he shouldn't.)

Hat Lady's green. She can land on green squares. But she can also land on a blue square if Grampa's already there.

You're pink. That's the bestest color of all. You can move anywhere you want.

Sometimes you land on a magic square. Magic squares are see-through, like Hat Lady. They look like ordinary colored squares till you land on them. That's when the coolest stuff happens—sort of like balloons and confetti and streamers and candy!

So, the space that was normal on the last roll of the dice might blow your mind on the next one. That's the deal with magic: you never see it coming.

Nobody can jump other pieces or capture them or send them back to Start. There's no Start anywhere on the game board. No Finish either.

Nobody wins. Nobody loses. Everybody keeps moving around the board, avoiding penalties and collecting prizes, till the sand in the timer runs out.

Then the timer flips over again, all on its own. Like it's held by an invisible hand.

GRAMPA'S BENT OVER, holding his knees. Hat Lady wants to get into one of his jacket pockets, like Aladdin when he was still a thief. But her hand keeps passing through the cloth.

She could probably use a little help.

"What's in there?" Olivia asks Grampa, pointing at his pocket.

"In where?"

She points again. "There!"

He pulls out a brown paper bag. Inside the bag is a big-people book with a title as long as a train.

"What's '*dee*-men-*tee*-uh'?" she asks, sounding out the longest word in the word train.

"Dee-*men*-shuh," Grampa corrects her.

Hat Lady's trying his other jacket pocket now. She sure doesn't give up.

"What's dee-*men*-shuh?" Olivia asks again, saying the word his way.

Grampa heaves a giant big-people sigh. He removes her gloves.

"You better put these back on, Miss Pink."

Hands on her hips. "Don't you know what that big word means?"

"Sure I do." He jams the book back into his pocket. "Derives from the Latin root *demens*, meaning 'out of one's mind.' "

"*Demons*? You mean, like, soldiers of Satan?"

His eyes go all scrunchy. "Wherever did you hear about *them*?"

"Charley says they're falling angels."

"*Fallen* angels. Your Charley would do better to teach you Latin."

"What's Latin?"

He smiles. "Just forget the demons, okay?"

She slips on her pink gloves, happy for her fingers. "So . . . what's dee-*men*-shuh?"

"It's when your brain doesn't work quite right."

She peeks into his brain through her binoculars. "Your brain looks fine and dandy to me!"

"Thank you for your expert opinion, Dr. Pink. However . . . you know what a computer is?"

"Silly Grampa—everybody knows that!"

"Ever been on a computer when it crashed?"

"Yeppers!"

"Ever lost what you were doing before the crash?"

"Like, *poof!*"

He chuckles. "Yes, like poof. That's the problem with my brain—the memory part of it, anyway. Goes poof all the time, and I forget what I've been doing and with whom I've been doing it."

She tilts her head to study him better. So *that's* why he thinks all the squares are blue. He forgets what color's what. Or whose color is whose.

"I think we should fix you up," she says in her best doctor voice. "Get that dirty dee-*men*-shuh all out of your brain."

His eyes go all red and wet, like it's raining inside his poor, sick head.

"You're an excellent doctor, Dr. Pink. But someday you'll learn—what's broken can't always be fixed." He covers her gloved hand with his bare one. "Now, listen. Don't be afraid, but my brain's sure to crash soon. When it happens, I won't know who you are."

"Never again? Like, never *ever*?"

"It'll be okay. When it happens, just tell me your name, and I'll tell you mine, and we'll start being friends again. A happy reboot! Got it?"

Hat Lady isn't in his pockets anymore. She's as close to him as a see-through person can be, her hand all up in his heart.

OUT OF MIND

3:57 P.M.

SEATED at her computer in the bistro office, Abby closes her spreadsheet with a sigh, done at last with the inventory. Every task on today's to-do list has taken twice as long as it should. She can't seem to focus.

She picks up a framed photo from her desk. The best picture she has of her father. A photographer from the *Daily Register* had shot it for a feature story on him, back when he gave up his faculty post, but it could almost pass as recent.

He's actually smiling in this one. That tinned, lopsided smile of his.

Her mother had called her first thing this morning. "Hi, hon," she'd said—only two syllables, but they were so cracked and weepy that Abby had braced for trouble.

Her father had suffered a brief episode in the night. For the first time, he'd been disoriented, didn't know where he was.

"He thought I was a total stranger, holding him prisoner," her mother had said, sniveling.

"How long was he out of it?"

"I don't know . . . five or ten minutes. But it felt like an eternity."

"What finally brought him around?"

That's when her mother had broken down.

"Fritz," she'd managed to say.

Abby replaces the photo next to her computer, thinking of her father and his red hands in the flames of her dream.

She hadn't mentioned the nightmare to her mother.

· · ·

89

"His brain has suffered some sort of accident," Dr. Chonkar says from behind her L-shaped desk.

Abby looks at her father. He's gazing out the plate-glass window, where a late-spring snow is dribbling down on April flowers.

For this latest appointment, her mother has dressed him in his best suit—his one and only suit, in fact. The same double-breasted black pinstripe suit he has worn for decades of weddings, christenings, funerals—every formal purpose under heaven not requiring academic regalia. He looks remarkably dignified for a guy so indifferent to appearances.

Her mother has dressed herself to match in a three-piece black pant ensemble. When in public, she seems to use clothing as a binding agent, the self-possessed artist shoring up her socially awkward scholar husband.

Their attire blends seamlessly into the monochromatic palette of Chonkar's office. Here, no grays exist. The space is a cold black-and-white fable.

"An 'accident'?" her mother says to Chonkar. "You mean, like a stroke?"

"I can't say for certain. Blood clot, brain bleed, inflammation . . . the tests are inconclusive. But the accident has resulted in a form of dementia."

"Dementia." Her mother shifts irritably in her sleek chair. "What a horrible word! It has no dignity. My husband has not lost his mind, I assure you."

Her father cups his veiny hands around his better knee. "Referring to the meaning of dementia in the original Latin," he says, as if explaining to the snow. "Out of mind."

"You're sure it isn't Alzheimer's?" Abby asks Chonkar.

The doctor gathers her long black hair in one hand and lets it fall. Like the other two specialists with whom Abby and her parents have consulted, Chonkar studies the firing of neurons in brain tissue, much as Abby's father had once studied fossils encased in rock. Both disciplines try to account for the present by discerning the past. But sometimes the evidence yields only partial answers.

"Your father's short-term-memory loss does suggest Alzheimer's," Chonkar says. "But his scan was negative, and he exhibits no other Alzheimer's symptoms. His long-term memory is excellent for his age. His reasoning is cogent. His language skills are intact. From what you and your mother have told me, you've seen no significant changes in his personality or behavior—only the memory issues. So no, not Alzheimer's. What it is, exactly, I can't say. Dementia is a tangled forest."

Hanging on Chonkar's wall is an impressive array of framed diplomas and medical certificates: Loyola, Ohio State, Johns Hopkins. Once upon a time, Abby knows, these credentials would have meant something to her father. They would have intrigued and perhaps reassured him.

A scientist himself, he values mastery of knowledge, scholarship, research. For years after retirement, he'd kept a tiny office on campus as professor *emeritus, with his own array of diplomas and honorary degrees still decorating the wall: University of Nebraska–Lincoln, Dartmouth, Columbia.*

But her father's days in academia are well behind him, his certificates probably stashed in a box in the attic.

Chonkar refers to a multicolored model of a human brain on one corner of her desk. "The hippocampus is here, in the temporal lobe." She taps a purple piece shaped like a shrimp. "It's our memory maker. It creates short-term memories and turns them into long-term memories for storage and retrieval elsewhere in the brain."

Abby steals another glance at her abstracted father. What's he thinking— this man who never cracks? Or rather, this man who never shows *his cracks? He's like plaster crazing behind layers of old wallpaper. The walls appear to be in fine condition until life scrapes off the paper and exposes what's underneath.*

She nudges his arm to summon him back to the conversation he'd clearly rather not be part of. He'd only agreed to keep this appointment because her mother had promised him two scoops at Cold Stone Creamery afterward.

"But when the neurons in the hippocampus are deprived of oxygen," Chonkar is saying, "the memory-making process is severely impaired—just as we're seeing with Simon. If I were to leave right now for lunch, he probably wouldn't remember me when I got back. Am I right?"

With her eyes, Chonkar directs her question to Abby's mother, then to Abby herself, completely skipping the man between them.

"And without memories of the recent past," Chonkar goes on, "Simon can't imagine the immediate future. He can't plan ahead or prepare himself for upcoming events without prompting. He can't anticipate."

"Can we reverse the damage somehow?" Abby asks. "Any new medicine or treatment we might try?"

Chonkar lays one palm atop the life-size brain. "Medically speaking, I'm afraid there's nothing more to be done—"

"Same old nonsense," Abby's mother says, shaking her head. "What about his diet? Keeping his mind active? Exercise? He takes a long walk every day. He's so faithful about his walks!"

"That's all good," Chonkar says in a measured tone. "However . . ." She laces her fingers together, her nails long, shaped, and polished. "I have the impression, Mrs. Richter, that despite exercise and other lifestyle interventions, your husband's symptoms have worsened since you first noticed signs of his condition. I'm sorry to say, he'll likely continue to deteriorate."

Abby can see her mother's nose blushing, her chin quivering. Reaching behind her father's chair, Abby touches the slope of her mother's shoulder.

"Look out . . ." her father says.

Abby assumes he's warning the room that his wife is about to weep.

But no. He's nodding outside at the once-dribbling snow, which has changed over to huge, heavy flakes, dripping straight and thick, as if on ropes. It's the most beautiful kind of snow, the kind that makes you stop and forget the rest of the world.

"Used to catch snowflakes like that with your tongue, didn't you, Gilly?" he says to Abby.

That silly pet name. It has always made her squirm.

She doesn't have gills. She isn't a fish wiggling on somebody's hook.

But now that he's gradually disappearing . . . the nickname's starting to grow on her.

He had raised her well enough. He'd put a roof over her head and food on the table. He'd paid for her accounting degree at a community college—all the schooling she'd wanted. He'd walked her down the aisle. Three times.

He had watched her grow up. She has watched him grow old.

So how is it they've never truly known each other?

Soon it will be too late. Dementia is fast closing the door. Maybe if she wedges herself against it, she can hold it open, just long enough.

"Whatever are we going to do?" her mother says, to nobody.

Her father stands up, grimacing at the old pain in his stiff knees.

"Why don't we just go home," he says, the ice cream bribe forgotten.

"Oh dear," her mother says, tearing up. She grabs one of his hands. "We've been going on this whole time as if you're not here!"

"I'm mostly not" —he smirks— "from the sound of it."

THE BISTRO PHONE rings on Abby's desk, startling her back from that wretched day at Chonkar's office into the present. The caller is yet another supplier, trying to drum up pandemic business.

Frank sticks his head in the office door. "Abs, you made that seafood run yet?"

Hold on, she mouths, her red pen filling her yellow legal pad with numbers from her negotiations.

Lockdown has forced her and Frank to shutter the front of the house. Bistro patrons now place their orders online or by phone, for curbside pickup.

Most of the staff have been laid off. So these days, she's not just the bookkeeper and marketer. She's also the errand girl, the janitor, the stocker, the dishwasher, the order taker, the bagger—pretty much anything except prep cook. Frank's well aware of her shortcomings in the kitchen.

She checks her wristwatch. If she hurries, she can still get to the fish market. Frozen seafood is cheaper than fresh, but Frank will source the best ingredients for as long as the pandemic allows.

"Go after your father," Abby's mother whispers once they're back from Chonkar's office. She points up the stairs. *"I don't want him to be alone."*

Abby slings her coat over a hook on the hall tree. Her mother would certainly go after him herself, but she does no more stairs than she must, due to her hip.

"Look in our bedroom," her mother says. *"That's where he goes when he's depressed."*

But her father hasn't gone to the bedroom. He's in the upstairs hallway, unfolding the attic ladder from the ceiling. He doesn't strike Abby as depressed. More like on a mission.

"What you want from up there, Dad? Tell me—I'll go get it."

He answers by leaning into the rickety ladder to lock its hinges.

He starts to climb. He's pretty sure-footed despite his bad knees. But near the top, he wobbles.

Abby scrambles up to steady him from behind, pressing her hand into the small of his back.

If he falls, *she thinks,* we're going down together.

At last, he clambers into the dark of the attic. He fishes for the chain on the light bulb and tugs.

Abby follows him into the gloom. Cobwebs drift in the rafters. Papery wasps' nests hang along one eave.

Despite the attic's dreariness, Abby feels a bloom of nostalgia for the countless hours she'd spent up here as a child. She and her mother had played dress-up and make-believe. They'd converted boxes and tarps into tunnels big enough to crawl through on their bellies, pretending they were creeping through caves. They'd painted flowers and clouds and stick people on the chimney. Some are still visible. Someday, maybe, she'll show Frank.

Her father shucks off his suit jacket. Is this the first time she's been up here with him?

"What you wanting up here, Dad?" she asks again. *"Can't it wait?"*

"Waited too long as it is."

He loosens his paisley tie and slips it over his head. He unfastens the top few buttons of his shirt, exposing the neck of his undershirt. He roams around cardboard boxes and vintage luggage, rolling up his sleeves, coughing a little on dust.

"Should I get a flashlight?" she suggests.

In semidarkness, everything looks like a ghost of itself. Framed diplomas and certificates. A rocking horse. A wooden high chair and crib. Plastic tubs of *holiday decorations. Several old typewriters, manual and electric. A bin of computer junk. Open boxes containing vases, canning supplies, and mismatched dishes. A set of golf clubs, though nobody in the family golfs. A tricycle. Carpet remnants rolled up and bound with tape. Clothes in garment bags on a metal rack. A console TV. Fishing and camping gear. Small appliances presumably in need of repair. Cross-country skis and snowshoes. A hulking green armchair so big she can't imagine how it had gotten up here . . .*

An American flag is tacked to a rafter upside down.

"Why's it hanging that way?" she asks.

"Signal of distress," her father says as he roots around.

As if that's an answer.

Dementia. *The word bursts into her awareness like a rain-swollen river breaking its banks. After three sober-headed consultations with specialists, she's suddenly drowning in the fact of it.*

Not that she'd ever doubted the diagnosis, first suspected by Doc Willard. Up from Philly once or twice a month, she'd noted the subtle changes in her father's behavior. How he would repeat a question for the umpteenth time. How he would forget what he'd just set out to do.

"Something's wrong," Abby would observe to her mother, in private.

"Nonsense," her mother would reply. "That's simply what happens as people age—they become more of what they always were. Your father's always been absentminded. We can expect these little senior moments."

Her mother's the family expert on aging. She has a pile of self-help books by the bed, a medicine cabinet full of dietary supplements—and when it comes to her husband, a storehouse of rationalizations at the ready. Even as the symptoms of his dementia grew more pronounced, she couldn't accept that he wasn't himself. Unhappy with Doc Willard's diagnosis, she'd insisted on shopping around for a more favorable opinion.

A half century of living with the same person can distort your vision. Prevent your seeing what's there. Make you see what isn't.

"So, Gilly," her father says now, picking his way toward the farthest, darkest corner of the attic. "Question for you: Would you rather be healthy in body but not in mind, or healthy in mind but not in body?"

That one again. How many times has he asked her?

"Don't make me choose," she says.

She flicks on her cell phone's flashlight and shines it in his direction. Its beam cuts the dark.

"Question for you, Dad: What are we looking for?"

She needs him to tell her. Any minute, he might forget, and they'll both be standing here, covered in dust for nothing.

He stops and puts his hands on his hips. "If it's anywhere, it'll be around here."

She maneuvers her way across the attic to join him.

"Stuff from the farm," he says.

"The farm?"

"The homeplace. Where I grew up."

"Where Grandma Iris lived?"

His stepmother Iris has always been little more than a curious story handed down in pieces, like orphan quilt blocks, faded and frayed. Over time, Abby has been slowly gathering and stitching the lonely blocks into a scrappy patchwork.

She knows that a sniper in Italy had picked off Iris's sweetheart—Ernie Blanchard—toward the close of World War II. As a war widow, Iris tried to support herself and her toddler son, first as a telephone operator, then as a hairdresser.

Less than a year after Ernie was shot dead, Iris married Grandpa Karl. Considering the twelve-year difference in their ages, Abby had a hunch that their union was more transactional than romantic. Iris needed a husband to provide for her and her baby boy, even if the man was much older and from a family of Krauts. And Grandpa Karl needed a mother for his son, who was then in grade school, even if it meant two extra mouths to feed.

The couple's circumstances fit together nicely, like the edges of two quilt blocks of similar size. Very neat. Very dutiful. Very practical.

Her father slivers the tape on a cardboard box with his pocketknife.

"After Iris's funeral," he says, "Colin took me into my old room—"

"Your stepbrother? Did I ever meet him?"

"Sure. Guess he didn't make much of an impression."

"Because he wasn't my real uncle, you mean? Like Iris wasn't my real grandma?"

"Oh, Iris was real enough."

He always calls her Iris, not Mother.

He parts the box flaps. "I was six when Pop married her. Out of the blue, I had a new mother and a new brother. Colin was a little squirt, just learning to walk. We never quite took to each other, him and me."

"So," Abby says, "after the funeral, Colin led you into your old room, and . . . ?"

"He said he had a bunch of stuff Iris wanted me to have. Said I should go through it and take whatever I wanted—the rest he'd haul to the dump. But I had a plane to catch. He ended up shipping it. Sent me the bill."

He lifts out a short length of model train track. "Well, lookee here—"

A loud sigh escapes him. His face softens.

"Pop bought this, our first Christmas alone. Had the train running beneath the tree when I got up Christmas morning."

He unwraps a locomotive from the funnies of a newspaper, yellowed with age. Then a boxcar. A tank car.

"Never knew how Pop came by such a train in the middle of the war."

Here's a caboose, bright red in the glow of her flashlight.

"He added more every Christmas," her father says. "Tiny tin buildings, bridges, crossing gates, streetlights . . ." He gives the caboose's wheels a jangly spin. "Colin never showed any interest in it. He could get away with that."

She tries to picture him as a motherless little boy with his widowed father, their first Christmas morning without his mother. Maybe he'd never wished for a train, only his mother alive again. Maybe he'd had no choice but to feign glee that morning—and every Christmas of his remaining boyhood.

But this train set had probably spared him and his father having to talk about the one subject—the one person—they couldn't bear to talk about.

In the end, Grandma Iris had packed up the train and let her stepson decide what to do with it. Unfinished business, to finish or not. It's been up here in the attic ever since, where he keeps so many things that can't be gotten rid of.

He rewraps the cars and sticks them back in the box.

"Someday," he says to Abby, "all this will be yours to deal with."

"Gee, thanks, Dad."

Abby sweeps the shaft of her light forward. It leads her and her father to a humpback steamer trunk, scarred from travel. The wooden trunk is decorated with brasswork tarnished with age.

"That's quite a trunk," she says, her light settling on RICHTER, *engraved on the lid.*

"Came over with Pop's parents on the boat," he says, unlatching it.

"Rup-perts-grün?" she says, sounding out the German word engraved beside the family name.

"Place they came from."

He tips the lid back. Piled inside are knotted comforters and raggedy quilts, smelling of history and mothballs. Practical cousins of her mother's art quilts, they'd likely been handstitched by long-dead kinswomen.

"Could be in here," he says, pawing through the contents. "Cushioned, for protection."

"You know, Dad, if only you'd tell me what you're looking for . . ."

"Iris kept everything. She was careful."

All at once, he's wrestling a bundle from the bottom of the trunk. A box-shaped object folded in a quilt and tied with twine. Sensing his excitement, Abby clears a small space on the floor for him to set it down.

He lowers himself to his old knees. Severs the twine with his knife.

"This quilt covered my bed as a boy. Mama . . . your grandma Vera . . . made it."

Abby crouches beside him as he peels back the folds. It's a star quilt. The eight-pointed star is formed of dozens of diamonds cut from pastel fabrics:

powder blue, baby pink, mint green, lavender. Its rays, tipped in butter yellow, spread in every direction love might ever go.

"Wow!" she says. "Mom should see this!"

But her father's attention is fastened not on the quilt but on the vintage instrument case that it had cocooned. He caresses HENRI SELMER PARIS, the instrument maker's logo, stamped in gold on the black leather. His hands tremble, as with palsy.

He fumbles with the two metal clasps. When he raises the lid, the lardy smell of cork grease thickens the air. Abby knows that smell from playing the sax as a kid. She'd never much liked the saxophone, but she'd been crazy for Stevie Fergus, the hunk who'd always sat first chair. To sit beside him, she had to be good.

Nestled in the case's emerald-green lining are the pieces of a clarinet: upper and lower joints, barrel, bell, mouthpiece. Abby does a quick appraisal. Time has done the instrument no favors. Its black body is dull with grime. Its silver keys have lost their luster.

"No sign of bugs," her father says.

"Whose clarinet?"

He takes one of the joints in each hand and weighs their feel. "Last time I played, I was just a boy. Thought I was a man, but I wasn't."

He returns the joints to the case. Then he fingers a delicate reed—thin as a Communion wafer, shorter than his pinky. It's warped and worthless now. But once, when attached to the mouthpiece, it would have been the clarinet's vocal cord, giving this black wooden stick a voice that moaned and cried, just like Stevie Fergus's sax, playing jazz.

Abby watches her father touch the reed's curved tip to his tongue, a tender taste, all lover and musician. At that moment, in the flashlight's glow, his face regains a flush of youth.

"Taste dusty?" she says.

"A mite."

"You wanting to play again?"

"Needs some fixing up first. Know a shop?"

She sizes up the clarinet again, more carefully. She's no expert, but it will require more than a good polishing. Sections will need to be recorked, keys straightened and repadded, springs replaced. Reconditioning the instrument won't be cheap.

"Don't worry about the cost," her father says.

Not fair. He always knows what she's thinking, yet she reckons him as inscrutable as a pile of prehistoric bones.

"It's really old, Dad. How about we buy you a new one instead?"

He shoots her that look over his glasses—the one meant to end all discussion.

"Okay, okay," she says. "But even if we fix it up, how will it sound?"

He closes the case. "Only one way to find out, Gilly. And I need to. While I still can."

"Abs?" Frank prods. "I need those scallops!"

Abby throws him a pleading look. He ducks back into the kitchen.

On her legal pad, her red pen has doodled vivid tongues of fire.

ALL THAT GLITTERS

4:11 P.M.

THE DARKER IT GETS, the better Olivia can see Hat Lady, right behind Grampa, a spooky glow in the Christmassy snow. That pink straw hat is still in Hat Lady's hand. She must love it a super lot to carry it all the time.

They've been tramping on this train track forever. Olivia leaps from tie to tie, leaning into her number rhymes.

"One, two, buckle my shoe . . . Three, four, knock at the door . . ."

In the beginning, the ties were like dark chocolate bars, lightly sugared with snow. But now the ground between the rails is like one skinny white cake with lumps in the frosting. It goes on forever.

At "nineteen, twenty," she spins like a penny on her pink twinkle toes. She starts back at "one, two" just as the dwindling daylight turns the falling snow into glittery fairy dust. It's like the three of them are inside a snow globe with a gazillion sugar sprinkles and God's shaken it super hard.

"Wowzies!" she exclaims just as the glitter fizzles. "You see that, Grampa?"

"See what?" he says.

"Too late!"

That's what happens. If you don't watch out, you miss stuff. Especially if you're pooped.

STRETCH MARKS

4:17 P.M.

"SY? YOU THERE?" Fee calls with hope, reentering the house after driving the streets.

The Shaker pegs in the hall are still empty.

His black sneakers are still missing from their spot beneath the bench.

Oh, Bestie—why didn't you wear your boots?

She shuffles past the pegs to the front door. She flicks on the porch light and the yard light—beacons that might guide him home.

She peers out through the door's glazed window at the snow-dusted porch, the snow-crusted steps, the snow-blanketed brick walk. She gazes as if she might have the power to raise a trace of his footprints in the unbroken white.

Mindlessly, she jams her knit hat and gloves into her coat pockets, then sheds her coat and stuffs her neck scarf down one sleeve. She drops the coat over a hook on the hall tree.

She looks toward the dark kitchen. Toward the dark living room. Toward his dark den.

There's nowhere in this house that she wants to be without him.

The answering machine isn't blinking. No messages.

She hits the play button, just to hear his voice, recorded years Before Diagnosis.

"Congratulations," his terse greeting says. "You've reached us. So talk."

Not rude but to the point.

She should let Abby know that he's gone again. She should call Mikey and Victor. She should recruit the neighbors.

She should. But she can't. Yet.

She mounts the dark stairs, vexed at the agony in her hip. Vexed at Fritz, crowding her feet on the steps, threatening to trip her. Vexed at the man she has loved so long yet not long enough to always know how.

Upstairs, she enters their bedroom, shutting Fritz out. The moocher whines in the hall, pawing at the door.

She eases herself onto the edge of the carefully made bed.

Years ago, when she'd worn her hair longer, her Bestie would sit with her here at bedtime and brush it in the dark, throwing sparks.

She lies back onto the quilt, then flounders onto her side to face the shallow crater in the mattress, where he sleeps. He's always slept closer to the window, which is latticed now with frost and snow.

She lays her palm on his body's place.

She imagines herself with him between the flannel sheets, dragging her rag of a body into the shelter of his spare frame. The comfort of his disappearing flesh against hers. His familiar arms around her shoulders. Their legs loosely, gingerly twined, one of his crazy-long royal toes protruding against her ankle.

She wants the familiar scent of him. His warmth. His dear lips tasting her wilted breasts. Brushing her ancient stretch marks.

FREE RIDE

4:31 P.M.

"MY NAME'S SIMON RICHTER," Olivia hears Grampa shout at her, into the wind. "I have a condition that causes me not to remember very well—"

"Yeah, I know!" she shouts back. "Dee-*men*-shuh! You told me!"

His bare hands must be super cold. They're all balled up in his coat sleeves.

"Do I know you?" he yells.

"I'm Olivia Pink. You're my grampa. We reboot every time your brain crashes. Like, over and over and *over*!"

He looks stumped—just like Lucy did, back when Olivia had crawled out her bedroom window. Olivia's getting used to that look.

"You cold, Olivia Pink?" Grampa yells.

"A little!" More like, she's a *lot* cold. And a lot pooped. And a little scared.

She can't tell where to step in the snow anymore. She had to stop counting railroad ties, like, the *longest* time ago.

If only she could sail over the ground like Hat Lady!

Hat Lady glides along behind Grampa like nobody alive. She doesn't look too happy to be out here. But happy is for clowns. (That's what Charley says.)

At least Hat Lady doesn't look like a popsicle, like Olivia and Grampa do. And Hat Lady doesn't look the least bit tuckered out either.

"Got to get you home, missy," Grampa says. His black sneakers are two Little Engines That Could, chugging through the snow. His breath's all puffy.

Olivia thinks about her room. About Lucy. About the red numbers on her digital clock. About her wide-open window. About the pizza her mom was supposed to bring for supper.

By now, maybe Charley knows she's gone.

She'd promised Charley and God always to be a good girl. But she doesn't want to be good if it means going home.

Not yet.

Maybe not ever.

So what if it's getting dark?

So what if she's cold and pooped and scared?

So what if Grampa's brain is broken?

So what if—

Grampa's yelling at her again.

"What'd you say?" she yells back.

"Where do you live? What's your address?"

"I don't remember." Pretending her brain's broken too.

There's his stumped look again.

God doesn't like tiny fibs any more than whoppers. But God wouldn't want her to leave Grampa all alone out here. Especially with a broken brain.

"Remind me," Grampa yells, "which way to town from here?"

"I don't know."

This isn't a lie. She's all discombobulated. Before the railroad, Grampa had them walking every which way.

Big people are supposed to know where they're going.

"You mean we're lost?" he says, sounding more like a little boy than a grampa.

"My dog, Lucy, was a stray," she yells, "till Charley brought her home and let me keep her. She wasn't lost. She just wasn't found yet."

Grampa doesn't say anything. Not for the most very longest time.

"Where are we trying to get to?" he hollers.

"The train." That's what he'd told her before the last crash.

Grampa stops. Hat Lady stops right behind him.

"We've got train tickets?" he says.

"Oh no," she says. "We get to ride for free. You're supposed to play jazz for the passengers. Remember?"

STUCK

5:49 P.M.

In the middle of the night
I go walking in my sleep
From the mountains of faith
To the river so deep

ABBY, back from the fish market with the bistro's order, parks the loaded dolly near the walk-in refrigerator while Billy Joel's gospel pounds in her ears.

I must be looking for something
Something sacred I lost
But the river is wide
And it's too hard to cross

If only she could take time for a run. A few miles would ease her mood.

Frank waves at her from the wait station, where he's plating a line of takeout containers.

She turns off her earbuds.

"Sorry to hit you with bad news," he says, "but your dad's gone missing again."

"No way!" she cries.

"I'm just off the phone with your mom."

"She called *you*? Did I miss her somehow?"

Abby unlocks her phone. No notifications from her mother.

"That's weird."

Frank swirls a serving of hummus and tops it with a glug of olive oil. "She wanted me to be the one to tell you."

A sense of foreboding engulfs her. She and Frank have been so busy all day, she hasn't yet told him about last night's dream or her father's spell of disorientation.

Now *this.*

"What's so bad this time," she asks, "that Mom couldn't tell me herself?"

Frank holds his gloved hands in midair like a surgeon who has just scrubbed in.

"She said a nor'easter's moving in."

"That's not really an answer to my question."

"It's already snowing hard."

Abby's stomach turns. "Maybe we should call nine-one-one. Maybe file a missing person's report."

His forehead wrinkles above his thick Italian eyebrows. "Don't you have to wait twenty-four hours?"

"Only in Hollywood."

"Then do it!"

In her Favorites on her phone, she taps the entry for her mother's cell.

"I tell you, Frank, I hate being stuck down here in Philly when shit like this happens." She paces the tile floor in her designer sneakers. "Come on, Mom! Pick up!"

"Why don't you hop on Zoom?" Frank says, motioning toward the office. "Stay there with your mom as long as you need."

"You can't manage orders all by yourself! And I haven't put away the seafood yet—"

"Don't worry yourself. I'll handle things. Just find him!"

LOCK AND LOAD
5:52 P.M.

VICTOR MIXES a Manhattan and drops a cherry in the martini glass.

Helluvan anniversary.

He dices carrots, turnips, and parsnips for a roasted vegetable stew. Mikey'll like that, whenever he gets home. Right now, he's still stuck in a ditch over by Martinsburg, waiting for a wrecker to winch him out.

Victor's starting on the sweet potatoes when his cell phone rings.

Mikey, he thinks with hope, laying down his knife.

No. Mikey's a texter.

He towels off his hands.

Jim, maybe.

Last Victor knew, Jim and Frieda were on the highway, bound for an open hospital bed in neighboring Connecticut.

Fiona, says the caller ID.

"Victor!" her voice bursts into his ear. "Thank heaven I got you!"

He lowers himself onto a barstool next to the kitchen island. "Fiona—what's wrong?"

"I've looked everywhere!"

Simon. Again.

"I hate to ask you," she says, "especially in this weather, but . . ."

His mind races ahead of Fiona's words, assessing his options. On a farm, you can't just leave evening chores to heaven. How will he ever find enough help on short notice to cover the work?

Somehow he has to.

His Marine mind-set locks and loads.

"I'll be there, soon as I can. Mikey too. But Fiona, this time we *really* need to involve the police—"

"Oh, Victor—I have to go. Abby's trying to reach me. Hurry, won't you? But do be careful of the roads. Whatever would I do without you boys?"

TWIN CULVERTS

6:22 P.M.

SIMON'S EYES sweep the surreal landscape. The shadowy snow cover is painted in blues and purples. Charcoal silhouettes of full-bodied evergreens and thinly dressed deciduous trees break the orangish-black cloud cover. The world is nightmarish. Nothing looks as it should.

In an embankment to his right, he spots a jaggy hole. Against the twilit snow, it has the hue of a Turkish black rose.

"There!" he yells at Gilly, shoving her toward it with such force that she tumbles to her knees.

He rushes to hoist her up. "So sorry. Upsy-daisy!"

He gathers her into his arms. She coils herself around his middle as he lurches forward.

The hole, he sees now, is the remains of an old stone culvert built into the slope of a shallow gully. At one time, it had probably channeled water beneath a roadbed.

At the culvert's mouth, he sets Gilly down and brushes the caked snow from her clothes.

"A cave!" she exclaims.

Out of breath, he doesn't bother to set her right.

"Scoot inside!" he tells her with a gentle push, just as he notices a twin culvert nearby, altogether collapsed, drifting with snow.

"You got to come, too!" Gilly whines.

He gropes in his pants pocket for his Swiss Army knife. His fingers, numb with cold, are clumsy on the handle. "Need to collect branches. Cover the opening."

"Don't leave me!"

"I'll come right back."

"But your brain is broken!" She sounds ready to cry. "You'll forget where I am!"

She's right, Fee says in his brain. *You might get lost.*

"If I take you with me," he says to Gilly, "you've got to remember where this place is. Can you do that?"

Her hooded head bobs.

"Okay." He grabs her gloved hand. "Scuff your feet like this—watch me now! Make deep tracks. And don't lose sight of our cave."

ENDANGERED

6:35 P.M.

"FIONA RICHTER?"

Fee cracks the front door a titch further. "Are you the police?"

The white man under the porch light isn't in uniform. Tall and gaunt with woolly brows and dull, sunken eyes, he'd pass for Abe Lincoln if he swapped out his mask for a stovepipe hat.

"Detective Mitchell Parrish from the APD," he says, flashing a badge. He gestures to the woman behind him. "That's Miguelina Bragg, a licensed social worker with our community response team."

Bragg's skull cap is pulled low over her brow. A mask hides all but her brown button eyes.

"I don't need a social worker," Fee says, raising her own mask higher on her nose.

"Ms. Bragg is a valued member of the department," Parrish says.

Bragg steps closer, her shoulders square in her duty jacket. "We're here to gather more information so we can bring your husband safely home," she says.

The woman has a slight accent. Mexican maybe. But her features don't look Mexican.

Detective Parrish draws the door toward him, opening it wider. "Mrs. Richter, given the weather and the late hour, every minute counts. Please, let us come inside."

BRAGG SEATS herself with Fee at the kitchen table and pulls off her knit cap with a crackle of static electricity, spilling coppery-brown hair. Parrish stays on his feet, nosing around.

"How would you prefer we address you?" Bragg asks.

"Fiona is fine." Fee repositions her laptop so she and Bragg can both view the Zoom window. "This is Abby, my daughter in Philly. She's been with me for the last hour or so."

"How are you holding up?" Bragg says, introducing herself to Abby as she flips open a tablet computer. Her fingernails are perfect ovals painted a glittery gold. A disco-ball manicure.

"We're eager to know what's next," Abby says.

Parrish turns away from the wall calendar with its neat November week of Xs. In one Abe-Lincoln stride, he's leaning over Fee's shoulder, smelling like coffee and cigarettes, with a whiff of Old Spice and onion rings.

"Abby," he says into the screen, "I'm Detective Mitchell Parrish. How about you and I talk in another room while Ms. Bragg asks your mother some questions?"

"Oh no!" Fee protests. "I want Abby in on everything!"

"I'm afraid I must insist," Parrish says, commandeering Fee's laptop. "It's procedure."

He disappears with the computer into the dining room.

"I don't much care for your 'procedures,'" Fee says to Bragg.

"The faster we work, the sooner you and Abby can be together again. Sound good?"

Maybe she's from the Middle East.

"That mask muffles your voice," Fee says.

"I'm sorry," Bragg says, dialing up her voice's volume a bit too far. "I'll speak up."

"You don't have to shout."

Bragg unzips her jacket. "The first two hours after someone goes missing are critical, especially if they're considered endangered like Simon."

"Endangered?"

"Don't be alarmed—anyone with dementia falls into that category. We've already issued a missing endangered person alert. Have you and Abby reached out to relatives and friends, in case they've heard from your husband?"

"Everyone we could think of." Fee folds her hands to hide their trembling. "Nobody's seen him."

"How about area hospitals?"

"Nothing." Fee cradles her forehead in her hands. "I can't believe this is happening. I just dozed off . . ."

"It's not your fault," Bragg says in a saccharine tone. As if she has *any* idea.

Fee raises up with a glare. "Of *course* it's my fault! Who else?"

Bragg shifts her weight. Her chair creaks. "How about a drink of water?" she suggests. "A nice cup of tea?"

"You think my *husband* is someplace nice and warm, drinking tea?"

Instantly Fee regrets being snippy.

"I'm sorry to be short-tempered, Officer. I'm in such a state!"

"You're worried. I get it." Bragg's sparkling fingers flip open a notepad. "By the way, I'm not a police officer. Just call me Miguelina."

"Oh."

Bragg aligns the notepad on the table in perfect symmetry with her tablet computer, a peculiar redundancy in writing instruments.

"Do you have any recent photos of Simon?" she asks Fee.

"Oh, dear . . . I'm not sure I do. He *hates* having his picture taken. Besides, with the pandemic, who's taking photos?"

"Maybe Abby can help." Bragg types a message into her tablet.

Out in the dining room, Parrish's cell phone pings.

"As soon as we have a good photo," Bragg says, explaining to Fee, "we'll send it, with Simon's description, to the media and other community partners. With your permission, of course. Now I'd like to ask you some questions that weren't answered in the initial report."

"Fine."

"Does your husband go by any nicknames?"

"I call him Sy."

And Bestie, she decides not to say.

S-Y, Bragg scrawls with her pen—like a snake and a tree branch. The woman's a leftie.

"Does he carry any money? Credit cards?"

"Not anymore."

"Any places in town he likes to go?"

"They're all closed because of COVID."

The tip of Bragg's pen freezes on the paper. "Is *he* aware of that?"

"Well . . . no . . . I guess you'd better check his favorite hangouts— McClure's Books, the Daily Grind, Main Library."

Scribble, scribble. And now the clicking of those shimmery nails on black keys.

"Has he ever lived anywhere else in town? Someplace he might go back to?"

"Just here."

"Workplaces?"

"The university. I suppose you'd better look around Sneed Hall. Geological Sciences. Across the quad from the music building."

"Got it." Hints of a smile play around Bragg's eyes as she records this detail. "Lovely old part of campus. I hung out on the quad a lot."

"You were a student there?" Fee asks in surprise.

Bragg doesn't elaborate. "How about houses of worship?"

"We keep faith with each other, thank you."

"Any other places Simon might have an attachment to? Special eateries? Getaway spots?"

"Sy's not the sentimental sort."

Bragg lays down her pen. She plants her elbows on the tabletop, either side of her keyboard. "Fiona, would you say that Simon is . . . happy?"

"Would *you* be happy, in his condition?"

Bragg sweeps her hair back from her face. She traces one spangly fingertip over one dark eyebrow. "Let me put it another way: Has he seemed depressed lately?"

"No more than usual. Though the dementia sometimes brings him quite low."

"Have you ever worried that he might harm himself?"

Fee hesitates. "I don't think I should answer that question."

"Fiona, if he's a danger to himself, we need to know."

Fee wrestles with what to say. And how.

"It's not time," she says finally.

"Meaning?"

"Sy has asked me to . . . well . . . He wants certain measures taken . . . at a certain point . . . to do what must be done. But not yet. When the dementia is more advanced." She sneaks a nervous glance at Bragg and finds herself under tight surveillance. "That's all I'm willing to say."

Bragg picks up her pen again.

"Not yet?" she says, waiting on Fee's next word as if it were scripture.

"Not yet."

Bragg writes something in her notepad. Underlines it. Twice. Then scratches it all out.

"Does Simon ever become violent with you? Hard to handle?"

"Never."

Bragg gazes at her, sizing her up. Fee holds herself steady as a nightlight in the wee hours.

"That's good," Bragg says, then. "With dementia, there's no predicting. Now, when did you last see Simon today?"

"I was up in my studio, working on a quilt. He was down here in his den, practicing his clarinet. That's the only place he'll play his music. He thinks nobody can hear him. But you can—one end of the house to the other. You can hear everything in this old house."

Fee slips off her right shoe and reaches down to massage a light spasm in her fallen arch. Her foot's not easy to get to, what with her hip. If Sy were here, he'd rub out the cramp. He has the touch.

"For a dabbler, Sy's quite good at his music," she tells Bragg, digging into her sole. "You'd be amazed. Today he was grinding away at 'Memories of You.' You know the song . . . ? No, of course you don't. You're a young thing. Anyway, he was playing the same tune, over and over. He does that with every song."

"Practice makes perfect!" Bragg says with a conductor's flourish of her pen.

"No—that's not it." Fee wedges her shoe back on. "The endless repetition isn't about Sy trying to play better. It's the dementia. Every ten or fifteen minutes, it's like some cruel finger presses a reset button in his brain, and he forgets everything that's just happened. Like an odometer, resetting to zero. He always thinks he's just getting started."

Bragg's back to typing again with lightning speed. "What time was this, his practicing?"

"Around two, I think. I was listening to NPR. Korva Coleman was coming on with the news. I was thinking how, for supper, I'd fix sauerkraut, bratwursts, and noodles, topped off with a German chocolate cake—for his birthday, you know. Abby would join us by Zoom. And maybe Frank, too, though he's so busy, trying to keep the bistro afloat—"

Bragg's fingers pause. Her eyes flick to Fee. "Frank?"

"Abby's husband. He's *so* good to Sy, though Sy doesn't have a clue who he is. Sy thinks Abby's still married to Gabriel."

"Did Simon know about the party tonight?"

"I told him. Many times. For all the good it did." Fee lifts her tortoiseshell glasses to dab at her eyes with a tissue. "I had to keep reminding him that today was his birthday."

Fritz leaps onto her lap. He settles into the furrow between her thighbones.

" 'Why bother with a party?' I kept asking myself." Fee rakes her fingers through Fritz's plush gray fur. "I mean . . . Sometime between the main course and the cake, we'd have to remind him what day it was and what year, and then he'd say, 'Oh, right. I'm eighty.' " Stroking Fritz. Forgetting all about Bragg. "And we'd sing him the birthday song and urge him to make a wish. He'd give the candles a big blow, and we'd all applaud, and he'd begin to cut and serve. And for a moment, it

might feel almost like Before Diagnosis. Then, all at once, he'd stop—
I can just see it! He'd look down at the half-eaten cake and say, 'I'm
sorry, but what's all this fuss about?' "

Bragg's as still as a mannequin in a shop window.

"I'm telling you, Officer," Fee says, as eerily calm as the air right
before a big rain, "it's enough to break your heart."

ACCOMPLICES

6:36 P.M.

SIMON BLOWS into the hollow of his cupped hands. As his eyes adjust to the dark, he takes stock of the derelict culvert. A century old, if not two, it's formed of tightly wedged fieldstones. It arches well above his head, maybe to seven feet. In width, it's merely half that and cluttered with debris.

Hunched on the rubble opposite him is the girl. Together they've just finished heaping pine branches and scrub brush in front of the culvert.

Outside, she'd told him her name is Olivia Pink. "We wanted to ride the train," she'd added, "but there was too much snow."

She reminds me of Gilly, he tells Fee. *Why's she with me? What train is she talking about?*

He unhooks the strap of his clarinet to ease the strain on his neck. He'd prefer to set the instrument in some safe, out-of-the-way place, but it needs the warmth of his body. Otherwise, the wood might crack.

Should have never brought you out here, he says to the clarinet, in apology. *Don't know why I did. Was I trying to get on the train to take you home?*

He tightens the metal cap over the mouthpiece, then claps his palms to move the blood, careful to avoid his painfully numb fingers.

"Your turn," Olivia says, fumbling toward him. She presses her sodden gloves into his hand as if she has lent them to him before.

"Thank you," he says, trusting the gloves to fit.

"Grampa?"

We're not related by blood. She just calls me that.

Yet he senses that the two of them are connected somehow.

Companions. Accomplices. Headed for the same place. Or searching for the same thing.

"Can I come sit with you?" she says. "On your lap, maybe?"

Poor child, Fee says in his brain.

MAGIC SQUARE

6:49 P.M.

Olivia fishes a smushed box from Grampa's pocket.

"What's in here?" she says, giving it a shake.

Of course, Grampa can't see the box in her hand, because it's night, and they're stuck in this cave, and caves are always darker than the stomach of Jonah's whale.

She herself can see pretty much everything, though, because she, unlike Grampa, can see Hat Lady. And in this pitch-black cave, Hat Lady is as bright as a glow stick.

That's how it is. Sometimes you can see the light, sometimes you can't. All depends on the color of your square on the game board.

"The box says 'matches,'" Olivia tells Grampa, setting it in his gloved hand, real easy, so his frozen fingers don't break like his brain.

Her fingers are frozen too. If only she could have her gloves back. But Grampa needs them more.

It stinks, wanting two opposite things at once. It's kind of like patting your head while rubbing your tummy—any Muggle can do that. But you'll get all discombobulated if you try switching which hand's doing what, out of the blue.

"Don't matches start fires?" she says to Grampa.

He slides the box open.

"Can't see a fool thing," he says, pawing at the contents. "But I don't think there's any matches."

She peeks into the box. Across from her, Hat Lady peeks in, too, with her magic glow.

"Grampa, I think my eyes see better in caves than yours do. I

mean . . . you're right, there's no matches. But there's this thingy."
Olivia lifts out a little plushie by the leg. It's covered all over in teensy-weensy red beads. "A stuffed toy, maybe?"

Hat Lady's wearing a big happy smile. She has to be the shiniest see-through creature ever.

This is what Hat Lady wanted. This is why she kept poking Grampa's pocket.

Now Hat Lady's smiling straight at *her.*

Olivia's tummy does a frightful somersault.

Holy Oculus Reparo! We've landed on a real magic square!

"You can *see* me?" she whispers to Hat Lady, trying not to be a big fraidy-cat.

"No better than you can see me," Grampa says, as if Olivia has meant the question for him.

She feels like she's on the most ginormous teeter-totter *ever.* She wants to stay high up in the air and never come down.

Hat Lady points at a leather cord dangling from the beady thingy.

"Maybe it's not a toy," Olivia says, now holding the plushie by the cord. "Maybe it's a necklace. Yeah. A *turtle* necklace."

She loops the cord around her neck and tucks the turtle down the front of her shirt. It slides down toward her belly button—an outie, Charley says.

Hat Lady dims out. Like when you're on the computer, and suddenly the screen goes kind of pale, like the computer's going to faint or crash or die.

On a hunch, Olivia pulls the necklace back out of her shirt.

Hat Lady goes all bright again.

JAZZ AND CLASSICAL

6:52 P.M.

FRITZ HEADBUTTS FEE'S HAND. She scratches his chin.

"So," Bragg says to her, "you last saw Simon around two this afternoon?"

"More like, that's when I didn't *hear* him. These walls were so quiet—my heart fell straight into my stomach."

"Did anything happen today that might have prompted him to leave the house?"

Fee twiddles with the lockbox key at her neck. "It was just an ordinary day. Ordinary for *us*, anyway."

"Tell me everything you remember. Nothing's too trivial."

"Shouldn't you be out *looking?*"

"Trust me. Our team's already organizing the search."

"Well, we got up . . . got ready for the day . . . had breakfast. We have our routine, see?"

After breakfast, she sits Sy down in front of his computer—the big-screened one in his den. Back when he first got on his music kick, Abby had put together a playlist of clarinet videos: Artie Shaw and Benny Goodman and Pete Fountain and Sidney Bechet and Anat Cohen and Acker Bilk . . . More clarinet music than you could ever possibly want.

Since then, Sy's watched that clarinet playlist dozens of times, but he doesn't remember. So to him, every morning is like Christmas. The videos rev him up, and pretty soon, he's itching to play.

This morning, she's about to leave him to his listening, when, out of the

*clear blue, he says from his desk chair, "Remember when we saw Eddie Daniels
play live at Lincoln Center?"*

She's amazed. It's like her old Bestie is back again.

"You remember that?" she says.

"Course I do! Jazz Meets Classical, wasn't it?"

*Tears well in her eyes. It's as if he's been gone for months on expedition,
without any reliable means of communication, then suddenly, without warning, he's home again. And whole.*

"That show was the fusion of two opposites," she says. "Just like we are!"

"But which of us is which?" he teases.

*"Oh, that's easy," she says with a laugh. "I'm jazz. And you, Bestie, are a
classic."*

When she's done reciting the story for Bragg, Fee realizes she's been
mindlessly folding a clean tissue into ever smaller squares. It can't be
folded any smaller. She covers it with her palm.

"You sure you don't want to take a break? Have something to eat?"
Bragg asks. "You need to keep your strength up."

"I'm fine," Fee says. "Are *you* hungry? I can fix you a sandwich—"

"No, thanks."

"What about that detective?" Fee says, nodding toward the other
room. "You think he's hungry?"

"Don't worry about us, Fiona. *Please.*"

Bragg flips to a new page in her notepad. Fee frowns to think that
the meager details she has provided the officer could have somehow
filled a sheet of paper.

"Now," Bragg says, "did you have any visitors today?"

"You and that detective are the first souls I've allowed inside this
house since lockdown!"

"No deliveries? No meter readers?"

"Well . . ." Fee looks up and broods on the lazy turning of the fan as
it brings heat down from the ceiling. "Victor dropped by this morning.
But he didn't come in."

"And Victor is . . . ?"

"Victor Curliss. We buy our milk and eggs from him and Mikey
Harper. Maybe you know them—Dinky Creek Farms, out near the
reservoir? Usually their girl Frieda delivers, but this morning it was
Victor. I saw him out the kitchen window."

Bragg switches from her notepad to her computer tablet. Her mouth
silently forms "Dinky Creek Farms" as she types. Maybe she's searching
online.

"What time was that?" she asks Fee.

"Eight thirty or nine."

"We'll need to talk to him."

Fee crushes the tissue enfolded in her hand. "You can't seriously believe that Victor's involved somehow!" she says crossly.

"Just following every lead. Anybody else?"

"Well, of course, the mail came, before lunch."

So much nonsense, Fee thinks with impatience. Even the ceiling fan seems to be turning too slow. *Wasted effort. Wasted time.*

"What's your carrier's name?" Bragg says, typing.

"Why would I know that?" Fee says. "She's a black girl."

EVERY LAST ONE

6:52 P.M.

If only Abby could see more of Detective Parrish than those flat, bothered eyes and those pointy ears sticking out from the loops of his mask. Through a computer screen, she can't tell whether she trusts him.

"Your dad ever gone missing before?" he asks her.

"Never like this. Late getting home from his walk is all—three times lately, that I know of. I'm not sure Mom tells me everything."

"How long was he gone those other times?"

"Four, maybe five hours."

He taps his pen idly on his notepad. "Been at least that now, looks like."

His tone is impersonal—even robotic. Walling off his emotions might help him do his job, but couldn't he display a modicum of kindness?

"After Dad retired, you could almost set your watch by him," Abby says. "A real stickler for routine. He'd leave the house at four on the dot. Get home by five, five-thirty at the latest." She's fighting back tears. "Not anymore. Not today."

That pen of his, tap, tap, tapping. A damn drumstick.

"How about you?" she asks, foraging for his human side. "Are your parents still living?"

"They head to Florida this time of year. They like it hot."

She thinks again of her dream—in hindsight, a clear portent of trouble. No point mentioning it to Parrish, though. However much he might resemble Honest Abe, he doesn't seem the sort to share Lincoln's sturdy belief in premonitions.

"Have you worked a lot of missing cases like this, Detective?"

123

"Too many."

"Have you solved most of them?"

"Every last one," he says, dotting the air with one spindly finger.

She doesn't ask how many of the missing he has found alive.

"Your folks argue much?" Parrish asks then. "You know . . . maybe your dad, he gets mad, stomps out of the house to let off some steam—"

"They're not like that!" Abby says with weepy indignation.

He crosses his arms over his hollow chest. "*Every* couple's like that."

"You don't understand. My dad . . . he'd be absolutely lost without Mom. That was true even before the dementia. She might be the only person in the world he really trusts."

The only person he really *loves*, she'd almost said.

"Got to be hard on her, the way he is," Parrish says. "Maybe she's bushed, loses her temper, ticks him off—"

"No way!" she erupts at the screen.

"I've seen it before."

"You don't know them!"

Her heart's high in her throat with rage. She tells herself to calm down.

"With all due respect," she says, feeling little respect for Parrish at all, "you just don't get it. My mom's a guard dog. Anybody who hurts my dad is in big trouble. That goes double for her. If she ever did anything that got him hurt, she'd beg you to haul her away."

Abby pours green tea into two mugs and sets them on the coffee table, a salvaged wooden door painted the same fire-engine red as the exterior of the house. Downstairs, her father's tooting away on his newly refurbished clarinet. It had taken Bernie, the Vintage Horn Doctor, more than a month to swedge and countersink the instrument's keys, resurface the tone holes, tighten the posts, rehydrate the wood . . .

Over the years, many of her most memorable talks with her mother have taken place right here on this sofa, in front of this table. It's her favorite spot in her mother's studio, which is her favorite room in the house.

The studio is tucked away like a secret chamber in a fairy tale. The only way in is through a pocket-sized door in Abby's old bedroom, just left of the wrought-iron bedstead. Painted the same sage green as the plaster walls, the door is all but invisible but for a beaded pull-string dangling through a bitty hole.

Pull that string, and a latch lifts on the other side of the door. The door swings forward, and you can step inside. If you've outgrown your childhood, you'd better duck as you pass through, or you'll smack your noggin against the low doorhead.

The long, narrow room you enter is sunny white, flooded with natural light. Occupying its center is the Beast, as Abby's mother calls it with affection—a twelve-foot longarm quilting machine. It's flanked by two sewing machines.

Bins of thread and embroidery floss, paints and dyes, buttons and beads line the entirety of one wall. Along the opposite wall is the Vault: a storehouse of fabrics sorted by color in open cubbies. Here are the usual cottons and linens and flannels. But you'll also find prized endek from Bali, shema from Tibet, Mapuche cloth from Chile, khadi from India, yūzen from Japan . . . extraordinary textiles, all either collected by her mother on her travels or gifted by admirers of her art quilts.

The sofa squats in front of the dormer window, here at the far end of the room. The window frames the procession of the seasons: shades of green in spring and summer; a rich palette of dying leaves in autumn; black branches, drab skies, and brilliant snow in winter. Views from this window have inspired not a few of her mother's nature quilts.

Abby kicks off her sandals and draws up her legs. The intoxicating scent of peonies wafts in through the screen behind her.

Over at the worktable, her mother is cutting fabric tiles for a mosaic quilt meant for a charity raffle, another of her countless causes. She's been laboring on that same quilt for months and has made little progress since Abby's last visit.

This, Abby realizes, is mainly because of her father. He requires loads of supervision. With each trip up from Philly, she marks the worsening of his condition. In many ways he's still his pensive, impossibly private self. But more and more, his old-man body shelters a little-boy mind in need of oversight and direction. He has to be told. And told. And told again. The endless repetition and virtually round-the-clock surveillance exhaust her mother.

"I never know which Simon I'm with," her mother had confided, just this morning. "Is he the one I can trust or the one I can't? Sometimes he's both at the same time."

Only during one of his rare naps can her mother enjoy a few moments of uninterrupted time in her studio. And whenever Abby spells her for a weekend, as now, her mother savors the extended opportunity to create, free of worry. She laps it up like a cat with a fresh bowl of milk.

Right now, long-toned scales and halting arpeggios are seeping up through the floorboards from her father's den, below. If he takes to the clarinet again— and sticks with it—his music-making will offer her mother additional respite.

Abby stirs a heaping spoonful of sugar into her mug. "Mom, your tea's getting cold."

"In a minute, hon," her mother says, her nose still into the cutting.

Abby fans her fingers across a vibrant royal-blue and orange cloth slung across one arm of the sofa. "This fabric is gorgeous," she says in a bid for attention.

"Isn't it, though?" Her mother glances over at last. "That's kente cloth from Ghana. Handwoven from silken yarn, not the usual cotton. I was thinking I might use the cloth in this quilt, but I can't bear to cut it. The design has a message, you know. Kente cloth always carries a message of some sort. That's one reason it often gets passed down as an heirloom."

"So what's the message in this?" Abby says, fondling the strip of cloth.

" 'Something that hasn't happened before.' That's what I was told, anyhow. By tradition, the cloth would have been woven on a loom by a man. A master weaver."

This is no knock-off factory print. Abby can feel every thread in the weft and warp of the tight, heavy weave.

"No wonder you don't want to cut it," she says.

Downstairs, her father is walking up a chromatic scale—certainly "something that hasn't happened before" in her lifetime.

The kente cloth seems like a sign. A green light.

Sitting cross-legged on the sofa, Abby pats the seat beside her. "Come sit with me, will you, Mom? I have some questions about Grandma Vera."

"Vera?" Her mother straightens in her chair. "For heaven's sake! After all this time?"

"Is there some statute of limitations I don't know about?" Abby jokes.

Her mother isn't amused. "Why ask me? Why not your father?"

"I'm afraid of upsetting him."

Her mother perches her tortoiseshell glasses atop her head. "What's eating at you, honey?"

"Come. Sit." Another slap on the cushion.

Her mother maneuvers out of her chair, protective of her hip. "Don't tell me you're dressing up an old skeleton you found in the back of the closet."

That's when she laughs. A short, nervous burst.

She's not far from the truth, though.

As her mother hobbles over to the tattered sofa, Abby ponders where to begin. It's never easy to broach a delicate subject, and for some reason, her mother already seems keyed up.

From the mist of Abby's imagination, a tiny cemetery materializes. It's out on the prairie, on the edge of nowhere, though the small town of Hardin, Nebraska, must be nearby. You get there by driving a straight dirt road toward a vanishing point in the cloudless sky. Unmaintained, the road is basically two ruts, as if it had been cut into the ground by the wheels of covered wagons.

The cemetery is just as forsaken as the road. No trees around to catch the wind. Only weeds. Weeds and weathered headstones, all of them out of true.

This is where she must start.

"You went with Dad to Grandma Iris's funeral, didn't you?" Abby asks.

Her mother frowns. "Of course. You know I did."

Abby hadn't made the trip herself. She'd been in community college. She'd had a job. Besides, she'd barely known the woman.

"Did they bury Iris beside Grandpa Karl?"

"No. Next to her first husband."

"Ernie Blanchard."

Her mother dribbles cream into her mug. "I'm surprised you remember his name. He's on the fringe of your father's family history."

"So," Abby says, pressing on, "if Iris is buried beside Ernie, is Grandma Vera buried beside Grandpa Karl?"

"Yes. Both couples are interred in the same cemetery, there in Hardin. Why?"

Abby tries to picture KARL and VERA on a single RICHTER gravestone.

"You're absolutely sure?" she asks. "Vera is with Karl?"

Her mother's spoon rattles vigorously against the well of her mug. Usually she's a swisher, not a clinker. "Of course! Why wouldn't they be?"

"Well, way back when, that cemetery was whites only."

Just as Hardin had been, come sundown. According to the internet, a sign posted on the edge of town had declared so.

"Whites only?" her mother says with a peculiar air. She deposits her brash spoon on the tea tray. "Whites only," she says again, this time as if settling a debate. "I honestly don't see how that concerns us, hon."

"Let me show you . . ." Abby opens the photo app on her phone. "Bernie, the guy who restored Dad's clarinet, found two old photos hidden in the lining of the instrument case."

Her mother parks her tea on a quilted coaster, then pulls her glasses back down on her nose.

The first image is sepia-toned and washed out from overexposure. But without doubt, the boy is Abby's father—maybe five years old, wearing knickers and knee socks, swimming in a jacket several sizes too big. He's adorable. But pouting. Just behind him is a bone-thin woman in a puff-sleeve dress.

"Oh, Abby," her mother murmurs. "I've never seen a picture of the two of them together. That is his mother, isn't it?"

The woman drapes her arms around the boy's shoulders, pulling him back against her body. She has removed his cap, maybe to make the photographer happy. She clasps the cap in front of him, along with his little hands, as if holding him still for the camera. Her dark hair looks crimped with an iron. It flies wild in the wind.

Mother and son are standing in somebody's yard—at the homeplace in Hardin, maybe. The paint on the frame house behind them is peeling.

Vera is smiling half-heartedly for the camera. A lopsided smile, to the left.

Abby recognizes that smile. Her father has it too.

"He favors her, don't you think?" she says.

Her mother chuckles. "Looks like he hated getting his picture taken even then."

Downstairs, her father is still climbing up and down that chromatic scale, but now at a faster tempo, his tongue testing articulations on the tip of the reed. Buzzing. Slurring. Playing staccato . . .

What kind of man might her father have been, Abby wonders, if Vera hadn't died so young? Her unnatural passing had altered him forever. He'd never had the chance to form an identity apart from its shadow. He wouldn't even talk about it, beyond saying there'd been a freak "accident in the woodshed."

"Just guessing," Abby says, "but if Dad was only five when Vera died, this photo must have been taken shortly before."

"So heartbreaking," her mother says with a protracted sigh. "I honestly don't want to think about it. You said there were two photographs?"

"Right. This next one is even older . . ."

Abby swipes to a sharp black-and-white, the work of a professional. It shows a dinky orchestra seated in two rows on an auditorium stage. The musicians are of high school age, on the cusp of adulthood.

Half of the musicians hold violins. There is also a pianist at a baby grand, a string bassist, a trombonist, a trumpeter, a snare drummer, a bass drummer. The young men are clad in conservative suits and neckties; the young women in identical dresses, formal and dark, with sailor collars.

Then there's one conspicuous clarinetist. Garbed in white, she's seated center stage with her instrument across her lap. Among the other musicians in their somber attire, she shines bright as a streetlight. The featured performer.

"This is Vera, too, isn't it?" Abby says to her mother. "Here in the white?"

"Sure looks like it."

Abby zooms in on Vera's clarinet. "I'm thinking this might be the same clarinet that Dad's playing."

"Really?" her mother says, voice sharp with intrigue.

"It all adds up. Bernie, the repair guy, told me Dad's clarinet was manufactured in Paris in the '20s, give or take—around the same period as this photo."

Her mother contemplates the photograph in silence.

"It could be the same instrument, couldn't it?" Abby prods.

"Honey, I've no idea. I never even knew your father had a clarinet till you two brought it down from the attic."

Abby, changing her tack, restores the full view of the orchestra. "Do you see anything distinctive about these musicians?"

"No. Why?"

"Please. Just . . . look at them."

With her artist's eye, her mother will surely notice the high cheekbones. The more or less dusky complexions. The short dark hair. The wide-set eyes. The gravity of the faces.

"I don't know what you want me to see," her mother says listlessly.

Abby bottles up her impatience. She zooms in on the bass drum suspended in the back row. It looks beat to hell, as if it belongs to a marching band, not an orchestra. Painted on its discolored head are a few words in capital letters. Between the chipped paint and the angle of the shot, the words are tough to read. Abby enlarges the image as far as she can.

"Genoa Indian School?" her mother reads in astonishment.

Finally, Abby thinks.

"Impossible!" her mother exclaims. "You're saying Vera was an Indian?"

"That's the only explanation."

"But if that's true, then maybe—"

Her mother breaks off abruptly. She kneads her forehead with her gnarled fingers, like when she's mulling over a quandary with a quilt. Then she exhales through pursed lips.

"Sy's always told me his mother . . . was an orphan."

"So?" Abby says. "Maybe she was!"

Her mother shifts her weight on the sofa. "Well, he's never said anything about any Indians!" Clipping every syllable of every word. "His mother had to have been white. Her burial in that cemetery proves it!"

Abby's speechless. Her mother knows a little about a lot, and a lot about more than a little. How could she say such a harebrained thing?

Her mother skews away from Abby, mumbling about being "uncomfortable."

"Here." Abby slips a throw pillow behind her mother's lower back, to support her hip. "Better?"

"A little."

Outside the window, a bird brawl has broken out atop a nearby beech tree. A red-tailed hawk has a blue jay clutched in its talons. A trio of other jays are dive-bombing the hawk, attacking the larger bird with their beaks before swooping away. The air fills with furious jeers and screeches, drowning out her father's music. Feathers fly.

"Shut the window, will you, hon?" her mother says. "I can't stand the ruckus."

Abby unfolds her legs. "It's pretty important knowing who your parents are," she says, leaning back to crank the handle. "Knowing who you are."

Her mother consults the well of her mug as if she were divining tea leaves. "Sometimes it's better to forget."

Abby searches her mother's powdered face. "What in the world do you mean?"

"Sometimes the past just isn't worth raking up. It can be such a burden. Best to let it go." She holds out her mug like a peace offering. "A warmer, hon?"

"I need you to do something for me," Abby says now to Detective Parrish. "Could you check today's mail? I sent Dad a gift for his birthday."

Parrish shoots her a curious look. "You think that might be relevant to his disappearance?"

"I hope not."

Parrish scrapes back and leaves the dining room table. All that's visible on the Zoom screen now is the wall behind the chair where he'd been sitting—her father's chair, at the head of the table.

Displayed on that wall is one of her mother's art quilts: a tree of life.

Every branch, an outstretched hand of a different color.

Each hand, twining with the next.

DON'T FORGET

7:10 P.M.

FEE STANDS in the den with Detective Parrish and Officer Bragg, anxiously fiddling with Eileen's handle. As usual, Sy's desktop is perfectly neat. His mail is tidily stacked in a basket. His bookshelves are arranged according to subject and author. His satchel is in its customary place, atop the vertical file. After a half century of use, its leather still has a lovely patina. He used to oil it every week; now he oils it whenever he *thinks* it's been a week.

Only the hardwood floor is in disarray, littered with sheet music and typewritten pieces of paper. The music stand has been toppled near the side window, as if some sort of dustup.

Fee picks her way through the litter to the music stand and stoops with a grimace to right it.

"Stop!" Parrish says, his raspy voice echoing in the room. "Don't touch anything! We need to preserve the scene, just in case . . . "

He whisks out some black disposable gloves. "Why didn't you tell us about this mess?" he says to Fee, crossly.

Fee shoots him a look. "This is the first time I'm seeing it."

Parrish snaps on his gloves. "Didn't you come in here hunting for your husband?"

"I *never* come in here unless *he's* here!"

"He could have been passed out on the floor this whole time!" Parrish says, sweeping an arm toward his feet.

"Do you *see* him passed out on the floor?" she fires back, bristling. So much nonsense. As if Parrish knows *anything*. "Look, I can always tell when Sy's in here. He always shuts the door, for one thing. And he's almost always playing!"

"His clarinet, she means," Bragg explains to Parrish, working her right hand into a tight rubber glove. "Music's a passion of his."

Fee prods the five-footed clarinet stand with Eileen's tip. "This is all wrong," she murmurs.

Bragg steps closer as she gloves her left hand. "*What's* wrong?"

"His clarinet isn't where it should be."

Fee casts a glance toward the instrument case. "Detective, since I'm not supposed to touch anything, would you please check that case, there under the window?"

Parrish whips out his cell phone. He shoots a photograph of the small black case where it sits, then lifts it high by its handle.

"Empty!" he announces.

"How do you know without looking inside?" Fee says, mocking him.

He totally misses her point.

Lips pinched in exasperation behind her mask, Fee pivots on Eileen to scan the wider room. "So strange. His clarinet's not *anywhere.*"

"Maybe he took it with him," Bragg suggests, hands on her wide hips.

"Whatever for?" Fee asks, incredulous. Sy never plays anywhere else. Or for anyone else.

Parrish is treading the scene with care, inspecting it with his doleful Abe Lincoln eyes, flashing picture after picture.

"Bragg," he says without stopping, his cell phone shuttering like an antique camera, "message dispatch that our MEPA might be carrying a clarinet. Somebody might notice a screwy detail like that."

"Got it," Bragg says.

A leatherbound notebook is splayed open on the floor beside the upended music stand. It's the type Sy had always used to record his field notes while on expedition.

"Hand that to me, would you?" Fee says to Parrish, pointing Eileen.

"Not till you put these on," he says, producing another pair of gloves.

Fee bridles. The latex in such gloves irritates her skin. But she can't bother with that now. Sy's all that matters. She can manage the rash.

After photographing the notebook, Parrish picks it up and transfers it to Fee.

She folds back a bent page. Flattens the crease.

"Anything that might help?" Bragg asks, her shoulder brushing against Fee's.

-16-

Fee sets the world in order.
Has our whole life.
Gives me a safe place to be.
She'll always be my Girl.

But where I am now she can't come,
even when she's sitting right beside me.

S. C. R.
Fritz in my lap

Fee closes the notebook. She relinquishes it to Bragg.

I can't do this, she tells the officer with her eyes.

Bragg accepts the notebook, her expression solemn above her mask. She leafs back to the opening page. She begins to read its contents aloud.

Fee absorbs the weight of the words. Being on page one, they're presumably the oldest in the notebook.

Clearly the entry originated After Dementia, but how long ago? A year? A month?

The words themselves reveal nothing of their timing. They float. Defy history. Perhaps even chronology. Her Bestie could have written them this very day, seated at his desk, earnest as a schoolchild, the tip of his tongue curling over his lower lip.

-1-

Other than Fee and our baby girl, my life hasn't amounted to much more than a collection of worthless fossils. Still, there are things I don't want to forget. Things worth remembering.

Writing them longhand helps them stick.

This is my last season in the field. Digging through the strata of my own mind. What's left of it, anyway.

I'll keep this notebook on my music stand. Seeing it there, in this Desert of Forgettery, may prompt me to write.

Maybe this is where you'll find the last facts of me, once I'm gone.

I love my life. More than I knew, for too long a time.

If you happen to think of me once I'm gone, kindly remember to love your life too.

Ne obliviscaris.

S. C. R.
It's morning in the house

"Ne ob-livis-car-is," Bragg reads, tripping on her delivery. "What's that? Latin?"

Fee nods. "That notebook's probably full of it."

"I thought it was a dead language."

"Dead doesn't mean lost."

Bragg taps the handwritten entry. "So, what's this *ne oblivis-caris* mean? Do you know Latin?"

"Yes, I do." Fee turns to face the wall. "It means 'Don't forget.' "

GOOD DAUGHTER

7:25 P.M.

FRANK RUSHES into the office between orders, a big puffy cloud in his chef's whites. Smooth as a waiter, he serves Abby a simple charcuterie board with a glass of wine.

"Love you," he says. "For now, all I can do is feed you. Please eat."

Then he's gone, back into the kitchen.

Alone at her desk, Abby tears a short baguette with her teeth, waiting for Detective Parrish to rejoin the Zoom. Breadcrumbs dribble like flakes of snow down her front.

If she fills her mouth, maybe she can keep from crying.

She swirls the merlot, then sets the goblet down on the desktop. Tears of merlot weep down the inside of the glass.

Food is Frank's native love language. Hers is work. Fixing. Solving.

Ask her how to keep a bistro open during a pandemic. How to scour the books for corners to cut. How to shorten a "consistently good, modestly inventive" menu (awarded four stars, right before COVID) to the most popular fare . . . then shorten it again. How to lay off staff with a sense of decency.

Such things she can do.

But don't ask her how to be a good daughter. Not while she's staring into a vacant screen in Philly, her father vanished into Massachusetts snow.

Her thoughts surge back to that momentous afternoon in her mother's studio, when slivers of the past, so painfully embedded in the present, had been allowed to fester.

. . .

136

DOWNSTAIRS, done with scales and arpeggios, her father's playing an actual piece of music. Classical. Maybe an étude from the intermediate student book Abby had bought him. She should have purchased the advanced book instead.

She drains the teapot, wipes the spout with a napkin, then returns her attention to her mother, on the sofa beside her.

"Best to let the past go"? Did those words really just come out of her mother's mouth?

Abby has always admired her mother for speaking her own mind and striving to do right (even when her high-mindedness could be totally maddening). For never giving up on the Good (as she understood it). For exhorting others not to give up on it either.

So when had her mother become conventional and timid?

To be in the dark about Vera's identity all along—that's one thing. But to believe that being in the dark, and staying in the dark, is perfectly fine . . . ? (Just as it had been perfectly fine to believe for almost a year that her husband was suffering from "senior moments" despite unmistakable evidence of dementia?)

"This Genoa Indian School," her mother says, startling Abby out of her swirl of speculation. "Any idea where it is?"

Now here's a glimmer of her true mom. The bands of anxiety in Abby's chest ease somewhat. "Nebraska. What's left of the school is a museum now."

Her mother grabs her forearm. "But honey—Sy's from Nebraska! Is that school anywhere near Hardin?"

"Yes." Abby locates Genoa in her maps app. She zooms out until Hardin pops up to the southeast. "A couple hours away, tops."

"It would have been farther in those days, what with the slow cars and the bad roads." Her mother's hooked now. Her face is opening. Her voice has verve. "Do you know anything else about the school, hon?"

"It was an off-reservation boarding school. One of the first."

"Like Carlisle, in Pennsylvania?"

"Exactly," Abby says. "Where'd you learn about Carlisle?"

"A documentary, on PBS. The government used schools like that to force Indians to assimilate. 'Kill the Indian, save the man.' All that nonsense. The same thing happened up in Canada."

"Right." Now she and her mother are getting somewhere. "From what I've learned online, Genoa was among the biggest of all those government boarding schools. It operated from 1884 to 1934. Thousands of Indian kids passed through, up to six hundred in a single year."

"And Vera was one of them. Bless her heart."

Abby can hear in her mother's voice that Vera's story is as true for her now as the message in the orange-and-blue kente cloth, though its precise meaning is just as obscure.

"The whole idea," Abby says, "was to take the Indian kids away from their families and put them in these boarding schools, where they'd be Christianized and taught to live and work like Americans . . . or I should say, like white Americans." She grimaces, dismayed at how readily she still falls into biased language. "The schools punished kids who tried to hang on to their culture. By and by, the kids were all meant to disappear into the great American melting pot. That was the government's hope, at least."

Her mother gathers up the length of kente cloth. Shakes it smooth.

"Maybe that's what Vera was doing when she married Karl," she says wistfully. "Maybe she was disappearing into the world of whites."

She rolls the fabric into a bright, neat scroll.

"Keeping secrets," she says, "can take a toll on a person . . ."

She hands the cloth scroll to Abby.

You can't intend for me to keep this, Abby wants to say, taken aback. You know that such precious cloth would be wasted on me.

But before Abby can object aloud, her mother asks, "Any idea where Vera might have lived before the school?"

Abby shakes her head. "Not yet. Her student records will tell us, if we can find them. I'm working on it, but the school's paperwork is stored in archives all around the country. Native kids were shipped to Genoa from more than a dozen states."

The two of them sip their tea as music percolates up from the den. Outside the window, the bird battle between the hawk and the jays is over.

Abby smiles to herself, feeling lighter, no longer alone with the few facts she has uncovered about Vera.

"Mom," she says then, "how do you think Dad will react when we tell him? He's never been one for surprises. Especially since he got sick."

"Tell him?" Her mother rips off her glasses. "Why ever would we do that?"

Stung by her mother's sudden withdrawal back into a timid shell of herself, Abby sets aside her mug. She may not be alone with the facts, but she and her mother are not yet together.

They may never be.

Abby's entire life, this is how their family has been. It's like she's in a solo skiff, out on the water, while her parents are close by, in another boat loosely tethered to hers. Her mother, rowing. Her father, surveying the shore through binoculars. No way for Abby to join them. No room in their boat for a third.

They've loved her. She knows that. But they've always loved each other more.

On impulse, Abby unwinds the kente cloth. She wreathes it around her neck like a scarf.

"Lovely," her mother says. "It suits you."

Abby reaches for her mother's hand. She plants a kiss on a knobbly knuckle.

"Mom," she says gently, "Dad deserves to know. He has a right to the truth, even if he's old and losing his mind."

Her mother's eyes narrow. "He is not losing his mind! He still works the Sunday puzzle, for God's sake!"

Their eyes lock. Their joined hands tighten like a vise.

Abby draws a deep breath. Relaxes her grip on her mother's arthritic fingers.

Her mother's wedding band is loose. It should be resized.

"Mom, all I'm saying is, doesn't the possible good—the rightness—of telling Dad the truth outweigh the potential harm?"

"No." One curt, businesslike word, as if Abby were five years old again and sneaking another cookie from the jar.

"Why not?" Abby protests.

"Because . . ." Her mother lifts her eyes to the skylight, as if appealing for help from beyond the clouds. "Because if the roles were reversed, your father wouldn't tell you."

"How can you say that? He can't abide lying."

Her mother's expression goes to flint. "He'd lie to protect you."

"No way!"

Abby leaps in her mind to her father's defense: He's many things, but not a liar. He might not say much, but what he does say, you can bank on.

But somehow she can't give evidence on his behalf. She's tongue-tied on the stand. A terrible witness.

"Hon"—her mother, the only witness in this case with any credibility—"he's been lying to you since you were born."

The world heaves on its foundation. Abby clings to the crumbling.

Her mother barges ahead. "You know that story he told you about how Vera died . . . ?"

"An accident," Abby says hoarsely. "In a woodshed."

"It wasn't an accident. She hanged herself."

Abby drops her mother's hand. "That can't be true!"

Her mother caresses Abby's forearm. But Abby steels herself, not willing to be soothed. Not yet.

"You lied to me," she cries. "Both of you!"

"Perhaps we shouldn't have," her mother says, her fingers like lost feathers on Abby's skin. "But your father thought it best. He made me promise not to tell. To protect you."

Her mother rests a cool, clammy palm on Abby's cheek.

"Honey, you mean well, and I love you for it. But we can't go back and undo what's been done. Who Vera really was, what happened to her—I'm afraid it's just too late."

"But what if it isn't?" Abby holds up her phone. "What if these old photos have surfaced now because now *is precisely when the truth's meant to come out? Every last bit of it!"*

Downstairs, her father has abandoned the étude book for a delicate, poignant tune, full of vibrato. His playing is beautiful. Disarming.

" 'Somewhere Over the Rainbow,' " her mother says in a whisper, marveling. "Did you buy him the sheet music?"

But Abby can tell he's improvising, playing either by ear or from indelible memory. She and her mother hang on every note as he wends his way to the end.

"It's like he's been playing his whole life," her mother says under her breath as the last note decays.

Maybe he has, Abby thinks. First, as a boy, by playing vicariously, watching his mother's lips on the mouthpiece, her fingers on the keys. Then, after she died, by making her instrument his own and unearthing her talent in himself.

But his mother didn't just die, Abby corrects herself with indignation. She killed herself.

Why did you ever give up? she asks him. Part accusation. Part lament.

He starts back at the top, with more surety in his tone.

A tear is leaving a track in her mother's face powder. "For now, honey, let's not tell your father any of this nonsense about Vera. Let him have his joy."

No, Abby thinks, gnawing at her baguette, don't ask her how to be a good daughter.

For most of two years, she'd honored her mother's wishes. She'd let her father "have his joy."

Meanwhile, she'd plugged away at her detective work, successfully locating a number of digitized documents and letters about Vera in government archives. From that smattering of records, she'd been able to sketch the faint outlines of her grandmother's life as a student at Genoa Indian School. She'd begun to penetrate the stony eyes of that inscrutable girl seated in the orchestra. The troubled eyes of that melancholic woman bundled around her son.

Then the time had arrived to tell her father.

His eightieth birthday.

So, had the papers arrived today, as she'd planned? And had her father opened them?

Detective Parrish will soon supply the answers. There's a chance she could still intercept the papers. Prevent her father from ever seeing them, once he's safely home.

But *should* she?

FATHER'S JOY

7:35 P.M.

DUE TO THE WEBCAM ANGLE, Abby can only see half of her mother's face on her computer screen. That one eye is squeezed shut, as if blocking out a hideous sight.

Their Zoom session has just resumed, back in her mother's kitchen. Detective Parrish is briefing Abby on the mess they'd discovered in her father's den. He brandishes a fistful of papers—those she'd sent by Priority Mail.

Abby's thoughts are a jumble, her heart flayed open. If only she hadn't sent those documents to her father. If only she'd handled the matter some other way.

Parrish slips off his mask, unwraps a stick of gum, and plugs it into his mouth. "As a precaution, I'm calling in a crime scene unit to make sure your father left the house of his own free will."

"You really think that's necessary?" Abby says, flustered.

"Another thing," Parrish says, letting her question hang like the mask still low on his chin, "your dad's clarinet is missing. You ever known him to take it out of the house?"

"No, but . . . Hey, Mom—" she says, to rouse her mother.

The one eyelid flutters open. "What's that, hon?"

"Does Dad ever take the clarinet out of the house?"

"Never."

Parrish takes to tapping his infernal pen again. "Either of you have any idea why he might have taken it today?"

Abby shakes her head. Her mother is still not all there.

Abby wants Parrish to stop with his pen. She wants him to raise his mask. She wants him to have no reason to be in her mother's house.

She quaffs the rest of her merlot.

"Detective," she says then, "please—I can barely see my mom."

"Sorry," Parrish says, adjusting the laptop's position.

"And while we're at it," Abby says, "pull your mask back up."

"Sorry," he says again, a regular apology machine, not sounding sorry at all as he replaces his mask. "But Abby, help me get this straight: When your father's condition was diagnosed, he suddenly wanted to play clarinet?"

"Yes. He'd played as a boy."

"And somehow, while getting his clarinet fixed up, you learned his birth mother was some sort of Indian?"

Some sort of Indian.

"She was a Dakota woman, yes," she says, playing nice. As if Parrish would ever call a white person *some sort of European.*

"And you and your mother decided not to tell him?"

"Actually," her mother interjects, suddenly feisty, "Abby and I decided to *wait.* We agreed that would be best—"

"*Actually,*" Abby says to her mother, cutting her off, "I just let you have your way till I could learn more. I told you then, and I'm telling you now: Dad has a right to know."

Her mother wags a mishmash of papers. "And you thought today— his *birthday*—would be the best time to tell him?"

"How long was I supposed to wait? Till he totally loses his mind? Or catches COVID?"

Her mother shuffles until she locates the note Abby had clipped to the documents. "Here," her mother says, flaunting it at the webcam. "You wrote 'Don't show Mom.' Why go behind my back? Why keep secrets from me?"

"That's rich," Abby mutters, shoving her empty wineglass away. "*You* complaining about *me* keeping secrets!"

"Abby! Honey!" her mother fumes. "Whatever's in these papers of yours made your father run off!"

Abby's eyes rim with tears. "We don't know that!"

"Fiona, Abby . . . we need to focus," a calm, grounded voice says. "Let's all take a deep breath."

The voice belongs to the social worker, sitting off-screen. Her hand, sheathed in a black disposable glove, is the only visible part of her.

Abby watches the hand massage slow circles into her mother's shoulder.

Abby wants that kind hand to be hers.

"I need a minute," she says, tipping over the edge. "Be right back." She flees the Zoom.

THE BISTRO IS DESERTED except for Frank. Still, Abby locks the restroom door behind her.

It's chilly in here; the thermostat is set low without patrons in the house. The chic ceramic vases have no cut flowers. The bougie candles are unburned. The red-and-white checkerboard floor remains spic-and-span from the last time she mopped, forever ago.

She splashes cold water on her teary face, over and over. Counts to five. Ten. Fifteen.

When she straightens in the glossy lighting to towel off, her reflection in the gold-gilded mirror is her mother minus thirty years. A fair complexion with a web of fine lines and a couple of well-earned wrinkles. Short salt-and-pepper curls, trending fast toward plain salt.

But a mirror tells only that part of the truth you're willing to show.

If she could bring herself to smile, her face would morph into her father's. A crooked smile, just like his. And as she now knows, just like Grandma Vera's. A smile that changes everything.

Back in her teens, Abby had actively suppressed her smile so as not to resemble him so much. She'd resented how much he was away—gone on expedition or holed up in his laboratory or flying off to conferences. When he *was* at home, he wasn't truly there. Not with her, anyway. If he wasn't outside cultivating his rosebushes, he was sequestered in his den, grading papers and writing up his research. Much like her mother these days, Abby had known he was around mostly by the sounds bleeding through his den door: the clickety-clack of his Smith Corona typewriter or the thumping of his rubber ball as it bounced off the wall in rhythm with his jazz LPs.

Some years back, as if making amends for him, her mother had told her that Abigail means "father's joy."

"Your father and I chose that name," her mother had said, "more for its sense than its sound."

Father's joy. Yet he'd never called Abby anything but Gilly.

Growing up, Abby had felt fatherless—or at least born to the wrong dad. Nothing seemed to matter to her father except his work, his roses, and his wife.

In one of Abby's earliest memories, she's around two years old, screaming bloody murder against his shoulder, struggling to break free of his arms.

He had her, but he didn't want her. She'd divined it, even then.

This is the story she'd told herself over the years. She'd worn it out like a scratchy old record, accounting for how things had been between her and him.

Then came her two failed marriages.

Years of inner work.

The inevitable ups and downs with Frank.

Her father's decline.

The pandemic.

She's wising up now. In some measure, every story you tell yourself about those you love—or those you want to love but can't, or those you want to feel loved by but don't—is dreamed up. Distorted. Incomplete.

Maybe only one aspect of any love story is true: loving is hard work, with no guaranteed payout.

Oh, and this too: there is sometimes joy in loving, but there is inevitably grief.

One of Abby's earrings clatters into the basin of the sink. The back rolls straight down the drain, but she saves the stud, pinning it against porcelain.

She breaks into a chill. Her skin goes to gooseflesh.

When was the last time she'd lost an earring? Why today, of all days? And why *this* one—a screwback from a set her mother had mailed her last Father's Day? "So you'll always remember how much your father loves you."

A tiny rose. Delicate, blushing petals.

Yes, she has always wished that her father could be other than who he is. Just as she'd allowed herself to wish after the onset of his illness that his condition might be treatable, if not curable. She'd kept wishing even after she realized all wishing was in vain.

Because she has always loved him. And he has always loved her. His deepening vulnerability during the "long goodbye" of his dementia—as well as her readiness to hang with him instead of going MIA during that agonizing goodbye—has taught her that much.

She never would have walked away from him. She never will.

And now she understands that the troubles between her and her father are traceable to a root cause much older than either of them: the sins committed against his mother. Each fact Abby has unearthed about Grandma Vera has assured her of this.

Organized bigotry. Institutionalized hate masquerading as government, as church, as boarding school. Aggressions against the body, mind, and soul. All this had been transmitted, in some form, from mother to son—from the very start, as he rode in her belly. The disease of trauma had infected him as if through the umbilical cord.

Unwittingly, he had then carried his mother's woundedness across the desert of his own life. He had lived emotionally isolated from almost everyone but his wife, inhabiting a private melancholy, afraid or unable to trust, loathe to express affection.

This is the story Abby tells herself now.

She shoves the petite rose earring into her pants pocket, then runs water over her wrists, as hot as she can stand, trying to warm herself.

She'd believed it only proper to out the truth, to make Grandma Vera more visible against the backdrop of history. True, Abby couldn't right any of the wrongs done far back in time. But by excavating the facts, by acknowledging them without flinching, and by absorbing them as best as she was able, she'd hoped to restore, in part, what she and her father had both been deprived of: the capacity to love, and to be loved, without fear. She'd wanted to shift the family's axis, help realign its spine.

It was the work of repair.

She'd meant well, sending her father those papers. But he might not survive her good intentions.

You haven't killed him, says the wet gleam in her eyes.

You can't save him, says the trembling of her lip.

CHARLEY MEADOWS

7:40 P.M.

THE DOORBELL DING-DONGS for the fourth time. Charley knocks back his shot of bourbon and slams the glass down on the island.

He can't deal with visitors right now. Olivia's gotten out.

He marches on spindly legs across the living room, erect like a flamingo. At the bay window, he sneaks a peek out the curtain.

Holy crap.

It's a cop. Burly black guy, spotlighted on the front stoop.

Charley hesitates at the door. He pops a mint to cover the bourbon, grinds it between his teeth.

Help me, Jesus, he prays, twisting the knob.

He unlocks the frosted glass storm door and props it open with a polished toe of one of his wingtip shoes.

"Can I help you, Officer?" Courteous. Honorable.

"You Charles Meadows?" the cop says.

"Yes, sir. How can I help?"

"I'm Officer Denton with the APD. How you doin' tonight?"

"Truly blessed. What's this about?"

"Could I bother you to put a mask on?"

Flying flip.

"Sorry. Don't have one handy." Charley tightens the knot of his red tie with a deliberate air of poise. "I'm not used to people just dropping by."

"Here's a fresh one you can use," the cop says, slipping a disposable mask out of a pocket in his duty jacket. "Appreciate you wearing it."

"Anything for a man in blue," Charley says, accepting the mask.

146

Then, discreetly, he lets his hand fall to his side and crushes the flimsy mask in his fist.

"Mr. Meadows—" the cop says.

"Call me Charley." Friendly, but not *too* friendly. He mustn't arouse suspicion.

"Okay, then," the cop says, his gaze traveling down to Charley's fist. "*Charley.*" He thumbs his duty belt, stony faced.

Charley's dander is up. Cop or no cop, he's not using a frigging mask.

"We're conducting a search for your neighbor Simon Richter," the cop says. "He went missing this afternoon. Mrs. Richter says you've helped hunt for him before?"

"Just being neighborly, you know," Charley says. "But I can't help tonight. Sorry . . . Hate to say it, but if you ask me, that guy belongs in an old folks' home."

The radio on the cop's belt squelches and chatters. He flicks off the volume switch. "I'd still like to ask you a few questions," he says. "Just take a minute. But first, I need you to mask up!"

Charley scrutinizes the gear buckled around the cop's hips. The hinge cuffs. The black holstered pistol. He'd like to have a belt like that.

"Look," Charley says, "I don't know anything, okay? I was at work all day."

"Yeah? How about your wife?"

"Her too," Charley says, popping another mint, this time to hide his aggravation.

By God's grace, Peg is still out searching for Olivia. No telling what she'd say or do if she were here at home, a cop at their door.

"So, you and your wife both work outside the home?" the cop asks.

"Yes, sir."

"But don't you have a daughter? Says here"—he consults his notepad—"she's maybe eight or nine?"

Charlie stiffens at the reference to Olivia. One problem with cops, they're nosy. Whatever they know, or *think* they know, it's never enough.

"What of it?" he says.

"So, who takes care of her when you're at work?"

Who the flying flip does this guy think he is? The frigging parent police?

Charley combs his fingers through his slicked-back crop cut. "Peggy and me, we coordinate schedules so one of us is always here. Can't leave the kid home alone, you know!"

"But you just said you were *both* working today."

Charley's starting to sweat. Maybe this cop isn't just here about the old man.

"My wife's only part-time," Charley says.

The cop eyeballs him like he's pulled Charley over for speeding but just maybe the car's trunk is loaded with drugs.

"Peg and me, we work different hours," Charley says.

The cop thrums his notepad on his palm. Then he slides it into his pocket. "Got a boy about the same age as your girl," he says, suddenly chummy. Maybe *too* chummy. "He's bored out of his skull, stuck at home since school went online."

Charley shrugs. "We've always homeschooled."

"That right?" The cop cranes his neck for a look inside the house. "Could you ask your wife to join us, please?"

Frick.

"And put on that mask I gave you," the cop says, crabby now. "I've got a mask for her too."

Charley grits his teeth so as not to say something stupid. As he presses the crumpled mask to his mouth, the Holy Spirit falls upon him with such power that he almost drops to his knees with a cry of *Hallelujah!*

Tell a righteous lie. That's what he hears.

A lie like the Israelite midwives told the evil Egyptians, to save the boy babies.

In God's eyes, any sin done with heavenly purpose is no sin at all.

Thank you, Jesus. Praise be.

Charley holds the mask loosely above his chin. "Look, Officer . . . Sorry . . . what was your name again?"

"Denton."

"Yeah, well, my wife's not here, okay? She ran to the store. For medicine. My daughter's, like, spiking a fever. Might be the virus—"

Lucy barges past him, out the door.

"*Hey!*" Charley cries. "Grab her collar!"

The cop wheels around. Lucy barrels into the dark.

"Sorry," the cop says. "Didn't see her coming! Ran right through me!"

"*Lucy!*" Charley shouts, braving the cold in his shirtsleeves. "You dumb bitch! Get on back here!"

From out in the yard, beyond the halo of light on the front stoop, he hears a high-pitched yelp. The prongs on Lucy's collar have delivered a jolt.

There's a second squeal.

Then all Charley can hear is hushed loping in fresh snow.

With a swift, mighty kick at the drifted stoop, Charley sends white powder flying. "She breached it," he says. "Muscled through."

Silence.

"One of them invisible dog fences, huh?" the cop says.

"Isn't worth squat!"

First Olivia. Now Lucy. In a frigging snowstorm.

At least now he can get rid of the cop.

"I'm sorry, Officer, but I've got to go—she's a devil to catch when she's loose." Charley tosses the mask back to the cop. "Hope you find the old man. He always turns up, you know?"

BODY HEAT

7:55 P.M.

ABBY REJOINS the Zoom just in time to see her mother drop hard into her chair.

"That was Gertie," her mother announces. "On the phone," she adds for Abby's benefit. "She was just calling to ask if I got the book she sent home with Sy today. She had no idea he's missing. How'd we ever forget to call her . . . ?"

"She *saw* him?" Abby blurts.

Her mother is rocking back and forth in her chair. "Around two o'clock . . ."

A taste like metal spills warm through Abby's mouth. "God, he's been gone even longer than we'd thought!"

"She said he seemed like his usual self," her mother continues, hugging her sides as she sways. "She assumed he was just taking his walk early to beat the storm. She gave him the book and told him to hurry on home."

"Who's this Gertie?" Parrish asks.

"Our friend Gertie McClure," Abby says. "She owns a bookshop on Main."

Parrish is typing a text. "I'm canceling the CSU. Clearly he left here on his own."

"Do you think he was aware of the forecast?" Bragg asks offscreen, so far from the mic that Abby must strain to hear her. "Could that be why he might have left for his walk earlier than usual?"

"I never told him about the storm," her mother says.

"Even if you had, he wouldn't have remembered," Abby says.

"Well, *something* made him leave earlier," Parrish says. "Any deviation from routine is significant."

He twirls his pen in his fingers. Taps. Finally, he levels it at Abby on the screen.

"Those papers you mailed—"

Her mother slaps the tabletop, startling Abby and Parrish both. "Enough of this nonsense! I don't care what made Sy leave the house— I just want him back! All this time, he's been out there in the cold and snow!"

The accountant in Abby has already done the math. Six hours on the streets. Maybe seven. Or even more. Wearing only his field jacket and his bush hat for warmth. No gloves. No boots. No scarf.

And no memory.

"Maybe he took shelter somewhere," Abby says, trying to project optimism she doesn't feel.

"We've initiated a door-to-door search in your neighborhood," Parrish says. "If we have to, we'll canvass the entire route he typically walks."

"He could be anywhere by now," her mother says wearily, her face drawn taut.

"If door-to-door doesn't turn him up," Parrish says, "we'll deploy reinforcements and expand the search. Our K-9 unit can trail Simon's scent in the air and on the ground—"

"In a nor'easter?" Abby asks skeptically.

"One time," Parrish says, "the dogs found a girl, four inches of fresh snow. Wind can complicate matters, but the handlers know how to work it."

Abby is ready to burst. "Then why don't you just bring the dogs in now?"

"Trust us. We know what we're doing."

"Fee," Bragg asks, still so far offscreen that she's barely a murmur, "can you give us an article of Simon's clothing for the dogs, just in case? It's best to be prepared."

"Try the laundry basket," Abby's mother says. She points weakly toward the utility room. "There—around the corner, next to the washing machine. A load of dirty clothes."

A chair creaks as Bragg leaves the table.

"Nine times out of ten," Parrish says, scratching at his face through his mask, "we find someone like Simon safe and sound within a couple miles of home—often in a place they have some sort of attachment to."

"That close by?" Abby says in surprise, with an upswell of hope.

"But there's no predicting," Parrish says. "Sometimes when they wander off, they can get pretty mixed up, disoriented. They might crawl under a nearby bush and stay put, or they might walk and walk till they can't go on. One old guy, we found him behind an abandoned truck stop, eight miles out. Another lady, she was *twelve* miles away."

Abby wishes that Parrish would stop with his stories. They aren't at all reassuring. He's like a surgeon who leaves the operating room in the middle of a procedure to tell you all the complications that might befall your loved one, who's still on the table.

He's like a clone of Dr. Chonkar, only male. No bedside manner.

Mercifully, her mother seems to have tuned him out.

Maybe, with her mother caught up in her own thoughts, this is the moment for Abby to scrape up enough voice to ask the unaskable.

"I've been wondering," she says to Parrish, "what with the storm and all . . ."

She can't finish.

Parrish apprehends her meaning. "You want it straight?" he asks.

"Gertie said he had his clarinet with him," her mother says, as if engaged in a different conversation. "Did I tell you that? Why would he have taken it?"

"That's a mystery for sure, Mom," Abby says, like a parent placating a child who won't stop asking questions. "But at the moment, I'd like to hear more from the detective. That okay?"

Her mother peers offscreen, in the direction of the utility room. "Officer, bring me that load out of the dryer, will you? They're probably a wrinkled mess by now."

Bragg's not an officer, Abby thinks. She decides not to correct her mother.

"Go ahead," she tells Parrish, as if the two of them are alone. "Give it to me straight."

"Best case?" Parrish says. "He's got twenty-four hours. After that, chances of finding him alive and well drop by half."

Abby shudders.

They've already lost a quarter of that time. Maybe even a third.

On the screen's edge, Bragg sets a small basket of clean laundry on the table. Abby's mother begins to fold, her face expressionless, devoid of emotion. Maybe she hadn't caught what Parrish said. Or hadn't understood. Or is choosing not to.

Abby rarely regards her mother as "old," even at eighty-three. But suddenly, right in front of Abby's eyes, her mother is downright elderly. A cracked eggshell held together by a thin membrane.

"Weather's supposed to break by midmorning," Parrish goes on. "If we still haven't found your dad by then, we'll call in a chopper with an infrared device—detects body heat. I don't expect him to wander beyond the city, but if we have to expand the search into the county, the chopper will help."

But a body only has heat when alive.

Abby pushes the thought away.

She watches her mother match clean socks. Pair the cuffs. Roll the socks into neat little balls.

"We're already knocking on doors," Parrish says. "If we have to, we'll knock on every door in a ten-mile radius. No stone unturned."

There's supposed to be comfort in that.

FIRE STARTER

7:59 P.M.

In the dark of the culvert, Simon feels an object being pressed into his hands. A book, he decides.

"Let's read!" the little girl says, as if he could switch on a lamp to see by.

"Where'd you get this?" he says.

"Your pocket! Remember? The book about broken brains . . . ?"

Paper, Fee says in his brain, *can make fire.*

"Oh, missy!" He jostles the girl off his lap and groans to his feet.

"You're not leaving me, are you?" she whines.

The poor child, Fee says. *Reassure her.*

"Not a chance." He hands the girl his clarinet. "Hold on to this. Hug it against you. Keep it warm."

"Like a doll baby?"

"Yes, just like a doll baby." He bends down and gives her shoulder an approving, even affectionate, squeeze. They're on such friendly terms that he's too embarrassed to ask what her name is.

Straightening from the girl in the shadowy black, he loses his balance. Keels hard into the craggy wall of the culvert.

His blind hand catches a crevice, stopping his fall.

Dammit.

On blood thinners, there's no such thing as a little scrape. But he can't worry about that now.

He pulls himself vertical. Still bracing himself on the wall, he blindly gropes the rocks in the arch overhead, trying to gauge their stability. His fingers tell him that the mason of yore had dry-laid every stone: splitting, sizing, chipping, lifting, fitting, leveling, all the while balancing a volatile mix of competing forces. The mason had done himself proud.

Even without mortar, this stonework had held up across generations of depressions, wars, riots, presidential assassinations, elections of fools . . . all manner of meanness. But now the culvert's barely hanging on, crumbling with age just like he is. Rubble has already sealed its outlet.

If Simon isn't careful, the rest of the culvert might cave in, as its twin had, and bury him and the girl forever.

He tests the ceiling with the main blade of his Swiss Army knife. He can't scratch it, judging by the sound.

Could be granite, he tells Fee.

If he lays the right kind of fire, in the right place, the culvert should bear up to the heat.

If, he repeats to Fee.

HE DISMANTLES the crude windbreak at the culvert's mouth. He must have cobbled it together earlier to block out the weather, but he doesn't remember. Maybe the girl had helped.

He kicks and scuffs at the deep snow, clearing a small spot by degrees, down to crusty grass. He encircles this bare spot with rocks from the ruins of the twin, to throttle the fire and capture the heat.

"What you doing out there?" the girl calls, like a cherub from within a grotto.

Who the hell is she? he asks Fee. *Where the hell are we? Why are we out here?*

He listens in vain.

His Girl can pick the damnedest times to go quiet.

He huddles on crotchety knees beside the fire ring. If only he had more light to see by than obscure starlight and the uncanny glow of snow. He can't distinguish colors, can't appreciate details. He perceives only the contrasts of downy whites and blackest blacks, the merest outlines of shapes and suggestions of form.

A bleak world in which to be trapped.

In places, the void looms.

You can do this, Fee says, back in his brain again.

If, in fact, he can get a fire going, it must slowly feed itself with a minimum of fuss through what remains of the night. In case he forgets to tend it. Or isn't able.

Yes, the architecture of the fire is key.

For the sake of the girl, it must burn from the top down.

He lays his biggest pieces of deadwood at the base. On these, he layers tapering strata of heavy sticks. He tops the pyramid with ample kindling.

All he needs now is a tinder nest at the apex.

He rips a handful of pages from the book. He tears them into strips and scrunches them onto the kindling. Into the paper he shaves wood with his knife. As an experiment, he adds a smattering of pine needles, perhaps too wet to burn. Over all this, he erects a tiny tepee of delicate twigs.

"Grampa?" the girl says, spying on him from just inside.

"Hold your horses!" he says too gruffly.

"But I'm cold!"

She's clutching the clarinet as if about to play a tune, though her fingers must be icy sticks.

He peels off his pink gloves. "Here—put these on! Then move back where it's warmer!"

Once the girl's gone, he breathes into his hands. The moisture of his breath only makes the exposed skin colder.

Quickly now, Fee says.

He unfolds his Swiss Army scissors. He snips a piece of cloth from the bottom hem of his undershirt, the size of an eye patch.

He swaps the scissors for his knife.

He hunches over a table of a rock in the fire ring, his body a shelter against dripping snow and gusts of wind. He stretches the patch of cloth taut between his thumb and index finger. With his free hand, he strikes his knife blade against the rock's edge, right next to the cloth.

Tzick Tzick

He strikes again and again. Metal on rock.

Tzick Tzick Tzick Tzick Tzick

"What you doing?" the girl says.

Dammit.

"Back inside!" Not looking up.

Come on, he begs like a Neanderthal coaxing out his first fire.

Tzick Tzick Tzick Tzick

TzickTzickTzickTzick

The insistence of his hand and his appetite for a spark spools him back into the past . . .

You're a five-year-old sitting on Pop's lap at the kitchen table.

"Come on!" you beg. "Let me try!"

Pop glances into the hall, then rips out another match. "Let's be quick. Your mother won't be happy!"

He takes up your wee hand in his paw.

"Hold the match like this. See . . ."

Zip! goes the red tip of the match down the striker.

It fails to catch.

You giggle.

Pop's a match wizard. He can light a match by flicking it across the room. He can light a candle with a match without touching the wick. He can swallow a lit match without a blink.

But not even Pop is perfect.

You'll perform match tricks of your own someday. But first you have to learn how to spark a match head.

Pop helps you zip the match a second time, just as Mama walks into the kitchen.

Another dud.

"Karl, what've I told you about those matches?" Mama scolds.

Another strike. This time the match flares between your fingers.

You drop it on the yellow linoleum with a shriek.

"See?" Mama says to Pop as he grinds out the match with his shoe. "What are you teaching him?"

"Do it again!" you exclaim, clapping in delight.

"Your mother says we're done."

"But Mama!" you cry. "Please?"

"Good boys," she says, hands on her hips, "don't play with matches!"

You always try to be a good boy. But after touching off that one match with Pop, you can't stop thinking about the red coffee can on the top shelf in the cupboard, next to the jars of pickles and peaches. That's where Mama stores the matches.

The next morning breaks nippy, blustery, and gray. After the milking, Pop gets ready to head into Lincoln.

He cranks down his window as the truck engine sputters to life. "See to the chickens while I'm gone," he tells you. "And start stacking the pile in the woodshed. I'll bring you back a surprise."

He gives the horn a toot as he drives off.

You watch the black Ford bump up the gravel road. The moment the dust trail settles, you scamper into the house.

Mama's still upstairs, changing the beds. You make sure of that before untying your shoes.

You clamber onto a kitchen chair in your stockinged feet. From there, you step up onto the countertop. On your tiptoes, you can just reach the coffee can with a fingertip.

Inside the can are a few matchbooks. And clear down at the bottom, a huge matchbox, kind of smushed. It must hold hundreds of matches. A thousand, even.

You fish out the big matchbox. You give it a shake.

It doesn't rattle. But you can tell it isn't empty.

Hugging the coffee can with one arm, you slide the matchbox open, revealing some sort of stuffed doohickey. You lift it out by a stubby leg.

It must be a toy. It's shaped like a baby turtle but covered with tiny red beads—

The muffled scrape of bed legs directly above you makes you scrunch the red turtle back into the matchbox and chuck it back into the can.

You steal a slender matchbook and skedaddle.

You make for the barn. You scramble up the ladder into the loft.

You sweep loose straw from a section of floorboards. In the center, you heap a handful of dry old stalks. Just enough that you'll be able to warm yourself a bit.

From your knickers pocket, you produce the matchbook. You rip out a match.

"Chasker!" Mama yells from the house, just as you scratch the red tip down the black strip.

Flame bites your finger.

With a yowl, you plug your nipped finger into your mouth.

You hadn't expected success on your very first try.

You're standing there, sucking your finger, certain that Pop would be so proud, when you smell the burning, like when Mama forgets her bread in the oven.

The lit match. You'd dropped it, just like Pop had in the kitchen.

But this floor isn't yellow linoleum.

Fire is smoldering in a dune of straw outside the circle you'd brushed clean on the planking. You stamp at it, finger still in your mouth.

Tendrils of white smoke begin to rise and drift. Straw blackens in a creeping patch.

Your thin chest is thudding. You forget your smarting finger.

"Mama!" you howl.

Baby flames lick up.

"Mama! Fire!" Tears on your cheeks.

It's forever before she tops the ladder. Slung over each of her bony shoulders is a sopping wet burlap feed sack, water dribbling down.

She shoves you away. "Get out!"

She flings the sacks over the burning straw and tromps them down. The hiss of water fills the air.

At the ladder, you're transfixed.

The fire has *to die out.*

Maybe it'll go out on its own.

Maybe it'll go out because Mama's smart and always knows just what to do.

"Go to the house, Chasker!" she shouts at you, now beating at the fire with a tarp. "Run!"

Snow gusts in Simon's face. His blade's still striking, fervent as prayer, spitting random sparks on the scrap of cloth.

TzickTzickTzickTzick

You're slouched at the table, nursing your angry red finger, when Mama marches into the kitchen, all wet and grimy, smelling of smoke.

You burst into tears all over again. "I'm sorry, Mama! I won't do it ever again! Never, ever, ever!"

She thrusts a fistful of charred straw under your nose.

"Do you know what you could have done?" she screams. "Burned down the barn! Killed all the cows!" She hurls the straw.

"Pop can spank me when he gets home!" you wail.

She yanks you out of your chair. "And what might have happened to you!"

"Please don't hit me, Mama," you plead through your sobs. "Pop can use his belt! I'll bend over and grab my ankles—"

"I told you to stay away from those matches!" She's cuffing your ears. "Fire can kill!"

You dive under the table. She lunges and catches an ankle.

"Mama, no!"

She hauls you out and jerks you to your feet. She spins you around and around, a slapping tornado.

You slip free. You collapse and curl into a ball on the linoleum.

"I wish you were dead!" you yell at her.

From between your fingers, you see her hand freeze midswing. Her eyes go glazed and fixed, like the glassy eyes of the deer Pop had shot in Donus Dalloway's field.

I take it back! *you want to bawl at her.* I didn't mean what I said!

But she isn't staring down at you. She's staring at the doorway.

At Pop, just back from Lincoln.

At last, at last, a glimmer.

TzickTzickTzickTzickTzickTzick

A feeble orange. A single fiber. The faintest hope.

Simon bends lower to caress the glow with his breath, resisting the urge to puff.

Patience, he tells himself.

He's a student of fire—all those campfires lit in the field while searching for fossilized bones and eggs trapped in the earth. History pressing down. The crushing gravity of being.

With trembling hands, he transfers the wee cloth with its winking orange to the tepee of shavings, pine needles, twigs, and paper. Gently, gently, he nurses the kindling to flame.

THE PAPERS

8:15 P.M.

"WE'LL GIVE YOU A RUNDOWN, soon as there's news," Detective Parrish assures Abby on the Zoom, wrapping up the interview. "Call us if you think of anything else."

He rises from his chair, almost entirely out of Abby's view. His hand drops a business card on the kitchen table.

"Don't bother getting up," he tells her mother. "We can show ourselves out."

After Parrish and Bragg have gone, Abby's mother occupies the left side of the screen. She appraises the detective's business card like it's a foreign bill of uncertain worth.

"Maybe hang it on the fridge so you don't misplace it," Abby suggests. "And while you're there, fix yourself a bite."

"I'm not eating till you tell me what's in these," her mother says, skewering the papers with a fingertip. "Maybe that will help me get inside your father's head."

"Okay, okay . . . Where do you want to start?"

"At the beginning! Where else?"

"Maybe you should put them in order first," Abby says, imagining how they'd been scattered around the floor of her father's den, as if he'd forgotten to close his window during a violent storm. "Arrange them by date."

Her mother shoves aside a jumble of unfolded socks. She licks her finger and begins to sort. "Give me a minute."

Those gnarled hands might still be deft with fabric, but they're clumsy with paper—and curiously tentative. Putting this document here on the tabletop. Picking it up again. Putting it over there.

The strain of circumstances may be clouding her mother's mind.

If only Abby could reach through the screen and be of use.

"By the way, Mom," she says, "I'm sorry."

"For what?" her mother asks, engrossed, organizing the documents in columns like she's playing solitaire.

"For what I wrote Dad in that note. About keeping all this from you."

"Spilt milk."

With Abby and her father, her mother never holds a grudge for long. With everybody else, she's never quick to let go.

Her mother lays two papers to one side. "I see you enlarged those old photos of Vera."

"Yeah. The rest are copies of the records I've located so far about her time at the Genoa Indian School. I accessed them online in various digital archives. The earliest document is her Application for Enrollment."

Her mother snatches up a form from the bottom of the pile furthest to her right. "It's several pages long," she says, thumbing through.

"And a complete joke," Abby scoffs. "A form like that was supposed to be completed for any Indian child attending a government boarding school away from their home reservation. But as you'll see, it wasn't really an *application*, at least in Vera's case."

Her mother tips the document into the webcam. "What's this scribbling mean at the top—'Henceforth Vera Whiteman'?"

"So listen, Mom—this is crazy." Abby leans toward the screen. "Vera Whiteman wasn't Grandma's real name. On the next page, you'll see her birth name listed as Chekpawee Walks Like Thunder."

"Chek-pa-wee?" her mother says, testing the name on her tongue.

"The school must have renamed her Vera Whiteman."

"Whiteman . . . as in *white man*?" her mother exclaims, her lips curling with disgust.

Abby lets her mother's words hang like a pall.

"According to government policy of the period," Abby continues then, "the school would retain a student's birth name after admission only if it was 'of a proper sort.' Whatever that meant! Otherwise, the school would assign the child a new English first name. For the family name, it would use a rough English translation of the name of the child's father."

"So, if I understand you, honey," her mother says, "by rights, Vera's last name should have been Walks Like Thunder, not Whiteman."

"Not exactly. By *policy*, that's true. But by *rights*, Vera should have remained Chekpawee and never have been stolen from her family."

"Well, of course," her mother says. "You know that's what I meant."

But no, Abby doesn't know. Not for certain.

Her mother's eyes return to the enrollment form. "Says here she arrived at the school in September 1918, from the Sisseton reservation in South Dakota . . . That was about the time World War I was ending. And the Great Flu was starting."

That's her mother, knowing a little about a lot.

"Pretty ironic, right?" Abby says. "Here we are in another global pandemic! There's a long arc stretching from then to now."

"How old was Vera when she got to the school?"

"Look further down the page. The clerk filled in the details."

Her mother squints through her tortoiseshell glasses. She's been complaining about needing a stronger prescription, but with COVID, an eye exam will have to wait.

" 'Seven or eight' years old, it says. The daughter of 'full-blood' members of the 'Sisseton-Wahpeton band of the Sioux tribe.' " She glances up at Abby. "But didn't you tell me that Vera was Dakota?"

"Right." Abby smiles at her mother's powers of recall, even for details she might rather forget. Maybe her mind isn't as muddled by stress as Abby had thought. "The Sioux commonly refers to a confederacy of the Dakota, Lakota, and Nakota peoples."

"Oh, I think I've heard that." Her mother turns back to the application. "Vera's mother is listed as She Who Holds Up the Sky . . . deceased. Her father was Chaskay Walks Like Thunder. Such strong names!"

"More about Chaskay's name in a minute," Abby says. "For now, do you see where it asks for the signature of 'Parent, guardian or next of kin'? That's where Chaskay should have signed, as Vera's only living parent."

Her mother frowns. "But it's blank! Why would that be? Maybe he couldn't write?"

"If that were the case, he would have at least made a mark," Abby says. "On later documents, you'll see that he used his thumbprint. But not here. At least on paper, *no responsible party* consented, in writing, to Grandma's attending the school, even though the intention was for her to enroll there for at least three years."

Her mother studies the application further. "Then who's this J. L. Suffecool, who *did* sign off, saying it was in the 'best interests of the child to attend'?"

"The superintendent in charge of the Sisseton reservation. A bureaucrat. Despite the incomplete paperwork, he certified with his signature that a lawful party had granted consent for Vera's enrollment."

"By 'lawful party,' you mean her father, Chaskay."

"Right."

"Such nonsense," her mother says in a huff. "These lines for witness signatures are also blank!"

She chucks the application onto the table, as if capitulating. "Maybe that was simply how the government dealt with Indians back then. Business as usual!"

"Don't give up yet," Abby pleads. "There's more. Look at page three—the physician's certificate. It asks for all kinds of details about the student's health: height, weight, condition of the eyes . . . That's all blank too. I'll bet no doctor ever examined her. It's like the bureaucrats didn't care enough to follow their own procedures."

Her mother slips her glasses on top of her head. She peers thoughtfully at Abby. "Just out of curiosity, hon, how far is Sisseton, South Dakota, from Genoa, Nebraska?"

"You mean, how far is it from Grandma's home reservation to the school? I wondered the same thing. It's around three hundred and fifty miles."

"Good Lord! In those days, the school might as well have been on the moon."

Abby tries, as she has so often, to put herself in little Vera's place. "Mom, just imagine if, when I was seven or eight, the government had shipped me off to a place you'd never heard of, so far away . . . all without your say-so."

Her mother is shaking her head. "For how long, again?" she asks quietly.

"The term of enrollment was supposed to have been three years. But the government was free to ignore that stipulation. Vera, for example, seems to have been at the school for *thirteen* years. There's no evidence she was ever allowed to go home—even for a visit—between her admission in 1918 and her discharge in 1931."

"What do you mean by discharge? Did she graduate?"

Abby tosses her hands. "I can't say. So far, I haven't found anything like a diploma. All I know for sure is that, by 1931, Grandma had nobody left to go home to. All her close relatives were dead."

Fritz must be back on her mother's lap. His gray tail, flicking contentedly in the air as she pets him, gives him away.

She gazes at Abby intently. "Weren't you going to tell me something more about the name of Vera's father?"

"Yeah. Frank figured this part out, not me." Abby recalls how the idea had struck him while he was stirring ladlesful of broth into a risotto on simmer. Inspiration tends to visit him in the kitchen. "So," she says, "Dad's middle name is Chasker, right?"

"Yes."

"Well, how many other men do you know by that name?"

"Zero," her mother says with half a smile. "It's pretty old-fashioned."

"Maybe not just old-fashioned . . ."

Her mother's forehead knits in puzzlement.

"Maybe," Abby says, "Chasker was the closest name in English that Grandma Vera could come up with for Chaskay."

Her mother removes her glasses. She folds them with great deliberation.

"Maybe," Abby rushes on, "she chose that name to honor Dad's Dakota blood, with none being the wiser."

"You're suggesting," her mother says slowly, "that Vera secretly named Sy after her own father?"

"No, it's more than that." Abby rubs her temples, pondering how best to explain. "By custom, as a Dakota man, Vera's father had two names. One was his given name—translated into English as Walks Like Thunder. He probably received that name as an adult."

She draws a deep breath, as if breathing for the sake of generations.

"His other name, Chaskay, was a birth-order name. It identified his position in the family. It means 'firstborn son.' "

Her mother scoops up some loose socks. "So," she says after a moment, sifting for pairs. "you're thinking . . . ?"

Abby's throat tightens. She can't prove Frank's theory, but somehow it's as true to her as math. "I think Grandma gave Dad the middle name Chasker to mark him as her Chaskay. Her first baby boy."

Her mother lifts a dusty-blue argyle dress sock by the toe. "I can't find the mate."

"Oh, Mom . . ." Abby breathes.

She can no longer endure the distance between them.

"There aren't any more trains from Philly tonight," she announces. "But Frank and I will be there, soon as we can, in the morning."

"But what about the virus?" her mother protests, collapsing forward, her face distorted by proximity to the webcam.

Abby touches a fingertip to her mother's glass cheek. "We'll mask up. We'll be as careful as we can. But we're coming!"

NOODLES
8:46 P.M.

THE FIRE POPS like a fat balloon stuck with a pin. Olivia, nestled against Grampa, jumps out of her skin.

"You hungry?" she says then, picking herself up. "I got noodles."

"You playing games again?" Grampa sounds super tired, like Charley when he gets home from the office. Will Grampa get grumpy too?

She shuffles outside and gives the fire a poke like she's seen Grampa do, stirring it with a stick about as big as her Mystical Magical Mermaid Wand. The fire crackles and spits sparks that the wind whisks away.

Back inside the cave, she crumbles the cake of ramen she'd pocketed before crawling out her window. She squeezes through the wrapper to break up the noodles.

"Hi-*yah!*" she yells, splitting the package along its center seam. (She's a regular ramen ninja, Charley says.)

By the light of Hat Lady, she bites open the silvery seasoning packet. Shrimp.

Not her favoritest flavor. It tastes like sucking on a penny, only fishier.

She sprinkles the powdery stuff over the noodles in the open wrapper and stirs with her pointer finger.

"I'm a wicked cook! See?"

But of course, Grampa can't see because he still can't see Hat Lady. He's as much in the dark as ever.

"Have some," she says. "They're scrunchy. Like potato chips."

166

But Grampa's nodding off. He doesn't know it but he's resting against Hat Lady's shoulder. His body's all mixed with hers in her glow.

HIS LITTLE GIRL

9:11 P.M.

SIMON ENFOLDS Gilly in his jacket for warmth, the clarinet cushioned between them.

Two peas in a pod, Fee says in his brain.

A fire is smoldering at the mouth of the culvert. Gilly says he'd started it "forever ago," so he figures he must have. She never lies. Not to him. She knows better.

The fire blunts the bitter edge. But cold is cold.

At least the wind isn't sweeping smoke inside.

Remember when Gilly was a baby? he asks Fee. *She'd wail like a banshee whenever I picked her up. Give her to you, she'd stop, like you'd flipped a switch.*

She was afraid of you, Fee says.

I was afraid of her.

"You're bleeding again," Gilly says, cutting into his thoughts.

He holds his gloved hand in front of his face. He can barely discern its shape.

"How can you tell?" he asks.

"That red spot on your glove," she says, brushing a fingertip against his palm.

"You've got the eyes of a cat, you know that?"

"It's growing."

"Just a scratch," he says.

Damn blood thinner.

"I'm thirsty," she says, cuddling into his upper body, an easy fit in his arms. "Let's suck on snow."

"Your belly will turn into an ice chest," he says.

He touches his lips to her crown, then raises her hood.

"Go back to sleep," he says. "Sail away on a lovely dream."

He nuzzles her head. Their breaths crest together and sink, crest and sink, as if keeping time with the same slow metronome.

"I want a song," she says drowsily, as if they're back home and he's tucking her into bed.

As if he—not Fee—is the one who always does the tuck-ins. And the storybooks. And the lullabies.

"Shh, child," he says.

From the day Gilly was born, he'd sworn never to beat her like his folks had beaten him. So far, he has kept his vow—by staying away. He'd been on a dig in Utah when she took her first step. Missed her first laugh too. Her first word.

Even when home, he has kept his distance.

Maybe that's hurt you too, he tells her in his brain. *Far worse than a belt.*

Wind can't blow backward. Snow can't unfall. A symphony, once performed, can't be unplayed. Not one measure of it. Not a single note.

"Forgive me," he murmurs.

Somehow, he has to keep his eyes open. Somehow, he has to remember enough of what he knows about this world to keep his little girl alive.

Dum spiro spero. While I breathe, I hope.

DRIFTING

9:36 P.M.

"JUST GOING to rest my eyes, Gilly," Olivia hears Grampa say.

He sounds like he's drifting underwater.

"Just for a spell," he says before she can ask who Gilly is.

She snuggles tighter against him, the top of her hood in the hollow beneath his scratchy chin. He smells all smoky and sweaty and sweet.

"Love you," she says, rubbing an eye with her fist.

"Love you," he says, in a see-through voice.

They might be the only real people left in the whole snow-globe world.

VIGIL

12:23 A.M.

FOR THE PAST FOUR HOURS, Victor has followed his van's low beams up and down the city streets in whiteout conditions. The wind is pumping its fist and pushing snow around like the president, believing it can do whatever it wants. Who can stop it?

Now, past 0000h, he's calling it quits. Mikey's just texted him to say that he's finally made it back from Martinsburg. He's at the Richters'. Victor will rendezvous with him there and bivouac for the night on Fiona's floor.

On Division Street, the Richters' house is lit up despite the late hour, like any household in crisis. Victor parks behind the Jeep, grateful that it's still drivable after Mikey's spinout. Mikey had told him on the phone how the rear of the Jeep had swung around and struck a deer-crossing sign with enough force to send the vehicle careening into the ditch. Fortunately, the spare tire mounted on the back had taken the brunt of the impact.

Inside the house, Victor grabs up Mikey in a bear hug. Their anniversary night could have been a helluva lot worse.

Fiona is masked and timid. Mindful of the COVID, she maintains a safe distance, depositing a pile of bedding in front of the fireplace. She then withdraws into the hall and lingers there as Victor and Mikey get situated.

On the mantel is an orderly array of family photographs. Among them, one frame is leaning precariously against a potted philodendron, as if knocked askew by the cat. In the oval frame is a sepia-toned portrait from bygone times. A wedding photo, but not a happy one. The

171

doughy-faced woman is wearing a plain dark wraparound dress with a skimpy corsage. The groom, obviously much older, is an ordinary-looking fellow with a pitted complexion. Neither newlywed is smiling.

Victor sets the portrait straight.

"That's Sy's father and stepmother," Fee explains in a shivery voice.

Framed in the doorway, she's clutching a sheaf of papers against her bosom, looking pale and spooked.

"Love you boys!" she says then. "Crack a window while you sleep, will you?"

FRAGMENTS

HOUR UNKNOWN

AT THE BIG HOUSE. *Sitting with Grandpa Richter on the porch swing. Listening to birdsong.*

You're three years old, maybe.

Grandpa's long-stemmed pipe. His bushy white mustache, stained by tobacco.

"Kardinal," he says. Thick, precise German.

"Cardinal," it sounds to your ears.

Understanding each other.

The coiled metal springs of the swing, creaking, creaking.

NESTLED *in Mama's arms on the love seat at the Big House. Grandpa and Grandma are there. And Pop. Uncle Pete. Others too. The old ones all jabbering in German, like they do. Especially around certain ears.*

Maybe Mama picks up their meaning, more than they know. Maybe, like you, she's good at pretending.

Like now. You're playing possum. Eyelids closed but loose so they don't flit. Deep, slow, even breaths.

Even Mama thinks you're fast asleep.

Her fingertips. Idly stroking your face and hair. Light as the wings of a fluttering moth.

So happy. So lost in the powdery scent of her long, distracted caresses.

. . .

OSTERSONNTAG. *At the Big House. Soft wall of fog, hovering over the low bushes along the porch. Can't see anything out there.*

Crouching on the porch swing, gripping its chains. Getting it to sway hard to your sing-songy chant:

"Führer . . . Jews . . . Nazis . . . Reich!"

Launching out over the shrubs. Feet first. Into nothing.

WALKING *the gravel road with Pop.*

(After Mama. Before Iris.)

Legs so short. Hard to keep up.

Pop slumping like there's a boulder on his back.

You reaching for his hand.

Him burying his hand in his pants pocket.

"Pick up your feet, boy. You're scuffing your shoes."

Two men. The one before. The one after.

BURNING UP WITH FEVER.

Hair plastered to your forehead. Sweat seeping salty into the corner of your mouth.

Iris lowering you into a tub, full apron over her housedress. Cold water running from the tap. Iris's hand dribbling it over your head and neck.

Ice cubes clinking, floating in the tub.

Shivering with chills. So hot. So cold.

Retching again. A white metal bowl with a red lip.

She presses her brow against yours.

Tears crawling down her face, dripping from her chin. Like Mama.

"Please don't cry," you say.

How you still love her.

POKING *at fresh roadkill with a stick. Dead mama possum.*

Wanting to see how death is.

The hairy white face and pointy pink snout. The vacant eyes. The mousy whiskers. The rope of a tail. The jaggedy teeth. The belly pouch, empty of babies.

Once, she must have been happy. Before she came to this road.

Didn't make it even halfway across.

Dragging her beyond the ditch into the broken field. Covering her with dirt.

Hands sticky with blood you can't wipe off.

. . .

"*WHAT DO YOU MEAN, you saw your mother in the casket? You couldn't have. The lid was closed! Tight as a vault!*"

"*But Pop . . . she was in her best dress, remember? And the pillow was light pink—*"

"*Boy, I'm telling you—*"

"*And I saw her sit up! Plain as day! Me and you, we were across the room—*"

"*You just saw what you wanted to see!*"

"*And she put her finger to her lips, like I should be quiet. Only I couldn't be quiet. I had to tell you! But you—*"

"*Simon! That casket lid was closed! You hear me?* Closed!"

POP WHIZZING his bike down the bald hill.
    The heat of summer. The dirt road packed hard.
    You on the handlebars. Flying free.
    Old enough not to let go.
    Young enough you don't think he can wreck.

STRADDLING Pop's shoulders in the farm pond. Chicken-fighting Uncle Pete.
    Pete's thick mop of curls wet and flat against his scalp.
    His muscles.
    His easy laugh.
    You want to be just like him, someday.

ET LUX in tenebris lucet et tenebrae eam non comprehenderunt. And there is a light in the darkness, and the darkness could not comprehend it.

SMOOCH
HOUR UNKNOWN

A PINPOINT of light shines pink through Olivia's eyelids, so bright it hurts. She presses her face into Grampa's chest.

After a minute, she turns her head to the side and rests her cheek on his heartbeat.

The light's still there.

She lifts her head and squints at the light between her gloved fingers.

It's Hat Lady. She's pointing.

At Olivia.

At Grampa.

At Olivia again.

"You want the clarinet?" Olivia says to Hat Lady in a whisper, not wanting to wake up Grampa.

Hat Lady shakes her head. She points again at Olivia. At Grampa.

A guessing game.

"The necklace thingy?" Olivia whispers.

Hat Lady smiles.

Olivia transfers the turtle from her neck to Grampa's, so gently he never knows. Then she drops a kiss on the ice-cold tip of his nose.

"That," she tells Hat Lady in her top-secretest voice, "was a smooch from you."

NEWSBREAK

HOURLY, ALL NIGHT

POLICE ARE ASKING THE COMMUNITY'S HELP IN LOCATING A FORMER UNIVERSITY PROFESSOR WHO WAS REPORTED MISSING FRIDAY AFTERNOON FROM HIS RESIDENCE ON THE 900 BLOCK OF DIVISION STREET.

EIGHTY-YEAR-OLD SIMON RICHTER SUFFERS FROM DEMENTIA AND IS CONSIDERED AT-RISK. A FAMILY MEMBER REPORTED HIM MISSING AROUND 6:00 P.M. FRIDAY. HE WAS LAST KNOWN TO BE AT HOME SHORTLY BEFORE 1:00 P.M.

OFFICIALS SAY RICHTER LEFT HIS RESIDENCE ON FOOT. HE IS BELIEVED TO BE CARRYING A CLARINET.

RICHTER IS DESCRIBED AS A WHITE MALE, 5'9" TALL AND 170 POUNDS. HE HAS WHITE HAIR AND HAZEL EYES AND WEARS WIRE-RIMMED GLASSES. HE WAS LAST SEEN DRESSED IN A FOREST-GREEN POLO SHIRT, BURGUNDY SWEATER, KHAKI PANTS, AND BLACK SNEAKERS. HE IS ALSO BELIEVED TO BE WEARING A BLUE HAT AND A HEAVY KHAKI JACKET.

FAMILY REPORTED RICHTER MISSING WHEN THEY COULD NOT LOCATE HIM IN OR AROUND HIS HOME. WHEN POLICE ARRIVED ON SCENE, THEY GATHERED INFORMATION AND

CONDUCTED A THOROUGH SEARCH OF THE RESIDENCE AND PROPERTY. NO FOUL PLAY IS SUSPECTED.

POLICE OFFICERS AND FAMILY FRIENDS HAVE BEEN ACTIVELY SEARCHING RICHTER'S NEIGHBORHOOD AND THE ROUTE ALONG WHICH HE OFTEN TAKES WALKS. THEY HAVE FOUND NO SIGN OF HIM AT AREA HOSPITALS, JAILS, OR TRANSIT STATIONS. THE SEARCH HAS BEEN SUSPENDED UNTIL SATURDAY MORNING DUE TO HAZARDOUS WEATHER CONDITIONS.

MEMBERS OF THE PUBLIC WISHING TO AID IN SATURDAY'S SEARCH SHOULD GATHER AT 6:00 A.M. AT THE REAR ENTRANCE TO MCCLURE'S BOOKS ON MAIN STREET. AUTHORITIES WILL PROVIDE SEARCH ASSIGNMENTS AT THAT LOCATION.

WEAR COLD-WEATHER GEAR. BE PROPERLY MASKED, AND MAINTAIN SOCIAL DISTANCING.

ALL RESIDENTS ARE URGED TO CHECK THEIR PROPERTIES AND TO BE ON THE LOOKOUT FOR A MAN MATCHING RICHTER'S DESCRIPTION. ANYONE WITH INFORMATION ABOUT THIS CASE SHOULD PLEASE CALL 911.

THIS INDIAN DOES NOT
KNOW HOW TO WRITE

HOUR UNKNOWN

AN INTERMINABLE NIGHT. Bereft and sleepless on her side of the bed, Fee peers through a handheld magnifying glass at the documents Abby had mailed Sy. She returns again and again to a letter dated October 18, 1918. To the thumbprint near the bottom, red as old blood—the mark of a Dakota man named Chaskay Walks Like Thunder.

Sy's maternal grandfather.

Under her lens, that thumbprint's smudges and loops and whorls are proof of life and lineage. They evidence a family story about which she knows little and understands even less—a story that she'd once wanted no part of.

Simon's mother was named Chekpawee, not Vera. She had a twin brother, Chekpa. When the twins were seven, the authorities removed them—stole *them*—*from their home on the Sisseton reservation in South Dakota. The children were transported to Indian boarding schools in two different states, far beyond the family's reach.*

In the Old Testament, King Solomon once threatened to cut a baby in two with his sword—a ruse he'd employed in wisdom, to determine which of two women claiming to be the child's mother was telling the truth.

In the case of Chekpawee and Chekpa, the government's sword had actually swung, but not to reunite. To sever. To separate two siblings who had cuddled since their first flutterings in a shared womb. To cleave them from their kindred, their hearth, their people. To rip apart the truth of their lives.

179

LAW OFFICE OF
RALPH D. PRESCOTT

SISSETON, SOUTH DAKOTA.

October 18, 1918

Hon. Commissioner of Indian Affairs
Washington, D. C.

My dear Commissioner:

I am writing you about my son, Chekpa Walks Like
Thunder, who is now at the Wahpeton Indian School in
Wahpeton, No. Dak., and my daughter, Chekpawee Walks Like
Thunder, at the Genoa Indian School, Genoa, Neb.

My children were lately sent to these schools without my
consent. They are just seven years of age. They were taken
from my home by J.L. Suffecool, the Agent of the Sisseton
Reservation, when I was not present. My parents, who live
with us and were providing care, objected to their removal.

I wish to have my children back. When they are older, I
will allow them to attend the day school here on the
reservation. We live within two miles of that school.

I am willing over time to repay the fares the government
will have expended, first to transport my children out of
state and now to return them.

I believe it is wrong for my son and daughter, who are
twins, to be separated. It is wrong for them to be parted
from their family.

I also believe that I should not burden the U.S.
government and taxpayers with the costs of keeping my
children in schools where they do not wish to be, and where
I as their father would not have them.

Please arrange for their speedy return and advise me of the
sum of money I owe.

                                    Very truly,
                                    Chaskay Walks Like Thunder

I, Ralph W. Prescott, Esquire, wrote on behalf of this Indian
because he does not know how to write.

THE TWINS' father, Chaskay, had presumably understood little about American laws and customs. And he hadn't known English well enough to write a letter, if at all. Yet he'd managed to secure an attorney, Ralph Prescott, who wasn't without skill.

In Fee's estimation, Prescott's appeal on Chaskay's behalf to the commissioner of Indian Affairs had been pretty fair gamesmanship for a white lawyer living in a dinky South Dakota town adjoining an Indian reservation in 1918. Prescott hadn't dwelled on the ethics of the twins' seizure or the fact of their family's heartache. Instead, he'd stressed that restoring the children to their father would benefit the government. He'd painted Chaskay as a "good Indian" who was willing to educate his kids in a reservation school, concerned about the prudent use of taxpayers' money, and fully prepared to repay his debts.

Prescott had seemingly hit the right notes to impress an Indian Affairs bureaucrat of his era. In the end, his silver tongue hadn't mattered one whit, of course. But how had Chaskay ever found him? How had he ever *afforded* him?

Fee sets her index finger on the paper beside Chaskay's thumbprint, as close as she dares.

This letter is the only document in the dossier that Abby had reproduced in color. It was a deliberate and unmistakable invitation on her part, bidding Sy to press his eighty-year-old thumb on his grandfather's thumbprint and ponder what it meant.

HERE ARE THE ENLARGEMENTS of the vintage photographs that Abby had pulled up on her phone.

Sy and Vera in the yard.

Vera in the school orchestra, with that telltale drum in the back.

Fee scrutinizes every inch of the pictures through her glass, thinking back to the afternoon in her studio when Abby had first shown them to her.

You told Abby to let it all go. You told her not to make a fuss.

Another memory flashes in from decades earlier, forcing Fee to put down her lens.

She's giving Abby a bath, hunched over the sea-green tub on young-mother knees, swabbing folds and creases of chubby baby flesh with a terry washcloth. Sy's behind her, waiting to swaddle Abby in one of those hideous floral bath towels that comes free in king-size boxes of detergent.

"You know," he says, out of the blue, "my mother didn't die in a freak fall."

He has this irksome habit of starting conversations in medias res. Without warning, you're in the thick of the skirmishes in his mind.

"Please, Sy," she tells him, lathering the washcloth over Abby's scalp, front to back. "Can't we discuss this later, after I'm done?"

He sidles closer. Out the corner of her eye, she can see him wringing the towel as if it were soaking wet and he had to make it bone-dry. "She must have been sick. To do it, I mean."

"Do what?" she says, hands full of wiggly, slippery baby.

"String herself up in the woodshed."

For one hideous moment, his words blot out Fee's vision. No baby. No water. No suds. No tub.

Nothing but a noose.

"For God's sake, Simon!" she says once she recovers herself, squeezing honey into her voice so she doesn't terrify Abby.

"On Easter, if you can believe it," he says.

Fee lowers the back of Abby's bald head into the shallow water, muffling the dainty ears.

"Using the rope from my sled—" he says.

"Not in front of the baby!" Fee says with a glare over her shoulder so icy and absolute that it freezes Sy's mouth midsentence.

He looks like a petrified little boy, eyes bugging out of his head, as though he's convinced he was to blame. He must have been carrying the shame of this throughout his life. Like an ugly birthmark that never fades.

A port-wine stain, that rarest of birthmarks, will actually darken and thicken over time. It can be passed between generations.

So—Fee is certain—can shame.

"Not now!" Fee declares to Simon, their daughter sloshing and cooing in the filmy water. "Not ever!"

Let it all go, she might as well have said to him that night. *Don't make a fuss.*

Just like with Abby.

You're history, repeating itself.

Chaskay's thumbprint on Prescott's letter glowers at her like an accuser in court.

She can't bring herself to touch it.

II

WAKINYAN SE MANI

I SING OF CHASKAY, firstborn son of those the white man called Iron Foot and Turtle Woman. Their true names cannot be spoken in White Talk. Their names in White Talk are noise, the flapping of wings in air.

When he was grown, our people gave Chaskay the name Wakinyan Se Mani. In the noise of White Talk, he was Walks Like Thunder.

Next to his horse, Chaskay stood short and slender as a boy. But brave blood throbbed in his veins. Even white people seemed to sense his power. When he walked down the street in Sisseton, the white man's town, they parted before him like water before the bow of a canoe.

White men knew Chaskay as a skilled hunter. They hired him to guide them in the chase.

Our people knew him as a maker of red cedar flutes.

Men in his family had made flutes for as long as our people could remember. Father taught son; son became father and taught his son. A great circle, unbroken.

They carved flutes through seasons of hardship and war with our enemies. They carved flutes as white settlers advanced. They carved flutes as the blue coats humiliated our people and forced us onto reservations. They carved flutes beneath the boot of the white man's laws, which forbade us to play our music and dance our dances.

As a boy, Chaskay had to learn the art of the flute from his father in secret.

Iron Foot had shown him how to offer tobacco and sing prayers before harvesting a branch from a tree. In this manner, they honored its gift of wood.

"The red cedar tree is not like other trees," Iron Foot told him. "When the snow is white on the ground, this tree is still green. It does not die. This quality will live in the flute we bring forth from the wood. It will live in the songs of the man who plays it."

Chaskay would watch Iron Foot take up a bare, fresh branch, about the length of his arm. With sure hands, his father would split the branch in half along a straight seam, end to end. Laid open, the red heartwood yielded a sharp, sweet aroma.

Iron Foot would hollow out each half of the branch and smooth the walls with his knife. Then he would glue these pieces together and bind them with rawhide straps until they knit together.

"When a man plays the flute, he must put the heart back into the wood," he told Chaskay. "This is the promise we make to the wood as we bring forth the flute. We may remove its heart with our knives, but we will put its heart back with our songs."

The first flute Chaskay ever made was small, as he was. Its body was no longer than his stubby arm. He bored its six finger holes close together, so his little-boy fingers could cover them.

As Chaskay grew toward manhood, his flutes grew with him. Their bodies lengthened. Their voices deepened.

He learned to turn out two sorts of flutes. The first sort he fashioned from inferior wood. These flutes were dead. They didn't sing; they only made noise. He painted them with idle designs and decorated them with trinkets.

In the white man's town of Sisseton, there lived a trader. His white name was Karl Nordenson. Our people called him White Hair. He had a shock of long hair the color of clouds. The same white hair bristled all over his face. He spoke Dakota better than most of our young people, whose tongues had been crippled in the Reading Houses.

Chaskay gave White Hair his dead flutes to sell. The same white men who punished our people for making and playing our flutes would pay much money to possess them. They displayed them in their houses like trophies won in battle. They presented them to their women as tokens of affection. They sold them to other white men in faraway places.

White Hair would return to Chaskay a fair share of the gain from the dead flutes. He had a good heart. Chaskay trusted him like few others of his kind.

The other sort of flutes that Chaskay made were traditional singing sticks. No two were exactly alike. Yet all were close relatives, having sprung from the same maker. They sang for Chaskay as trees sing for the wind.

Chaskay gave his singing sticks to Dakota men, as was the custom of our people. Some flutes he offered in exchange for firewood, a shovel, a saw, a new knife. Others he presented as gifts.

"Abandon the white man's firewater," he would tell the men. "Live with honor. Keep the old ways alive."

The flute had lived among our people since long, long ago. Yet many of our men had never heard its music. The white man's laws had stopped their ears.

"I will teach you to play for the woman you would have for your wife," Chaskay told them. "I will teach you to play for the ceremonies the white man has forbidden."

These were words of war. And Boss Farmer had ears everywhere.

THE READING HOUSES

I SING of Chaskay's children, Chekpa and Chekpawee—Twin Boy and Twin Girl, in White Talk. They lived in a one-room log house in the bush with their father and grandparents.

Their mother was Mahpiya Wakun Yuzawee, or She Who Holds Up the Sky. She walked on to the spirit world not long after the twins had taken their first steps. She perished from a sickness unknown to our people.

In those days, our children had to attend the white man's Reading House. They had to speak the white man's tongue. They had to worship the white man's god. They had to mold their lives to the white man's ways. The white man's laws decreed it.

In the beginning, our people resisted these laws. We did not want to lose our children. We did not want our children to forget who Great Spirit had created them to be.

Our people banded together to keep our children safe. We did not report the births of new babies for the reservation rolls. We hid our young ones from the authorities. We refused to send them to the Reading House.

The superintendent was the government man in charge of the reservation. Our people called him Boss Farmer. His heart became hot. He withheld our rations of food, clothing, and supplies. He imposed fines we could not pay. He put our men in jail.

Our children were crying from hunger. Our old ones were wasting away.

Our people gathered in council.

"Perhaps we were wrong," some said. "Perhaps our children should go to the Reading House. If they are to survive, they will need to know more than we do about the white man. They can learn to use the club of the white man's wisdom against him."

Others disagreed. "The white road is not the road of the old ones, passed down to us through the pipe. We must not walk in it. A Dakota who takes up white ways no longer has a face."

Our people tried to appease Boss Farmer by giving up our orphans.

He was not satisfied. "You must follow the law," he told the elders. "You must send *all* your children to school."

Next we gave up our children who were weaker in body or mind. Then we gave up the children whose parents did not properly tend them.

We did not want to do these things. It was not our way. But we hoped to save the many by sacrificing the few.

Boss Farmer still was not happy. "*Every* boy and girl who is old enough *must* be in school. And they must attend *every day.* If they miss classes too often, I will send them on the iron horse to Reading Houses that are far away. You will not see them for *many* winters."

Tribal police came to round up our children. We pleaded with them to remember their blood. "You are our sons, our brothers, our cousins! Have a good heart!"

When our begging proved futile, we bargained. "Take one of our children, but leave us three." Or "Take our two oldest. When they return home, they can teach the others." Or "Take only the boys. Our girls are less able to protect themselves."

The tribal police would not negotiate. They had ears of stone.

One by one, our families submitted. They enrolled their children in the reservation Reading House. Some even consented to their children's removal to Reading Houses beyond the reservation boundaries.

When permitted, we prayed over our sons and daughters before they left us. We exhorted them to be brave and to safeguard one another. We asked Great Spirit to bring them home someday.

"Learn all you can from the white man's books," we told them, "but never forget your blood. We will be waiting to welcome you back."

The parents among us who would not yield suffered the greatest punishment. Their children were seized and bound with ropes or handcuffs. They were dragged away without prayers. They were loaded into wagons and put onto the iron horse. They were made to disappear over the rim of the world, to faraway places whose names were strange on our tongues.

Carlisle, in Pennsylvania.

Haskell, in Kansas.

Genoa, in Nebraska.

There were many such Reading Houses.

As winters passed and more of our children disappeared, the white names of those places became familiar. But we did not like to speak of them.

Many of our children died in those places. They were buried in ground that did not know them or their ancestors. They had no kin to grieve at their graves. They had none of their people to help their souls walk up the spirit road.

The children who came home from those places were not who they once had been. Sometimes they came back after three winters. Sometimes they came back after six winters. Or even more. Returning after so long, they did not resemble the sons and daughters of our memory. They had grown big. They wore their hair as white people do. They dressed as white people do. They walked and talked as white people do.

Often the children did not recognize their own kin. They walked past their mothers as if unacquainted. They shook hands with their grandmothers as if they had never met. They scowled at the talk of their closest relatives, unable to understand the language born on their tongue.

"You live bad," some of these children told their families in White Talk. "You are savages. You are the devil's tribe."

These ghost-children hovered between worlds. Many were ashamed of their own blood and did not want to be Dakota anymore. Yet they were not white enough for white people ever to accept them. They had nowhere to belong.

Some of our children could not bear the emptiness. They drank. They raged. They fled to the white man's towns. They became like earth upon which nothing good can grow.

Many of them ended their own lives. To this day, they wander the earth, weeping.

To all this, the twins' father said no. Like his father and mother before him, Chaskay vowed that the white man would never take his children to the Reading House.

OWLS AND BEARS

I SING of the bravehearts who readied for battle but wore no paint.

When the twins were five winters, Chaskay made ready for the day when Boss Farmer would try to steal them for the reservation's Reading House. He and his father dug a secret lair in the dirt floor of their log house. They covered it with a stout latticework of branches. Over the branches, they spread buffalo robes and other bedding, as if this were a sleeping place.

"In the old days," Grandfather told the twins, "this is how we protected our families when enemies attacked our camp. Those who could fight fought. Those who could not fight hid beneath false floors in our lodges."

"If white men ever come to our house," Chaskay told them, "my children must hide here at once."

The dugout was deep enough for the twins to lie down and curl up together. Chaskay showed them how to slither down into the hole, then replace the bedding on the branches above them, leaving no trace.

"When my children hide here," he said, "you must be as quiet as Moon shining on water. You must be as patient as River waiting for the spring thaw. You must be like Rabbit in its burrow. Come out only when we tell you it is safe."

THE TWINS WERE seven winters when Chaskay was summoned to the agency office.

"According to the day school inspector," Boss Farmer told him through an interpreter, "you have been seeking every means possible to keep your son and daughter out of school. I am out of patience."

He tapped the White Talk papers on his desk.

"Because of your truculence, your children will be enrolled at government boarding schools far from this reservation. Your son will go to Wahpeton, in North Dakota. Your daughter will go to Genoa, in Nebraska. You must make your mark of consent."

Few children so young were dispatched to Reading Houses so distant. But Chaskay did not reveal his surprise. He revealed nothing at all. Nor did he step forward to ink his thumb.

"You cannot properly raise your children without a wife," Boss Farmer said.

The interpreter translated.

"I will find a woman," Chaskay said in Dakota. "When I choose."

"You are away from home too often to be a good father to your children," Boss Farmer said, inventing another reason.

"Their grandparents tend them, as is our custom."

By now, Boss Farmer's pale face was redder than pipestone.

"What about your heathen dancing? Your ceremonies? The sweat lodge you built in secret, back in the hollow, to the west? Are you prepared to burn your pipe—all your pagan possessions—and join the church?"

Here was the true source of the heat in Boss Farmer's heart. For generations, the white man's missionaries had pitted our people against one another with their talk of sin and salvation. Now the black robes had the white man's government and the power of its laws at their back. For our people, it was a terrible wind.

"It is an offense to the Creator for a father to raise his children outside the love of Jesus Christ." Boss Farmer's words whizzed like arrows.

Chaskay respected the holy man Jesus, whom Great Spirit had long ago set upon the earth across the sea. But had Great Spirit not also sent White Buffalo Calf Woman to teach our people how they were meant to live? Had Great Spirit not chosen her to bring us the sacred pipe?

Chaskay would not renounce the wisdom of our ancestors. He would not abandon the pipe.

He would not dip his thumb into the red ink. He would not put his mark on the Reading House papers.

BOSS FARMER's heart blazed up. He ordered his clerk to reduce Chaskay's rations of sugar, coffee, beef, and flour.

Chaskay's family was prepared for the infliction of this penalty. They had never relied on the government's meat, which was gristly and often spoiled, nor the government's flour, which was wormy. They had carried on what old ways they could.

The life-giving buffalo had vanished into the earth, but Chaskay and his father stalked deer, prairie chickens, rabbits, and other scarce reservation game. They fished and caught turtles. They trapped an occasional muskrat.

Grandmother scratched out a garden of beans, squash, corn, turnips, and potatoes. She foraged for nuts, berries, chokecherries, wild grapes, and plums. She dug roots and collected herbs.

By eating little and preserving much, the family had buried enough small caches of food to survive stretches of serious lack. When Boss Farmer withheld their rations, they did not starve.

MOONS PASSED. Chaskay ignored a series of summons to enroll the twins in the reservation Reading House. Chekpa and Chekpawee practiced hiding themselves in the secret place beneath the floor.

"Do not move," their grandparents told them. "Do not make a sound."

The twins would lie like stones until their tiny muscles were cramped and their tiny throats were parched.

"Stay still," their grandparents encouraged. "Bad white people prey upon little children like owls and bears."

Our people began to believe that Wakinyan Se Mani had defeated Boss Farmer. Some took pride in his victory. They sang songs in his honor, as they had for warriors in the old days.

But jealous hearts filled with resentment. They believed Chaskay should relinquish his young ones, just as they had.

They harbored a dark desire for his undoing. He was a mighty tree, but they knew how the twins could be split from his trunk.

It is said that someone among the jealous betrayed him.

IN THE MOON WHEN THINGS
RIPEN

I SING of the day Chaskay's children were stolen.

It was in the Moon When Things Ripen. The twins were eight winters.

On that morning, in the cool blue of daybreak, Chaskay rode off for a stand of cedar trees. He left First Dog at home to help guard Chekpa and Chekpawee.

Sun rose higher. The twins were playing stickball. Their grandmother was seated on a stool in the shade of her tipi, next to the cabin, grinding dried prairie turnips into flour.

First Dog barked toward the west. Grandmother shielded her eyes and squinted into the distance.

The silhouette of a horse-drawn wagon was trundling toward her, wheels raising dust. She counted two men in the driver's box. Behind the wagon were four shadowy men on horseback, riding as white men do.

"Hide, my grandchildren!" she ordered from her stool.

The twins sprinted for the cabin. At the rickety door, they slipped past Grandfather, emerging with his shotgun.

THE WAR PARTY that set out to abduct the twins numbered six men. Of these, none were tribal police.

Children are the closest of all two-leggeds to the spirit world. They are gifts of Great Spirit. Their hearts are as pure as rain.

The hearts of twins are the purest of all. Twins jump together through the hoop of fire. They enter this world already old, possessing the balance and wisdom of white-hairs.

Surely Great Spirit would punish any man who harmed a twin.

This is what the tribal police believed. They were always careful to do Boss Farmer's bidding, but on this day, they were brothers of one mind: they would not touch the twins born to Wakinyan Se Mani. If this bad thing must be done, white men must do it themselves.

In this war party of six, only one man was Dakota.

He wore the black robe of the white man's god.

GRANDMOTHER SIGNALED First Dog to be quiet. She resumed her grinding, crushing pieces of dried root beneath her pestle, all the while singing a song of protection.

Grandfather trudged past her stool. He nestled the gunstock against his shoulder, leveled the barrel at the advancing wagon, and waited. At Grandmother's command, First Dog joined him.

The wagon groaned to a stop in front of Grandfather. Black Robe was driving. Beside him in the wagon box was Boss Farmer.

First Dog growled through bared teeth. One of the full-rumped horses, a sorrel, fidgeted in the harness, pawing at the turf, nostrils flaring.

"I greet you with a good heart," Boss Farmer said to Grandfather in broken Dakota.

Grandfather acknowledged the customary greeting with a scornful grunt. After so many winters on the reservation, Boss Farmer should have been able to speak better Dakota. But he was only interested in Dakota people speaking better White Talk. His heart was bad.

"Mr. Iron Foot," Boss Farmer said, switching to his own tongue, relying on Black Robe to translate, "I'm sure you know why we are here."

Grandmother put down her pestle. Ignoring the men, she stirred to her feet and waddled on wide hips toward the cabin.

"The Creator wants your grandchildren in the Reading House," Black Robe said to Grandfather, speaking now for himself, in Dakota. "There they will learn White Talk. Twin Boy will learn how to farm. Twin Girl will learn how to keep house. One day they will be as civilized as any white children. The Creator will look upon them with favor. They will have a good life."

Grandfather's shoulder ached from holding the gun. Many winters had passed since he'd had an enemy in his sights.

"We have given your son fair warning," Boss Farmer said, closing

Black Robe's argument as if his white ears had fathomed the Dakota words.

Grandfather's finger tightened on the trigger.

Boss Farmer removed his hat. He wiped his brow on his sleeve.

"Your son isn't here, is he." A statement, not a question. He replaced his hat. "That's a shame. It truly is."

He pivoted in his seat and wagged his hand at the men on horseback.

The four riders charged their mounts at Grandfather. One horse knocked him down. The old man's gun fired as he fell.

The shot spooked the yellow paint that had struck him. The horse reared up with a squeal, spilling its man from the saddle.

The paint lunged into a gallop. The white man, sprawled on the ground, flopped over onto his back. He swiped at his cheek, where the bullet had grazed him. His hand came away red.

He sat up in the dust. He shoved himself to his feet.

With one loud breath to collect himself, he set upon Grandfather. His boots pummeled the old man's groin and belly, his side ribs, his neck.

Grandfather tucked his head against his chest. He drew his knees toward his chin. But he could not shield himself from all the blows.

Suddenly the white man howled. First Dog's snarling fangs were sunk into his right leg.

"Get it off! Get it off!" the man screamed to the others, collapsing.

A second man tried to beat off First Dog with the butt of his rifle.

"Goddamn it!" roared the man on the ground, flailing against First Dog. "*Shoot!*"

The second man swung his rifle up and fired.

First Dog crumpled.

Beside him lay Grandfather, limp and senseless.

"BE BRAVE, MY GRANDCHILDREN," Grandmother told the twins in a hushed voice as they trembled in their lair beneath the bed of buffalo robes. "Be still. Be silent. Whatever happens, remain hidden."

Grandmother waited behind the closed door of the cabin, hatchet poised overhead. She waited as the injured white man cried over his leg. She waited as the other men bound his torn flesh, loaded him into the wagon bed, and poured liquor down his gullet. She waited as they left him with the silver flask. She waited as they strode past her beaten husband, toward the house.

When the cabin door finally swung open, Grandmother brought her hatchet down with a war cry upon the first man through. It was Boss Farmer.

He blocked the blow with his gunstock and slammed her against the log wall. Two of his men subdued her. The cabin filled with her high-pitched ululations.

GRANDMOTHER'S tremulous wails thrilled and terrified Chekpa and Chekpawee. They had never heard any such sounds escape her mouth.

Be brave, they told each other in their thoughts, clutching the beaded amulets they had worn around their necks since birth. Chekpa's was a lizard, beaded green and yellow. Chekpawee's was a red turtle.

The twins clung to each other, their two hearts throbbing in unison, as boots treaded the earthen floor above. Household goods were being tossed about. Men's voices were grumbling in gibberish.

White Talk, the twins thought.

This was the first day they had heard it spoken.

Be brave.

GRANDMOTHER SANG AND SANG, writhing against the hands restraining her.

"Shut her up!" Boss Farmer yelled.

A handkerchief was crammed into Grandmother's mouth. It only muffled her, so two white men dragged her, gagged and singing, out the door. They dragged her, gagged and singing, past Grandfather, still motionless on the ground. They dragged her, gagged and singing, past the wagon where the man was moaning over his mangled leg.

THE SINGING STICK THAT
DID NOT WANT TO SING

I SING of the singing stick that did not want to sing.

Down in their hole, Chekpa and Chekpawee pressed their foreheads together. They expected the buffalo robes to be flung back at any moment and for monstrous figures to appear, swooping them up like owls or falling upon them like bears and devouring them whole.

They could not see Black Robe above them, seating himself on a primitive ladder-back chair with a deer-hide seat.

BLACK ROBE SURVEYED the crude one-room cabin with its earthen floor. In his eyes, it was a curious mix of worlds.

A table stood with three more chairs like his own. A pearly abalone shell rested atop the table, gray with ashes from the family's prayers. Settler-style clothing hung on nails. Iron pots waited near the fireplace. Narrow sleeping platforms lined the walls, with colorful trade blankets and dried grass for mattresses. Another bed of buffalo robes and fox-skin pillows occupied the floor. Sack curtains framed the lone grimy window.

A workbench, overflowing with curly wood shavings, was crowded with an assortment of knives, rawhide thongs, and a ball of sinew. Suspended above the workbench was a painted rawhide bag. Fringe hung from its edges like tresses of hair.

Black Robe was Dakota enough to recognize this bag as the lodge where Flute lived. He had reckoned Chaskay a worthier adversary—

one who would have stowed the forbidden instrument in a secret place, along with the family pipe.

If Flute was so near at hand, perhaps the twins were too.

Black Robe swung around on the chair to face Boss Farmer. "I know what must be done. Leave me."

Boss Farmer plugged tobacco into his cheek. He was unaccustomed to being ordered around, especially by a red man masquerading as a churchman.

"You got five minutes," he said to Black Robe, then he marched out of the cabin with his last man.

THE TWINS HEARD the cabin above them quieten, as after an intense storm.

Our enemies must have left, they thought together.

They pressed their ears against the sides of their hole. They listened for footsteps retreating to the wagon and the rumble of turning wheels.

But there was nothing.

If we peek out the window above us, Chekpawee said to her brother in her thoughts, *we might see the white men going away.*

We must not come out until we know we are safe, Chekpa said to his sister. *We must be certain, as Grandfather Sun is certain of his place in the sky.*

BLACK ROBE CREPT across the room to the workbench. He collected Flute's pouch from its nail.

He unlaced the rawhide ties and removed Flute. Then, draping the empty pouch around his neck like a Sabbath vestment, he eased himself back onto his chair.

Flute's hand-carved body was old, featuring a duck motif. Its song was meant to issue from the duck's open beak, once painted red. Most of the paint had worn away.

Black Robe blew softly into each of the six finger holes, warming Flute with his wind. Then he positioned the instrument in his hands to play. His fingers were relaxed, as from cherished acquaintance.

But Flute did not want to sing for him.

FLUTE HAD SUNG for only three men since being born. The first was Chaskay's grandfather, He Who Steals Many Ponies. That man had brought Flute forth from a cedar branch. He had fashioned Flute's mouth pipe from a bullet shell casing.

In his last winter of life, He Who Steals Many Ponies had given Flute to his firstborn son, known as Iron Foot. In time, Iron Foot had given Flute to his firstborn son, Walks Like Thunder, that he might woo She Who Holds Up the Sky. One day, Walks Like Thunder would give Flute to Chekpa.

This was Flute's lineage. Black Robe did not belong.

Flute did not dislike Black Robe. But it surmised his purpose.

When the stranger's lips closed around the brass mouth pipe, Flute quailed from his breath before it arrived.

BLACK ROBE LIVED as a white man. He had gone to a white man's Reading House, many days away by the iron horse in the direction the sun rises. There, when he came of age, he married a white woman who wished to bring the Christ-road to red people. So he studied to serve the white man's god and be the woman's helpmeet. He learned to speak White Talk almost as if white blood flowed in his veins.

Yet now he was making Flute sing as only a true Dakota could.

WHO TAUGHT *you to play so well?* Flute wondered, struggling against Black Robe. *How can you know how to bend my pitches? To flutter your tongue? To play these rapid ornamentations?*

Flute could tell that Black Robe wanted it to sing like a winged one. But Flute resisted, deadening every warble and trill and pop. It darkened its tone. It tried to sing like a wolf.

Stay where you are, Flute tried to sing to the twins, even as Black Robe made it sing *Come.*

It is not safe, Flute tried to sing, even as Black Robe made it sing *All is well.*

WHEN THE TWINS had lived inside their mother, Flute had sung to soothe them. And when their mother walked on to the next world, Flute sang her memory into their hearts. Whenever they were visited by sickness, Flute sang them medicine songs. Whenever they were unable to sleep, Flute sang them into the place of dreams.

They knew Flute's voice as well as they knew their father's.

But on this day, frightened and confused in their hole, they did not notice how unnatural Flute's singing was. They heard no hints of warning. They heard only sweetness and light.

Our father is back! they thought with relief, already smelling the pungent scent of red cedar that always lingered on his hands. *Our father has chased all the white men far, far away.*

They nosed up through the buffalo robes.

IT WAS NOT their father who greeted them.

It was a woman, clad in a dress as black as death.

She leapt at them like a wild cat, shouting in White Talk—like a man. She aimed Flute straight at them, as if to shoot bullets from its mouth.

The horrified twins dropped back into their hole. What manner of enemy was this?

They were like fish snared in a river trap, no way out. Above them, white-man boots were charging into the log house. White-man spurs were jingling.

Bedding and branches were being pitched aside as white hands ripped apart the false floor. White arms thrust down to snatch Chekpa and Chekpawee.

Even those who hide can fight, the twins told each other.

They kicked and flailed. They spat and bit and scratched and punched.

They were seized by their long hair. They were hoisted out of the hole, yowling in pain.

They were hauled from the cabin, thrashing and shrieking.

"Grandfather, save us!" they cried, passing Grandfather, lying next to First Dog's lifeless body.

Roused by their distress, the old man managed to prop himself on an elbow but then fell back in a daze.

The twins were thrust headfirst into a cage in the wagon. Beside the cage lay a white man with a mutilated leg. He looked as if he were dreaming darkly.

The cage door screeched shut. A key turned the lock. A heavy blanket was spread over the pen. All went black.

The twins bawled and bawled in utter darkness. The blanket smothered all sound.

Even Great Spirit cannot hear us, they thought together.

AT THE CABIN'S lone window, Black Robe watched the twins being caged like animals in a white man's zoo. Flute ached from the clench of his grip, fearing he might smash it into pieces against Chaskay's workbench.

By the white man's laws, that was precisely what Black Robe should have done. But he laid Flute on the table with the beautiful pouch that was its lodge.

He wiped his palms down the front of his robe. Then he went out to Grandmother, still gagged and tied to a tree, tears coursing down her leathery cheeks.

"It did not have to be this way, my grandmother," Black Robe said to her in Dakota, speaking as a man should speak to an elder. "But this is the day to which the Creator has brought us."

He tugged the handkerchief from her mouth and freed her from the rope.

"Go now," he said. "Bless your grandchildren—while you can."

THROUGH THE IRON GATE

I SING of Chekpawee and the day she passed through the iron gate.

On the reservation, she had sometimes spotted an iron horse at a distance, spewing a plume of smoke, pulling a line of small dark boxes across the prairie on shiny metal tracks. Now she was inside one such box, wrapped in a scratchy gray blanket and clinging to a rattly wooden seat.

The landscape rushed past her window. The iron horse screeched and bellowed. Its headman was a portly white man in a blue uniform with bright brass buttons.

Chekpawee had last seen her brother on a wooden platform near the white man's town of Sisseton. Boss Farmer's men had put him on an iron horse headed north, the direction of harsh winter winds. They had put her on an iron horse headed south, the direction from which all life comes.

She didn't know where the iron horse was going or how long it would take to get there. Brass Buttons might have tried to explain, but she couldn't understand his White Talk. She didn't *want* to understand. She wanted Chekpa. She wanted Father. She wanted Grandmother and Grandfather. She wanted home.

What had the white men done to her grandparents after the wagon had rolled away? What had they done to her father upon his return?

Across the aisle from her were two white children, a girl and a boy. They were traveling with a woman who might have been their mother.

From the corner of her eye, Chekpawee saw the children pointing at her, whispering and giggling.

She cloaked her head with the blanket. She bit its edge between her teeth.

She closed her eyes. She felt safer with them shut.

Inside her tipi of cloth, she clasped the red-beaded turtle hanging by a thin rawhide strap around her neck. Her amulet contained the dried stump of the birth cord that had once joined her to her mother. It connected her life to all that had gone before and all that would ever be.

Chekpa wore an amulet too. His was a lizard, beaded green and yellow.

"The two of you," Grandmother had said, blessing them inside that cage in Boss Farmer's wagon as Black Robe looked on, "discovered each other before you were born, in that land in the sky from which all children come. You leapt together into this world, through the circle of fire. You are gifts from Great Spirit."

What did it mean, Chekpawee wondered now, that white men could seize her and Chekpa from their home and separate them so cruelly? Was Great Spirit angry with their family?

The iron horse chugged on and on, never tiring. Naked wooden poles, tall and straight as trees and lashed together by long ropes, marched past Chekpawee's window.

White men had planted them all.

THE SUN WAS on the other side of Chekpawee's traveling box when the iron horse hissed and squealed to a stop at a platform like the one she had set off from. But this one was girdled by black bars.

At the door of Chekpawee's box, Brass Buttons swung her down into a band of children who were much like her in appearance, only bigger. At eight winters, she might not have been the youngest of them, but she was the littlest.

She felt her connection to Chekpa stretching thin, like the path of a star that had fallen from the sky. Had his iron horse delivered him to such a place?

We must be brave now, she told him in her thoughts. *As brave as we had been when hiding from our enemies.*

White men and women funneled Chekpawee and the other fresh arrivals through an iron gate. The men were dressed in black, and the women in gray. They were assisted by a few older boys and girls who, apart from their matching settler-style clothes, closely resembled their charges.

"Greetings, my sister," one of the older uniformed girls said to Chekpawee as they walked beneath an arch with peculiar markings.

To Chekpawee's amazement, she could understand the girl's tongue fairly well. It sounded like a relative of her own language.

"Welcome to Genoa Indian School, a white man's Reading House," the girl went on. "My name in White Talk is Helen Washington."

Helen, by introducing herself, was indirectly prompting Chekpawee to do the same. But Chekpawee kept her eyes low.

This is the land of white people, Chekpawee heard a voice say. *Do not reveal your name. It is your shield.*

This voice was not Chekpa's. It was a voice in her spirit that, until now, she had never heard speak.

"*Hel-en,*" the girl drawled. "Try to say it."

Do not give anyone the satisfaction of eliciting sound from your mouth. Whoever possesses your voice possesses you.

"I am Oglala Lakota," the girl said, "from the Pine Ridge reservation."

Chekpawee did not say who her own people were. She did not say where she was from.

She had arrived at the place where all speaking ended.

She raised her silence like a war club.

THE WHITE PEOPLE and their uniformed helpers herded the bewildered children up a cobbled street, toward a huge white-man house with tall windows. Chekpawee had never witnessed such spectacles. She was tempted to flee from them even as she dragged her feet, marveling.

Do not be deceived, the voice in her spirit said.

Just ahead, a white man with a hairy face and big round glasses was bustling about, barking in White Talk. He pointed at this girl, at that boy, lining up the children in two lines against a brick wall. Time and again, he thrust his finger at the storm clouds gathering in the sky.

Hairy Face grabbed Chekpawee by the shoulders. He forced her into the center of the front row.

Then he retreated behind a brown box seated atop three long legs. With gestures, he instructed the children to stand very still and focus on the enormous glass eye on the face of the box.

With his right hand, he lifted a flat bar on a short stick. With his left, he held up three fingers . . . two . . . one . . .

Pop!

Light flashed from the stick, showering sparks. Chekpawee and the other children erupted into wails of terror. Who was this white man who could command fire from the sky? Might he use his power to strike them all dead?

The panicked girls were hurried inside the imposing building behind them just as the first raindrops came pelting down. The boys, no less unnerved, were rushed across an expanse of grass toward another brick structure.

"This building is where you will sleep," Helen said as she propelled Chekpawee through the massive door. "In White Talk, it is called a *dormitory.*"

The glare inside the dormitory forced Chekpawee to screen her teary eyes. She studied the lights on the ceiling through slivered fingers, her alarm slowly yielding to awe.

Her gaze slid down the plaster wall to a stack of wide wooden boxes. The stack sloped away to a summit beyond seeing. Its polished brown surface glimmered with reflections of the light bulbs.

"That is called a *staircase* in White Talk," Helen told her in Lakota. "Try to say it: *stair-case.*' "

Chekpawee did not speak.

White women shepherded the new girls toward another stack of boxes that went down into the floor. This staircase led to a much darker place.

Peering down, Chekpawee felt dizzy, as if she were on a lofty outcropping of rock.

"Hold this *banister,*" Helen said, placing Chekpawee's right hand atop the railing. "You will not fall."

She grasped Chekpawee's free hand and showed her how to step down.

Chekpawee did not want to step down. She did not trust the staircase. She did not trust Helen.

A white woman with a big stick yelled up at them from below.

"The matron said you must move faster," Helen told Chekpawee. "Come!"

Helen tugged Chekpawee's hand. But Chekpawee did not want to move faster.

"Quickly!" Helen said, jerking Chekpawee's arm. "Or something bad will happen!"

Chekpawee thought of Hairy Face and his spark stick.

She stepped down.

IN THE BASEMENT, Big Stick sorted the girls roughly by age and dispatched them with supervisors through various doors.

Helen dragged Chekpawee after the younger girls into a large white room partitioned by dingy open stalls. Along the far wall of each stall was a bowl, perched on a pedestal, the color of a wood duck's egg.

"*Toilet*," Helen said, baring Chekpawee's bottom.

She hoisted Chekpawee onto a bowl.

"Make water," Helen ordered in Lakota.

The instant Chekpawee's feet found the floor again, the toilet flushed with a roar to shake the world. She ran in terror, hands clapped over her ears.

From behind Helen caught her up by the armpits and raised her into the air. Chekpawee's legs churned in fright.

"Do not be afraid," Helen said. "The big sound will stop."

And so it did. The roaring was already dying away, just as another toilet flushed. And another.

"It is as I told you," Helen said. "I speak the truth."

Helen carried Chekpawee into another room. This one contained a tribe of metal tubs.

"Take off your clothes, my sister," Helen said.

Chekpawee stood like The Star That Stands In One Place.

"Look around you," Helen said. "All the other little girls are brave."

It was true. They were undressing beside their tubs.

Chekpawee wouldn't be deemed a coward. She took off her frayed moccasins. She shed the shawl that Grandmother, singing a blessing, had slipped through the wires of the cage. She removed her belt and stripped off her calico dress.

At last, she was naked except for Turtle, her only remaining defense.

When Helen went for Turtle, too, Chekpawee slapped the girl's hand away.

"This creature is strong," Grandmother had often said, teaching Chekpawee about Turtle. "With her tough, protective shell, she is difficult to kill. Even after she dies, her heart can beat for days."

A white-man's cross was gleaming at Helen's neck. Chekpawee squeezed her amulet in her fist.

"Guard Turtle with care," Grandmother had also told her. "She will help keep you safe until you walk on from this world."

Turtle did not belong with Helen. Chekpawee backed away.

"I will give Turtle back when we finish," Helen said, her voice like maple sugar.

A low growl escaped Chekpawee's throat.

Helen sighed. She knelt on the floor.

"Come, little sister," Helen said, coaxing. "For now, you may keep your amulet. But I must wash you. You are a dirty little girl!"

Chekpawee stayed put.

Helen doused a rag with water from a glass bottle. Then she inched forward, toward Chekpawee, humming a strange but enchanting song, until finally she was close enough to clasp an arm.

Chekpawee screwed up her nose at the sharp stink from the rag. The white man's water reeked.

"Hold your breath," Helen told her.

Helen scrubbed Chekpawee's birdlike body with one hand while firmly controlling her with the other. Chekpawee struggled as the *alcohol* on the rag burned the scratches and scrapes she had suffered in her battle with the white men. Soon she was coughing and wheezing from the vapors in the room—so many girls, so many bottles. She wiped at her smarting eyes.

"Stand still," Helen said, "or I will take Turtle."

She loosened Chekpawee's braids and shook out the interwoven strips of ribbon. Then she soaked her rag with more alcohol.

"Now I must kill the bugs on your head," she told Chekpawee. "Squeeze your eyes tight."

Alcohol tingled into Chekpawee's scalp. Helen vigorously rubbed it in before raking her rag through strand after strand of Chekpawee's hair, root to tip, humming all the while.

WATER GUSHED FROM A METAL PIPE. Chekpawee watched the water level creep up the side of the tub as Helen's fingers splashed, testing its warmth. Steam began to rise.

One last slosh of her hand, then Helen scooped up Chekpawee and lowered her into the *bath*. At the prickly heat, Chekpawee stifled a whimper, cupping Turtle in her hands, well above the water.

Helen scrubbed her down with a brush and carbolic soap. Chekpawee felt like Snake losing its skin.

"Your hair and skin are not so dark as some," Helen said reassuringly. "This will be to your advantage."

CHEKPAWEE FIDGETED in her blue dress uniform. She scratched at the ruffle, tight as a rope around her neck, and flicked the great wings of her collar. She picked at the white braid trim on the poofy sleeves tapering from her upper arms to her wrists. Every movement of her body swished and swooshed.

She pulled at the white buttons sewn at a diagonal from the bottom of her collar to the waist of her pleated skirt. These buttons were merely decorative. But the buttons stitched in a line down her spine offered a means of escape from this fancy animal trap. If only her fingers were longer! Stretch as they might, they could unfasten only two buttons.

Helen pressed Chekpawee into a single file of other new girls. The column trembled together as if one creature, with one skin.

Just ahead was a door. Every few minutes, it would creak open to admit one girl. Each time, Helen would grip Chekpawee's shoulders from behind and force her a couple steps forward.

Chekpawee clutched Turtle as shrieks and howls filtered through that door. Images of dead dogs and black robes and spark sticks crowded her mind. What awaited her and the other girls in the room beyond the door?

"You must take off Turtle now," Helen whispered when Chekpawee was only two girls from the threshold.

Chekpawee clenched the amulet against her chest.

"If you wear it into that room," Helen warned, "they will cut it off your neck and throw it into the fire."

Who is behind that door? Chekpawee wondered frantically, her little heart drumming against Turtle's belly. *What is about to happen?*

"Hurry!" Helen insisted when Chekpawee was next. "Give Turtle to me! I will keep it safe!"

Chekpawee did not want to part with Turtle. She did not trust Helen. But she trusted that door even less.

She drew Turtle over her ruffled collar, then over her head. Helen snatched Turtle away and thrust it into her dress pocket, just as the door swung wide.

There, in the room beyond, stood Hairy Face behind a tall black chair, holding shears instead of his spark stick. On the floor all around him lay thick clippings of black and brown hair.

This man has a bad heart.

Chekpawee launched herself like a wildcat toward a door in the wall opposite the one she had entered. But there in front of her, blocking her path, was the brown box on three legs.

Chekpawee stumbled, trying to avoid the box. Big Stick, the matron, snagged her by the waist and swung her into the barber's chair.

Chekpawee kicked and clawed as if she were back in the hole in the cabin floor.

Big Stick locked her fat forearms on either side of Chekpawee's tender neck. She pinched Chekpawee's scrawny legs between her own skirted knees. Her breath heaved into Chekpawee's face, sour as apples after a frost.

"Do not fight a battle you cannot win," Chekpawee heard Helen say, the traitor's voice not far away.

Cold shears brushed against Chekpawee's skin. She moaned.

No blade had ever been so close. Her hair was as long and alive as her eight winters. It was sweet brown grass that had sprung from the soil of her spirit.

Hair was her medicine, just like Turtle. Now it was falling away in clumps, dropping to the floor. With every crisp snip, Chekpawee's strength seeped away, like the cloudy water that had gurgled down the drain of the tub.

When the ordeal was over, Chekpawee spread her hands over her shorn head. It felt like a wretched patch of sky in which no birds would ever want to fly.

Big Stick muscled Chekpawee off the black chair.

Once on her feet again, Chekpawee flounced toward Helen, jabbing her finger into her palm, wordlessly demanding the return of Turtle.

Helen ignored her.

"Now we must take your picture," the Lakota girl said.

Helen was as much Chekpawee's enemy as the black-robed woman who had played her father's flute in the cabin. As much as the white man who had dragged her to the cage in Boss Farmer's wagon.

Chekpawee tore the cross necklace from Helen's neck and hurled it against the black chair.

Exploding into White Talk, Big Stick cuffed Chekpawee on the cheek. Then Big Stick wrenched Chekpawee down onto a short stool, obliging her to sit and face the box on three legs.

"Look at the camera!" Big Stick commanded.

"Look at the Big Eye," Helen repeated in Lakota, "or you will never see Turtle again!"

Hairy Face raised his spark stick.

I will grow my spirit back, Chekpawee vowed in her mind. *I will have my revenge.*

III

REVEILLE TO TAPS

AUTUMN 1918

CHEKPAWEE LEARNED to jump out of bed at *reveille.*

She learned to mark the passage of time by the calling of bugles, the clanging of bells, the shrieking of metal whistles, the blasting of the steam whistle at the powerhouse. She learned to divide time into the *minutes* in an hour, the *hours* in a day, the *days* in a week, the *weeks* in a month, the *months* in a year, and the *years* before and after the birth of *Our Lord Jesus Christ.*

She learned that if she made water in bed, she would have to tote her soiled mattress to classes and endure the taunts of her fellow students.

She learned upon rising to make her cot *like a soldier,* squaring the corners and tucking the bedding so tight that Big Stick's coin would bounce.

She learned to dress fast in her *unmentionables,* her black cotton stockings, her uniform, and her stiff lace-up shoes. The leather shoes, loose and heavy, rubbed her heels raw and raised blisters on her toes.

She learned to march around the school in those same insufferable shoes.

She learned the meaning of *no.*

The meaning of *yes.*

Of *Start over.*

Get in line.

Stay in line.

"Left . . . left . . . left, right, left!" her *captain* would snap, drilling her *company* in precise *formations* on the parade grounds at 6:00 a.m. as the

American flag flapped on its pole. Chekpawee struggled to lift her knees high while matching the strut and cadence of older girls. The captain was quick to kick her shins.

She learned to *stand at attention* without moving, even as girls fainted all around her.

She learned to salute *Superintendent Davis*. He was Boss Farmer of this Reading House—*Genoa Indian School*.

The school was a sprawling village. She learned to identify its buildings and to navigate their labyrinths of drafty corridors: Dormitories. Administration hall. Classroom building. Gymnasium that doubled as an auditorium. Superintendent's house. Employee cottages. Print shop. Mechanics shop. Carpentry shop. Harness shop. Blacksmith shop. Tailor shop. Mending room. Mess hall. Bakery. Laundry. Dairy, cattle, and horse barns. Cheese factory. Powerhouse. Baseball diamond. Hospital. Cemetery.

She learned to march into the mess hall for meals, stand in her place, bow her head, close her eyes, and wait through a white man's *prayer* to the white man's *god*. At the screech of a pea whistle, she and the rest of the room scraped back their chairs to sit.

She learned the proper use of *cutlery*. She learned to eat white man's *gravy* and *hash* and *rice* and *prunes*. She learned to fight for her share of food. She learned to ignore the dead *mice* in the milk pitchers and the *worms* in the bread. She learned that if she were late arriving at the mess hall, for any reason, she wouldn't be admitted—or fed.

She learned that those black bones that white people pressed against their ears were *telephones*. That those white pots on the wall that spurted water were *drinking fountains*.

In class, she learned *Miss McDougall* was the *teacher of the little people*, of which Chekpawee herself was one.

She learned from Miss McDougall that the iron horse was a *train*. It had delivered her to a town called *Genoa*, along the *Loup River* in a *state* called *Nebraska*, in the *heartland* of the *United States*. She learned how to use a *globe* to find the United States in *North America*, one of seven *continents* on a *planet* called *Earth*.

She learned to smile when she didn't understand White Talk or how she was expected to behave.

She learned to smile when she *did* understand, to make white people believe she didn't.

She learned to be glad that she, like Helen Washington, was a mixed-blood *breed*. Her complexion and hair were lighter than a full-blood *skin*'s. Though she wasn't as *near white* as many breeds, her *less savage* appearance generally assured her better treatment.

She learned to retire at *bedtime* to her dormitory room, crammed with forty cots and rats running across the floors. She learned to change into a long white *nightshirt*, kneel at her bedside, and place her palms together while Big Stick recited another white man's prayer in monotone.

She learned at the bugling of *taps* to crawl under the covers. She learned to listen to the voices of the dark after *lights out*. All around her, girls whimpered into their pillows or whispered among themselves in their native tongues, risking severe punishment for *talking Indian*. Her ears strained in vain for words in Dakota.

She learned to talk with Chekpa in her mind until she dropped into dreams of home.

All this she learned to do. But she didn't speak a word.

VEER-AH WHYT-MAN

AUTUMN 1918

CHEKPAWEE LEARNED THAT *VEER-AH WHYT-MAN*, a string of four sounds, meant *her*. As if she weren't Chekpawee, daughter of Mahpiya Wakun Yuzawee and Wakinyan Se Mani.

She learned that when Miss McDougall took the roll, students would spring to their feet when they heard their name called, stand straight and tall at their desk, and declare themselves "Present!"

So Chekpawee would listen for *veer-ah whyt-man* to issue from Miss McDougall's mouth. She would rise from her chair. She would stand like a tipi pole. But she would not speak.

Because she would not speak, Miss McDougall made her draw a chalk circle on the blackboard and press her nose against it. Chekpawee learned to stand there, sucking in chalk dust, without slouching or leaning. The slate would darken with the moisture of her breath.

When this method didn't compel Chekpawee to speak, Miss McDougall enlisted the services of Mr. Peniska, one of the school's disciplinarians, charged with enforcing order.

He made Chekpawee bend over and grab her ankles.

"Count the licks with me," he told her, striking her rump with his paddle, air whooshing through holes drilled in its wood. "One . . . two . . . three . . ."

She clamped her jaws. She made no sound resembling speech.

The blows intensified, raising welts.

"Seven . . . eight . . . nine . . ."

Tears pooled in her eyes and dripped on the floor, her bottom on fire. She had never been struck before. It wasn't her people's way.

"You have to cry hard!" girls whispered to her at night from their beds. "If you cry hard, he will stop!"

She learned to understand what the girls were saying. She learned to begin bawling after the first few blows, because the whispers were true. Once her tears were flowing, Mr. Peniska would show her a measure of pity he never afforded a boy.

When the paddle proved ineffective, Miss McDougall tried to make Chekpawee talk by forcing her to stand throughout the class period on one foot.

Then Miss McDougall tried to make Chekpawee talk by washing out her mouth with lye soap. This, Chekpawee knew, was the usual punishment for sassing back. So, whether you talked back or didn't talk at all, you would soon be eating soap.

But Chekpawee could stomach soap. After all, she had eaten the school's wormy bread.

So Miss McDougall reversed herself, like a wind that suddenly shifts. Now she tried to make Chekpawee talk with bribes from the faculty dining room—a slice of bacon, a fistful of raisins, a pat of butter for her hash.

When Chekpawee would have none of it, Miss McDougall tried to make her talk by locking her in a cage exhibited on the green, where other students could poke her with sticks and call her ugly names.

But Chekpawee had survived another cage.

She did not speak.

In due course, Miss McDougall gave up. *Veer-ah whyt-man*, she declared, was a *mute*.

DIRT

AUTUMN 1918

CHEKPAWEE STUDIED Helen Washington like a wolf studies its prey.

As an older girl, Helen didn't sleep in the crowded main dormitory room. She shared a double with her friend Maude, down the corridor. Early each morning, right before Big Stick's white-gloved room inspection, Helen would scuttle down to the lavatory in the basement to complete her toilette.

One morning, after Helen and Maude had disappeared downstairs, Chekpawee crept into their room. She had a pillowcase of dirt scraped up from the frosty bare patches beneath the swings on the playground.

Helen's bed was left of the washstand with its bowl and pitcher. Chekpawee sprinkled the dirt all over the top.

Helen was busted for the mess. Big Stick put her on latrine duty for two weeks and confined her to quarters when not in class.

Chekpawee exulted in Helen's humiliation. Like the brave men in Grandfather's stories, she had struck a blow against her enemy and escaped unhurt. She had wounded her enemy's pride.

She was only a little girl, but like a warrior, she deserved an eagle feather for counting coup—the highest form of valor among her people.

Surely Helen would know that it was Chekpawee's hand that had counted coup on her. Surely she would know the reason why.

Surely Helen would feel disgrace and admit defeat before more than her honor was injured.

Helen was like a river frozen under ice. Chekpawee waited for the thaw.

But Helen didn't give Turtle back.

DEPARTMENT OF THE INTERIOR

UNITED STATES INDIAN SERVICE.

Genoa Indian School, Nebraska,
November I4 - I9I8.

Hon. Commissioner of Indian Affairs,
Washington, D. C.

Dear Sir:

Replying to your letter of November 5th, relative to the
request of Chaskay Walks Like Thunder for the return to the
reservation of his daughter Chekpawee, enrolled here at Genoa, I
have the honor to state that so far as I can determine, there is
absolutely no reason for this girl to leave us.

Many Indians are indifferent to, or indulgent of, the whims
of their children. Such parents need to be discouraged in their
efforts to secure the release of pupils attending off-reservation
schools. There are a lot of good and intelligent Indians on the
Sisseton reservation, but as your Office knows, there are also
some pretty tough ones living there. We must retain their
children in schools away from the reservation, or most will end
up in the penitentiary.

It would be a bad thing for this girl to return home. I am
told by J.L. Suffecool, the Sisseton Agent, that despite
assurances to the contrary, her father will never send her to
school there. We should make every effort here at Genoa to make a
decent citizen of her.

Please note for future correspondence that the pupil records
for this girl Chekpawee Walks Like Thunder are filed under the
name Vera Whiteman.

Very Respectfully,

Sam B. Davis
Superintendent.

DEPARTMENT OF THE INTERIOR

OFFICE OF INDIAN AFFAIRS

WASHINGTON

November 26, 1918

Mr. C. Walks Like Thunder
    Care of Ralph Prescott, Esq.
        Box 3, Sisseton, South Dakota.

My dear Mr. Walks Like Thunder:
    This has reference to your letter of October 18th, in which you reported that your son and daughter, Chekpa and Chekpawee Walks Like Thunder, were taken to the Wahpeton Indian School and the Genoa Indian School, respectively, without your consent.
    A report has been received in this matter, showing that application forms covering their enrollment were properly submitted. Your children joined two parties of pupils at the railroad station in Sisseton, along with their escorts, Mr. Fahey and Mr. Dunn, respectively, and subsequently traveled to the schools of record. Upon arrival, your children were examined by physicians and found to be in good physical condition, with the exception of the fact that they have trachoma. This condition, an infection of the eyes, can lead to blindness if not attended. The physicians treated your children's eyes and will continue to do so until they are soon cured of this trouble.
    You will be happy to know that your son gained two pounds and your daughter four pounds in October.
    While you state that you live near a day school on the reservation where your children might attend, it is noted that they have never attended a single day of classes there, though they are of age. It is therefore believed that in justice to your children, they should remain where they are.

Very truly yours,

E. B. Meritt
Assistant Commissioner of Indian Affairs

VERA WHITEMAN

AUTUMN 1918

CHEKPAWEE LEARNED TO GRIP A PENCIL. To press its tip to paper while moving her hand. To bear down on the paper without causing it to tear.

She learned to replicate on paper the strange white man's markings Miss McDougall drew with chalk on the blackboard. She learned the markings were called *ABCs* and *numbers*.

Then she learned to imitate the markings in her tattered copy of *First Lessons for the Deaf and Dumb,* a white man's book used by the students in her class.

She learned to write *Vera Whiteman,* the string of sounds and letters that meant *her.*

She learned to write *Vera Whiteman* on tags of cloth she then stitched into her clothes.

She learned to write *September 23, 1911,* the date on the white man's calendar when, according to the white man, she had been born.

All this she learned to do. But she didn't speak a word.

GLASS

AUTUMN 1918

CHEKPAWEE HARVESTED a triangle of broken glass from the school's trash heap. Two edges of the glass were as dull as tree bark. The third was as keen as her father's carving knife.

She bided her time until the day she could sneak alone into the school laundry. It took all her courage to set foot there. A clothes-wringer had recently chewed off the arm of an older girl on work duty.

Chekpawee hastily sifted through the big girls' blouses that were waiting to be ironed. She inspected their tags for a name she couldn't yet sound out but whose written form she'd memorized.

Once she spotted *Helen Washington,* she put her sliver of glass to work, ripping up all of her enemy's blouses.

She had counted coup again.

She dreamed of another eagle feather in her hair.

She dreamed of Helen surrendering to her, in the presence of every girl in the dormitory.

But Helen seemed beyond shaming. She didn't give Turtle back.

THE CRYING TREE

AUTUMN 1918

CHEKPAWEE LEARNED about the Crying Tree, a towering cottonwood situated between the slide on the girls' side of the playground and the hand bars on the boys'.

Back home, a cottonwood tree like this had sheltered Grandmother's tipi. Chekpawee remembered how its heart-shaped leaves would rustle in the barest breeze. That rustling was the tree's voice. She could hear it singing prayers.

But all the Crying Tree did was wail.

She remembered how, at home, she and Chekpa would play in the cottonwood's immense shade. Sometimes they would fashion a handful of its leaves into toy tipis and erect them in a tiny village.

She dared not do that with this tree's leaves.

She remembered when, back home, Grandfather had cut open a dead cottonwood branch that had dropped in the wind. He had shown her and Chekpa what was hidden inside: a five-pointed brown star, running throughout its core.

She didn't look for stars in the Crying Tree's windfall.

Trees, Grandfather used to say, were a nation with powerful medicine. They lived in three different worlds at once: underground, on the earth's surface, and in the air. They bore within them the spirits of sun, wind, wood, and water.

Could all this be true of the Crying Tree, watered by the tears of children?

DUNCE

WINTER 1919

CHEKPAWEE'S HEART was thumping against her ribs. A classmate's tongue had just slipped out of White Talk.

"English, young man!" Miss McDougall said. "Or you know what will happen!"

The boy was William, a dark-skinned Ojibwe.

"I make *one* word bad," he said, punching the chairback of the student in front of him.

"Are you quarreling with me?" Miss McDougall asked, upbraiding him.

Chekpawee couldn't comprehend every word being said. Nor could she easily sympathize with an Ojibwe, a traditional foe of her people. Still, she understood enough to be afraid for the boy.

William burst to his feet. "I make good talk one way whole life! I make good talk now!"

Mr. Peniska, the disciplinarian, sprang from his chair in the back of the classroom. He was Ponca. A former Genoa student. He strode toward William with his paddle.

William spun to confront him, only half the man's size.

"You gone beat?" William said, sticking out his chin. "You like beat boy? Like big boss white man?"

Mr. Peniska grabbed a fistful of William's shirt.

"You gone beat?" William repeated, his chin even higher. "Gone beat dead? I die make good talk!"

His lips let loose a fierce stream of Ojibwe.

"That will be *enough!*" Miss McDougall snapped.

226

"You heart bad!" William spluttered at her.

Mr. Peniska strong-armed William to the front of the room and wrestled him onto a tall stool. There he compelled the boy to roost, wearing a tipi-shaped hat stamped DUNCE in bold red letters.

"As I've told you so many times before," Miss McDougall said to the class, "this word, *dunce,* is a badge of dishonor. It means idiot. Stupid person. A rebellious attitude is a clear sign that someone lacks intelligence. As a reminder of this, William will wear the dunce cap until I say otherwise."

Dunce, Chekpawee thought, *must be a medicine word of rare power.*

She copied the word onto a scrap of paper, laboring over each letter.

Later, she slid the paper under Helen Washington's door.

Helen didn't give Turtle back.

WHERE YOU BELONG

WINTER 1919

CHEKPAWEE LEARNED that any girl singing softly in her own tongue in the night might well be expected to run away.

She learned girls and boys of all ages routinely absconded, even in the Time When the Snow Lives. They ran alone. They ran by twos and threes.

She learned that most runaways were soon caught. The school paid a hefty $5 *bounty* for each *deserter* who went *AWOL*—every day, so many new words.

Matthew Long Elk, a light-skinned Ponca, was Helen Washington's sweetheart. The day he deserted, a farmer captured him tramping through the snow along the railroad tracks, only a couple miles beyond the school fence. Helen said he'd been making for Columbus, Nebraska, the next station on the Union Pacific line.

"The farmer had a gun," Helen reported to her circle of girls in the dormitory. "He tied Matthew's wrists by a long rope to the rear bumper of his truck. He pulled him on his feet all the way back to town."

White people in Genoa had gawked from the snow-covered boardwalks as the farmer, intent on collecting his reward, dragged Matthew down Main Street. By the time the truck reached the school gate, Matthew had lost a shoe and was caked with icy mud.

"I saw everything," Helen said. "I was in town for the dentist."

"Is Matthew all right?" asked her roommate, Maude, one of the palest faces of them all.

"He's in the Hole."

"What 'hole' is?" a Mohawk girl asked in halting White Talk.

228

"A little room in the attic of the classroom building," Helen said. "You live all alone in the dark with the rats. You never see another person. You never see the sun. You eat only bread and water."

"How long he there?" a pudgy Wyandotte girl said.

"Two weeks," Helen said. "Fourteen sleeps."

Her eyes rested on Chekpawee, though not as an enemy's should. "Let this be a lesson. This school is your home now. This is where you belong. You must learn to be happy here."

Chekpawee didn't speak a word.

FIREBUG

SPRING 1919

CHEKPAWEE LEARNED that boys and girls weren't allowed to mix without a chaperone. But she broke the rule to seek out Sid, an older boy who often smoked on the sly behind the dairy barn. He was Dakota like her, though not from her reservation.

Chekpawee offered Sid a carrot she'd stolen from the root cellar in trade for four of his matchsticks.

Sid tilted his broad-brimmed hat back on his head. "Little sister," he said in their shared tongue, "have you ever made fire with a match?"

Chekpawee shook her head.

He spent one of her matches, showing her how to strike it on a tiny box.

"Fire is a gift from the Creator," he told her. "Be careful how you use it. Do not burn what is not meant to burn."

SHE GUARDED her last three matches like little Turtles, especially after Sid disappeared.

Some students said he'd deserted. Some said he'd transferred to an Indian school called Haskell. Some said he'd been shipped home in a pine box after taking ill with the white man's flu. Some said he lay beneath a pile of fresh dirt in the school cemetery, down by the river.

Chekpawee didn't know which of these stories, if any, was the truth.

Maybe Sid was in the Hole with the rats.

After several uncertain weeks, she decided that her big Dakota brother was gone for good. She chose to believe that he was still alive somewhere, and happy.

With a bent nail, she etched the three letters of his name into the foundation of the dairy barn, the first brick above the ground. Next to it, she gouged CHECK PAW WE, the best white spelling she could give the birth name that had marked her as a daughter and a twin.

ON THE PARADE GROUNDS, as her cohort was falling in to march to dinner, Chekpawee raced up to her captain.

I have to make water! she signaled with urgent hands.

"Permission granted," her captain said.

Chekpawee scampered into the girls' building. But she didn't go down to the lavatory in the basement.

No girl, she'd learned, should ever go down to the basement alone. But the truth was, she didn't need to make water.

She flew up the stairs, not down—all the way up to the third floor, where she slept.

If I give my enemy another push, she thought of Helen, *she may return to me what was never hers to take.*

At her cot, Chekpawee pulled from beneath the flimsy mattress a pillowcase she had filled loosely with dry straw and wads of paper.

She retrieved her tiny box of three matches.

She struck a match. Struck it so hard it broke in half.

Two matches left.

In her mind, she watched Sid showing her how to make fire.

You must hold the match lightly, she heard him tell her, *like a white man's pencil.*

She struck another match, so gently it didn't spark.

She tried that same match again, but harder, with trembling fingers.

Again. Again. Again.

The second match was played out. She tossed it away in anger.

Only one matchstick remained.

CHEKPAWEE DIDN'T KNOW that all the fire escapes and windows of her dormitory had been bolted fast—an effort by Big Stick to keep the "wild girls" in and the "wicked boys" out.

Nor did she know that "the babies"—two four-year-old Poncas who had arrived by train the day before—were napping together in a single cot, inside her room of forty beds.

Had she known, she never would have tossed her flaming bundle into the linen closet adjoining Helen's room.

Had she known, nobody would have died.

THE BABIES, dead of the smoke, were wrapped in a winding sheet and buried in a single white box near a sad bend of the Loup. As the box was lowered into the ground, Chekpawee fastened her eyes on the sand-choked river. Hundreds of minnows were stranded in shallow pools along shore.

She had not wanted this. All she had wanted was Turtle.

Investigators from the Genoa Fire Department ruled the incident *arson*. Chekpawee waited in terror, expecting to be chucked into the Hole for the rest of her life, or maybe buried in her own white box on the riverside.

Just a little fire. That's all she'd meant.

LET THIS BE A LESSON, Helen had said to Chekpawee and the other girls after Matthew's runaway attempt. *You must learn to be happy here.*

The fire department closed its arson investigation without turning up the *firebug*. But Chekpawee felt dead inside.

Helen, she now knew, would never give Turtle back.

Her enemy had won.

LAW OFFICE OF
RALPH D. PRESCOTT

SISSETON, SOUTH DAKOTA.

June 30, 1919

Hon. Commissioner of Indian Affairs
Washington, D. C.

Dear Sir:

I wrote your office on June 18th in relation to my
children, Chekpa and Chekpawee Walks Like Thunder, asking
that they be permitted to return home from the U. S. Indian
schools at Wahpeton, No. Dak. and Genoa, Neb., respectively,
during the summer vacation period. Up to this date I have
failed to hear from your office about this matter.

I was told after my children were taken from my home
last year that they would be permitted to visit home during
the summer at my expense, so long as I returned them to
school likewise before the start of the academic year. I
have written both school superintendents requesting such a
visit. The Supt. P. Carter at Wahpeton has not answered. The
Supt. Mr. S. B. Davis at Genoa states he has no permission
from your office to allow pupils out of the state to return
home. I herein request that such permission be granted.
Please favor me with an early reply.

> Most respectfully yours,
> Chaskay Walks Like Thunder

I, Ralph W. Prescott, Esquire, wrote on behalf of this Indian
because he does not know how to write.

TWO WORLDS AT ONCE

AUTUMN 1919

CHEKPAWEE WADED DEEPER into the fast-flowing stream of White Talk. She exhibited a facility for reading, writing, and comprehension.

"You may be mute," her new teachers told her, "but you aren't dumb."

I hate white people for stealing us from home, Chekpawee told Chekpa in her thoughts. *I hate them for sending us far from each other. And I have tried to hate their language. Even now, after so long, I will not speak it.*

Still, my spirit soaks up White Talk as if it were light. Sometimes it dazzles me, like sunbeams on water. Sometimes it twinkles like stars. Always it changes, like the glow of the moon.

Are you in school, as I am? she asked him. *Are you learning White Talk too?*

He didn't answer. He rarely did anymore.

Maybe he never really had. Maybe their conversations had only ever taken place in her imagination. Maybe, here at school, she had only made up their talks because she missed him.

That idea chilled her blood.

How many other things that seemed so real had never actually happened?

We are children of so few winters, she told Chekpa. *I fear that the white man can easily pry us apart.*

No answer.

Many of our people's words, she told him, *have no close relative in White Talk. But even when white words and our words seem to mean the same, in truth they can be worlds distant.*

234

That's where you and I stand: between worlds.
Perhaps we must cling to both worlds at once?

All this, and more, she told Chekpa in her mind, even if he couldn't hear.

STARS OF MEMORY
WINTER 1920

GRANDFATHER'S GRANDMOTHER *was the wife of a Frenchman,* Chekpawee told her brother in her thousand-petalled thoughts.

It was getting harder and harder to summon Grandfather's stories down from the stars of memory.

The Frenchman was a fur trader who had a post on the Cloudy River. Our people called him Yellow Teeth, for the gold in his mouth.

When Grandfather's mother was still small, the Frenchman left to explore farther west. He never returned.

My brother, when you and I were learning to hide in the hole, my nights filled with dreams of ugly white men with yellow teeth. Do you remember?

The Frenchman was our ancestor. I never thought of him that way. I never considered his blood our blood. I never observed the fairness of our hair and our skin next to Father's.

But I did notice your eyes, my brother—how their color would change from green to blue to gold, depending on the light. Sometimes all those colors would shimmer in your eyes at once.

One day I asked Grandmother why your eyes were so strange.

"Your brother," she said, "has the same eyes as you. They are the eyes Great Spirit gave you."

Now I wonder, my brother: Do we have the Frenchman's eyes? Is our paler skin the Frenchman's skin? I do not know. But the ugly white men with yellow teeth have disappeared from my dreams.

I do not know how it is in the place where you are. But here, in this place, my fairer features gain me better treatment. That drop of white man's blood has preserved my life.

All this, and more, Chekpawee told Chekpa, even if he didn't talk back. To nobody else did she speak a word.

THE GREATS

SPRING 1920

CHEKPAWEE LEARNED to write personal letters in White Talk on white paper with fine blue lines.

She wrote to Chekpa. She wrote to her father. She wrote to her grandparents.

She wrote to them about "approved subjects" listed by the teacher on the blackboard:

- ✓ the school's great herd of dairy cows
- ✓ the great quantities of milk, butter, and cheese sold annually by the school
- ✓ the great produce raised in the school garden
- ✓ the great homemaking skills the school taught its girls
  - ✓ cooking
  - ✓ canning
  - ✓ laundering
  - ✓ sewing
- ✓ the great Genoa Indian School marching band
- ✓ the greatest American presidents
  - ✓ George Washington
  - ✓ Andrew Jackson

Her letters were collected and inspected, then mailed by school staff. Chekpawee didn't know to where. She had no address for her father and grandparents. Back on the reservation, who had ever received mail? Even if her letters home had somehow arrived, what would it matter? She had written them in White Talk, which nobody there could read.

That left Chekpa.

Where was he?

What English name had he been assigned?

The day the two of them were stolen, he had been hustled onto a northbound train, presumably to a school like Genoa. If his student information had ever been reported to Superintendent Davis, the clerk had probably filed it in one of the cabinets in his office. Those cabinets stood higher than Chekpawee's head.

There was no hope of a letter from anyone.

Still, at mail call, Chekpawee always hung back, yearning to hear Big Stick call "Vera Whiteman." She would wait there until every last envelope had been handed out.

DEPARTMENT OF THE INTERIOR

UNITED STATES INDIAN SERVICE.

Sisseton Agency, South Dak.
August II, I920.

Supt. Sam B. Davis
Genoa, Neb.

Dear Sir:

It has been reported here on the reservation
that the father of Vera Whiteman is contemplating
sending her money. The family is anxious for her
return, as her brother is recently deceased, having
been run over by a boxcar after deserting Wahpeton.
Presumably he meant to make his way home. This
letter is written you in order that you may guard
against the girl either receiving the money or
making any use of it by likewise running away.

Respectfully,

J. L. Suffecool

J. L. Suffecool
U. S. Agent in Charge

MANNERS

AUGUST 1920

CHEKPAWEE SAT in front of Superintendent Davis's mammoth desk, her feet dangling well above the floor. The leather of her chair reeked of body odors and tobacco smoke. She reached to pinch her nose against the stink.

"Hands!" Big Stick admonished her from behind.

Chekpawee clasped her palms politely in her lap. After two years at Genoa, she knew the drill.

Over behind his desk, the superintendent stubbed out his cigar in a brass ashtray. Then he dipped into his jacket pocket for a peanut. He always had a stash.

"So here we are," he said to Big Stick, shucking the nut. "On this day, at least, we may be glad that our mute papoose can't speak."

He popped the peanut into his mouth and flipped the hull into a waste can. Then he pushed himself up from his seat, a big box of a man in a three-piece suit and colorful striped tie.

Chekpawee was certain he could see her heart hammering against the wall of her chest, even through her uniform. Superintendent Davis could see *everything*.

"How much does the girl understand?" he asked Big Stick, circling his desk with a piece of paper.

"She has her wits," Big Stick said.

"And her English?"

"She follows well."

"Excellent. Quite so. The younger we get them, the better."

He stopped only inches from Chekpawee's chair. "Miss Whiteman,"

241

he said, snapping his paper with a knuckle, "this is a telegram. Do you know what a telegram is?"

The blue pools of his eyes peered down at her. Chekpawee gave no sign.

"No, of course, you don't," he sighed. "So let me put this in the simplest terms possible." He thrust the telegram under her nose. "This is a message from the authorities, informing us that your brother is dead."

Chekpa!

Chekpawee stiffened, anchoring the slab of her little body to the bottom of her chair.

Dead!

The rock of her spirit broke loose and tumbled down a ravine. It landed with a clatter in a dry creek bed, split into pieces.

The superintendent swatted with the telegram at a fly buzzing around one of his wild sideburns.

"The fool boy was trying to hop a train. Misfortune always creeps in when rules are disobeyed."

My brother!

The superintendent shelled another peanut.

Chekpawee glared up at him, hatchets in her eyes. She swung her short legs defiantly against the confines of her skirts.

"Manners!" Big Stick said from behind. "This is *not* the playground!"

Chekpawee stopped moving—but not because she'd been rebuked.

Some scrap of her had suddenly quit the superintendent's office and was swooping like a swallow through a dark night, with a fast-moving train just beneath her. She dove on pointed wings into an open boxcar. She swept the air around two white men in overalls.

One white man had a lantern. The other man, a club.

This second man was grappling with a puny boy with darker skin—*Chekpa.*

"Nothing to say even now, Miss Whiteman?" she heard Superintendent Davis say, as if he were in the train, too, just as the two white men shoved her brother out the door.

THE BLACK STICK

AUTUMN 1920

On the first day of the new school year, Chekpawee and the rest of the student body filed into the auditorium for a special assembly. On the elevated stage that doubled as a gym floor was a musical ensemble, their chairs arranged in a semicircle. The musicians were dressed in school uniforms.

Once the summoned throng had settled into the theater seats facing the stage, Superintendent Davis strode in from the wings. The packed auditorium rustled down to quiet.

"We at Genoa are so proud of our marching band!" the superintendent bellowed. "For years, the band has been living proof of what you students can do if you submit to proper instruction and apply yourselves. Quite so!"

A round of courteous applause.

"This academic year," the superintendent continued, "an illustrious bandmaster will lead our marching band. He's none other than 'the red rival to Sousa,' Mr. James Riley Wheelock!"

Wheelock joined the superintendent on stage to a tepid ovation. Chekpawee sat on her hands. Like most of her schoolmates, she had never heard of any Sousa, let alone his "red rival."

"Mr. Wheelock is a model Indian," Superintendent Davis said. "An Oneida from Wisconsin, he graduated from Carlisle in Pennsylvania, one of our sister schools. Many of you have relatives who attended there."

The bandmaster's fancy red uniform with gold braids impressed

Chekpawee, as did his bearing. He was tall and stout as a bur oak, with broad shoulders.

"After graduating from Carlisle," the superintendent prattled on, "Mr. Wheelock attended the prestigious Dickinson College Preparatory School. He then returned to Carlisle, succeeding his brother Dennison as school bandmaster. During his summers off, he took the helm of the United States Indian Band, the only professional red man's band in the world."

Chekpawee yawned. The superintendent had a habit of using twenty words when one was plenty.

"During the late European war against the kaiser," he droned on, "Mr. Wheelock served in the army as a second lieutenant attached to the 808th Pioneer Infantry. He conducted an all-black regimental band that was judged the Best Infantry Band in all the American Expeditionary Forces. The group won the signal honor of playing for President Wilson before he sailed home from the Paris Peace Conference."

By now, Chekpawee was testing how far up she could tip the bottom of her seat before the crack at the back would gobble up her skinny rump.

"During Mr. Wheelock's time overseas," the superintendent yapped on, "Carlisle Indian School closed its doors. The elimination of his former post has conspired to our great fortune. Quite so."

He pivoted to the bandmaster.

"Chief Wheelock, you've lived an exemplary life. A red man *can* succeed in the white man's world! Welcome to Genoa!"

This round of applause was warmer. The new bandmaster bowed.

Chekpawee had often observed this act of bowing at school plays and concerts. Like a salute to student officers, it was said to be a gesture of respect. But why did no one seem to bow except when on a stage? And why did Mr. Wheelock bow, but not Superintendent Davis?

"I'm honored to join the faculty here," Mr. Wheelock said. "As Mr. Davis told you, I'll be leading our renowned band. But today my purpose is to boost the orchestra." He gestured to the musicians behind him. "As you can see, our orchestra is no bigger than a family of wolves."

Mr. Wheelock then jumped off the edge of the stage.

A collective gasp went up in the auditorium. *Nobody* was allowed to do that.

"Who can tell me the difference between a band and an orchestra?" the bandmaster asked, strutting along the front row of theater seats.

An older boy raised his hand. "A band marches. An orchestra sits."

Laughter rippled through the assemblage.

Mr. Wheelock grinned. "Indeed," he said. "A band often marches while playing! If you have trouble doing two things at once, the orchestra is by far your better choice!"

More laughter.

Chekpawee sat up straighter in her seat. This Oneida man from Wisconsin had her father's kind of voice—a voice everyone with a good heart wanted to listen to.

"I know what else!" a girl said. "Only boys can be in the band!"

"Correct," Mr. Wheelock said. "So, young ladies, if you wish to make music, the orchestra is your ticket!"

"Will we get to wear natty uniforms like the band members do?" another girl asked.

"Even better! We'll outfit you in the finest formal attire our tailor shop can produce." The bandmaster paused. "How else do the band and orchestra differ? Anyone?"

His gaze ranged from one side of the auditorium to the other, as if he were memorizing every face.

"A band has three families of instruments," he said when nobody answered. "Brass, woodwinds, and percussion. An orchestra may have all these. But it also has a fourth family: the strings. Would you like to hear some of these instruments played?"

Chekpawee edged forward in her seat.

"I've asked each of our current orchestra members to perform a few bars from 'America' by Theodore Moses Tobani."

The bandmaster stepped aside with a nod to the first musician.

This boy, a *bassist,* stood up as he played. He rubbed a stick across a set of strings attached to a huge wooden box balanced on a peg on the floor. The instrument's voice was so low pitched and resonant that it shivered Chekpawee's seat.

A *violinist* played a much smaller stringed box, cradled beneath the chin. Its voice was high and smooth.

A *harpist* plucked strings stretched in a wooden frame that resembled a massive hunter's bow. Her fingers produced a magical cascade of sounds.

Helen Washington, Chekpawee's enemy, was the *pianist.* She pressed black and white *keys* on a sort of table. Some keys produced tones as soft as a river's lapping against the bank. Other keys rolled like thunder.

A *percussionist* beat an upright *bass drum* that reminded Chekpawee of forbidden tribal drums. But this drum seemed lonely. The throb of its voice was muffled and feeble. If only the drum could be laid at the heart of a circle of drummers and singers, and the power of the Creator brought down!

"Orchestral music is richest when we're able to unite all the instruments," Mr. Wheelock said after the last demonstration. "To prove that, we'll conclude our brief program by performing 'America' as a group. We have only eleven members, so our music will sound weak and 'full of holes,' as we musicians say. To plug those holes, we need you to join us! You don't need any prior musical knowledge or experience, merely the desire to learn."

Then he held a black stick aloft in one hand—another instrument.

"Before our finale, though, I want you to meet one last member of the woodwind family. This clarinet and I have been friends since my school days at Carlisle. We've traveled the world together. To Leipzig, Germany, where I studied music. To London, England, where I was in an orchestra. To the front lines of the Great War, where we played for troops as they headed into battle."

The bandmaster propped the *clarinet* against one shoulder.

"For however long I'm alive," he said, "I aim to contradict, with all my being, the old saying that 'the only good Indian is a dead Indian.' I intend to show the world that, with proper training, Indians can master music, the highest of all the arts. If we are equal to our white brothers and sisters in music, we can be equal to them in *anything*."

The auditorium burst into spirited applause. A few students, forgetting themselves, even whooped, earning them instant reprimands.

Superintendent Davis stalked back onto the stage. His face was a storm cloud above his red-striped tie.

"What Mr. Wheelock *means* to say," he said, "is *not* that you can be *equal* to white people but that if you give the same *effort,* you'll enjoy a *degree* of success. Quite so. Am I not correct, Bandmaster?"

Mr. Wheelock replied by lifting his clarinet to his lips.

At that moment, in Chekpawee's eyes, the bandmaster wasn't a famous musician come to teach at the school. He was her father, holding the neck of Flute. He was her father, blowing into Flute's brass mouthpipe. He was her father, opening and closing Flute's finger holes. He was her father, warbling birdsong through Flute's open beak.

Can you hear this music, my dead brother? Can you hear?

MEDICINE

AUTUMN 1920

IN THE BAND ROOM, Chekpawee lowered her eyes before Mr. Wheelock's steady gaze.

"This child," Big Stick said to the bandmaster, "wishes to be in your orchestra."

"Oh, she does, does she?"

The bandmaster was even taller up close than he'd looked on stage—a craggy mountain of a man.

He'd been oiling a *trombone*. Now he rested the shiny brass instrument on its bumper and folded his hands atop the tuning slide.

"What's your name, little one?" he asked Chekpawee.

"Vera Whiteman," Big Stick said.

"Vera Whiteman can't speak for herself?" he said.

"The girl hasn't spoken since the day she arrived, two years ago now. But she's smarter than she seems."

"How old are you, Vera Whiteman?" Mr. Wheelock asked.

"Eight, maybe nine," Big Stick said, her rubber-soled shoes squeaking on the polished floorboards as she impatiently shifted side to side.

"You must eat more meat," he told Chekpawee.

"She's always been sickly," Big Stick said.

Mr. Wheelock smiled coolly at the matron. "Thank you for the introduction. You may go."

Big Stick's shoes squeaked out of the band room. Mr. Wheelock detached the trombone's bell from the slide and deposited each part in an instrument case.

247

Then he pulled up two folding chairs. He seated himself in one and directed Chekpawee to the other.

"So, 'Vera Whiteman, eight, maybe nine,'" he said, mimicking Big Stick, "you want to join my orchestra. Tell me why."

She said not a word.

Mr. Wheelock leaned back and crossed his legs. "I'm prepared to wait."

Chekpawee let her eyes roam. Instrument cases. Metal music stands. Sheets of paper covered with black lines and dots and squiggles. A wooden music desk on a conductor's rostrum. The ivory baton Mr. Wheelock had waved in the air while directing "America," flapping his arms like a graceful man-hawk.

And there—

His clarinet, erect on a three-footed stand. Next to it, a leather instrument case stamped with gold White Talk.

She rose from her chair and made her way to the gorgeous black stick with its glistening silver keys. She touched it timidly, expecting Mr. Wheelock to yell at her.

He didn't.

She hoisted the clarinet from its perch.

"Take the cap off the mouthpiece," he said.

Somehow, she understood. She gently removed the shiny metal cap and set it aside.

The black stick was heavier than she'd expected. Onstage, its cylindrical shape, plus how it was held, had reminded her of Flute. Now it seemed clumsy and foreign.

And forbidden.

Among her people, only men would play such an instrument.

All you need, the bandmaster had said in the assembly, *is the desire to play.*

Chekpawee closed her eyes. She tried to picture how Mr. Wheelock had clutched the stick. In her mind, he kept shape-shifting into her father. So she imitated what her father had done with Flute. She positioned her left hand at the top of the instrument and her right hand at the bottom.

Forming her mouth around the clarinet's tip, she discovered a strange slice of wood attached to the back of the mouthpiece.

"That's called a reed," the bandmaster said.

She tightened her lips, bit down, and blew.

The only sound that came out the clarinet's bell was her own wind.

"Try again," Mr. Wheelock said. "This time, relax. Don't bite."

Wind again.

"Don't feel discouraged, child. That reed isn't for beginners. It's a number five—the thickest, hardest, toughest reed to play. Your breath support has to be strong."

She blew again with all her might.

Wind.

"A remarkable beginning, Vera Whiteman," Mr. Wheelock said, extracting the clarinet from her hands. "Next time, we'll try a one and a half. Maybe a two. But I must tell you, the reed size is not our fundamental problem."

She stared down at his shiny black shoes as she waited for him to say more. The shoes seemed a perfect fit for his enormous feet. She doubted he'd ever had blisters or sore heels or bent toes.

"Look at me when I talk," he said, not unkindly.

To her, the white man's custom of looking people in the eye still seemed disrespectful. But already she wanted to please the bandmaster. So she ratcheted up her gaze from his burnished shoes, to the sharp crease of his pants, to his bright-red suspenders, to the buttons parading up his crisp white shirt, to his dark chin, to his brown eyes boring down.

"Every musical instrument," he said, "is a mirror of the person who plays it. This clarinet won't speak until *you* speak."

Mr. Wheelock loosened a couple of screws on the mouthpiece and slipped off the fragile reed. He raised it in front of her.

"This is the clarinet's vocal cord. It's a piece of cane. When you breathe over it, it vibrates, like this." Fluttering his hand. "This causes all the air moving through the instrument to vibrate too. And that vibration produces sound."

He curled his fingers over the reed so that it disappeared.

"No reed, no vibrations. No vibrations, no music—no *voice*. Do you understand?"

She felt like she was listening to one of Grandfather's stories.

"The day you arrived at this school, you decided not to speak." He patted the front of her throat. "You threw away your reed. Am I right? No reed, no speech—no *voice*."

Taking up one of her hands, he laid the tough yet delicate reed in her palm and closed her fingers around it.

"I've got a beat-up clarinet over there in that closet," he told her. "I'll let you play it, but only if you resume talking. Understand?"

His eyes were an eagle's, bold and piercing.

"That's the deal," he said. "When you're ready to find your voice, come back and see me."

Her fist tightened around the reed.

"Now you should go to class," he said.

She didn't move.

"Do you require an escort?" he said.

She wagged her head no.

"Words, please, Vera Whiteman."

Chekpawee's mouth was on fire. She gulped down the flames.

She could feel the reed singing in her hand. She could feel its medicine.

"*Hiya*," she whispered in Dakota. As if the bandmaster weren't Oneida. As if a Reading House hadn't cut out his native tongue.

"In English, little one."

She moistened her lips. She coughed up air, making room for speech.

"No class," she said to Mr. Wheelock in a croak, the first words she had uttered in two years. And her very first words in White Talk.

"I . . . stay . . . here."

X	SERVICE WANTED					
	TELEGRAM				CHECK	
	DAY LETTER					
	NIGHT MESSAGE				TIME FILED	
	NIGHT LETTER					

TELEGRAM
UNITED STATES DEPARTMENT OF THE INTERIOR
OFFICIAL BUSINESS

(TELEGRAPH CO.)	SEND OFFICIAL TELEGRAMS	To Washington, D. C., and other charge-account points .... Collect, Government Rate	X
		From Washington, D. C., to all points .... Paid, Government Rate, Charge	METHOD USED
		From charge-account points to all points except Washington, D. C. ..... Paid, Government Rate, Charge	
		All other official telegrams .... Government Rate, Pay in Cash	
Bureau of		Appropriation	

Sisseton Agency, So. Dak.,
November 29, 1920.

Supt. Sam B. Davis,
Genoa School
Genoa, Neb.

CHASKAY WALKS LIKE THUNDER FATHER OF VERA
WHITEMAN HAS DIED OF INFLUENZA

Suffecool.

BELONGING

1920–1921

V ERA LEARNED to assemble her beat-up black stick. She learned to attach a reed to the mouthpiece using the metal ligature. The vibration of that reed, caused by her breath, created sound.

"In time," Mr. Wheelock told her, "you'll develop your wind and learn to control your clarinet's voice. That begins with your posture. No slouching."

She learned to sit up straight, relax her shoulders, and hold the stick at a forty-five-degree angle from her body. Her grip on the stick had to be firm yet loose enough to keep her fingers nimble on the keys.

"Your hands will become stronger," Mr. Wheelock promised. "Your fingers will become longer."

She learned her stick had *holes* and metal *keys*. By blowing into the mouthpiece and manipulating her fingers, she could produce twelve basic musical *notes*, in lower and higher *octaves*.

She learned notes could be read off a page, like words in a book. Or—you could dream them up.

She learned that, with practice, musical technique could be mastered, like doing sums in arithmetic class. *Breath + fingering = tone*. But good music required more than technique. It was more like cooking class, where you made the most of the ingredients on hand.

"Whatever music you have," Mr. Wheelock told her, "you must find your own way to play it. All I can give you is a place to start."

She learned to alter the sounds she made by changing her *embouchure*—the way her lips closed around *the sweet spot* on the mouthpiece. Or by altering the flow of her breath. Or by changing her *tonguing* and *phrasing* . . .

She learned to build a note of music in her body and in her mind before offering it her breath and finishing it in the air.

She learned that no matter the competence she gained, there was always more to learn. Mr. Wheelock, accomplished as he was, still practiced daily.

She learned in orchestra class to watch Mr. Wheelock's baton out of the corner of her eye while reading the sheet music on her stand. She learned to follow the baton's pace as well as its cues about *dynamics* and other matters of *interpretation*.

She learned to appreciate the voices of other instruments and how to make her clarinet sing with them, contributing her part to the whole. She learned that playing music with other musicians—even with Helen Washington, pounding on the piano—was much more satisfying than playing alone.

She took a private lesson with Mr. Wheelock nearly every day. She visited the band room whenever she could contrive it, simply to be where he was. In his presence, she felt safer. Like she mattered. And belonged. She learned to be comfortable speaking aloud.

Having the bandmaster at the school was a little like having a father again. And having music was like being born again, with a new voice. This voice came on the breath of the Creator, who in White Talk she was learning to call *God*.

INTERRUPTION

SPRING 1921

VERA WAS ALONE in the band room, practicing her upper register, when Mr. Wheelock walked in.

"Vera Whiteman," he said matter-of-factly, as he did each day when greeting her for the first time.

He swung his leather satchel onto his desk. His big hand paused on the handle, as if reluctant to let go.

"May I interrupt?" he said then.

As he wended through the throng of folding chairs and music stands to join her, she happily laid her clarinet across her lap. She relished his interruptions.

He sat down next to her. For a moment, he seemed lost in thought.

"I know this will make you sad, and I'm sorry," he said at last. "But I want you to hear the news from me."

News?

She often heard news on the radio that played in the dairy barn. The Great Flu. The Depression. The Allied occupation of German cities. The national popularity of President Harding.

What news from the bandmaster could possibly make her sad?

"I'll soon be leaving," he said.

A gut punch. All breath went out of her.

"Leav-ing?" Struggling to say the word, as if it were still foreign.

Beside her, he was so upright in his chair that he might have been a puppet with a string pulling his spine straight. "Yes. At the end of the school year."

"How long you are going for?" Choking on the question, though she already knew the answer.

The toe of his shoe was tap-tap-tapping the floor, as if keeping time with a tune she couldn't hear.

"I never meant to stay here, Vera. I just needed a place to land after the war, until I could revive my band and go back on tour."

What was he doing? Abandoning her, even as her father had? She had heard not one word from her father—or anyone else in her family—since her admission to Genoa in the fall of 1918. All those letters she had written . . . for nothing.

She bottled up her feelings, trying to be brave. "But what will happen to—to—the orchestra?"

"You don't have to worry about that, Vera. I'm sure the school will hire another bandmaster."

She put the metal cap on the mouthpiece of her clarinet. "And *me*? What will happen to me?"

"You have a special talent, Vera. Such as I've never seen in someone so young. If you work hard, someday you'll be playing in Europe."

Europe. A place far over the water, beyond the reach of any train. The place of the white man's Great War. The place of the white man's greatest music.

She couldn't picture herself there. Ever.

She could only picture herself here.

Because of him.

Yet here he was, tossing her away, like garbage onto the manure pile behind the hog barn.

"*No!*"

Blind with fury, she flung her precious, beat-up clarinet to the floor and burst out of her chair. She stormed cross the band room, kicking aside chairs and knocking over music stands, finally slamming through the double doors.

GRANDE RÉVÉRENCE

SPRING 1921

VERA'S POWER of speech tumbled down into the dark well of her spirit. She didn't care to haul it back up.

Her old clarinet was the only voice she had left. Miraculously, it had suffered only more scratches when she let it fly. Now she poured her grief down that black stick. At the Crying Tree. In the mow of the dairy barn. In the school cemetery, down by the Loup.

She avoided the band room except for orchestra practice and her private lessons, from which Mr. Wheelock declined to excuse her. When there, she went through the motions of making music as if she were back on the train that had delivered her to Genoa—her head cloaked by a blanket, her teeth biting the edge.

The prospect of the bandmaster leaving was like death.

IN MR. WHEELOCK'S final week at Genoa, Vera stood before the full-length mirror in her dormitory.

"When musicians acknowledge applause, boys bow, and girls bob." This is what he'd once told her, when beginning to realize her talent. "But a soloist—which, young lady, you will one day be—gives what the French call *grande révérence*."

There at the mirror, Vera rehearsed the dramatic curtsy as he'd coached her, molding her grief to her little frame. Her grande révérence had to be perfect. It had to say *Thank you*. It had to say *I respect you*. It had to say *I don't know how to go on without you, but I will*.

She practiced until she could perform the graceful movement as naturally as Mr. Wheelock could play a wild jazz riff.

AT HER LAST PRIVATE LESSON, Vera held out her palm to the bandmaster. There lay the #5 reed he'd given her at their first meeting, now nicked and split from a year in her skirt pockets. She cherished it as much as she'd once cherished Turtle.

"Take it," she said, her first words to him—to anyone—since he'd announced he was leaving. "To remember."

She lowered her head. She tucked one foot behind the other and gave a slow, deep flourish to her maestro, as if he were royalty.

When she straightened again, on the verge of tears, she hiked her little-girl skirts and ran.

The next day, his family's cottage was empty.

BAYOU VOODOO

AUTUMN 1921

VERA CAREFULLY OBSERVED MR. MUMBLEHEAD, the new bandmaster, for weeks after his arrival. Once she decided he was harmless, she began to speak to him beyond formalities and to play for him outside of rehearsals.

Mr. Mumblehead was a Cherokee, born in Tennessee. Like Mr. Wheelock, he was a graduate of the now-defunct Carlisle Indian School, once the flagship of the entire Indian boarding school system.

But in no other respect did he resemble the music teacher Vera had cherished. He was a much younger, scrawnier man, tense and withdrawn, with a pencil-thin moustache. Less talented, less experienced, less traveled than Mr. Wheelock, he lacked presence on the podium. He couldn't command attention in the band room or inspire excellence on the stage.

His instrument of choice was the cornet, similar to the bugle that blared reveille to rouse the school at 6:00 a.m. every morning. The cornet's brass tubing was, like Mr. Mumblehead himself, tightly wound. Vera hated the sound.

She might have forgiven Mr. Mumblehead his flaws if he'd shown any fondness for the jazz music she loved. Black at its roots, jazz was getting to be all the rage. It was the kind of music for which Mr. Wheelock's regimental band had been famous during the Great War.

"White men call it 'bayou voodoo,' " he'd often warned Vera and his other jazz-loving students. "To them, it's no better than tribal music. Don't let Superintendent Davis get wise to you!"

The new bandmaster didn't attack jazz outright. He ignored it as he would a student with no ability, unworthy of his regard. He drilled the band and orchestra instead in classical, sacred, and martial music.

Vera played his preferred styles to her best ability, to win his favor. What she played in secret was another matter.

PERIODS

SPRING AND SUMMER 1922

VERA LEARNED to crawl into bed with Milly, a Lakota girl, the instant the lights went out. Mr. Silas, their arithmetic teacher, prowled the dormitory at night. He couldn't paw two girls at once.

She learned to look Mr. Silas in the eye whenever he called on her in class, despite his many "sins of the flesh."

She learned to suffer through the night hours with a full bladder rather than descend in the dark to the toilet. Things happened down there that no girls spoke aloud.

She learned to sweep and oil the wood floors of her building.

She learned during assigned work periods in the sewing room to hem dishtowels and pillowcases, to darn socks, to patch gingham dresses and dungarees.

She learned to weasel passes from Mr. Mumblehead that exempted her from work periods in the sewing room.

She learned to report her monthlies to Mrs. Biegert, the matron who had replaced Big Stick. Mrs. Biegert said she wasn't at the school to be anybody's mother. But the girls were soon calling her Mrs. B, almost as if she were.

With Mrs. B's help, Vera learned which officials in the government to write letters to, in her best longhand, begging for any news of her father and grandparents, begging for even a brief visit home.

Mrs. B also finagled Mr. Wheelock's address out of the school clerk. The bandmaster was living with his wife, Emma, and their children in Philadelphia, Pennsylvania—on the United States map, half the country away.

Every living soul who had ever meant something to Vera seemed to have forsaken her. What memories she still had of her family were a tangle of weeds.

If she wrote to Mr. Wheelock and he never wrote back, she didn't know if she could bear it.

Some kinds of pain pass. Others don't.

She ripped up his address beneath the Crying Tree.

LAW OFFICE OF
RALPH D. PRESCOTT

SISSETON, SOUTH DAKOTA.

June 7, 1922.

Hon. Commissioner of Indian Affairs
    Washington, D. C.

Dear Sir:
    I will write another letter to you, asking you
again if my granddaughter Chekpawee Walks Like Thunder
of the Genoa Nebraska Indian School can come home.
    I had written a letter to you last June wanting
her to come home. I need her home very much. If you
will please let her come home as soon as possible I
will be obliged to you.
    I would ask Mr. Davis, the school superintendent,
but I thought it best to ask at the head department of
Indian schools.
    My husband and son are dead. Chekpawee is my only
surviving grandchild. I expect much work from her. I
hope she will come home soon.
    I have asked this man to write for me. I am
learning to read and write your language but not fast
enough. I want my granddaughter home.

                        Yours respectfully,
                        Turtle Woman

I, Ralph D. Prescott, Esquire, wrote on behalf of this
woman because she couldn't write for herself.

Genoa Indian Sch.
Nebraska.
June 14, 1922

Mr. C.F. Hauke

Dear Sir:
Would you please let me go home on a visit as I have been gone for nearly four years and want to go home for a while.

I want to stay a week at home and then come back to school. All the rest of the girls got to go home and I didn't.

I have been good and I have always minded the rules.

Resp. yours,
Miss Vera Whiteman
Genoa, Nebraska.

DEPARTMENT OF THE INTERIOR

UNITED STATES INDIAN SERVICE.

Genoa Indian School,
Genoa, Nebraska,
July II, I922.

Hon. Commissioner of Indian Affairs,
Washington, D. C.

Dear Sir:

Replying to your letter of June 27th,
relative to the request made by Vera
Whiteman, pupil enrolled from Sisseton,
South Dakota, I have the honor to state
that owing to her home surroundings and
conduct of her family, who are not
progressive Indians, the Agent at her
reservation advises that we try and keep
her here until she finishes her course of
education.

As for "staying a week and then coming
back," that is merely a ruse to get home.
If allowed to go, the girl will never
return.

Very Respectfully,

Sam B. Davis
Superintendent.

DEPARTMENT OF THE INTERIOR

OFFICE OF INDIAN AFFAIRS

WASHINGTON

July 18, 1922

Miss Vera Whiteman,
    Genoa, Nebraska.

My dear Miss Whiteman:

    With further reference to your letter
of June 14th, requesting that you be
allowed to return to your home for a week,
you are advised that it is believed best
for you to remain at Genoa.

                Very truly yours,

                E. B. Meritt
                Assistant Commissioner

THE SWITCH

SUMMER 1922

HEADED ACROSS THE GREEN, Vera gave Superintendent Davis a quick salute and hastened on by. The day was a scorcher. The band room, though stuffy, would offer relief from the stifling heat.

"Not so fast, young lady," the superintendent said.

Vera rolled her eyes before she did an about-face. "Yes, sir, Mr. Davis?"

Unlike her, he was in no hurry. He was dawdling in the shade of an elm, overseeing two boys as they washed and waxed his Hudson motor car. His cheek was plugged full of peanuts. Peanut shells littered the lawn around his two-tone shoes.

"You know," he said, bidding her to come closer, "you must stop troubling officials in Washington with your letters. They have no interest in such trivial matters."

"Then let me go home!" she blurted.

He glowered at her as if she had just blasphemed the Lord Jesus Christ.

Aghast at her own temerity, she cast her eyes about for anything he might use as a switch. The superintendent was notorious for displaying his power in the open-air theater of the green. Sometimes he'd swing the rod himself. Other times, he'd corral students into a gauntlet, arm them with sticks, and order them to rain blows on the miscreant he forced to run between them.

One of the boys slammed the hood of the Hudson.

"Easy!" Mr. Davis growled. "And shine up that grill! I want her spotless!"

"Yes, sir," both boys muttered.

Vera felt sorry for them, sweating through their work shirts. But she was also glad they were there, distracting from her own impudence. The superintendent loved his Hudson. If anyone would be getting the switch on the green today, she decided, it wasn't apt to be her.

"Every student wishes to go home, Miss Whiteman," Mr. Davis said, rejoining their conversation. "Quite so. But this school doesn't operate according to Indian whim. Your duty isn't to question my decisions. Your duty is to obey."

"Yes, sir," she mumbled, choosing to submit. He meant to beat her down with words instead of a switch. A verbal whipping she could tolerate.

"I didn't hear you. Speak up!"

"Yes, sir, Mr. Davis!"

He seemed to relax at her show of deference. He fished a handful of peanuts from his jacket pocket, then husked them, one by one, squeezing them until they cracked.

"It's necessary to remind you, Miss Whiteman, that owing to your musical talent, you have been afforded certain liberties. *Exceptional* liberties, I should say. Quite so. During the school year, you have been excused from many vocational classes. Your hours on work details, even in summertime, have been greatly reduced, that you might focus more rigorously on your clarinet. This can all turn in an instant."

The shelled peanuts were now a lump in his jowl.

"Your time is *mine*. Your clarinet is *mine*. The orchestra you play in—*mine*. What's to become of you is fully at my discretion. I will therefore say it again: no more letters to Washington. Do I make myself clear?"

"Yes, sir, Mr. Davis."

"You're dismissed."

She resumed her beeline toward the band room, fuming inside. All she'd asked for in her letter was a short visit home. She was entitled. Every student that wasn't "outed"—apprenticed to a white family to learn a skill over the summer months—was to be granted leave. The school's rulebook said so.

But somehow the rules didn't always apply. Not to her nor to those boys waxing the Hudson nor to so many other students still confined to campus, owing to the superintendent's "discretion."

Then again . . . maybe it was true, what some of her girlfriends had tried to tell her before they caught a wagon or train bound for home. Maybe Mr. Davis was actually doing her a favor by detaining her. A stint back on the reservation wouldn't exactly be a cakewalk, especially after a considerable absence. Too much would have changed.

"Oh, and one last thing," the superintendent said, interrupting before she'd gone a half-dozen paces.

She spun on her heel.

"Yes, Mr. Davis?"

He spat out a scrap of peanut hull.

"I remember your brother's folly a couple years back," he said, thumbing his suspenders beneath his beige linen jacket. His suit was a perfect match in color for his Hudson. "It was terrible, having to afflict you with such sad news."

At his mention of Chekpa, her mouth went sour.

"It's terrible, Miss Whiteman, my having to afflict you with additional sadness. If it were in my power, I'd spare you. But due to your letter-writing, I'd best not coddle you further . . ."

She braced herself. He wasn't done with his thrashing of her.

"I'm sorry to tell you," he said, "that, like so many of our students, you have lost kin to the Spanish flu."

She waited with dread for him to continue.

"Your father," he said finally. "He expired some months after your brother's accident."

The air went out of her. All the world's colors bled into grays and browns.

The superintendent was gauging her reaction, as if to land his next blow for greatest effect.

"And your grandparents," he said, "have expired too. Not surprising, at their advanced age."

She clenched her jaw. Stiffened her back.

Maybe he was running her through a gauntlet of lies. If she could just stay on her feet until the end of this ordeal, maybe he'd confess his cruel bluff.

She firmed her knees. Curled her toes in her shoes.

"You have nobody left to go home to," the superintendent said then. "So you see, Miss Whiteman, there's no need for any more letters."

No. He wasn't lying. He was relishing this moment too much for it not to be the truth.

Silently she swore at him. For withholding, until now, information to which she'd had a natural right. For wielding it like a scourge.

To him, some people simply didn't matter enough to be mourned.

If only she could retaliate. An eye for an eye, a tooth for a tooth. That's what the white man's religion preached.

But she'd learned her lesson the day she set the fire that killed the babies: someone like her had no means of getting even.

DEPARTMENT OF THE INTERIOR

OFFICE OF INDIAN AFFAIRS

WASHINGTON

July 22, 1922

Mrs. Turtle Woman
    Care of Ralph Prescott, Esq.
    Box 3, Sisseton, South Dakota.

Madam:

The Office has your letter of June 7th, requesting the return of your granddaughter Vera Whiteman from the Genoa Indian School, where she is now in attendance after having been regularly enrolled there for four years.

This request is denied on the grounds that it would be for the best interest of your granddaughter to allow her to complete her studies at the Genoa School. You are advised that the Office is not aware of any circumstances which would justify a change in the current situation. Therefore your request cannot be approved.

Respectfully,

C. F. Hauke
Second Assistant Commissioner

CALL TIME

SPRING 1923

ALMOST TWELVE MONTHS had passed since Superintendent Davis had ambushed Vera on the green. With no evidence to contradict his sorry news about her family, she'd redoubled her dedication to her schooling and her music. She was now all alone in this world.

During her time at Genoa, Vera had learned that white people loved to watch Indian students give music recitals and act on the stage and play baseball and shoot hoops—anything that white people found entertaining. She'd also learned that she loved performing for them, especially during commencement week.

Held in June, commencement week was the pinnacle of each academic year. Townspeople thronged the school for military drills on the parade grounds, guided tours of campus, special worship services, literary recitations, exhibitions of student handiwork, music concerts, theatrical productions, and grand ceremonies.

This year, on Thursday before graduation, the school orchestra would accompany a staging of *Pocahontas*. The operetta sold out well in advance. Its leading lady was none other than Vera's old nemesis— Helen Washington, one of the forty-nine members of the class of 1923.

At call time, Vera took her seat in the woodwind section. She was chilling from nerves. During dress rehearsal, Mr. Mumblehead had once again miscued the violins at a critical moment in the finale, bringing them in too early. His conducting mistake had caused a chain reaction through the strings, then the woodwinds, then the drums, then the brass, until the entire orchestra was out of time. She dreaded that he might botch up during the actual show.

She collected her instrument case, stowed beneath her folding chair, to assemble her clarinet.

Inside the case she found a penny-candy bag.

Inside the paper bag was Turtle.

Memories streamed through her mind of all the petty and terrible ways she'd tried to win Turtle back during her first year at Genoa. Sometimes she still dreamed about the two little ones she'd killed by setting the fire in the dormitory. Their faces were always missing, as if they'd been born without any.

What other sins might she have committed in desperation, if not for Mr. Wheelock? Her plunge into music had distracted her from the loss of Turtle and all it had represented. Without realizing, she'd gradually surrendered any hope of recovering it. She'd supposed that Helen had destroyed it.

But no. Like a good sister, Helen had jeopardized her own future to keep Vera's forbidden amulet safe. Now, graduating from Genoa, Helen was transferring Turtle—and the risk of possessing it—back to Vera.

Turtle was Vera's last material connection to her family. Strangely, she didn't know what significance, if any, it yet carried. She wasn't who she once had been.

She crumpled the bag and stuffed it back in her clarinet case.

That night, from her seat in the orchestra pit, Vera watched Helen Washington play a near perfect Pocahontas. Stumbling on only two lines, the "Indian princess" saved the English adventurer John Smith from execution by her own people and then sailed away with him to a happy life in a distant land.

At the curtain call, Helen floated out to center stage. When she curtsied, the audience of townspeople leapt to their feet in wild applause. Mr. Mumblehead screwed up the finale again, just as Vera had feared. But it didn't matter. The cheering drowned out the orchestra's flop.

Down in the pit, Vera left off playing to shout "Brava!"

Mr Royal C. Johnson, Congressman, Washington D.C.
  My Dear Congressman: —— With very happy heart in
getting your answer I am old indian woman do not know
white man way. No write good. I am old lady live alone
I am glad again when hear from you I am think one good
white man living yet. I am told you very simpathitic
white man. You have very good mother or grand mother
You know mother feelings please get my grand daughter
home for summer I am old I raise her from baby she is
only thing I have in my heart. With happy heart I close
thank you for answer. I know you help me with all you can.

                    I am say goodby from old grandma

                        very truly
                        Turtle Woman

DEPARTMENT OF THE INTERIOR

UNITED STATES INDIAN SERVICE.

Genoa Indian School,
Genoa, Nebraska,
June I3, I923.

Hon. Commissioner of Indian Affairs,
Washington, D. C.

Dear Sir:

Replying to your letter of May I6th,
relative to the request made by the grandmother
of Vera Whiteman, pupil at this school, I have
the honor to state once again that the girl
should not be allowed a visit home.

This girl is doing splendidly in her school
work and is an excellent musician. She is very
nice and quite an attractive young girl. In
fact, she is too pretty and inexperienced to
make the trip alone from Genoa to the Sisseton
Reservation. I suggest that you write the
Superintendent of the Sisseton Agency for any
further information desired.

Very Respectfully,

Sam B. Davis
Superintendent.

TEA PARTY

AUTUMN 1927

"YOUR DISHES ARE SO PRETTY," Vera said to Mrs. Davis as a maid deposited the porcelain tea set on the tea table. "They aren't at all like the dishes in the mess hall!"

Vera avoided the maid's eyes. It pained her to be waited on by a friend.

Four years had elapsed since Helen Washington's triumph as an Indian princess. Vera and Milly, now sixteen by the white man's records, were old enough to share a double room in the girls' dormitory. By night, they remained each other's refuge against Mr. Silas's wicked advances. By day, Vera was off after classes to the band room, while Milly reported for training at the superintendent's house, dressed in the blue-striped cotton shift and white waist apron of a domestic servant.

"Milly," Mrs. Davis said, "you may leave us now and retrieve the item we discussed earlier."

The girl bobbed a curtsy and disappeared.

Mrs. Davis unfolded her linen napkin and draped it across her lap. "Please, Vera—your napkin? Do as I do."

And of course, Vera did.

Florence Davis, with her caramel complexion and genteel bearing, could pass as a white lady. But everybody on campus knew that the superintendent's wife was a mixed blood from Alaska. Like Mr. Wheelock and Mr. Mumblehead, she had graduated from Carlisle Indian School.

"My dear," Mrs. Davis said to Vera, "I presume you know you're one of our stars here at Genoa. How long have you been with us?"

"Ten years, ma'am."

"You're to be commended for the tremendous personal progress you've made." Mrs. Davis added a cube of sugar to her teacup, then a thin slice of lemon. "Your turn, child."

Vera imitated the woman's movements.

"Over time," Mrs. Davis said, "you will have to experiment with the taste. If you wish to use milk rather than lemon, for instance, add it before the tea is poured. *Never* use milk and lemon together."

Mrs. Davis tipped the floral teapot. Tea streamed elegantly from the spout.

"When stirring," she said, "gently swish with your spoon, back and forth. *Never* clink. When you're finished, place the spoon on your saucer —like this."

"Yes, Mrs. Davis." Very careful not to clink.

Milly reentered the parlor, carrying a shallow lidded box.

"Deliver it to Miss Whiteman," Mrs. Davis told Milly.

Vera abandoned her tea to the table. She awkwardly accepted the box and another curtsy from her friend.

"I'll have you stay a minute longer," Mrs. Davis said to Milly. Then, to Vera, "Go ahead, dear—open it."

Nestled in tissue paper within the box was a delicate cream dress. It was fancier than any dress Vera had ever seen, except perhaps on the boardwalks in town.

"This is for your special performances," Mrs. Davis explained. "See what hard work wins you?" She smiled at Milly, underscoring her point. "*Now* you may leave us."

As Vera watched Milly go, she fondled the dress's buttons. "I . . . don't know what to say."

"A simple 'Thank you' is sufficient."

"Then . . . thank you." Vera was still uncertain. Such a lavish gift would doubtless have strings attached—and not of the orchestral kind.

"Those buttons are genuine mother of pearl," Mrs. Davis said. "The fabric is called voile."

"Like 'foil'?" Vera caressed the dress's silky front.

"Yes, but spelled with an *e* on the end. I did the hand-embroidery myself. If the dress requires alteration, take it to Lisbeth in the tailor shop. Now, set it aside. I'll freshen your tea."

Vera cradled her newly warmed cup, aware of Mrs. Davis's scrutiny. The woman was like Mr. Mumblehead, tutoring his beginners in the band room on the proper use of their hands.

"Dear, not that way! You must pinch the handle of the cup between your thumb and your first finger—like this. Tilt your pinkie, for balance." She nodded approvingly. "That's it. But Vera, always take *dainty* sips. *Never* gulp like a fish."

"Yes, ma'am." Wiping her nose on her napkin.

"Vera!" Mrs. Davis scolded. "Ladies *never* do that!"

"But the tea's making it run!" Vera protested.

"That's what your hanky is for!"

"But I don't have a hanky!"

"Then you must make yourself one," Mrs. Davis said, unimpressed. "In time, you will master these necessities, even as I once did."

Vera wondered how long it had taken Mrs. Davis to learn all these necessities and who had taught her. The list of necessities, like the rules of etiquette, seemed as endless as a train track.

"Today I'm serving tea sandwiches with jam," Mrs. Davis said. "You may eat them with your fingers. For the jam, spoon a small amount onto your plate, then use your knife to spread the jam on the bread, which is already buttered—like this. *Never* use the serving spoon to spread the jam."

"Yes, Mrs. Davis."

Vera helped herself to a heaping spoonful.

"Vera! You must *never* appear greedy."

"Yes, ma'am." Vera gobbled down her petite white triangle. "May I have another sandwich?"

"Learn to take dainty bites, dear."

"Yes, ma'am. But . . . may I? Have another?"

"One more, I suppose."

Vera nibbled this sandwich, studying Mrs. Davis's comportment. In what place had this woman stopped being Indian and begun to be white? Did the final line of demarcation appear on any map? Had she realized when she was crossing over?

"Now, child," Mrs. Davis said, "I have a specific matter to discuss with you, on the request of my husband."

"Yes, ma'am." The exact nature of the string attached to the dress was about to be revealed. But Vera wasn't ready. "Please, may I have more tea?"

"You may, if you serve yourself properly."

Vera wanted three sugar cubes for her tea. And she wanted so much milk that her tea would turn near white. But she settled for one cube and a splash of milk, so as not to appear a "greedy" Indian.

"My husband and I read your recent essays in *The Indian News* with interest," Mrs. Davis said, referring to the school's monthly publication.

Two of Vera's compositions, having won best-in-class, had been featured in the latest editions. In reply to the topic "Should Indian

Tongues Be Preserved?" Vera had argued that Indian languages, which had no orthography, were inferior to English: "A tongue that cannot be transmitted in writing is doomed to die." Then, the very next issue, in addressing the question "Should Indians Be Absorbed into the White Race?" Vera had elaborated upon the thesis "Such is our purpose in attending this school."

"Many of our benefactors," Mrs. Davis said, "are curious about the everyday lives of our students. Mr. Davis would like you, along with a few other exceptional boys and girls, to write letters to these donors, elaborating upon the benefits of your schooling. This would win you much admiration, while bringing good fortune to the school. Are you willing to do this for us?"

"Yes, ma'am."

"Very well, then."

Mrs. Davis picked up the napkin from her lap. "This is how a lady signals the end of teatime. You should respond by lifting your own napkin—at the center—and laying it on the tea table, to the left of your plate."

"Yes, ma'am." Vera gulped down the rest of her tea. She scooped up her napkin, then paused, her hand hanging in midair. "But I have a question, please, Mrs. Davis."

"Yes, child?"

"If I write these letters, may I please have more sandwiches with jam?"

DEPARTMENT OF THE INTERIOR

UNITED STATES INDIAN SERVICE.

RULES FOR LETTER-WRITING

I. Don't write at all unless you have something good to say. Having said it, stop.

2. Don't give reasons or explanations unless they are called for.

3. Don't write anything in a perfunctory way but remember always that each letter or endorsement should bear impress of the writer's dignity, courtesy, and intelligence.

4. Don't hesitate to say "no" if that is the proper answer; and having said no, don't attempt to suggest an alternative aimed to circumvent your own "no."

5. Don't discuss people; discuss things.

6. Don't write anything quarrelsome. (It would probably never be mailed.)

7. Don't get excited; or if you do, don't record the fact on paper.

8. Don't use long words when they can be avoided (and they generally can).

9. Don't say "shall" or "must" or "should" if you mean "will;" "verbal" when you mean "oral;" "amount" when you mean "quantity;" "in reference" when you mean "with reference;" "in accord" when you mean "in accordance;" "hardly" when you mean "scarcely;" or "with the view of" when you mean "with a view to."

Sisseton, So.Dak.
Hon. Cato Sells, Commissioner of Indian Affairs.
January 2, I929.

You send letter December 20. I say you look into indian
rule book. You say any indian boy or girl go school 6 to I8
years old. When reach I8 they get share of Sioux benefit.
You run over rule. My grand daughter Chekpawee Walks Like
Thunder is reach I8 years now. Time you send her home. I
need her very bad but you keep her. Old Prescott walk
spirit road but I find good white man make law suit against
Supt. Davis. Make petition for Chekpawee. I hear from grand
mother of other girl Chekpawee have much sickness. She
might to die. Too much extra work she do. She no need keep
in school so long. She is I8 years. Supt. Davis is no
permit her come home. I will to write President Hoover. I
want my grand daughter home. She is not prisoner. Lots of
girls come home. If Davis wise man or care for children why
him no help? He is no wise gentle man. I find lawyer. I
pray you help. Will close now. You help us. Why not you
send doctor to look at Chekpawee? Supt. Davis is not
doctor. I hope hear from you soon.

Turtle Woman

Mrs. Turtle Woman
Cardiff Store, Box I5, Sisseton, So. Dak.

DOWNWIND

SPRING 1931

IN THE COOL thick of night, as migrating birds babbled across the face of the moon, Vera met up with her chums in the grassy field beyond the fence along Lover's Lane.

This patch of pasture, downwind from the main campus buildings and sheltered by a windbreak, was their open-air speakeasy. Their gig? Jazz. Their audience? Sleepy cows. Tonight, they'd even filched half a bottle of booze.

Solomon was a beast on double bass. Paul, legit on trombone. Annie mostly faked it on flute. Vine laid down the beat on field rocks. A snare drum would be too noisy. A bass drum, too tribal. Should their crazy combo ever be caught, their unsupervised use of a bass drum would cause extra consternation.

During a breather, Vine parched field corn for them in a dust pan over red-hot coals. Vera liked him for that. And she liked his swagger. He could cuss a blue streak better than a white man.

The boy could shake a leg too. Sometimes when she'd sneak off to the dairy barn to listen to the radio—Duke Ellington, Mamie Smith, Louis Armstrong—Vine would already be there, almost like he'd been waiting for her. He'd coax her to dance until she caved. She wasn't a dancer, but he knew how to win her over. Make her laugh.

"You're so serious, girl," he'd say, her head falling against his shoulder during a slow one. "Brain's so heavy you can't hold it up."

He was right. She was always thinking. She couldn't seem to stop. Even now, here in the pasture, she was distracted, her playing full of clams and clinkers.

In a few months, she'd graduate—a milestone that many students at Genoa never even aspired to, let alone reached. She was among the seniors who had already carved their names and graduation year on a beam in the dairy barn. VERA WHITEMAN 1931. Other such inscriptions dated from way back, into the 1880s.

So much lay behind her. But what might lie ahead?

Girls who graduated from Genoa were meant to become housewives to the men on their home reservations—like Helen Washington. Or servants in the homes of white folks—like Milly. Or employees of the Indian Service—like Florence Davis, before she'd married the superintendent.

The prospect of going back to the reservation distressed Vera. Memories of her life there—of herself as Chekpawee—were like frayed knots. Faded. Complicated. Fragile.

Besides, who was left to receive her?

Chekpa had been run over by a train.

Her father and grandparents had died of influenza. Truth was, they'd been practically dead to her even before the superintendent had informed her—well after the fact—of their demise. Never once had they sent her any mail. Never once had they tried to gain her release. Never once had they paid her fare home in the summer. Never once had they made their way to Nebraska to visit her.

Had she never mattered to them at all?

No, she couldn't picture a happy return to the Sisseton Agency.

Maybe she could hatch a life for herself in white society. As Vera Whiteman, she dressed white. She read and wrote white. She talked white. She cooked and sewed white. She prayed white. She even dreamed white. And she played white music on a white man's instrument, except when she sinned by playing jazz.

In short, she could very well live white—as Genoa had been training her to do every day for thirteen years.

But she also knew, as Genoa kept insisting, that she could never *be* white. Only *near* white, like her skin.

Vine's drumsticks were wild on the rocks.

She wanted him dancing against her. Kissing her silly. Making her forget what hadn't happened yet.

She blew louder. Her fingers flew.

They were totally crushing it now.

Her troubles melded with the jazz. She felt as if she were guzzling life from some bottomless ancient sea and blowing it out into an unbreakable bubble—a transparent second skin, in which she could safely float. Resting inside the music, she had a chance in this world.

Long ago, to save herself, she'd stopped talking.
Then she'd learned to save herself, singing with her stick.
But not even this clarinet was hers.

PROBATION

SPRING 1931

FROM VERA'S VANTAGE POINT, Superintendent Davis was almost indistinguishable, lounging behind his ornate desk. The shade of the window behind him was lowered to the precise position where she was blinded by the sun's glare. This was likely on purpose. Mr. Davis did nothing slapdash. He was a shrewd, calculating man, always seeking an advantage.

Next to her, Mr. Mumblehead had skewed his chair to one side to save his eyes. His stony face, with its fine trace of moustache, offered no clue as to why she might have been summoned. Superintendent Davis never called a student into his office for a casual chat.

Nearly a decade had passed since Mr. Mumblehead had succeeded Mr. Wheelock. During his tenure, the music program had steadily declined in quality, even while Vera, as a performer, had ascended in status and reputation. She was Genoa's "red prize." Costumed in chic dresses bestowed by Mrs. Davis, she was regularly paraded with her clarinet before philanthropists, preachers, and politicians—especially, it seemed to her, when the school was either underfunded or under investigation. In other words, almost always.

So what had she done to warrant this summons on the brink of graduation? Which of her furtive transgressions might the superintendent have uncovered?

Turtle was knotted in a stocking and nested between a rafter and a ceiling joist, high up in the dairy barn. She doubted that any student, let alone a member of the school staff, could have chanced upon it, hidden so long in such a spot. Even if someone had found it, Turtle couldn't have been traced to her.

She glanced out the corner of her eye at Mr. Mumblehead.

It must be the jazz. Someone has ratted us out.

"You may remember Mr. Wheelock," Superintendent Davis said from across his desk.

Still blinded by sunlight, she heard him touch off one of his fat cigars with his fancy gold lighter.

"Yes, sir." She was so rattled by her predicament that those two syllables were almost too many.

"Quite the wandering type, that Indian was," he said.

She thought of her name, whittled into the beam with her graduation year.

You jinxed it, she scolded herself now. *You should have waited.*

The superintendent was drumming his pudgy fingers on the desk blotter. That much of him—his fingers—she could see.

"It seems that Mr. Wheelock remembers you too. Quite so."

In a minute, Mr. Davis would be reaching for his damn peanuts.

"We find ourselves at the juncture of remarkable events," he said. "Mr. Mumblehead, will you explain?"

The bandmaster shifted slightly toward Vera. He didn't look her straight in the eye. He was still very Cherokee in that respect.

"Since leaving Genoa," he said, "Mr. Wheelock has written me, on occasion, to inquire after your progress. Of course, my reports have been flattering."

Vera's posture softened. She couldn't help but smile. Mr. Wheelock, traveling the world with his band, had bothered to ask after her. More than once. And he'd met with glowing praise of her.

She wasn't in a jam at all. To the contrary. She was in a sweet spot.

Mr. Mumblehead brought a black leather clarinet case from beneath his seat. HENRI SELMER, PARIS was stamped on it in gold letters.

Her heart leapt in recognition.

"To congratulate you upon your graduation," Mr. Mumblehead said, "Mr. Wheelock wishes to make you a gift of his clarinet."

Vera hugged the clarinet case to her chest. Mr. Wheelock had been at Genoa for a single school year. But that one year had saved her life. He'd helped her reclaim her voice and carve out a space to belong. He'd ignited in her an obsession for the clarinet that had been nearly matched by her natural ability. He'd been her truest—at the time, *only*—friend.

He didn't forget me.

She heard Superintendent Davis puffing. Blue smoke rolled toward the ceiling.

"I assure you," he said, "this gift will be ballyhooed in the next issue of *The Indian News*. Quite so. But that's not the end of the story. We're not yet finished."

Curious, she fidgeted in her chair until she could finally see the superintendent better against the sun. Squinting, she watched him remove a document from an envelope and flatten its folds.

"Mr. Mumblehead—with my full blessing, of course—has engineered a generous arrangement with Mr. Wheelock whereby you might continue your musical studies at the University of Nebraska. We've just received confirmation from the School of Music. Needless to say, you will accept?"

Vera's mind went giddy. Her body flushed hot.

The superintendent's hand disappeared into his pocket.

"Speak up, girl!" he said loudly, leaning across his desk, the top of his head eclipsing the sun. He wasn't a patient man.

"I'm happy to accept," she said.

"I should hope so."

The superintendent relaxed back in his chair. Cigar between his teeth, he took to shelling peanuts.

"I must say, you've done well for yourself," he said. "We've watched you grow from a wild child too timid to talk into a lovely young woman without a trace of reservation accent. You could almost pass as a white girl. Quite so."

"Thank you, sir."

"You must know, Miss Whiteman, that it was never our intention to keep you here so long. Our only hope was to save you from disaster. Unlike most of our students, you weren't an undesirable pupil. We could see you had a chance at a real future. To have sent you home, at any point, would have been a bad wager, because no decent soul was there to support you."

"I understand, sir. Thank you, sir."

She spoke mindlessly, from habit, stunned as she was by her good fortune. All at once, she could conceive a real future for herself—not as a misfit but as a woman fully capable of fashioning her own life.

My dear teacher. Bless you.

The superintendent was neatly banking raw peanuts on his desk beside a growing pile of shells. "You should be aware that, despite your superior musical talent, to which both Mr. Wheelock and Mr. Mumblehead attested in their letters of recommendation, the university has questioned your academic qualifications. This is to be expected of an Indian student. The School of Music has therefore admitted you on probation. You will have to prove yourself."

"Yes, sir. I will."

The sun had moved. Now she didn't have to squirm at all to see the superintendent and his yellow paisley necktie. Yellow was a ghastly color on him.

He tipped so far back in his office chair that it creaked a complaint. For a long awkward moment, his eyes raked over her. She should have been used to it by now, but she still clutched the clarinet case tighter against her breasts, blood rushing to her cheeks.

The superintendent coughed his throat clear. "I must warn you, Miss Whiteman: these are unusual circumstances. You will be the only Indian attending the School of Music—perhaps even the entire university. Surviving its rigors will require every civilized skill we have striven to instill in you. Everything you do, every word you say, will reflect upon this school. Do not disappoint!"

IV

MAKING HERSELF UP

APRIL 9, 1945

VERA STEPPED out the door of the farmhouse with Karl and Simon. Tightlipped, she settled the strap of her white leather purse in the crook of her arm. She'd dressed in her Easter best, but she'd wait to put on her happy-daughter-in-law face. At the moment, appearances didn't matter one whit, cloaked in fog so dense that the sun couldn't pull it up.

She lifted a white-gloved hand. Could barely see it in the thick haze.

The fog had kept them from driving to church this morning. But it wouldn't keep them from dinner with Karl's parents at the Big House, a quarter mile away. Easter dinner was on the family's interminable list of command performances.

Already this week, on Maundy Thursday, a houseful of relatives had gathered for Mutti's green soup. On Good Friday, for her bockwurst, sauerkraut, and green cabbage. Today, *Ostersonntag,* it would be diced lamb with onions, green beans, and potatoes.

Vera could picture the scene: Mutti would once again have laid an extra-long table with starched white linens, china, and silver. At the center would be a bouquet of pussy willows and budding tree branches, all decorated with hand-painted eggshells, bits of ribbon, and tiny birds' nests.

Try to have a good time—that's what Karl had advised her to do. And she was a good pretender. She could act well enough to fool them all. By now, she could even fool herself.

Ahead of her on the road, Karl was a ghost, leading the way. She listened for the crunch of his dress shoes on gravel. Now and then, she glimpsed the back of his leg, his camera case, the picnic hamper.

"We almost there yet?" Simon said.

She tightened her grasp on her boy's hand, steering him away from the invisible ditch. For weeks, she'd been trying to patch things up with him. As if he'd never set the fire in the barn. As if she'd never beaten him in the kitchen.

They walked through the fog with no sense of where they were or how far they'd gone. Finally Karl bumped up against the mailbox mounted on its post in front of the Big House.

"Damn," he said.

Oriented now, they turned into his parents' short driveway. Any other Easter Sunday, it would have been a parking lot of vehicles belonging to Richter relatives. But today, only a red Chevy truck materialized in the murk.

"Uncle Pete!" Simon yelled in delight, recognizing the truck.

To Vera's surprise, the door of the Chevy swung open.

"Hey, Simple Simon!" Pete slid out from behind the wheel and flicked away a cigarette. "How's my favorite nephew?"

"Your *only* nephew!" Simon giggled.

"Happy Easter, Pete," Vera said, smoothing her hands down her light-pink dress.

"Don't you look pretty, even fogged up," he said.

He nudged her pink straw hat to a jaunty angle. She'd trimmed it with ribbons and flowers, for show.

"Nice bonnet!" he said.

Karl pumped his brother's hand. "You drove out from town in this soup?"

"Quick as a pig in mud." Pete rumpled Simon's hair, then gave him a dutch rub with his knuckles. "You do what you got to do, for family, right?"

AFTER THE FEAST, Vera helped Mutti clear the meal and wash the dishes. Cleanup didn't take long; only six people had eaten. The festive table had looked forlorn.

When Vera joined the men in the parlor, Vati was already snoring in his chair, one hand cupping the bowl of his pipe. She settled beside Karl on the loveseat. He and Pete were smoking cigarettes and drinking Storz, talking the war.

A couple of weeks earlier, the Allies had battled across the "uncrossable" Rhine River, a massive operation that had rivaled D-Day in scale. Allied troops were now thrusting into the heart of Germany, crushing all resistance, even as Russian forces advanced on Berlin from the east.

"What's a rhyme river?" her boy asked, riding horsey on Pete's knee.

"Not *rhyme*," Karl said, correcting him. "*Rhine*."

"Runs between France and Germany," Pete said.

Vera saw her boy's perplexity. In his short memory, America and Germany had always been at war. But he couldn't wrap his head around it. She could all but hear the haggling in his head.

Where are their armies, exactly? And why don't they like each other?

His grandparents had come over on the boat. They read German newspapers. They ate *Schnitzel, Sauerbraten,* and *Apfelstrudel.* They drank *Kaffee* and *Bier.* They celebrated *Ostern* "like good Germans." *Oktoberfest* and *Weihnachten* too.

Can people who speak German be true Americans?

A gang of Germans, on loan from the nearest POW camp, routinely labored in Vati's fields. They helped raise Vati's potatoes, his grains, his Great Northern beans, as their lone guard played solitaire beneath a tree.

Vati would read to the POWs from the *Lincoln Freie Presse,* loud as Pastor Hoff. He'd pepper them with questions about the *Vaterland,* pipe hanging from his lips.

Mutti, meanwhile, would whip up German dishes to supplement the prisoners' meager rations of apples and hard-boiled eggs. Once, she baked a *Kuchen* for a prisoner's birthday, and the man broke down and cried.

All this . . . yet Simon's dear uncle Pete worked on the assembly line at the Cushman plant in Lincoln, manufacturing scooters so more Americans could kill more Germans.

Which side's our family on?

We live in America.

Americans are the good guys. Right?

That makes the Germans the bad guys.

But . . . I'm both!

Vera sensed that her boy didn't like being both. He wanted to live in a box with clearly defined edges.

But life wasn't so simple. Especially for someone of mixed blood. *Tainted* blood, some would say.

"The other day," Pete was telling them now, "I was on my way to work, and some hooligans were throwing stones at three little kids, last name of Heinz. Calling them Nazis. Ran off when I pulled up to the curb."

"This is what I am always afraid of," Mutti said, tottering in from the kitchen on her cane.

She slapped Vati on the knee as she passed his chair. He woke with a snort.

"What is it you're afraid of, Mutti?" Vera asked, though she could feel the conversation sliding sidewise. In this house, the subject of the war was ever a minefield.

"Our being taken for Nazis. Traitors. Just because we love where we came from." Mutti flumped her well-padded frame into her upholstered rocker. She propped her cane nearby. "Can we not love Germany and also this country? Can we not braid all our loyalties together, as in a loaf of *Osterbrot?*"

Karl was mounting the flash on his new Kodak. "Hitler's made loving Germany impossible, Mutti."

"*Quatsch!*" Vati said, rallying his drowsy voice. "The *Führer* is a friend of Germans everywhere. I wish I were younger! I would have gone back home to fight!"

Here we go, Vera thought.

Vati touched off a match and circled the flame over the chamber of his pipe, puffing to char the tobacco. "In the *Vaterland,* I could speak my mind, in my own tongue, to people who live and believe as I do—"

"Enough, Franz!" Mutti chided. "It is a poor bird that dirties its own nest."

Too late, Vera thought.

Karl aimed the Kodak at his father. "You'd actually have gone back to Germany to enlist?"

"*Natürlich,*" Vati scoffed. "Why would I not? The *Führer* has restored us to glory after the tragedy of the Great War!"

He leveled his pipe at the camera like a pistol.

Click went the shutter. *Pop* went the bulb.

Vera folded her arms in an angry sulk.

"A pretty short-lived glory, I'd say," Karl replied, soberly. "Won't be long now till Hitler goes down, and Germany with him!"

"Vati," Vera said, picking her words the same way she selected produce at the market, inspecting for bad spots, "I just don't get . . . how you can approve . . . of the unspeakable things . . . Hitler has done . . . to Jews, especially. We probably don't even know the worst of it!"

"Exaggerations!" Vati said with a dismissive wave of his pipe. "Lies spread by Franklin 'Rosenfeld' and the Jew-loving press."

"Ignore him," Mutti said to Vera. "He is an old man wishing for the return of spring."

Vera turned her head and looked helplessly at Karl. His eyes were just like his mother's, pleading with Vera to lay off.

The Black Forest clock on the wall chimed the hour. Vera wanted to hurl a throw pillow at the noisy cuckoo.

Vati fished his watch from his vest. "What time?" he said, as if the clock's commotion hadn't been enough to tell him.

"Not today, Franz!" Mutti scowled, obviously onto what he was thinking. "It's *Ostersonntag*!"

"*Ja, und*? We can all listen together!" Vati flung a finger at the radio cabinet. "Boy," he said to Simon, "tune that thing into Midge."

"Franz!" Mutti complained again.

"Stop him!" Vera implored Karl in a whisper, but Karl shrugged in resignation.

"You know how the boy loves the music!" Vati said.

Simon twiddled the radio dial. The golden needle landed on the "Home Sweet Home" broadcast just as its signature train whistle wailed in the distance, plaintive and homesick, to open the show.

"Good afternoon, women of America—and Happy Easter," said Midge's sultry voice through the cloth-covered speaker. "This is Berlin calling all you mothers, wives, and sweethearts! And when Berlin calls, it pays to listen, because this American girl sitting at the microphone has a few words of truth for her countrywomen back home."

"Louder!" Vati said.

Simon cranked up the volume.

"Girls," Midge said, "we're in a serious situation. Why am I still here in Berlin? The reason is this: I was brought up a one hundred percent American girl, conscious of her enemies. And our enemies are precisely those people who are fighting against Germany. A defeat for Germany would also mean a defeat for America and her civilization. That's why I'm staying here and having these little heart-to-heart talks with you. I'm only afraid it might be too late."

Can't be too soon, Vera thought.

Karl focused the Kodak on Mutti.

She screened her face with her hands. The ornate rings on her gnarled fingers caught the light.

"Point that thing at someone else!" she declared.

"But Mother, you look beautiful," Karl teased. "You know you do!"

Click. Pop.

"Especially now, at Easter time," Vera heard Midge saying in her honey radio-voice, "I can imagine how you're missing the man you love, worrying what has happened to him. Just imagine: you could be sitting with him on the porch in a sweet wicker rocking chair, listening to the birds. Instead, he's over here in Europe, far from home. And for

what? For Roosevelt and Churchill and their Jewish gangsters! Oh, girls
—why don't you wake up, for the sake of your men?"

Beside Vera on the loveseat, Karl leaned into her shoulder, silently
warning her against getting up and walking out of the room.

"*Der Jude,*" Vati declared, "*ist für das Land so nützlich wie eine Mause
für die Tenne.*"

Vera waited for someone to translate Vati's spate of German.
Somebody always did.

But not this time. Karl tinkered with his camera. Pete took a drag
on his Camel. Mutti rocked in her chair, back and forth, back and
forth.

Vera lost patience. "What did your father say?" she asked Karl in a
strained voice.

Vati spilled pipe smoke from his mouth. "I *said, meine Liebe,* 'The Jew
is as much use to the country as a mouse to the threshing floor.' "

"Girls, let's take a break," Midge suggested over the airwaves, as if
tuned into the tension in the Richters' parlor. "How about we listen to
the Merry Macs play some Glenn Miller? Are you ready for a
'Sentimental Journey'?"

A tinkling piano introduced the jazz ballad, with soft brushes on the
drums and a plunking bass. The music was obviously canned.

The brass was entering when Mutti said to Vera, "I realize the *Führer*
often says vile things—"

"*Says* things?" Vera said. "What about the things he *does*?"

"Shhh!" Simon said. "I want to hear the music!"

"But Adolph Hitler is not Germany," Mutti pressed on, "just as
Franklin Roosevelt is not America."

Pete sprang from his chair. "Hey, Vera, how about a dance? If my
brother will let me, that is." A wink at Karl.

"She's all yours!" Karl said.

Pete and his harebrained ideas.

Vera didn't want to dance. Especially not to canned music broadcast
from Nazi Germany. Certainly not in front of Vati and Mutti, who might
misinterpret any sign of pleasure.

But Pete obviously didn't care what Vera wanted. He pulled her up
from the loveseat and spun her into his arms. He held her in a slow
sway near the radio, humming out of tune to the sumptuous arrangement of the song.

"Why don't the Merry Macs ever play live anymore?" Simon griped.

"If they're smart," Karl said, eyeing the dancing pair through his
viewfinder, "they're on the run."

"But *Midge* is still on the air!" Simon said. "And she's a *woman*!"

The syrupy music had Vati nodding off again. Even Mutti's eyelids were drooping.

Vera turned slow, self-conscious circles with Pete. Karl wasn't a dancer. At their very first encounter, he'd made it clear that his love for music didn't extend to his feet.

Tommy Dorsey's in town with his orchestra at the Pla Mor Ballroom, along the railroad tracks on West O Street. On the margins of the crowded dance floor, Vera bumps into a stocky white man with heavily dimpled cheeks. In his dapper striped vest and trousers, he looks like a college guy, but his rolled-up shirt sleeves reveal chiseled arms with a farmer's tan.

Both of them are reluctant to dance. They hold back, making small talk about the orchestra's smooth ballads and the ballroom's magnificent chandeliers.

He's an Ag student at the university. About to drop out. Whatever he hasn't already learned about farming from his folks he figures he can teach himself.

"No disgrace in quitting," he says, bending into her ear to be heard. "Nobody in my family's ever gone to college. They don't see the point."

"Same for me," she says.

"I'll bet you're not studying Ag," he jokes.

A bashful smile. "Music."

"Cool!" he shouts over the band. "What kind?" Genuine interest in his face.

"All kinds! But I like jazz best."

No doubt he thinks she's white, just as her professors and fellow students do. She doesn't mean to deceive anyone. But on the advice of the dean of the School of Music, she allows everyone the right to their assumptions.

And why shouldn't they assume that she's white like them? The only place around here that she ever sees an Indian is in her own mirror—where she's become quite practiced at not really looking, except to make herself up.

"You sing?" the white guy says.

She rolls her eyes. "Like a woodpecker. At least till I pick up my stick."

"Your stick?"

"My clarinet."

"Name's Karl," he says with a grin. "Maybe you'll play for me sometime?"

Suddenly, Pete's hand in the small of her back felt as hot as a crimping iron. Just as the song ended, she twisted free of him with such force that she smacked against the radio console. A couple of potted plants skated toward the cabinet's edge. She lunged to save them from tipping over. Vati and Mutti stirred awake at the racket.

Pete reclaimed his chair opposite the loveseat. Ground out the stub of his Camel in an ashtray. Lit another.

"Shirley Smith," Midge said, picking up again after the Glenn Miller piece, "if you're listening tonight in Syracuse, New York, I want to tell you that I recently visited your husband, Ted, in a fine German hospital. He's had the most ideal treatment there, almost as if he were German himself."

The most ideal treatment. Almost as if . . .

Vera, leaning over the top of the radio, studied her indistinct face in the polished walnut.

It's a year after Tommy Dorsey. Karl's down on one knee, promising to save up for a ring.

"Don't know who I've fallen for, exactly," he says in a tease. "You or that clarinet of yours."

"You'd better get up from there and sit yourself down," she says to him, dead serious. "There's something I need to tell you."

"Your husband," Midge purred on through the radio, "showed me a little picture of your baby boy, Ernest. If you could have seen Ted's face, you would have cried! How you must be missing Ted! And he's missing you too! He's carrying you around in his pocket, right over his heart."

Vera imagined Karl soldiering in Europe, carrying a picture of her and Simon over his heart . . . maybe one of the photographs he'd taken that windy day in the yard, right after the fire in the barn.

Photographs full of lies.

"Ted has made a great, great sacrifice," Midge said. "And Shirley, so have you. So, be awfully swell to him when he gets home, even if he's not in one piece."

"Midge is a blabbermouth," Simon groused. "May I go outside and play?"

"Quiet, boy!" Vati said.

"One point I pride myself on," Midge went on, her words sticky as taffy, "is telling you girls the truth. And here it is: the lives of the men you love are being sacrificed for *nothing!*"

"*Please,* Mama, may I go outside?" Simon whined.

"Okay," Vera murmured, wishing that she could go with him.

"All you wives and mothers, you're on the wrong side of the fence,"

Midge said. "You might think America's winning this war, but Germany will *never* go down—"

"*Ja!*" Vati said, thrusting his dead pipe into the air, startling Mutti in her rocker.

Now that she has confessed the truth to Karl, Vera searches his eyes for any hint of trouble. He's searching her eyes, too, but for what?

"Look, honey," he says at last. "You know I don't care none what you are or where you came from. But what you just told me . . . we can't be telling nobody else. If my folks had their way, I'd marry a nice German girl from church. They ever find out what you really are, we'll be toast. You got to play white, good as you play that clarinet of yours—and you can't never stop!"

Over the ensuing weeks, Karl selects passages from Emily Post's Etiquette *for Vera to master, grooming her to fool his parents.*

Fundamentals of good behavior.

Conventions of courtesy.

Basics of hygiene and dress.

The proprieties of christenings and funerals.

Tips for keeping "a gem of a house."

She doesn't point out that she'd needed no help from Emily Post to fool Karl himself. She'd learned most of these lessons in boarding school. But she reviews the old and memorizes the new, rehearsing her role, anxious to earn a standing ovation for a performance that must never end. Karl directs her every move, though she doubts any man could ever be an expert in such womanly matters.

And no white man could ever be an expert in concealing an Indian's identity.

"This is Midge, signing off. I've got a heavy date, but I'll keep my man waiting long enough to sing that song you just love to hear me sing . . ."

Midge began to croon "Lili Marlene," the gooey German love song that closed her broadcasts.

"All these troubles will pass," Pete said, over her singing.

"When?" Vera said testily. "After every Jew has been rounded up and done away with?"

That's when she noticed a pale fingertip on the foggy windowpane. Simon, out on the porch, was drawing stick figures in the condensation. Planes dropping bombs. Soldiers shooting. Cows and children flattened. Images no boy his age should know how to draw.

"Do not dirty my windows!" Mutti scolded Simon through the glass, shaking a crooked finger.

The Black Forest clock ticked, tocked, ticked.

Through six years of marriage, Vera had been swimming in a sea of constant anxiety, no land in sight. Struggling not to go under. Sacrificing herself simply to stay afloat.

One slipup, and she would betray herself and bring those she loved most to ruin.

Now, amid heaving waves, she saw what she'd never allowed herself to see: sooner or later, the hungry waters would devour her, as surely as the Nazis were devouring the Jews.

And somehow the sea would swallow her boy along with her.

A storm was bearing down. Her own winds were whipping it up, even as she bade them *Be still*.

DON'T YOU WORRY
SEVEN MINUTES LATER

VERA PROWLED the side yard of the Big House.

"Simon!" she yelled through the muffling fog.

No reply from her boy. *Where could he be?*

She gathered her wind to yell louder. "*Si*-mon! Come to Mama! Right *now!*"

Ever since that blanket had fallen over the cage in the white man's wagon, she'd been living in shadows and haze, nothing to trust but her instincts.

Now, at last, she had vision.

"*Simon!* Where *are* you?"

What had she said, exactly, to the Richters in the parlor just moments ago?

Already, she couldn't remember. She didn't need to. The actual words she'd spoken mattered less than the fact that they'd broken free.

Here he was, finally—her Chasker, a phantom emerging from the direction of the walnut grove.

"We're leaving," she said, holding out his jacket.

"But I want to play soldier!"

"When we get home!" Wrestling his arms into sleeves.

"But Mama, we haven't had Grandma's *Kuchen* yet! Or lit the bonfire on the hill!"

She seized his hand. She marched him toward the road she couldn't see.

"What about Pop? Isn't he coming too?"

She remembered how Karl's square face had drained of color. Then how his cheeks had gone blotchy red.

That look in his eyes—like love mixed with hate.

"Don't you worry about your father. He can find his own way home."

TOO GODDAMN GOOD

FIVE HOURS LATER

THEIR CHAIRS CREAKED at the table, set for three. Their spoons clinked in their blue bowls.

Vera guarded her tongue. She knew her boy was miffed: No *Kuchen*. No bonfire. No Pop.

Just leftover cabbage and potato soup.

"Yuck," he said after an unhappy slurp. "Worse than succotash."

This afternoon at the Big House had been the perfect strain of conditions. All that vile talk of Hitler and the war. Of Germans and Jews. Of what was and wasn't "American." Of what a child was born to be—or should be made to become. Of German American children, like her own boy, being sent to Nazi summer camps, dressed in Nazi uniforms, taught to salute the Nazi flag, and marched around like young soldiers of the Reich.

The strain had split open the husk of her, and she'd spilled the truth like so much "bayou voodoo." She'd completely forgotten herself. By the time the procession of sound had finished with her lips, her spirit had been in an altogether different place.

The next move on the board was up to the Richters.

Vera scowled again at Karl's empty chair. He must have come home for the late-afternoon milking. Even in the middle of a family crisis, cows still need to be milked. But he hadn't stepped foot in the house. Not even to change clothes.

By now, he was surely back at the Big House.

She plonked her spoon down in her half-eaten soup.

"You know what we need?" she said to Simon.

"Music?" he said, brightening with sudden hope.

She leapt up from the table. "You finish eating, then meet me in the barn. I'll be out, soon as I take off my stockings!"

In the bathroom, she unclipped her artificial silk stockings from her garter belt. They were old, but they were her best, and they had to last. With the war, real silk was hard to come by. Nylon too.

She draped the sheer stockings over the sink. She'd hand-wash them later.

Most every evening, in mild weather, she'd play jazz for the cows. "Hello, my lovelies," she'd say, heading out to the pasture with her singing stick.

That was all it took.

They'd hurry after her, if cows could ever be said to hurry. Even the sleepy ones would get up from the trampled grass and lumber over to the oak that looked as old as the Tree of Life.

She'd seat herself on its exposed roots, and the cows would crowd around her in quiet, expectant rows. She'd woo them with standards like "Stardust," "Memories of You," "The Man I Love," "More Than You Know."

While she played, they'd sniff at her clarinet and snuffle around her feet. They'd watch her with moony jet-black eyes, chewing their cud. When at last she'd end her open-air concert, they'd moo for more.

The cows liked her music even more than Karl did, and he was always after her to play hymns at church with Mrs. Hoffman, the spidery widow whose face turned beet red as her tiny feet pumped the bellows of the organ. The cows liked her music even more than Pete did, and he'd once told her, "Forget church, Vera. You're too goddamn good for God. You should be on the radio!"

But not even the cows liked her music as much as her boy did.

TONIGHT, in the chill and oppression of the fog, Vera didn't go to the pasture. She headed for the red barn door painted with a big white X.

The wet country air was as still as a grave. No metal screech from the windmill. No breeze stirring the limbs of the trees or the shoots of the wild grasses. The birds, too, were silent.

She opened the door to the wafting of slow music—the radio always on, to soothe the cows. The only other sounds were meows from barn cats and snuffles from the horse in his stall.

"Beat 'cha!" her boy squealed, jumping out of the dark.

"You little rascal!" she said with a halfhearted laugh.

She switched off the radio and switched on some lights.

Beyond the fence, lounging cows pushed themselves up from the straw and ambled over. They didn't care what had happened this afternoon at the Big House. They didn't care about secrets. They didn't care about blood.

Simon raced off in pursuit of Possum, the orange-and-black calico. The cat who didn't trust people.

Her boy wasn't one to sit still. He preferred to roam rather than fidget among the cows. But she knew he was always listening to her music, wherever he went in the barn.

PINK HAT

TWENTY-FIVE MINUTES LATER

VERA WAS in the middle of "Somewhere Over the Rainbow"—where "the dreams that you dare to dream really do come true"—when Pete startled her from behind.

"Pretty as ever," he said in the dimly lit bay of the barn.

She broke off her music with a flinch, slicing her lower lip on the clarinet's reed. She pressed her tongue into the sting.

"Scared you, didn't I," he said.

"I didn't hear you drive up," she said, feigning nonchalance. "You headed home to town?"

"What? In this soup?" He produced her pink hat and white purse from behind his back. "You forgot these." He set the hat on her head.

She snatched away the purse, then shed the hat, in no mood to wear it. "Karl with you?"

"Nope."

She looped the handle of her purse over a fence post, then topped the post with her hat. "You expect he'll be coming home any time soon?"

"How the hell would I know?"

Pete leaned against the fence rail, right next to her, musky and smelling of Storz. *All these troubles will pass,* he'd said this afternoon, with respect to the war. He'd had no idea that troubles of another sort were about to tumble in from closer shores.

But now he knew everything. Mutti and Vati too. And these troubles wouldn't pass before muddling up the Richters' carefully laid-out lives.

Up in the rafters, a nest of owl chicks was screeching for food.

"The boy around?" Pete said.

"Chasker?"

An awful slip. She only ever called her boy by his middle name in private.

"What the hell kind of cockeyed name is that, anyhow?" Pete said.

Not even Karl knew that she'd hatched the name Chasker from Chaskay—"firstborn son," among her people. She most certainly wasn't going to share that tidbit of information with Pete.

"I haven't seen Simon in a while," she said, switching names to throw Pete off, but she knew that her boy had to be in the barn. He always stayed until her very last note. "Why you want to know?"

Pete straightened and turned square. "You and me's got us some talking to do that's not meant for his ears."

He plucked her straw hat off the fence post.

"Where's my favorite nephew?" he bellowed to the barn. "You around, Simple Simon? Give me a holler!"

The barn didn't answer. Vera felt relief. She felt worry.

Pete spun her hat aside. "Guess we're alone, you and me."

Get out, said a long-dormant voice in her spirit.

Vera sidled away from the fence. "I suppose Karl had his supper with you all at the Big House?"

"Supper? You think anybody's hungry after that bomb you dropped?"

She struck out for the door.

Pete scooted around, in front of her. "Hey, baby—where you rushing off to?"

"Don't 'Hey, baby' me!" She skirted around the tractor, putting more space between them.

"But we had ourselves such a nice dance after dinner! Let's have another go!"

She tripped over a grain bucket. Wind-milled. Pitched forward onto the barn floor. Landed on top of her clarinet, facedown in dusty oil stains.

Pete loomed above her. "You okay?"

She rolled over into a sitting position, her wind knocked out. She rearranged her dirty pink dress, pulling it down to midcalf. Blood trickled warm from one nostril. She wiped it away.

Against the glow of a light bulb, Pete offered a hand to help her up. She let it hang.

This wasn't the Pete she knew.

The Pete she knew was the handsome charmer. The elder Richter son, christened Simon Peter after the friend of Jesus. The fun-loving, affable fellow in whose honor she and Karl had named their firstborn.

This Pete with his hand out was a predator. Just like Mr. Silas, back at Genoa.

She gave her clarinet a slow inspection from mouthpiece to bell. Other than a chipped reed, nothing seemed bent or broken.

His hand stayed put. She had no choice but to take it.

"Thank you," she mumbled as he pulled her up.

Once she was on her feet, he didn't let go. She didn't like that one bit.

"How about we go inside?" she said, forcing her voice down, low and cool. "I'll make us some coffee. We'll wait for Karl."

He jerked her into his chest. "Don't want your damn coffee!"

Her face met the moist heat of his liquored breath. The clarinet, wedged between their bodies, jabbed her in the ribs.

"How'd you learn English so good?" More like a taunt than a question.

"School. Same as you." Trying to wrench free.

"You don't sound Indian," he said.

"You don't sound like a Kraut."

He lifted a strand of hair shaken loose from her bun. Gave it a tug. Let it fall.

"Don't touch me!" she hissed, finally wriggling out of his grip.

She retreated a step, glaring at him, heat mounting in her cheeks. "Everybody's passing as something, Pete—pretending to be somebody they're not, hoping to get by. Trying to *survive*, even. Maybe that's all anybody is—a collection of masks, till one day, maybe, the truth spills out."

She opened her arms wide, like Christ on a cross.

"Well, take a good look at me, Pete! This is who I am! And I've got as much right to be me as you've got to be you!"

His eyes twitched.

"What are *you* passing as, Pete?" she goaded, ignoring the hint of cruelty playing around his lips. "What piece of *you* are you holding back?"

He angled in, eyeing her mouth. "Who do you think you are? How dare you mingle outside your kind—and *marry*?"

"Karl and I love each other!"

"That so? Then why isn't he here with you instead of at the Big House?"

For this, she had no good response. "He just . . . needs time," she decided. "To make you understand."

306

Pete hawked and spat.

"What's your real name?" he said then. "Damn sure isn't Vera."

Suddenly she was a little girl again, arriving at the train platform in Genoa. The little girl who, for most of two years, refused to say a word, so as not to give up her power. The little girl who, even after recovering her voice, didn't utter her birth name to a living soul. Not even to Mr. Wheelock.

"Pocohantas?" Pete said with a sneer.

It is time, the voice in her spirit said.

"My name," she said with eerie composure, looking past Pete as if he weren't there, "is Chekpawee, daughter of Mahpiya Wakun Yuzawee and Wakinyan Se Mani of the Dakota people."

"You're nothing but a prairie nigger!"

Only weeks ago, she'd beaten her boy. She'd been stranded ever since in a desert of shame so immense that she still despaired of ever reaching the other side. But at this moment, she almost believed she could kill Pete Richter with no shame at all.

Yet the voice in her spirit said, *No.*

The voice in her spirit said, *Tame the righteous anger of your flesh.*

The voice said, *You cannot defeat this man with your bare hands.*

But you are Turtle, the voice said then, *and Turtle is strong.*

Vera thought of her red-beaded amulet, hidden in the coffee can, high in her kitchen cupboard.

Wake from the mud, the voice said. *Swim to the center.*

Vera withdrew into the shell of herself. She waited for the flood of her fury to subside.

It was then that an idea settled upon her, like a hymn in a minor key that resolves to a major, coming home on its final chord.

She saw a way to end this. Mr. Wheelock had shown her how.

"I have to leave this place," she said to Pete.

He thrust his hands onto his hips. "What do you mean, *leave*?"

"I tried to make Karl happy. I really did. But everything's wrecked now. Better if I just go."

He crossed his beefy arms. "Yeah, right."

She dusted her clarinet with the hem of her dress. "I could make it on my own," she said, not so much to Pete as to herself. "I could sign on with a band and work the clubs. Indian bands are playing gigs in dance halls all over this country. They're on the radio. Touring Europe, even—"

"You crack me up!"

"I'm good enough! You've said so yourself!"

"You'd actually trade in your boy for a band?"

She gawped at him like the Lord God had laid her out with a lightning bolt.

"*Trade* him?" she cried. "I'd take him *with* me! He's *mine!*"

"The hell you say! He's a *Richter!*" Pete's features contorted with contempt. "I won't let you ruin him!"

He started pacing in front of her, twisting her plan into a scheme of his own.

"You're gonna leave, yeah . . . But you're gonna leave the boy here with us. We'll say you ran off . . . took up with some lowlife. There'll be talk . . . But before long, it'll be yesterday's news."

He stopped, inches from her face, done with his ugly calculus.

"Nobody will ever know what you were. Not even the boy!"

She shuddered. "If I leave Chasker with you people . . . someday you'll all be looking at him the exact same way you're looking at me now."

This time, no slip of the tongue. Chasker was the finest thing she'd ever done in her life. From now on, she meant to call him whatever she damn well wanted to.

"You're a nobody," Pete said. He slipped a finger beneath the thin strap of her peachy-pink slip, her dress askew on her shoulder. "But one thing about nobodies—they have their uses."

He shoved her backward. She reeled into a wall, whacking her head.

For an instant, the barn went dizzy-black. Her insides went jiggly. Her hearing went wonky, as if she were buzzing inside a seashell.

She waggled her clarinet blindly at Pete.

For so long, she'd been under somebody's thumb. The matrons, the teachers, the disciplinarians, the superintendent, the dean of the School of Music, even the man she loved—they'd all impressed upon her the lie of a white life. The lie that, without whiteness, she *had* no life.

No more.

Pete blurred into focus.

IF ONLY HER clarinet had been as heavy as a baseball bat. If only she'd struck at the thinnest, weakest place in Pete's skull and had hit it square.

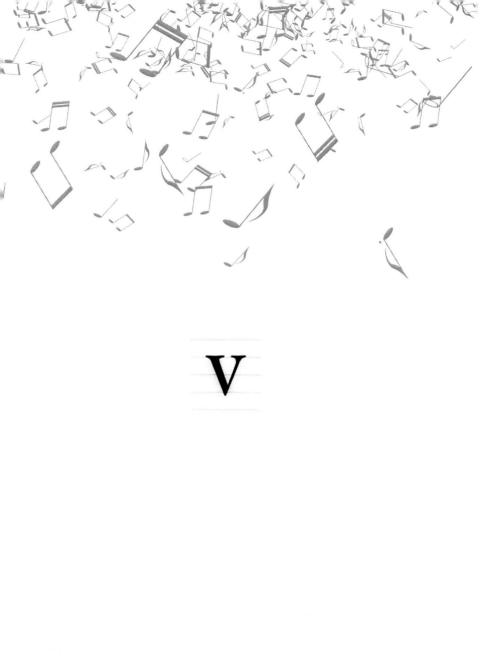

V

ON THE EDGE

SATURDAY, 0500H

FROM ACROSS THE KITCHEN, Victor watches Fiona stirring the batter for pancakes. Behind her glasses, her eyes are bleary and bloodshot. She looks like she hasn't slept in a hundred years, but the whisk in her hand is like an electric beater, propelling itself by long practice.

Mikey gently takes command of the whisk. Fiona moves to pour coffee into two thermoses.

"Volunteers will be mustering behind the bookstore around six," she says then. "They'll resume the search grid in town."

Under Mikey's eye, the cakes plump on the griddle. Victor retrieves sandwich fixings from the fridge to bag a couple of lunches.

"Sounds like they've got the town covered," he says to Mikey. "Maybe you and me should make for the country."

"You north," Mikey says, "and me south?"

"What about me?" Fiona screws the cap onto a red plaid thermos. "Where should I go?"

"Hold down the fort," Mikey says, "for when he comes home."

By 0530h, Victor and Mikey are defrosting their windshields, scraping ice, brushing snow. Victor will take the banged-up Jeep; Mikey, the van.

The predawn street is deserted, still waiting for a plow.

"Stay on the road," Victor hollers at Mikey through the blustering squall.

"Hang onto your turtle," Mikey hollers back, then slams his door shut.

The van groans past, fighting for traction, as Victor slides into the

Jeep. That's when he spots a vague figure inside the frosted-glass door of the next house. A woman, he guesses, by the slight build.

She gives him a you-might-not-want-to-see-me-but-I-know-you-do sort of wave.

"Shit," he says, his fingers itching on the keys in the ignition.

He climbs back out. Even the Jeep's door complains.

He plods up the woman's unshoveled driveway, past the white hulk of a buried car. As he hits the front sidewalk, or where he supposes the sidewalk to be, the woman steps from the house onto the drifted porch. She's dressed only in bathrobe and slippers.

"Need something?" he calls to her, not bothering to wade closer.

"You going out looking? For that poor man next door?"

"Yes, ma'am." Tightening the wrist straps on his gloves.

She hugs herself in the dark swirling snow. "I . . . hope you find him."

"Thanks."

When she doesn't say more, he starts back toward the Jeep.

"Mister, wait—"

He turns halfway around. The woman creeps to the edge of the stoop, curling even further into herself.

"Would you . . . I mean . . ."

She's talking like his mom, who, in her eighties, has trouble thinking of the words for what she wants to say.

"Could I ask you to look for . . ." The woman lifts the collar of her bathrobe higher on her neck. "I've lost her."

He almost can't hear her in the wind. "Lost who?"

"My daugh—"

Maybe she broke off midsentence. Maybe the words flurried away.

"What's that you say, lady?" Victor shouts.

"*Dog*," she yells. "I lost my *dog*. Lucy."

He can't be worrying about a dog.

"Sorry, but I've got to get going." Tracking away from the house.

"Just keep an eye open for her while you're out looking?" At the top of her voice. "She's a Rottweiler. Big, black, real friendly."

"Yeah, sure, okay," he yells back, marching on.

"Bless you! Her name's Lucy! Don't forget!"

NOT QUITE RIGHT

0540H

VICTOR LOOSELY TAILS a Ford Focus across town, his headlights slicing the slick, quiet streets. The Ford's tires are obviously bald, spinning at every stop, slipping and sliding, driving him insane. Headed down Orchard Avenue, the driver pumps the brakes all the way, but near the bottom of the hill, the car skids into the median, smack into the snow berm. Sticks fast.

"Shit," Victor says.

He can't just drive on by.

He eases up behind the stranded Ford and punches on his hazards. He's blocking the left lane, but traffic is nonexistent. At least for now.

After he finally digs out the Ford with his shovel, the woman behind the wheel rolls her window halfway down. She covers her mouth loosely with a mask, which reminds him to do the same—though out here, in this wind, the risk of transmission must be next to none.

"Thank you kindly," the woman yells, the snow blowing sideways, right into her face.

Victor angles in, screening her from the wind. She's dark skinned, with beaded dreads and hoop earrings. Huge eyes that drink you up.

"Your tires have seen better days," he shouts.

"That's the truth," she says, switching on her hazards. "Sure enough."

He notices her getup. "You work at the post office?"

Above her mask, her eyes crinkle into a smile. "Sure am! I deliver." Sounding proud. "Just headed into work now."

Victor pictures the woman hoofing it around town. Maybe noticing

313

stuff other people might miss. Vanity plates. Lucky pennies. Stray animals. Pedestrians who appear lost. Codgers carrying musical instruments.

"You out on your route yesterday?" he asks, checking the street again for oncoming traffic.

"Sure was! No itty-bitty storm gonna stop me!"

"Any chance you saw an old guy on the street with a clarinet?"

Her eyes widen. "You talking Simon? Dr. Richter, I mean?"

He huddles closer to her window. "You know him?"

"Sure do! Him and Miss Fiona!"

He can't believe his luck. "Maybe you've heard—he's missing."

"No way!" Her hand sags, and the mask with it, revealing silver studs in her nose. "For true?"

"Since yesterday afternoon."

She swivels her head, on the lookout for traffic. "Why don't you hop in here right quick, just for a spell?"

One more glance back up the hill, then he circles around to the passenger side.

HER NAME IS OLUBUNMI ADAMS.

"But everybody," she says, "just calls me Boo."

Her Ford's a beater. Flakes of snow drift in through the vents as she tells Victor about bumping into Simon, yesterday, around 1400h.

Gertie McClure had seen him around that same hour, by the timeline.

"I told him he should be getting back to Miss Fiona," Boo says, her mask now snugly strapped in place. "Why didn't the old man go on home?" She cranks up the heat another notch. More flurries fly into the front seat. "I've half a mind to call in sick, to go help you look."

"Got enough people searching," Victor reassures her. "We just need to catch a lucky break. And for this damn snow to stop."

"For true!" She swipes the steam from her window with her glove. Stares out at the storm. "Can't believe he's still out there."

Some mail carriers, Victor thinks, *carry more than the mail.*

"Well," he says then, "I should get going. Thanks for the intel." He grabs the door handle. "Watch yourself in this mess—"

"Wait a sec!" Boo exclaims. "Just thought of something! Let me reel it in before it's gone . . ." She closes her eyes. "Come on, come on, come on," she whispers, as if praying the memory back from oblivion. "Yessir, there she is—that little Meadows girl, on his heels, not far behind."

A snowplow rumbles by with an angry blast on the horn. The Focus is swallowed by a snow cloud cast by the plow's blade.

"Bad place for us to be stopped," Victor says as the white settles. "Gotta hurry. But tell me more about this girl Simon had with him—"

"Can't say she was *with* him. *Near* him, leastways. Lives in Nine Eighty."

"Next door to Simon's?"

"Yessir. Charles and Margaret Meadows—them's her folks. Girl's name maybe starts with an *O*. Strange thing is, I never seen her out much. Then yesterday, storm bearing down, she's out there all by her lonesome, like a puppy on the old man's tail."

"How old?"

"Seven, maybe eight. Pretty little thing, but she don't look well. I been thinking something's not quite right in Nine Eighty. And that dog! Lord have mercy! Big-assed Rott!"

Victor's mind spins back to the neighbor lady on the stoop. Her bathrobe snapping in the wind. Her face obscured.

"Dog," he says to Boo, "happen to be named Lucy?"

"Man, how you know that?" Boo says, cuffing him on the arm like a sister. "But don't let that dog's sweet name fool you none. She apt to eat you alive and chaw your bones!"

I've lost her, the woman on the stoop had said.

"So," Victor says, "if this Meadows girl—"

"Pink!" Boo cries, all amped up. "Her coat was bright pink! Boots too! Just now came to me."

"Okay, good to know," he says. "So, say this girl in a pink coat was out there *with* Simon. If *he's* missing, then—"

"She might be missing too!" Boo declares, capping his thought.

"Shouldn't her mom and dad be worried sick?"

"Sure enough should!"

He thinks of the car in the Meadowses' driveway, blanketed in snow that had fallen overnight.

"Shouldn't they be out looking?" he says. "Involving the police?"

"Like I said," Boo tells him, "something wrong in that house."

DEFINITELY OFF

VICTOR SWINGS the Jeep into a city lot that has already been cleared of snow. Idling the engine, he calls the APD on his cell. Says he has a tip on a missing person case. Is put on hold.

Dangling from his rearview mirror is a stone turtle—a gift from his mom, right before he'd shipped out to Iraq.

A couple months back, a cop with a thing against brown skin had pulled him over and cited him for his "mirror decoration." The judge had later tossed the ticket.

"Detective Parrish," rasps a tired voice over the phone, summoning Victor back from that morning in court.

"Yeah, I might have a lead on Simon Richter."

"Name?"

"Curliss. Victor. Need me to spell any of that?"

"No. Go ahead."

"Just talked to somebody who saw Simon uptown yesterday, around fourteen hundred."

"Nothing new there." Sounding pissed. Or exhausted. Sometimes you can't tell the difference. Sometimes there *is* no difference.

"Might have had a neighbor girl with him," Victor continues. "Seven or eight years old. Last name of Meadows. Don't know her first name. Might start with O—as in Oscar."

"Got an address for the kid?"

"Nine Eight Zero Division Street. Right next door to Simon's. Please confirm, over."

Parrish repeated the house number. "Thanks. We'll look into it."

316

"Roger that. Any kids by that name reported missing?"

"Like I said, I'll look into it."

"Without delay." Victor watches the wipers fighting back and forth on the crusty windshield. "I saw the girl's mother just a half hour ago. Something was definitely off."

BOY IN THE COUNTRY

0803H

VICTOR SWITCHES off his windshield wipers, the snow having tapered to flurries. He straddles the narrow two lanes in the Jeep, navigating by feel, not always able to distinguish the country road. The surface markings are buried beneath six inches of new snow and spotty monster drifts.

Where you at, Simon? Come on, buddy . . .

His search is drawing him along the main road toward home, six miles outside town. He can't explain why. No way Simon could have made it to Dinky Creek on foot. It was too damn far for an eighty-year-old man with bad knees to walk, even if he could remember how to get there.

But this isn't about logic. It's about instincts.

Not long before the pandemic had hit, he'd started taking Simon for Sunday-afternoon rides through the countryside. They'd drive slow for the scenery, each gazing out his own side of the Jeep. They didn't talk much, though Simon would always inquire about Dinky Creek—out of courtesy, maybe, to repay Victor for the ride-along. Or maybe the old man had genuine interest.

He wasn't your typical townie.

He'd grown up on a dairy farm. In Iowa, maybe. Or South Dakota. One of those states out west. He still had an eye for the maturity of a field crop or the quality of a heifer.

"You can take the boy out of the country . . ." he'd sometimes say, his monotone voice trailing off into the rattling of the Jeep.

318

But instead of capping off the cliché, he'd say, "I still wake up early—to milk the cows."

By the time of those outings, Fiona had confiscated Simon's keys.

"I get why she did it," Simon had said once as the Jeep plowed through a pelting rain. "I'm not a complete idiot. But . . ."

He'd left that *but* uncapped too.

Give me a clue, buddy. Where you at?

As a former Marine, Victor believes in the effectiveness of command and control; the duty to follow orders to accomplish an objective; and the need for appropriate tactics to fulfill a mission and win the victory, however long it takes.

But he also knows that the execution of proper procedures and techniques is seldom enough to achieve your purpose. You also need art. Intuition. Imagination. What his mom calls her sixth sense.

Let search and rescue use its grid. Let the police department follow its leads. It's all good.

His superpower is his gut.

He stays his course toward Dinky Creek.

Semper fi.

DEAD MAN'S MARBLE RUN

0900H

VICTOR ROTATES HIS HEAD, side to side, relaxing the kinks in his neck from hours behind the wheel. Won't be long before he has to gas up.

He hugs the road, approaching the steep series of hairpin curves down the last ridge before the entrance to the farm. Mikey calls it Dead Man's Marble Run.

The Marble Run is a dangerous stretch in any weather. The posted speed limit, all the way down, is fifteen miles per hour. You don't want to lose control here. If you crash through the guardrail on the outside lane, you'll plunge into the river gorge.

On a Sunday drive, Simon had referred to the Marble Run as "Walter's Wiggles."

"Damn straight," Victor had joked, familiar with the Wiggles, a deadly but dizzyingly beautiful section of trail in Zion National Park. Twenty-one switchbacks on a sheer cliff. Not for the faint of heart.

The old man claimed to have hiked the Wiggles a dozen times, all the way up to Angels Landing.

Maybe, Victor thinks now, the old man *could* have made it to Dinky Creek. His knees aren't in great shape anymore, but he's still a walker. His daily rambles around town are one of the constants in his life. "Peregrinations," he calls them.

"What the hell's a peregrination?" Victor had asked him once.

Simon isn't chatty, but if you pose an open-ended question on a topic he cares about, be prepared for a mini-lecture.

"From the Latin *peregrinor,*" he'd begun, "meaning 'to roam about' or 'to live as a stranger.' The *peregrinatio* isn't intent on a specific destination but on discovery. If he's lucky, the journey makes him less a stranger to his own life."

"How's that working for ya?"

"Verdict's still out," the old man had said with a smirk. "Anyway, that's what I do. Take my walks. Same route every day. But it's never the same route twice. My insides have no map."

Your outsides either, Victor says now to himself.

Just then, the Jeep hits ice.

Too fast! he warns himself. But too late, like when you enter a house you'd thought your buddies had swept clear of enemy, and you find yourself at the wrong end of a piece.

He hits the brake. The Jeep skates.

He wrenches the wheel into the slide. The Jeep swings back, flirting with hope, then fishtails into a spin.

Suddenly he's back in his high school junker, spinning on glare ice after speeding down a straightaway in a sleet storm, daring the Giver to kill him.

Enlisting in the Marines had been the same dare, on a different road.

Maybe loving Mikey is, too, he's thinking in the spin.

Then a calm, cool voice speaks into his ear from behind:

This is it.

Heat surges down his spine.

Impossible. He's alone in the Jeep.

Yet the voice is real as his bootlaces. Three words. Breath on his ear.

His foot lifts off the brake. His grip slackens on the wheel. He looks where he needs to go.

When the Jeep rocks to a stop, it's facing east, the opposite direction from which he'd come.

The stone turtle swings wildly on its leather cord.

By miracle, he's still on the road.

No traffic is approaching from ahead.
He checks his mirrors. No traffic behind.
He exhales with relief, long and loud.
The turtle falls still.

He cranks the steering wheel for a three-point turn, planning to resume course down the Marble Run.
But he doesn't step on the gas.
The Jeep idles in the center of the road.

This is it.
The sound of that voice is still as clear in his mind as the death on Meema's face, yesterday in the goat barn.
Whether the voice had been male or female, old or young, he can't say. It defies description.
But all such voices belong to the Giver.
Question is, what do the words mean?
He broods on his stone turtle, letting the message settle into its proper orbit . . .

It's not about you. It's about Simon.

THE SNOW-COVERED road has no berm. Victor cozies the right side of the Jeep up against the guardrail, shifts into park, and sets his hazards flashing.
He cinches up the laces on his tactical boots, zips up his parka, tugs on his gloves, and steps out of the cab. Inside his daypack are the thermos and sandwiches, a first-aid kit, some jerky and nuts, and a few other essentials. His water bottle, in the side mesh pocket, is three-quarters full.
He slings the pack over his shoulder, wishing he could call Mikey and tell him what's happened. But there's no cell service on the Marble Run.
Maybe this, too, is the way of the Giver. Not all stories are meant to be told. And even those that *are* meant to be told must be told in their proper time.
He pulls the bill of his Dinky Creek cap lower over his shades. His eyes range across the glistening landscape, seeking some sort of sign.

The snow has stopped. The sun is bright. The air is warming. *Improvise, adapt, and overcome.* That's what a jarhead does. He steps over the guardrail, dips down into the gorge.

AROUND THE BEND

1015H

HE's BEEN WADING for an hour through white powder, hankering for his snowshoes and poles. He hadn't expected a foot search in the hills.

He follows the burbling river around a bend on the margins of a pasture. The rock-strewn river is narrow and fairly shallow, but its current is steady. Around the curve, it has washed driftwood onto the banks and uprooted trees. A meandering mile or so on, it will dump into the Puhpeeg Reservoir.

By now, trained search-and-rescue teams as well as volunteers are fanned out across their assigned sections of the city. The search area will have widened since yesterday. Snowmobiles will have been brought in. The heat-seeking chopper, which had been on standby during the storm, is likely in the air.

His cold nose drips.

Half a klick off, against a sweep of whites and grays, a curious splotch of red rests atop a fence post. Too dinky and still for a cardinal. Too crimson for a stray clump of winterberries. Whatever it is, it looks out of place, like smoke curling from the chimney of an abandoned house.

Why isn't it buried in snow?

He picks up his pace. Maybe that strange spot of red will yield a clue to Simon's whereabouts.

A short distance beyond the post is a herd of Holsteins—a few dozen black-and-white-spotted cows, lined up at the pasture's edge, knee-deep in a drift. Their warm breath hangs in the air.

Funny, how they're all facing the river, into the wind. Usually cows turn their rumps against the weather.

He comes within spitting distance of the fence post—close enough to see a cow's frosty eyelashes . . .

But then his boot halts midstride.

Instantly he falls back, as if one more step might trip a wire. He's pierced by a sharp sense of trespass.

The red thing is an amulet of some sort, finely beaded, of considerable age. He can't be sure, but if he had to guess, he'd say it was shaped like a turtle.

How's it gotten way out here, atop this post?

That story isn't his to know. And the amulet isn't his to touch.

Such sacred objects know who they belong to. You've got to treat them with respect, or they lose their medicine and can no longer protect the one they were made for.

He looks beyond the amulet to the mottled row of Holsteins, their pink noses at attention. The cows are gazing through the taut wire fence as if it's spring and a thick stand of alfalfa is just beyond the water, dotted with sweet purple flowers waiting to be munched.

He turns to look with them across the river, into the trees.

That's where you need to go.

He fords the bitter river, rock by slippery rock.

HE SMELLS the smoke before he spots the charred, smoldering stain of a fire in the snow. Beyond the remains, peering out of a white bank of earth, is the black eye of a ruined culvert, weeping rocks.

As he advances toward the fire ring, a low growling emanates from the culvert. A large black dog emerges from the hole. Teeth bared.

"Easy, boy," he says in a soothing tone, averting his eyes to show submission. "Not going to hurt you."

As he inches off his pack and transfers it to his front for protection, he observes the menacing dog out the corner of his eye. Its feet are planted. Its clipped ears are pinned back and its chest puffed out. Its rust-colored throat is rumbling.

A Rottweiler.

He thinks of the Meadows lady.

And Boo.

That Rottweiler.

Maybe the dog's with the girl, and the girl's with the old man.

"Simon?" he says in a hush.

Maybe the old man had built the fire.

Maybe they'd all taken shelter in the hole.

"Simon?" he says again, a little louder, casting his voice toward the culvert. "It's Victor. You in there?"

The Rott springs forward with a bark, landing two meters from his boots.

Victor doesn't let himself flinch.

Big, black, real friendly, the Meadows lady had said.

She apt to eat you alive and chaw your bones, Boo'd said.

The dog barks twice more, nosing the top of the air, testing him.

Victor eases one hand into a side pocket of his pack and roots around.

"You Lucy?" With a flick of his wrist, he tosses a thick strip of jerky at the dog's feet.

The Rott sniffs, then nips up the jerky and sinks onto the snow with her prize.

"Good girl."

He edges around the dead campfire, still shielding himself with his gear. Lucy or not, the Rott can't be trusted. She's guarding *something* in that culvert.

You gotta go in.

His chest constricts. He needs to piss.

He doesn't want to go closer.

He can't deal with holes.

Just before Fallujah, his unit had been ordered into a cave complex to mop up enemy fighters. Nine fucking tunnels. Seven fucking hours. Two buddies of his, shredded to bits.

He peels off his shades, lets them drop on their strap.

He glances again at the Rott. She's paying him no mind.

"Simon," he calls again, stalling, "you in there?"

His ears strain for any signal that might save him from having to go in.

The Rott's still chomping away.

Get in there, jarhead. One quick look. For the old man.

THE HOLE

1030H

VICTOR'S PULSE is racing as he ducks into the culvert. He's panting like he's humped fifty pounds for thirty klicks. Nervous sweat rolls.

The flashlight on his phone stabs the gloom. The sight that greets him drives his fear to the back wall.

It's Simon, his arms around a dirty-faced girl, just a wisp of a child—dressed, like Boo had said, all in pink.

Their eyes are closed.

They're much too still.

"Simon! Hey buddy!" Victor's mind is racing, formulating a task list. "It's me—Victor. You okay?"

He squats beside the girl to check the pulse in her neck.

"Hey, little bug," he says, like she's his baby sister.

Behind him, toenails click and clatter on stone.

Shit.

Victor freezes in his crouch, swallowing hard. He never should have turned his back on the entrance.

But rather than attack, the Rott clambers into the culvert with a pitiful outpouring of whimpers. She ignores Victor entirely, nuzzling the girl, then slumping down beside her, close as she can. She rests her muzzle on the girl's hip.

"Hey there," Victor says to the dog, offering another piece of jerky. Can't be too careful. "So you're Lucy, huh? This gal your pal?"

"Grampa . . . ?" the girl says faintly.

Victor whisks off his parka and tucks it around her. She's obviously delirious from her ordeal.

"Name's Victor," he tells her while sliding his hand up to Simon's neck. He probes for a pulse with a wordless prayer.

Sometimes they fool you. Skin so damn cold, no pulse, no breath sounds. Then they come back.

"What's your name, little bug?" he says to the girl.

Her eyelids flicker. "You an angel?"

Lucy raises her head and cocks it to one side, adoring the girl.

Victor fetches his thermos, screws off the lid, and pours some steaming joe.

"Can you tell me your name?" he asks the girl again, breathing on the joe to cool it.

"Olivia . . . Pink . . ."

Pink? Not Meadows?

He brings the thermos lid to her lips. "Good girl, Olivia. Drink this for me."

"Thank . . . Hat Lady . . ."

Her eyelids close.

He gives her delicate shoulder a stiff shake. "Wake up! Olivia!"

She lies there, too quiet, too peaceful, too wan and willowy and washed out.

He swills down the joe himself, weighing his options, desperate for some sort of happy ending.

Maybe he should try plain water.

He twists open his water bottle. "Come on now," he says, lifting Olivia's head off Simon's chest. "This'll help . . ."

She rouses, but not enough to sip.

"Heaven . . ." she breathes.

"What's that you say, little bug?"

"Oh, Grampa . . . angel music . . . don't you hear . . ."

BARS

1037H

VICTOR CHARGES out of the culvert with his cell phone.

No bars.

He barrels through the snow-laden pines, retracing his heavy tracks to the bottomland along the river.

No bars.

He thrusts his phone toward the sky, turning in circles like a radar antenna.

No bars.

Winded, he doubles over with a groan, hands on his knees, fighting for air. Fighting to think.

Across the river, the dappled cows are watching him as if he's on center stage.

This is it.

The words he'd heard in the Jeep push his gaze back to the red amulet on the fence post. Like X marking the spot.

The thing that doesn't belong—maybe it's exactly where it needs to be.

Maybe it's exactly where *he* needs to be, to make this call.

This.

Is.

It.

SHAFT OF LIGHT

1115H

A SPECK APPEARS in the sky to the south. It dilates into a sleek blue-and-yellow bird with patches of black . . . the medevac chopper.

Beacon lights strobe on the chopper's landing skids and tail. The thumping air scatters the Holsteins from the fence line.

After a few sweeps around the pasture, high up, scouting the landing zone, the chopper holds overhead in a hover. A spotlight on its belly shines a vertical beam to flat white ground.

After a full minute, the chopper spiders down on that shaft of light. The rotor blades churn up blinding swirls of snow.

Victor hunkers down, shielding himself from the stinging whiteout. Waiting for the chopper to arrive had been torture. Waiting for it to land is almost worse.

The chopper touches down. Its blades are still turning when the cabin door slides open and two docs jump out in white helmets and royal-blue flight suits.

CALCULATIONS

BACK IN THE CULVERT, Victor watches as the docs assess Olivia and Simon with earnest calm. Their facemasks remind him to pull up his own.

He runs the calculations:

Number of casualties, Seriously Ill: two.
Number of docs: two.
Number of stretchers: one.
Minutes to load first SI: three.
Minutes to chopper: twelve.
Minutes to unload: three.
Minutes back to culvert: ten.
Minutes to load second SI: three.
Minutes back to chopper: twelve.
Minutes to unload: three.
Flight time to hospital: ten.
His analysis adds up to one result: AFU.
All fucked up.

Simon's on the stretcher, illuminated by a clip flashlight. One doc's doing CPR.

The other doc has stuffed heat packs in Simon's armpits and groin. Covered Simon with a forced-air warming blanket. Is pushing warm IV fluids.

"Stay with me," the doc that's pumping keeps saying. "Stay with me now."

"We've had worse who've come back," the other doc says to Victor, to buck him up.

Victor reruns the numbers.

Gotta shave minutes.

At his feet, Olivia's unconscious, wrapped in a shiny heat sheet. Beside her on the rocks is Simon's clarinet.

Victor hugs the girl up into the cradle of his arms. A limp rag doll.

"We're not waiting," he tells her.

He bolts for daylight.

Lucy's already ahead of him.

NOT SO EASY

1145H

Lucy's straining nonstop to get aboard the medevac, with Olivia. Victor strengthens his grip on the Rott's collar.

"Take the dog?" he yells at a doc over the chopper's engines.

He's crazy, asking the guy to evacuate a Rott. Without a leash. In a chopper already cramped with the crew, two patients on stretchers, and an array of monitors and tubes and tanks. A portable compression device is pumping Simon's chest.

"Service dog?" the doc yells back, behind his mask and visor.

Victor begs with his eyes. "Helped keep the two of them alive, you know?"

"Sorry, buddy!" the doc says. "Got to load and go!"

The chopper door closes.

Victor retreats with Lucy from the landing zone and throws a wave at the cockpit. The pilot gives him a thumbs-up.

Victor raises his shades to screen his eyes. He kneels beside Lucy, holding on to her for all he's worth.

Precious minutes tick by. The chopper finally eases off its skids. It nudges forward through flurries, then veers and lifts, nose down, into its climb.

When Victor can no longer hear the chopper, he lets go of the dog.

She stands beside him, tongue hanging out, looking lost. Snow dust is melting in her fur.

333

He tugs off his mask. Scratches her neck. "What you say, Lucy? We gonna get that happy ending?"

He looks again at the sky. It's unbroken except for an invisible jet sketching a white streak across the brilliant blue. The contrail is on a collision course with the sun.

Exhaustion presses down. Foreboding. Grief.

This is like the silence after battle. After flashbacks. After nightmares. So many years since Iraq, he still sleeps in his apartment behind the farm shoppe, alone, to spare Mikey his terrors.

Olivia will survive, most likely.

As for Simon . . .

Victor falls back from the murky edge, where hope's all mixed up with anxiety and doubt.

His attention gravitates to the fence post. The red turtle's still there, as impervious to rotor wash as to a nor'easter.

Tears collect in the corners of his eyes. He thumbs them away.

He folds his Dinky Creek hat and shoves it into his hip pocket. He settles Simon's grubby bush hat over his thick hair.

Now he's got to get to the hospital.

To Fiona. To Abby, who should have arrived from Philly by now.

To the police.

To Mikey.

"Let's go home," he says to Lucy.

He slogs off through the pasture in the direction of the Jeep, wading in his old footprints.

Lucy lopes alongside. Here and there, she throws herself down to roll in the snow, then bounds off with a yip, as if after a rabbit. She's moved on.

For him, it's not so easy.

NOBODY

1156H

VICTOR AND LUCY have gone maybe a klick when the pit drops out of his stomach.

You forgot his clarinet.

He doesn't want to hike back to the culvert. He doesn't want to go back inside that hole.

But that clarinet is part of Simon.

And a Marine leaves nobody behind.

CRACKED OPEN

1220H

NEAR WHERE VICTOR had first smelled the smoke of Simon's fire, Lucy points her nose skyward and lets rip with a howl.

"What's the matter, girl?"

Lucy will proceed no farther. She keeps up her baying, jawing at him like he should understand, her eyes round and brown and pleading.

"Come on," he coaxes, tugging her collar toward the culvert.

Lucy offers one last whine.

"Well, then," he says, yielding in frustration, "stay put!"

To his surprise, Lucy clams up and sits on her haunches, as if he'd issued a command.

He gives her a tired smile. "What a pooch!" he says, tossing her his last piece of jerky.

Lucy flumps down with her treat in the snow.

Ahead looms the hole. He'll have to go solo.

HE SPLASHES the slender beam of his flashlight around the inside of the culvert. There's no visible source of threat, but his hair's on end.

He screws his eyes shut to collect himself. In his mind, he nudges the stone turtle in his Jeep, sending it to and fro on its leather cord. Beneath its rhythm, he inhales from his belly.

His chest constricts. His panic is escalating. He's tempted to run.

He jerks his gloves off. He needs his hands bare.

Eyelids still battened down, he repeats the fifth general order as if it were a frenzied foxhole prayer: "I will quit my post only when properly

336

relieved. I will quit my post only when properly relieved. I will quit my post only when . . ."

The words bounce off the rocks. His heart's still hammering. The stone turtle's still swinging.

"*This is it,*" he says, abandoning the fifth order for a different mantra. "This is it. This is it. This is it . . ."

His breathing slows, becomes less jagged. Now he's beginning to win.

"This is it. This is it. This is it. This is it . . ."

He senses a reassuring presence beside him. Lucy must have gotten over her stubborn streak. He groans in relief, no longer alone with his demons.

Blindly he holds out his hand, expecting a lick or a nose-nudge. He meets only air.

"Here, girl," he says, adding a low whistle. "Where you at?"

No response.

He pries his eyes open.

No dog.

He swipes his light all around.

Not counting himself, the sole occupant of the ruined culvert is the clarinet, near where Simon and Olivia had lain, hugging each other for life.

The sight of the old man's clarinet spotlighted on the rocks catapults Victor into the past—an afternoon back before the pandemic.

He and Mikey have just finished upgrading the shelving in Fiona's studio. They're sitting with her at the kitchen table, polishing off some of her raspberry cobbler.

Simon's closeted in his den, practicing his clarinet. He never plays in front of people. Only in that room. Behind that closed door.

After a while, the chatter at the table leaves off. The three of them linger with their coffee, their forks resting on berry-stained plates. They absorb the music like bread soaking up soup.

In the reverie, Victor slips away and tiptoes down the creaky hall, toward the music. Nearing the den, he notices the door is ajar.

He hadn't expected this. He didn't wish to intrude, only to hear better.

But that cracked door is bait, luring him in.

He bends into a slight crouch. One squeak of the plank floor will betray him. He takes stealthy steps in his steel-toed work shoes, angling himself until Simon's profile fills the one-inch gap between the door and its frame.

The old man has removed his wire-rimmed glasses. His long-lashed eyelids

337

are closed; his bushy brows, arched in pleasure. He pours himself through the clarinet, swaying to the music as his fingers wag on the keys. Oblivious.

Victor freezes.

He then digs his phone from his jeans. Zeroes in. Waits.

Simon hits a loud, thrilling flurry of notes. Victor shoots a burst.

The old man never hears the snicks.

Back in the kitchen, Victor shows the sequence of photos to Fiona and Mikey—Simon so happy, yet so . . . alone.

Fiona tears up like an adoring sweetheart. Or a new widow.

Mikey wraps an arm around her shoulders and reels her into his side. She tips her head against his cheek. In that moment, they resemble mother and son—as if, at long last, Mikey has a mother who actually considers him worthy of love.

Mikey's been more Mikey *ever since.*

NOW, INSIDE THE CULVERT, Victor flips through his phone to find the one frame from that secret burst that he'd elected to keep—an image of Simon through a crack in time, turning himself into music.

Victor still can't explain why the door of the den hadn't been latched. Simon never would have neglected it on purpose. His music, like his peregrinations, is private.

Or who knows? Maybe that cracked-open door had been Simon's way of letting them all in.

The only way he'd known how.

Calmer in his skin, Victor lowers himself beside the clarinet. Beside it rests a grubby pink glove, spotted with blood. By its size and color, the glove must be Olivia's.

This stub of pink crayon must be hers too.

She's sure into pink, he thinks, pocketing the crayon in his parka.

The beam of his flashlight glints on the clarinet's tidy mess of silver keys and finger holes. To his untrained eye, the instrument appears to be in okay shape. Nothing that a clean rag and some polish can't fix.

He doesn't touch the clarinet. He ponders it like a new dad, unsure of the best way to hold his firstborn.

Timidly, he reaches with both hands to pick it up.

PRESENCE

TIME UNKNOWN

OUTSIDE THE CULVERT, somewhere far away, Lucy howls.

Out the corner of Victor's eye, a startling swish of luminescent pink.

He snaps his head to the side. Nothing's there.

He shakes out the cobwebs. Maybe he's too short on sleep. Or his blood sugar's low.

No—there it is again! The slightest movement in the shadows.

He shoots to his feet, nerves on fire.

There! A slight rippling in the daylight at the culvert's mouth . . . a *Presence*.

Just like that, it's gone. He doesn't see it leave so much as senses it.

He staggers out of the hole in pursuit, clenching the clarinet with both hands.

HER

TIME UNKNOWN

VICTOR SHIELDS his eyes against the dazzle of sunlight. When sight returns, he scans his surroundings for any shifting of shapes.

There.

He follows the Presence through the trees. It doesn't seem to be fleeing him, but it's so indistinct that it's hard to track. It flows like liquid glass. Every glimpse is see-through. A lady's pink hat, maybe. The skirt of a dress. A bare ankle.

He begins to imagine the Presence as *her.*

And he begins to suspect that whoever she is, or once had been, she's somehow linked to the clarinet. Why else would she have withdrawn from the culvert right after he'd picked it up?

He trudges after her, through the snow, toward the river.

This can't possibly be happening.

Of course it's happening. And it will alter you forever.

He stands under a tree at the river's edge, chest heaving from exertion, desperate for a telltale ripple of light or color.

Straight across, the cows are back at the fence.

The red amulet is gone from the post.

THE BIGNESS

TIME UNKNOWN

WHERE HAVE YOU GONE? Victor asks the Presence, surveying the landscape. But the only movement is Lucy, behind him in the trees.

Strange, this sugar maple beneath which he's standing. Despite the nor'easter's fury, the tree still possesses all its leaves, fiery red against the winter hues of the woods.

Dazzled by the foliage, Victor tilts back his head to stare up through the maple's canopy. When he reaches out a hand to steady himself on the trunk, the tree sings a note, as if he'd plucked a guitar string.

The world tips on a sunbeam.

"You hear that?" he says to himself, stupefied, trying to process the evidence of his own ears.

He experiments, easing his hand higher up the maple's trunk. The pitch of the tree's note slides up, like when his buddy Kadeem, before he got blown up, would run a finger up a silver string on his fretboard.

A single mesmerizing note, bending toward the sky.

But no—

It's not just one note.

Victor catches the hint of a melody, warm and melancholy. He can't be sure, but it seems to be emanating from across the river.

Maybe from the empty fence post.

Somebody's turning up the volume.

Somebody's mixing in more layers of sound, until, at last, there's only Song—pulsing, welling up from everywhere at once. From every needle on the pine trees. From every spray of light through the laden branches. From every crystal of snow. From every rock in the river. From every inch of wire in the fence. From every grommet in his boots.

Impossible music, produced from jostling and friction and dissonance.

"Do you *hear* it?" he exclaims again.

He's suddenly shaky on his feet. His entire body is vibrating—or is the air trembling?

Sometimes, in combat, he'd suffered dizzy spells. Immersed in horrors too grotesque to absorb, he'd lost his bearings. A dense, sickening vertigo would spin him to the ground, and he couldn't pull himself out of it. He always just had to get through it.

That vertigo, as he'd finally grown to understand, had been his private *No.*

But his loss of balance here—shin deep in fresh snow under this sugar maple, his flesh throbbing with waves of consummate sound—has nothing to do with terror or shock or his own barbarity.

He's tripping on the molecules of a cosmic *Yes.*

Random images boil up on the churning music: his mom lifting the stone turtle on its cord over his head, his buddies shooting hoops on base, Mikey's whiskered face asleep on the pillow, Meema licking a kid to its feet, Fiona sprinkling sugar over peaches, Boo Adams exclaiming "Pink!", himself spinning to a stop on the Marble Run, Lucy baying, Simon's arms clutching Olivia and not letting go—

Oh, the tenderness of it all!

His whole life, he's been waiting for this glorious Song to emerge from the world's noise. An irrefutable sign that he *belongs.* That he has a rightful, even necessary, place in this life. Wherever he is, *as* he is.

No code to crack. No privilege to earn. No worth to prove.

This is it.

The cows can hear the Song. Lucy too. Just look at them, all standing stock-still along the river, breathing in and out . . .

They're all part of it. Nobody's outside.

One of the cows on the fence line, anchored wide on her haunches, bellows at a billion-watt sun.

Following gravity, the Song drifts down and settles over Victor, an enchanted parachute of sound. With every inhalation through its gossamer silk, he draws more Song into himself.

Maybe every day is music, and you're an instrument of the Giver, shivering with dread and delight, life singing through you like breath through a hollow reed You sing—and are sung.

Some notes of the Song are givens. The rest you have to improvise, like Simon and his jazz that day through the crack in the door.

You, and everybody else, are making something more from what's already here, getting caught up in a groove, and being carried away into a Bigness beyond all time and place . . . Or maybe into a Bigness in which all times and all places coexist, along with all souls that have ever been and are and ever shall be.

He touches the maple tree again.

Nothing.

Silence, all around.

The Song's gotten all up inside of him.

It's never too late to be more you *than you were before.*

"Thank you," he tells the Presence, but he's almost certain that she has moved on. Like the amulet from the fence.

SCRIBBLED IN INK

TIME UNKNOWN

STILL IN A DAZE, Victor wills himself to move. He unzips his parka. He strips down to his long-sleeve crew, one of Mikey's old shirts. I'M JUST HERE TO PET THE GOATS, it says in bold block letters.

He peels off the crew, exposing his tattooed torso. Shivering, he swaddles the clarinet in his shirt, the polyester still holding the warmth from his body.

Like the turtle amulet, this clarinet has medicine. It's a special carrier of the Song. The Giver has made it to talk power on the wind, to put stories in the air for the world to swallow.

The clarinet doesn't belong to him, but the Giver has entrusted him with its keeping. By protecting it, he continues to protect the one it belongs to, until it's no longer needed . . .

He stands the bundled clarinet on end in one corner of his daypack. It's so long that it juts out the top. He closes the pack's zipper against it, for stability.

He slips back into his fleece jacket and parka. He shoulders the pack. He buckles its waist strap, for good measure.

Nothing's going to harm this clarinet.

Lucy trots up beside him and laps at his fingers.

Over in the pasture, the cows amble away through the snow, single file, like notes of music being scribbled in black ink across a fresh white page.

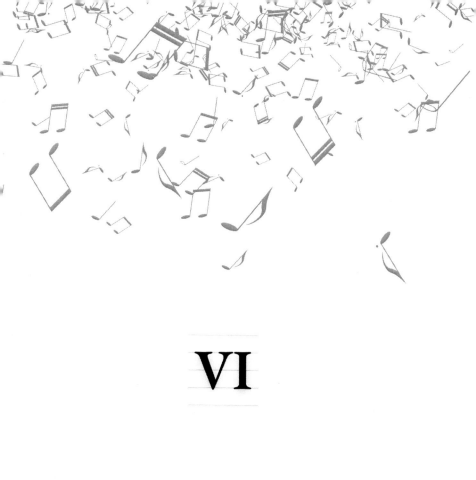

VI

NEWSBREAK

AN ELDERLY MAN SUFFERING FROM DEMENTIA HAS BEEN FOUND ABOUT EIGHTEEN HOURS AFTER HIS FAMILY FIRST REPORTED HIM MISSING FROM HIS HOME.

IN A JOINT STATEMENT WITH THE SHERIFF'S OFFICE, THE POLICE DEPARTMENT ANNOUNCED THAT EIGHTY-YEAR-OLD SIMON RICHTER HAD BEEN LOCATED NEAR THE PUHPEEG RESERVOIR IN RURAL ARONDALE COUNTY AROUND 11:00 A.M. SATURDAY. THE SITE WAS ABOUT SEVEN MILES NORTHWEST OF RICHTER'S RESIDENCE.

RICHTER HAD TAKEN SHELTER IN AN ABANDONED CULVERT. AN UNIDENTIFIED CHILD AND A DOG WERE FOUND WITH HIM.

RICHTER AND THE CHILD WERE AIRLIFTED TO MERCY HOSPITAL. THEIR CONDITIONS HAVE NOT YET BEEN RELEASED.

RICHTER'S FAMILY HAS BEEN NOTIFIED. IDENTIFICATION OF THE MINOR IS PENDING.

THE CANINE HAS BEEN PLACED IN THE TEMPORARY CARE OF ANIMAL CONTROL.

WE WILL PROVIDE UPDATES ON THIS SITUATION AS MORE INFORMATION BECOMES AVAILABLE.

A SPECIAL REQUEST

Thanks for reading *The Singing Stick*.

Please leave a brief review of *The Singing Stick* on your favorite book-loving sites. Just a sentence or two can help to raise the book's visibility and put it in the hands of more readers.

Care to suggest *The Singing Stick* to another book-lover or to your book club? Don't be shy. Good books make good friends.

Want to share your impressions of the book with the author? Email her here: phyllis@phylliscoledai.com.

BEYOND THE READING

Carry YOUR EXPERIENCE of *The Singing Stick* beyond the reading of the book. Consider these thought-provoking questions while listening to two music playlists curated by the author.

QUESTIONS FOR REFLECTION AND DISCUSSION

1. How do you interpret the book's title? In your view, what or who is the singing stick?
2. What role does the COVID pandemic play in the story? How would the story change if it were set in a different time?
3. Throughout the book, the author uses many points of view. What effect does this have? Which character's point of view do you wish had been included and why?
4. In what ways do Simon's experiences match the definition of *dementia* as "out of one's mind"? In what ways do his experiences defy that definition?
5. This story revolves around several major characters—but who is your favorite *minor* character? What impact did this character have on the novel and you as a reader?
6. In what ways is the truth hidden, revealed, and twisted in the story?
7. What effect does the truth have on different characters?
8. What strategies does Chekpawee/Vera use over time to cope with the various assaults on her cultural identity?
9. In one word, how would you describe the role Olivia serves in the story? Reflect on why you chose that word.
10. The novel features many letters, documents, and handwritten notes. How do these pieces impact the story and your experience as a reader?
11. In this transgenerational story, what changes from one generation to the next? What is passed down? What

transgenerational issues might you be facing in your own life?

12. How does music serve as a voice for different characters in the novel? How does music serve as a voice for people in real life, including yourself?

13. In what ways are characters interconnected in this story? In what ways are they disconnected? In what ways do you see connection and disconnection in your own community?

14. Reflect on the book's ending. How do you interpret it? How did it make you feel? Why do you think the author chose this ending?

15. To read a novel is to take a journey. How would you describe your personal journey with this book?

16. *It's never too late to be more* you *than you were before.* How does this quote apply to the different characters in the book? How does it apply to you and your own life?

MUSIC PLAYLISTS

These playlists are hosted by Spotify. To access a list, either scan its QR code or type its URL into your browser.*

NATIVE FLUTE PLAYLIST. Browse around four hours of native flute music in the Oceti Ŝakowiŋ tradition. The list features selections from Bryan Akipa, a member of the Sisseton-Wahpeton Oyate, whom the author consulted in her research. https://spoti.fi/3LI2JMM

JAZZ CLARINET PLAYLIST. Browse nearly six hours of clarinet music, primarily jazz. If you listen closely, you might hear Vera playing for the cows or Simon riffing through the cracked door. https://spoti.fi/3ADv7ZY

---

* To scan a QR code, first connect to the internet. Then open your device's camera app and point it at the code. Hold your device steady. In a moment, a notification will pop up asking you to open a link in your browser. Tap that link and the site will open. Spotify will then prompt you to login or create a free account.

AUTHOR'S NOTE

The Singing Stick is a work of fiction. However, Genoa Indian School (Genoa, Nebraska) actually existed, as did such associated characters as Samuel and Florence Davis, James Riley Wheelock, and James Mumblehead. Operating from 1884 to 1934, Genoa was the fourth-largest off-reservation boarding school established by the US Office of Indian Affairs to forcibly assimilate American Indian children by removing them from their families, communities, and nations of origin. The children at Genoa ranged in age from four to twenty-two years old; they came from over ten states and over forty tribal nations. The school's annual enrollment grew through the years from seventy-four to 599 students, even as the campus itself expanded to more than thirty buildings on 640 acres.

Today the Genoa US Indian School Foundation* preserves what remains of the school and interprets its history while seeking to promote awareness and healing. In addition, the Genoa Indian School Digital Reconciliation Project † provides "a space for telling the stories" of the children who attended there. Project members are locating and digitizing scattered government records about Genoa. Their efforts are "an act of archival reconciliation—of bringing history home." The project website, which was created after I had conducted most of my research, will be invaluable to tribal historians, academic scholars, descendants of the students, and more.

Readers wishing to learn more about the American system of Indigenous boarding schools and its impacts might start by consulting such books as *Boarding School Seasons: American Indian Families, 1900–1940*, by Brenda J. Child; *Education for Extinction: American Indians and the Boarding School Experience, 1875–1928*, by David Wallace Adams; *Away from Home: American Indian Boarding School Experiences, 1879–2000*, edited by K. Tsianina Lomawaima, Brenda J. Child, and Margaret L.

---

* genoaindianschoolmuseum.org
† genoaindianschool.org

Archuleta; and *Boarding School Blues: Revisiting American Indian Educational Experiences,* edited and with an introduction by Clifford E. Trafzer, Jean A. Keller, and Lorene Sisquoc.

John W. Troutman's *Indian Blues: American Indians and the Politics of Music, 1879–1934* was a groundbreaking work. It explores native musical practices and their relationship to federal Indian policy in three spheres: reservations, off-reservation boarding schools such as Genoa, and public performance venues. Boarding school students clearly turned many forms of music, including jazz, to their own purposes. Former students eventually toured across America and Europe in "all-Indian" musical groups. Then as now, music proved impervious to boundaries, a powerful experience of individual and cultural preservation, resistance, and hope.

ACKNOWLEDGMENTS

The Singing Stick, like many works of fiction, found its inspiration in actual life. The story began knitting itself together in my imagination late one night in March 2018, as I was flying home after a memorable visit with the poets Pat and Peter Schneider. At the time, they were wrestling with the painful realities of Peter's descent into dementia—a decline markedly eased by his playing of the clarinet, an instrument he'd abandoned long before. As it happened, I too had played the clarinet as a youngster. Our shared experience with the instrument and our mutual love of music made such an impression on Peter that, to some degree, he could actually remember me from one hour to the next. Pat was amazed and delighted. The Schneiders are now deceased, but my dear friendship with them infuses this novel.

So too does my relationship with the late Dakota elder Darlene Renville Pipeboy, a member of the Sisseton-Wahpeton Oyate. She and her twin brother, Darrell Fred "Toad" Renville, were born on September 22, 1940, near Sisseton, South Dakota. Her birth order name was Ćekpawiŋ (rendered as Chekpawee in the novel). It means "Twin Girl." Unlike their counterparts in this story, the Renville twins managed to evade boarding school.

The Schneiders and Darlene Renville Pipeboy remain present with me in spirit, continuing to encourage and guide me. I have written, in part, by their light.

I also owe a profound debt to Tamara St. John, tribal historian and historic preservation officer for the Sisseton Wahpeton-Oyate, for her generous time and sharing; Vine Marsh and Bryan Akipa (both Sisseton-Wahpeton) for imparting some of their immense cultural knowledge about the Dakota flute tradition and their personal experiences with that instrument; the late Sidney Byrd, tribal elder of the Flandreau Santee Sioux Tribe, for his stories about Genoa Indian School, having been sent there in 1926 at the age of six; Brenda J. Child (Red Lake Ojibwe), Northrop Professor of American Studies at the University of Minnesota, for her rich research on Indian boarding schools; and Maria

Yellow Horse Brave Heart (Hunkpapa/Oglala Lakota), president of the Takini Institute, for her expertise regarding historical trauma among native peoples.

I want to thank the following staff members and volunteers with the Genoa US Indian School Foundation for their assistance: Tammi Thiem, Linda Sass, Alyce Tejral, Nancy Carlson, and Tom Lawson. I especially remember their kindness when I visited Genoa for one of its annual "reunion and remembrance" events, during which I examined the museum holdings, walked what's left of the campus, and, most importantly, heard directly from descendants of Indigenous student-survivors.

I'm also grateful to Susana Grajales Geliga (Lakota/Taino), former tribal liaison and community outreach coordinator with the Genoa Indian School Digital Reconciliation Project. She is now the project's co-director.

My thanks to Elizabeth Burnes, archivist with the National Archives at Kansas City; various research staff at History Nebraska in Lincoln; and Peter Lefferts, professor of music emeritus in the Glenn Korff School of Music of the University of Nebraska-Lincoln.

I wish to pay tribute to the Honorable Deb Haaland (Laguna Pueblo), currently the secretary of the US Department of the Interior, for launching the Federal Indian Boarding School Initiative, a comprehensive review of the troubled legacy of federal boarding school policies and other past governmental measures to eradicate the languages, identities, and cultural practices of American Indians, Alaska Natives, and Native Hawaiians. As Secretary Haaland has said, the nation "will benefit from a full understanding of the truth of what took place and a focus on healing the wounds of the past."

A throng of other interviewees and authors endowed me with information and insights on an array of research subjects. There are too many sources to cite individually here, but their contributions live in these pages.

Big hugs to my editor, Angela Wiechmann (who also framed the thought-provoking questions for reflection and discussion). She understands my purpose, expands my vision, and hones my craft. She has become a true friend.

I've been buoyed in this writing by an ocean of personal good will. Special appreciation to members of The Raft, my online community, for their creative companionship. Deep bows to my mother, Carol Cole, and to my dear friends Mavis Gehant, Annette Grunseth, Ruth Harper, Don Mayhew, Claire Willis, and Ruby Wilson for their hearty confidence in me. Sue Grant, I bless your memory, recalling how you kept spurring me on, eager to read. I didn't finish in time.

Finally, I celebrate the steadfast love and support of my husband, Jihong, and son, Nathan. To a degree, every book I write somehow ends up being a journey that the three of us take together. How'd I get so lucky?

ABOUT PHYLLIS COLE-DAI

Phyllis Cole-Dai began pecking away on an old manual typewriter in childhood and never stopped. She has authored or edited more than a dozen books in multiple genres, seeking to "write across what divides us."

Originally from Ohio, Phyllis has lived for the past twenty-five years in Brookings, South Dakota, within the ancestral homeland of the Oceti Ŝakowiŋ—the "Seven Council Fires" of the Dakota, Nakota, and Lakota confederacy. Her novels reflect her desire to better understand the cultures of these nations and to grapple with the painful realities of Euro-American colonization, genocide, and forced assimilation.

As of 2025, Phyllis and her husband, Jihong, will make their home in Catonsville, Maryland.

Learn more at phylliscoledai.com. Explore The Raft, Phyllis's online community, at phylliscoledai.substack.com. To belong, all you have to do is step aboard.

Made in United States
North Haven, CT
07 December 2024

61849419R00224